About the author

Darrell Schweitzer is co-editor of the magazine *Worlds of Fantasy and Horror* (formerly *Weird Tales*) and has had his own short fiction published in various anthologies and magazines, including *Fear, Fantasy Tales* and *Interzone*. His previous books include *The Shattered Goddess, The White Isle* and *We Are All Legends*. He lives in Strafford, Pennsylvania, USA and is at work on a new novel.

The Mask of the Sorcerer

Darrell Schweitzer

NEW ENGLISH LIBRARY
Hodder and Stoughton

First published in Great Britain in 1995
by Hodder and Stoughton
A division of Hodder Headline PLC
A New English Library paperback

British Library Cataloguing in Publication Data

Schweitzer, Darrell
Mask of the Sorceror
I. Title
813.54 [F]

ISBN 0 340 64003 0

Typeset by Palimpsest Book Production Limited,
Polmont, Stirlingshire
Printed and bound in Great Britain by
Cox and Wyman Ltd, Reading, Berkshire

Hodder and Stoughton
A division of Hodder Headline PLC
338 Euston Road
London NW1 3BH

To the memory of my father,
Francis E. Schweitzer, 1924–1995

Contents

The Sorcerer Contemplates His Beginnings

Chapter 1: The Heron Boy   3
Chapter 2: In the Sybil's House   23
Chapter 3: Among the Dead   33
Chapter 4: Everybody and Nobody   41
Chapter 5: Sorcerer, Son of Sorcerer   67
Chapter 6: The Arrows of King Neoc   81

Interpolation: Three Brothers of the Air

Chapter 7: The Language of Corpses   109
Chapter 8: The Great River   135
Chapter 9: On to the City of the Delta   167
Chapter 10: The Murder of the Great King   185
Chapter 11: The Enigma of the Sorcerer   213
Chapter 12: The Inevitable Abomination   235

Interpolation: The Cup of Pain

Chapter 13: Time to Leave   267
Chapter 14: The Gatekeeper   289
Chapter 15: The College of Shadows   323
Chapter 16: The God of Sorcerers   369
Chapter 17: A Long Time Watching   389
Chapter 18: The Return of the Thorn Child   401

The Sorcerer to His Long-Lost Love

I have put on the mask of the sorcerer to hide my true self, but I am revealed, for the mask has become my own face.

– Tannivar the Parricide

The Sorcerer Contemplates His Beginnings

To think that once I was a child such as these,
a tumble of rags and dust in a village street,
or a trembling boy barely into his teens,
his heart thumping as he runs to meet
some sweetheart in the evening air.
The boy did not fear the darkness then,
nor ponder the mysteries of the Worm,
nor speak with thunder among the hills.
When did the fire begin to burn?

When he listened to whispers in the night,
and learned that death is but a door;
when demons raised him to some height,
promising kingdoms, gold, and more;
when first he walked a shadowed path,
quite unknown to most mankind,
seduced by sigils of the heart,
and inscrutable hieroglyphs of the mind.

Then the fire began to burn,
and sorcery sparked to life within.

> — *from the notebooks of Sekenre the Illuminator,*
> *but attributed to Vashtem of Reedland*

Chapter 1: The Heron Boy

Surely Surat-Kemad is the greatest of the gods, for he is lord of both the living and the dead. The Great River flows from his mouth; the River is the voice and word of Surat-Kemad, and all life arises from the River.

The dead return to Surat-Kemad, upon the waters or beneath them, borne by some secret current, back into the belly of the god.

We are reminded of Surat-Kemad daily, for he made the crocodile in his own image.

I, Sekenre, son of Vashtem the sorcerer, tell you this because it is true.

That my father was a magician I knew from earliest childhood. Did he not speak to the winds and the waters? I heard him do so many times, late at night. Could he not make fire leap out of his hands, merely by folding and unfolding them? Yes, and he never burned himself, for the fire was cold, like river water in the winter.

Once he opened his hands to reveal a brilliant, scarlet butterfly, made of paper and wire but alive. It flew around the house for a month. No one could catch it. I cried when it died and the light went out of its wings, leaving it no more than a trace of ash.

He made a different kind of magic with his stories. There was one in particular that went on and on, about a young heron who was cast out of his nest by the other birds because he had short legs, and no beak or feathers. He could pass for human, for all that he wasn't. So he wandered in lonely exile and had many adventures, in far lands, among the gods, among the ghosts in the land of the dead. Every evening for almost a year, Father whispered more of the story to me as if

3

it were a special secret between the two of us. I never told it to anyone else.

Mother made things too, but not fire out of her hands, nor anything that truly lived. She built *hevats*, those assemblages of wood and wire and paper for which the City of the Reeds is famous, sometimes little figures that dangled from sticks and seemed to come alive when the wind struck them, sometimes great tangles of ships and cities and stars and mountains which hung from the ceiling and turned slowly in a vastly intricate, endless dance.

Then a fever came over her one summer and she spent weeks working on a single, articulated image. No one could stop her. Father would put her to bed but she would get up again in her sleep and work on the thing some more, until a vast snaky creature of painted wooden scales writhed throughout every room of the house, suspended on strings just below the ceiling. At last she put a face on it – half a man, half a crocodile – and even I, six years old at the time, knew it to be an image of Surat-Kemad, the God Who Devours.

When the wind blew, the image writhed and spoke. Mother screamed and fell to the floor. Later, the thing was merely gone. No one would tell me what had become of it. When Mother recovered she could not recall anything that had happened to her.

One evening by a late fire, she explained that it had been a kind of prophecy, and when the spirit has departed, the seer is no more than an empty glove cast aside by some god. She had no idea what it meant, merely that a god had spoken through her.

I think even Father was frightened when she said that.

He told me one more instalment of the story of the heron boy the same night. Then the spirit of that, too, left him.

Father must have been the greatest magician in all Reedland, for our house was never empty in the early days. People came from all over the city, and from the marshlands; some journeyed for days on the Great River to buy potions and philtres or have their fortunes told. Mother sometimes sold them *hevats,* sacred ones for devotions, or memorials for the dead, or just toys.

I didn't think of myself as any different from other boys. One of my friends was the son of a fisherman, another of a paper-maker. I was the son of a magician, just another child.

But in the story, the bird-boy thought he was a heron—

As I grew older, Father became more secretive, and the customers came no further than the door. Bottles were passed out to them. Then they stopped coming.

Suddenly the house was empty. I heard strange noises in the night. In the earliest hours of the morning, Father began to receive certain visitors again. I think he summoned them against their will. They did not come to buy.

Then Mother, my sister Hamakina, and I were locked in the bedroom, forbidden to emerge.

Once I peeked out between two loose panels in the door and saw a bent, skeletal figure in the dim lamplight of the hallway outside, a visitor who stank like something long decayed and dripped with the water from the river below our house.

Suddenly the visitor glared directly at me as if he had known I was there all along, and I turned away with a stifled yelp. The memory of that horrible, sunken face stayed with me in my dreams for a long time.

I was ten. Hamakina was three. Mother's hair was starting to go gray. I think the darkness began that year. Slowly, inexorably, Father became, not a magician who worked wonders, but a sorcerer, to be feared.

Our house stood at the very edge of the City of the Reeds, where the great marsh began. It was a vast place, which had belonged to a priest before Father bought it, a pile of wooden domes and sometimes tilted, boxlike rooms and gaping windows fashioned to look like eyes. The house stood on log pilings at the end of a long wharf, otherwise not a part of the city at all. Walk along that wharf the other way and you came to street after street of old houses, some of them empty, then to the square of the fishmongers, then to the street of scribes and paper-makers, and finally to the great docks where the ships of the river rested at their moorings like dozing whales.

Beneath our house was a floating dock where I could sit and gaze underneath the city. The stilts and logs and pilings were like a forest stretched out before me, dark and endlessly mysterious.

Sometimes the other boys and I would paddle our shallow boats into that darkness, and on some forgotten dock or rubbish heap or sandbank we'd play our secret games; and then the others always wanted me to do magic.

If I could, I refused with great and mysterious dignity to divulge awesome mysteries I actually knew no more about than they. Sometimes I did a little trick of sleight-of-hand, but mostly I just disappointed them.

Still, they tolerated me, hoping I would reveal more, and also because they were afraid of Father. Later, when the darkness began, they feared him even more; and when I wandered in the gloom beneath the city, paddling among the endless wooden pillars in my little boat, I was alone.

I could not understand it then, but Father and Mother quarrelled more, until in the end, I think, she too was afraid of him. She made me swear once never to become like my father, 'never, never do what he has done,' and I swore by the holy name of Surat-Kemad without really knowing what I was promising not to do.

Then one night when I was fifteen, I woke up suddenly and heard my mother screaming and my father's angry shouts. His voice was shrill, distorted, barely human at times, and I thought he was cursing her in some language I did not know. Then came a crash, pottery and loose wood falling, and silence.

Hamakina sat up beside me in bed.

'Oh, Sekenre, what is it?'

'Quiet,' I said. 'I don't know.'

Then we heard heavy footsteps, and the bedroom door swung inward. Father stood in the doorway, his face pale, his eyes wide and strange, a lantern in his upraised hand. Hamakina turned to avoid his gaze.

He remained there for a minute as if he hadn't seen us,

and slowly the expression on his face softened. He seemed
to be remembering something, as if he were waking up from
a trance. Then he spoke, his voice faltering.

'Son, I've had a vision from the gods, but it is *your* vision,
by which you will become a man and know what your life
is to be.'

I was more bewildered than frightened. I got out of bed. The
wooden floor was smooth and cold beneath my bare feet.

Father was forcing himself to be calm. He clung to the
edge of the doorway and trembled. He was trying to say
something more, but no words came, and his eyes were wide
and wild again.

'*Now?*' I asked, hardly realizing what I was saying.

Father strode forward. He seized me roughly by my robe.
Hamakina whimpered, but he ignored her.

'The gods don't send visions just when it's convenient. *Now.*
You must go into the marshes *right now,* and the vision will
come to you. Remain there until dawn.'

He dragged me from the room. I glanced back once at my
sister, but Father merely closed the door behind me and barred
it from the outside, locking her in. He blew out his lantern.

The house was entirely dark and smelled of river mud
and worse. There was a trace of something burning, and of
corruption.

Father raised a trapdoor. Below floated the dock where all
our boats were moored.

'Down you go. *Now.*'

I groped my way down, fearfully, shivering. It was early in
the spring. The rains were nearly over, but not quite, and the
air was cold and full of spray.

Father closed the trapdoor over my head.

I found my boat and got in, and sat there in the darkness
cross-legged, my feet drawn up under my robe. Something
splashed nearby once, twice. I sat very still, clutching my
paddle firmly, ready to strike at I knew not what.

Slowly the darkness lessened. Out beyond the marshes, the
moon peered through thinning clouds. The water gleamed
silver and black, waves and shadow. And it was then that I
made out what seemed to be hundreds of crocodiles drifting in

the water around me, their snouts barely breaking the surface, their eyes sparkling in the dim moonlight.

It was all I could do not to scream, to keep silent. It was the beginning of my vision, I knew, for these beasts could easily have tipped over my boat and devoured me. In any case, there were too many of them for them to be natural creatures.

It was as I leaned over to slip off my mooring line that I saw, quite clearly, that they were not even crocodiles. Their bodies were human, their backs and buttocks pale as the flesh of drowned men. These were the *evatim,* the messengers of the river god. No one ever saw them, I'd always been told, save when he is about to die, or else when the god wishes to speak.

So my father had been telling the truth. There was a vision. Or I was going to die, then and there.

I paddled a short distance off, very carefully. The *evatim* parted before me. The tip of my paddle never touched one.

Behind me, in the darkness, I heard someone coming down the ladder onto the dock. Then something heavy splashed in the water. The *evatim* hissed, all as one. It was like the rising of a great wind.

I paddled for what felt like hours among the posts and pillars and stilts, groping my way with my paddle sometimes, until at last I came to open, deep water. I let the current take me a short distance, and looked back at the City of the Reeds where it crouched amid the marsh like a huge, slumbering beast. Here and there watchlamps flickered, but the city was dark. No one goes outdoors in the city at night; because the mosquitoes swarm in clouds at sunset, thick as smoke; because the marsh is full of ghosts who rise up out of the black mud like mist; but mostly for fear of the *evatim,* the crocodile-headed servants of Surat-Kemad, who crawl out of the water in the darkness and walk like men through the empty streets, their heavy tails dragging.

Where the city reached into deep water, ships lay at anchor, bulging, ornately-painted vessels come upriver from the City of the Delta. Many were ablaze with lights, and from them sounded music and laughter. The foreign sailors do not know our ways or share our fears.

* * *

In the City of the Reeds, all men who are not beggars wear trousers and leather shoes. Children wear loose robes and go barefoot. On the very few cold days they either wrap their feet in rags or stay indoors. When a boy becomes a man, his father gives him shoes. It is an ancient custom. No one knows the reason for it.

Father had hurried me out of the house without even a cloak. So I passed the night in quiet misery, my teeth chattering, my hands and feet numb, the cold air burning inside my chest.

As best I could, I steered for the shallows, in among the grasses and reeds, making my way from one patch of open water to the next, ducking low beneath vines, sometimes forcing my way through with my paddle.

A vision of sorts came to me, but all disjointed. I did not understand what the god was trying to say.

The moon seemed to set very suddenly. The river swallowed it, and for an instant moonlight writhed on the water like Mother's thousand-jointed crocodile image somehow glowing with light.

I set my paddle down in the bottom of the boat and leaned over, trying to make out the thing's face. But I only saw muddy water.

Around me, dead reeds towered like iron rods. I let the boat drift. I saw a crocodile once, huge and ancient and sluggish with the cold, drifting like a log. But it was merely a beast and not one of the *evatim*.

A bit later I sat in a stagnant pool surrounded by sleeping white ducks floating like puffs of cotton on the black water.

Night birds cried out, but I had no message from them.

I watched the stars, and by the turning of the heavens I knew it was no more than an hour before dawn. I despaired then and called out to Surat-Kemad to send me my vision. I did not doubt that it would come from him, not from some other god.

At the same time, I was afraid, for I had made no preparation, no sacrifice.

But Surat-Kemad, he of the monstrous jaws, was not angry, and the vision came.

9

The light rain had stopped, but the air was colder yet, and, trembling and damp, I huddled in the bottom of my boat, both hands against my chest, clutching my paddle. Perhaps I slept. But, very gingerly, someone touched me on the shoulder.

I sat up in alarm, but the stranger held up a finger, indicating that I should be silent. I could not see his face. He wore a silver mask of the Moon, mottled and rough, with rays around the edges. His white, ankle-length robe flapped gently in the frigid breeze.

He motioned me to follow, and I did, silently dipping my paddle into the water. The stranger walked barefoot on the surface, ripples spreading with every step.

We travelled for a long time through a maze of open pools and tufts of grass, among the dead reeds, until we came to a half-submerged ruin of a tower, no more than a black, empty shell covered with mud and vines.

Then hundreds of other robed, masked figures emerged from the marsh, not walking on the water as had my guide, but *crawling,* their movement a curious waddle, their bodies swaying from side to side as does that of a crocodile when it comes out on land. I watched in amazement as they gathered around us, bowing low at the upright man's feet, as if in supplication.

He merely spread his hands and wept.

Then I recalled one of my father's stories, about a proud king, whose palace was more resplendent than the sun, of whom the gods were jealous. One day a crocodile-headed messenger came into the glittering court and hissed, 'My master summons you, O King, as he summons all.' But the king, in his pride, bade his guards beat the messenger and throw him into the river whence he came, for the king did not fear the gods.

And Surat-Kemad did not care to be feared, only obeyed, so the Great River flooded the land, swallowing the palace of the king.

'That's not much of a story,' I'd complained to Father.

'It is merely true,' he said.

Now I looked on in awe, desperate to ask so many questions but afraid to speak. But the sky lightened, and the weeping of the standing man became merely the wind rattling in the reeds.

The sun rose, and the supplicants removed their masks and became merely crocodiles. Their robes were somehow gone in the shifting light. I watched their dark bodies sink into the murky water.

I looked to the standing man, but a long-legged bird remained where he had been. It let out a cry and took to the air, wings thundering.

The warm sun revived me. I sat up, coughing, my nose running, and looked around. The sunken tower was still there, a heap of dead stone. But I was alone.

It was midday before I got back to the City of the Reeds.

The city is a different place in the daylight, bright banners waving from towers, houses likewise bright with hangings and with designs painted on walls and roofs. The ships of the river unload by day, and the streets are filled with the babble of tongues, while traders and officials and barbarians and city wives all haggle together.

It is a place of sharp fish smells and strange incense and leather and wet canvas and unwashed rivermen who bring outlandish beasts from the villages high in the mountains, near the birthplace of the river.

By day, too, there are a thousand gods, one for every stranger, for every tradesman, for everyone who has ever passed through or resided or merely dreamed of a new god during an afternoon nap. In the street of carvers one can buy idols of all these gods, or even have new images made if one happens to be divinely inspired at the time.

At night, of course, there is only Surat-Kemad, whose jaws rend the living and the dead, whose body is the black water, whose teeth are the stars.

But it was by day I returned, making my way through the tangle of ships and smaller boats, past the wharves and floating docks, then beneath the city until I came out the other side near my father's house.

Hamakina ran to me when I emerged through the trapdoor, her face streaming with tears. She embraced me, sobbing.

'Oh Sekenre, I'm so afraid!'

'Where is Father?' I asked, but she only screamed and buried her face in my robe. Then I said, 'Where is Mother?'

Hamakina looked up into my face and said very softly, 'Gone.'

'Gone?'

'She has gone to the gods, my son.'

I looked up. Father had emerged from his workroom, his sorcerer's robe wrapped loosely over soiled white trousers. He hobbled toward us, dragging himself as if he didn't quite know how to walk. I thought there was something wrong with his legs.

Hamakina screamed and ran out onto the wharf. I heard the front door bang against the outside of the house.

I stood my ground.

'Father, where is Mother?'

'As I said . . . gone to the gods.'

'Will she be coming back?' I asked, hopeless as I did.

Father did not answer. He stood there for a moment, staring into space, as if he'd forgotten I was even there. Then he said suddenly, 'What did you see, Sekenre?'

I told him.

He was silent again.

'I don't know,' I said. 'It didn't mean anything. Did I do something wrong?'

For once he spoke to me tenderly, as he had in the old days when I was very small.

'No, faithful child, you did nothing wrong. Remember that the vision of your life goes on as long as your life does; and, like your life, it is a mystery, a maze, with many turnings, many things suddenly revealed, many things forever hidden. The longer you live, the more you will understand what you have seen this night. Each new piece of the vast puzzle changes the meaning of all that has gone before as you draw nearer and nearer the truth . . . but you never reach your destination, not entirely.'

The cold and the damp had given me a fever. I lay ill for a week, often delirious, sometimes dreaming that the masked figure in the vision stood at my bedside, barefoot on the surface of the black water while dead reeds rattled all around. Sometimes, as the sun rose, he took off his mask and a heron screamed at me, leaping into the air on thunderous wings. Sometimes it was my father beneath the mask. He came to me each dawn, put his hand on my forehead, recited words I couldn't make out, and bade me drink a sweet-tasting syrup.

After the fever had gone, I saw him very little. He retreated to his workroom, noisily barring the door. Hamakina and I were left to care for ourselves. Sometimes it was hard just finding food. We tried to assemble the leftover pieces of Mother's *hevats* but seldom got much for the results.

Meanwhile, lightning and thunder issued from the workroom. The whole house shook. Sometimes there were incredibly foul odors, and my sister and I would spend our nights outdoors, on rooftops among the beggars of the city, despite all the dangers. And once, as I crouched by the workroom door, terrified and holding back tears, Father spoke and I heard him answered by many voices, all of them faint and far away. One sounded like Mother. All were afraid, pleading, babbling, screaming.

At times I wondered where Mother had gone, and tried to comfort Hamakina.

But in my worst fears, I knew perfectly well what had happened to her. I could not tell Hamakina that.

There was no one I could turn to, for now Father was the most feared of all the city's black sorcerers, and even the priests dared not anger him. Demons of the air and of the river regularly convened at our house. I heard them scratching, their wings and tails dragging, while my sister and I huddled in our room, or kept to the rooftops.

In the streets, people turned away when they saw us, made signs and spat.

Then one day Father came to me, moving slowly and painfully, as if he were very old. He sat me down at the kitchen table and stared into my eyes for a long time. I was afraid to turn from his gaze. He had been weeping.

'Sekenre,' he said, very gently, 'do you love your father still?'

I could not answer.

'You must understand that I love you very much,' he said, 'and I always will, no matter what happens. I want you to be happy. I want you to do well in your life. Marry a fine girl. *I don't want you to become what I have become.* Be a friend to everybody. Have no enemies. Hate no one.'

'But . . . how?'

He took me by the hand, firmly. 'Come. Now.'

I was terribly afraid, but I went.

There was near panic as he came into the city, yanking me along, walking in his strange way with his whole back writhing and rippling beneath his sorcerer's robe like a serpent trying to stagger on heavy legs.

People shouted and ran as we passed. Women snatched up their children. A pair of priests crossed their staves to make a sign against us. But Father ignored them all.

We came to a street of fine houses. Astonished faces stared down at us from high windows. Then Father led me to the end of an alley, down a tunnel, and into a yard behind one of the mansions. He knocked at a door. An old man appeared, by his garb a scholar. He gasped and made a sign to ward off evil.

Father pushed me inside.

'Teach my son what you know,' he said to the old man. 'I will pay well.'

That was how I became an apprentice to Velachronos the historian, scribe, and poet. I knew letters already, but he taught me to make fine ones full of swirls and beautiful colors. Then he taught me something of the history of our city, and of the river and the gods. I sat with him for long hours, helping to transcribe ancient books.

Clearly Father wanted me to become learned, so that I would dwell in honor among the people of the city, and know at least modest comfort, as Velachronos did. The old man remarked on this once, 'You seldom see a rich scholar – or a starving one.'

But my sister was ignored completely. Once, when I came home after lessons and found Father outside of his workroom, I said, 'What about Hamakina?'

He shrugged. 'Take her along. It hardly matters.'

So Velachronos had two apprentices. I think he accepted us out of fear at first. I tried to convince him we were not monsters. Gradually he acquiesced. Father paid him double. I labored over the books. Hamakina, too, learned to paint beautiful letters, and Velachronos taught her something of music, so she could sing the ancient ballads of the city. Her voice was very beautiful.

He was kind to us. I remember the time with him fondly. He was like a grandfather or a generous uncle. He took us to the children's festival that spring, and rose from his seat to applaud when Hamakina won the prize in the contest of the masks and the sparrow-headed image of the god Haedos-Kemad leaned forward and showered her with candy.

I felt too old for that sort of thing, yet Father had never taken me to the priests to declare me a man. It is a simple rite unless parents want to make it elaborate. There is only a small fee. I had already had my vision from the gods. Yet Father did not take me and I remained a child, either because I was somehow unworthy, or he merely forgot.

Meanwhile his sorceries grew more extreme. At night the sky flickered from horizon to horizon, and sometimes he came out onto the wharf in front of our house to speak with the thunder. It answered back, calling out his name, and, on occasion, my name.

The stenches from the workroom worsened, and there were more voices, more terrifying visitors in the night. But, too, Father would sometimes stagger about the house, pulling at his beard, flailing his arms like a madman, like someone possessed by a frenzied spirit, and he would seize me and shake me so hard it hurt and plead with me, 'Do you love me, son? Do you still love your father?'

I could never answer him. It drove me to tears many times. I locked myself in my room and he would stand outside the door, sobbing, whispering, 'Do you love me? Do you?'

Then came an evening when I sat studying in my room – Hamakina was off somewhere – and a huge barbarian adventurer climbed in through the window, followed by a little rat-faced man from the City of the Delta.

The barbarian snatched the book from my hands and threw

15

it into the river. He took me by the wrist and jerked. My forearm snapped. I let out a little yelp of pain and the rat-faced man held a long, thin knife like an enormous pin to my face, pressing gently on one cheek, then the other, just below my eyes.

He whispered, flashing filthy teeth. His breath stank.

'Where's yer famous wizard da' who's got all the treasure? Tell us, brat, or I'll make a blind girl out of ye and tie yer guts fer braids—'

The barbarian merely grabbed me by the front of my gown in one huge hand and slammed me against the wall so hard that blood poured out of my nose and mouth.

I could only nod to my left, toward Father's workroom.

Later, when I returned to consciousness, I heard the two of them screaming. The screaming went on for days behind Father's door, while I lay feverish and Hamakina wiped my forehead but could do nothing more. It was only when the screaming faded to distant murmurs, like the voices I'd heard that one time before, like the voice that might have been Mother's, that Father came and healed me with his magic. His face was ashen. He looked very tired.

I slept and the barefoot man in the silver mask knelt on the surface of the water, sending ripples all around my bed. He whispered to me the story of the heron boy who stood among the flock in the dawn light and was left behind when the birds took flight, standing there, waving his graceless, featherless arms.

A few weeks later, Velachronos threw us out. I don't know what happened with him at the end. Perhaps it was just a rumor, or a culmination of rumors, or he might even have heard the truth about something I did not know, but one day, when Hamakina and I came for our lessons, he stood in the doorway and all but shrieked, 'Be gone! Get out of my house, devil-spawn!'

He wouldn't explain or say anything more. There was nothing to do but leave.

That night a vast storm came up from the mouth of the river, a black, swirling mass of clouds like a monster huge enough to smother the world, lumbering on a thousand flickering, fiery legs. The river, the very marshes, raged like the frenzied chaos-ocean that existed before the Earth was made, while the sky thundered light and dark; and for an instant you could see for miles across froth-capped waves and reeds lashing in the wind; then there was only utter blackness and stinging rain and the thunder once more, thunder calling out my father's name again and again.

He answered it, from within his secret room, his voice as loud as the thunder, speaking a language that did not sound like human speech at all, but shrieks and grating cackles and whistles like the raging wind.

In the morning, all the ships were scattered and half the city was blasted away. The air was heavy with the cries of mourners. The river ran beneath our house muddy and furious where before it had been mere shallows.

Many people saw the crocodile-headed messengers of the Devouring God that day.

My sister and I sat in our room, almost afraid to speak even to each other. We could not go out.

From Father's workroom there was only silence that went on for so long that, despite everything, I began to fear for him. I met Hamakina's gaze, and she stared back, wide-eyed and dazed. Then she nodded.

I went to the workroom door and knocked.

'Father? Are you all right?'

To my surprise, he opened the door at once and came out. He steadied himself against the doorway with one hand and hung there, breathing heavily. His hands were gnarled, like claws. They looked like they had been burned.

His face was so pale, so wild, that part of me wasn't even sure it was Father until he spoke.

'I am going to die,' he said. 'It is time for me to go to the gods.'

And, again despite everything, I wept for him.

'Now you must be a faithful son for the last time,' he said. 'Gather reeds and bind them together into a funeral boat. When you are done, I shall be dead. Place me in it and set me adrift, so that I shall come, as all men do, to Surat-Kemad.'

'No, Father! It isn't so!'

17

When I wept, I was remembering him as he had been in my early childhood, not as he had become.

He squeezed my shoulder hard and hissed angrily, 'Quite inevitably, it *is*. Go!'

So Hamakina and I went together. Somehow our house had lost only a few shingles in the storm, and the dock below the trapdoor was still there. My boat was too, but sunken and dangling from its line. We struggled to pull it up, dumped it out, and set it afloat. Miraculously, not even the paddles had been lost.

We climbed in and paddled in silence for about an hour, far enough into the marshes that the waters were again shallow and still and reeds as thick as my arm swayed against the sky like trees. With a hatchet I'd brought along for the purpose, I cut down several, and Hamakina and I labored throughout the day to make a crude boat. In the evening, we towed it back to our house.

I ascended the ladder first, while she waited fearfully below.

For the first time I could remember, the door to Father's workroom was left open. He lay inside, on a couch amid shelves of books and bottles, and at a glance I knew that he was dead.

There was little to do that night. Hamakina and I made a cold supper out of what we could find in the pantry. Then we barred the windows and doors, and pushed a heavy trunk over the trapdoor, lest the *evatim* crawl up and devour the corpse, as they sometimes do.

I explored the workroom only a little, going through Father's books, opening trunks, peering into coffers. If he had any treasure, I didn't find it. Then I picked up a murky bottle and something inside screamed at me with a tiny, faraway voice. I dropped the bottle in fright. It broke and the screaming thing scurried across the floorboards.

The house was full of voices and noises, creakings, whispers, and sighs. Once something heavy, like a huge bird perhaps, flapped and scraped against a shuttered window. My sister and I stayed up most of the night, lanterns in our hands, armed with clubs against whatever terrors the darkness might hold. I sat on the floor outside the workroom, leaning against the door. Hamakina lay with her face in my lap, sobbing softly.

Eventually I fell asleep, and Mother came to me in a dream, leaning over me, dripping water and river mud, shrieking and tearing her hair. I tried to tell her that all would be well, that I would take care of Hamakina, that I would grow up to be a scribe and write letters for people. I promised I wouldn't be like Father.

But still she wept and paced back and forth all night. In the morning, the floor was wet and muddy.

Hamakina and I rose, washed, put on our best clothes, and went to the priests. On the way, some people turned their backs to us while others screamed curses and called us murderers. In the square before the temple, a mob approached with knives and clubs, and I waved my hands and made what I hoped looked like magical gestures until they turned and fled, shouting that I was just as bad as my Father. In that single instant, I almost wished I were.

A whole army of priests followed us back to the house, resplendent in their billowing gold and silver trousers, their blue jackets, and their tall, scale-covered hats. Many of them held aloft sacred ikons of Surat-Kemad, and of the other gods too: of Ragun-Kemad, the Lord of Eagles, and Bel-Kemad, god of spring, and of Bel-Hemad's consort, Delivendra, the Lady of the Lantern, who sends forgiveness and mercy. Acolytes chanted and swung smoking incense-pots on golden chains.

But they would not let us back into the house. Two temple matrons stood with us on the wharf, holding Hamakina and me by the hand. The neighbors watched from a distance, fearfully.

The priests emptied out Father's workroom, breaking open the shutters, pouring bottle after bottle of powders and liquids into the river, dumping many of his books in after, then more bottles, then most of the jars, carvings, and strange specimens. Other books, they confiscated. Junior priests carried heaps of them back to the temple in baskets. Then it seemed the exorcisms went on for hours. They used so much incense that I thought the house was on fire.

In the end, the priests marched away as solemnly as they had come, and one of the matrons gave me a sword which had been my father's, a fine weapon, its grip bound in copper wire, its blade inlaid with silver.

'You may need this,' was all she would say.

Fearfully, my sister and I ventured inside the house. The air was so thick with incense that we ran, choking, our eyes streaming, to open all the windows. Still, the burners hung everywhere and we dared not remove them.

Father lay on the couch in his workroom, bound in gauze. The priests had removed his eyes, and placed amulets like huge coins in the empty sockets. I knew this was because they were afraid he would find his way back otherwise.

Hamakina and I had to get him down to the funeral boat. There was no one to help us. It was a terrible struggle. Hamakina was, after all, only eight, and I was fifteen. More than once I was afraid we would accidentally *drop* him.

One of the gold amulets fell out. The empty socket gaped like a dry, red wound. I was almost sick when I had to put the amulet back.

The funeral boat was hung with gauze and charms. Incense rose from a silver cup set in the prow. One of the priests had painted a symbol, a serpent swallowing its tail, only broken, on the stern.

In the twilight of evening, Hamakina and I towed the funeral boat out into the deep water beyond the city, among the crooked masts of the wrecked ships, and beyond.

The sky faded gently from red to black, streaked with the purple tatters of the last few storm clouds. An almost frigid wind blew out of the marshes. The stars gleamed, multiplied upon the rippling water.

I stood in my shallow boat and recited the service for the dead as best as I knew it, for my father whom I still loved and feared and did not understand. Then Hamakina let loose the line, and the funeral boat began to drift, first downstream toward the delta and the sea; but in the darkness, just before it disappeared, it was clearly going *upstream*. That was a good sign. It meant the boat had caught the black current, which carries the dead out of the world of the living, into the abode of the gods.

I thought, then, that I had time to mourn. When we got back, the house was merely empty. For the first time in many years, I was not afraid. It was almost bewildering.

I slept quietly that night. I did not dream. Hamakina, too, was quiet.

The next morning an old woman who lived in one of the first houses at the other end of the wharf knocked on our door and said, 'Children? Are you well? Do you have enough to eat?'

She left a basket of food for us.

That, too, was a good sign. It meant that the neighbors would eventually forgive us. They didn't really think I was as my father had been.

I took the basket inside slowly, weeping half for joy. Life would be better. I remembered my promise to my mother. I would be different. The next day, surely, or the day after, Velachronos would take us back and we could resume our lessons.

Only that night Father came to me in a dream, and he stood before my bed wrapped in gauze, his face terrible behind the golden disks. His voice was – I cannot truly describe it – *oily,* like something dripping, something thick and vile; and the mere fact that such a sound could form itself into words seemed the greatest obscenity of all.

'I have delved too far into the darkness, my son, and my ending can only come with the final mystery. I seek it. My studies are almost complete. It is the culmination of all my labors. But there is one thing I need, one thing I have come back for.'

And in my dream I asked him, 'Father, what is it?'

'Your sister.'

Then I awoke to the sound of Hamakina screaming. She reached for my hand, missed, caught the edge of the bed, and fell with a thump, dragging the covers onto the floor.

I always kept a lit lantern on the stand by the bed. Now I opened the little metal door, flooding the room with light.

'Sekenre! Help me!'

I stared incredulously for just an instant as she hung

suspended in air, dangling, as if an invisible hand had seized her by the hair. Then she screamed once more and seemed to fly through the window. For a second she grabbed hold of the sill. She looked toward me. Our eyes met. But before I could do or say anything she was yanked loose and hauled through.

I ran to the window and leaned out.

There was no splash; the water below rippled gently. The night was still. Hamakina was simply gone.

Chapter 2: In the Sybil's House

In the morning, the third after Father's death, I went to see the Sybil. There was nothing else to do. Everyone in the City of the Reeds knows that when the great crisis of your life comes, when there is truly no alternative but surrender and death and no risk is too great, then it is time to see the Sybil.

Fortunate is the man who has never called on her goes the old saying. But I was not fortunate.

She is called the Daughter of the River, and the Voice of Surat-Kemad, and the Mother of Death, and many other things. Who she is and what she is, no one has ever known; but she dwelt, fearsomely, the subject of countless terrifying stories, beneath the very heart of the city, among the pilings, where the log posts that hold up the great houses are thick as any forest. I had heard of the terrible price she was reputed to demand for her prophecies, and that those who visited her came away irreparably changed if they came away at all. Yet since time immemorial she had dwelt there, and for as long people went to listen to her words.

I went. For an offering, I had my father's sword, the silver one the temple matron gave me.

It was in the earliest dawn twilight that I slipped once more through the trapdoor beneath our house. To the east, to my right, the sky was just beginning to brighten into gray, but before me, toward the heart of the city, night lingered.

I paddled amid the wreckage left by the recent storm: planks, bobbing barrels and trunks, and, once, a slowly rolling corpse the *evatim* had somehow overlooked. Further in, a huge house had fallen on its supports, now awash and broken, its windows gaping like black mouths. Later, when the gloom lessened a bit, I came upon a capsized ship jammed among

23

the pillars like a vast, dead fish caught in reeds, its rigging trailing in the black water.

Just beyond it, the dark, irregular mass of the Sybil's dwelling hung suspended, undamaged by the storm, of course.

There's another story they tell about her: that the Sybil was never young, but was born an old hag in the blood of her mother's death, and that she stood up in the pool of her mother's blood, in the darkness at the world's beginning; and she closed her hands together, then opened them, and columns of flame rose up from her palms.

My father used to do that trick, and once he grew terribly angry when I tried it, even though I'd just sat staring at my hands, opening and closing them without understanding or results. It was enough that I had made the attempt. He was perhaps even frightened at first, at the prospect that I might try again and eventually succeed. Then his face shifted from shock to cold fury. That was the only time in my life he ever beat me.

But when the Sybil made fire with her hands she rolled the flames into balls with her fingers. She breathed on one to make it dim, and released them both – the Sun and Moon. Then she drank long and deep of the Great River where her mother's blood flowed into it, stood up by moonlight, and spat out the sparkling stars. And by starlight the multitude of gods awoke along the banks of the river and beheld the Earth for the first time.

As I gazed upon her house, I could almost believe the story. No, I *did* believe it.

The Sybil's house was more of an immense cocoon, like a spider's web filled to overflowing with debris and dead things, spun and accumulated since the beginning of time. It hung from the underside of the city itself, its outer strands a tangle of ropes and netting and vines and fibers stretching out into the darkness in every direction until I could not tell where the enormous nest began or ended.

But the core of it hung down almost to the water, like a monstrous belly. I reached up and tied my boat to it, slipped Father's sword under my belt, bound my robe up to free my legs, and started to climb.

The ropes trembled, whispering like muted thunder. Mud and debris fell in my face, splashing all around me. I hung on desperately, then shook my head to clear my eyes, and continued climbing.

Higher up, in complete darkness, I squeezed along a tunnel of rotting wood, sometimes losing my grip and sliding backwards for a terrifying instant before I found another hold. The darkness was ... *heavy*. I had the impression of an endless mass of debris in all directions, shifting, grinding as I wriggled through it. Sometimes there was an overwelming stench of decay.

I crawled over the upturned hull of a boat. It swayed gently beneath my weight. Something soft fell, then slithered against its side. All the while my hands and bare feet scraped desperately for purchase against the rotting wood.

Then came more rope, more netting, and in the dimmest twilight I was in a chamber where trunks, wicker baskets, and heavy clay jugs all heaved and crashed together as I crawled among them.

Serpents and fishes writhed beneath my touch amid reeking slime.

And yet again in utter darkness I made my way on hands and knees across a seemingly solid wooden floor. Then the boards snapped beneath me and I tumbled screaming amid ropes and wood and what touch alone told me were hundreds of human bones. I came to rest on heaving netting with a skull in my lap and bones rattling down over my bare legs. I threw the skull away and tried to jump up, but my feet slid through the net and I felt only empty space below.

I dangled there, clinging desperately to the rope netting. It broke and I was left screaming once more, swinging in the darkness while a cascade of bones splashed into the water far below.

One further story I'd heard came to me just then: that when someone drowns in the river, the *evatim* eat his flesh, but the bones go to the Sybil, who divines fortunes from them.

So it seemed.

At precisely this point she called out to me, and her voice was like an autumn wind rattling in dead reeds.

'*Son of Vashtem.*'

I clung tighter to the remnants of the net, gulped, and called up into the darkness.

'I'm here.'

'*Sorcerer, son of sorcerer, I await your coming.*'

I was so startled I nearly let go.

'But *I'm* not a sorcerer!'

'*Sorcerer, son of sorcerer.*'

I started climbing once more, all the while telling her about myself in broken, panting speech. Still a few bones fell, suddenly out of the darkness, striking me on the head as if in sarcastic reply to what I gasped out. But still I told her how I had never done any magic myself, how I had promised my mother *never* to be like my father, how I was apprenticed to the learned Velachronos, how I was going to be a scribe first, then maybe write books of my own, if only Velachronos would take me back when this was all over.

Then the Sybil's face appeared to me suddenly in the darkness above, like a full moon from behind a cloud. Her face was pale and round, her eyes inexpressibly black, and I think her skin *did* glow faintly.

And she said to me, laughing gently, 'Sorcerer, son of sorcerer, you're *arguing* with the dread Sybil. Now is that a brave thing to do, or just foolish?'

I stopped, swinging gently from side to side on the ropes.

'I'm sorry. I didn't mean to—'

'What you *mean* is not necessarily what you *do,* Sekenre. Whether or not you're sorry afterwards means nothing at all. There. I have spoken your name once. *Sekenre.* I have spoken it twice. Do you know what happens if I speak it three times?'

I said meekly, 'No, Great Sybil.'

'Sorcerer, son of sorcerer, come up and sit before me. Do not be afraid.'

I climbed up to where she was. I could barely make out a wooden shelf or ledge, covered with bones and debris. I reached out gingerly with one foot and my toes found, surprisingly, solid, dry planking. I let go of the ropes and sat. The Sybil reached up and opened the door of one box-lantern, then of another, and another. I thought of lazy beasts winking themselves awake.

Now light and shadow flickered in the tiny, low-ceilinged room. The Sybil sat cross-legged, a blanket with gleaming embroidery draped over her knees. A man-headed serpent with scales like silver coins lay curled in her lap. Once it hissed and she leaned low while it whispered in her ear.

Silence followed. She gazed into my eyes for a long time.

I held out my father's sword.

'Lady, this is all I have to offer—'

She hissed, just like the serpent, and for an instant seemed startled, even afraid. She waved the sword away.

'Sekenre, you are interrupting the Sybil. Now, again, is that brave or just foolishness?'

There. She had spoken my name thrice. I felt an instant of sheer terror. But nothing happened.

She laughed again, and her laugh was a human one, almost kindly.

'A most inappropriate gift, sorcerer, son of sorcerer.'

'I don't understand . . . I'm sorry, Lady.'

'Sekenre, do you know what that sword is?'

'It was my father's.'

'It is the sword of a Knight Inquisitor. Your father tried to deny what he was, even to himself. So he joined a holy order, an order of strictest discipline, devoted to the destruction of all things of darkness, all the wild things, witches, sorcerers, even the wild gods. He was like you, boy, at your age. He wanted so much to do the *right* thing. For all the good it did him. In the end, he only had the sword.'

'Lady, I have nothing else—'

'Sekenre – there, I said it again. You are very special. The path before you is very special. Your future is not a matter of how many times I speak your name. Keep the sword. You shall need it. I require no payment from you, not yet anyway.'

'Will you require it later, Great Sybil?'

She leaned forward, and I saw that her teeth were sharp and pointed. Her breath smelled of river mud.

'Your entire life shall be payment enough. All things come

to me in proper time, even as you, I think, come to me now, when your need is greatest.'

Then I began to tell her why I had come, about Father, and what had happened to Hamakina.

'Sorcerer, son of sorcerer, you are lecturing the Sybil. Brave or foolish?'

I wept. 'Please, Great Lady ... I don't know what I'm supposed to say. I want to do the right thing. Please don't be angry. Tell me what to do.'

'Sorcerer, son of sorcerer, everything you do is the correct thing, part of the great pattern which I observe, which I weave, which I prophesy. At each new turning of your life the pattern is made anew. All the meanings are changed. Your father understood that, when he came back from beyond the sea, no longer a Knight Inquisitor because he knew too much of sorcery. He had become a sorcerer by fighting sorcery. He was like a doctor who contracts the patient's disease. His knowledge was like a door that has been opened and can never be closed again. A door. In his mind.'

'No,' I said softly. 'I will not be like him.'

'Hear then the prophecy of the Sybil, sorcerer, son of sorcerer. You shall journey into the very belly of the beast, into the mouth of the God Who Devours.'

'Lady, we are all on a journey in this life, and when we die—'

'Sorcerer, son of sorcerer, do you accept the words of the Sybil of your own will, as a gift given?'

I was afraid to ask her what would happen if I refused. It wasn't much of a choice.

'Lady, I accept.'

'It is of your will then. If you stray from your path, if you step aside, that, too, changes the weaving of all lives.'

'Lady, I only want to get my sister back and—'

'Then accept these too.'

She pressed something into my hand. Her touch was cold and hard, like living iron. The serpent thing in her lap hissed, almost forming words.

I held my open hand up to one of the lanterns and saw two grave coins on my palm.

'Sorcerer, son of sorcerer, on this day you are a man. Your father did not raise you to manhood before he left you. Therefore I must perform the rite.'

The serpent thing vanished into her clothing. She rose, her movement fluid as smoke. I could only see her face and hands, like lanterns themselves floating in the half-light. She took a silver band and bound my hair as the men of the city bind it. She gave me a pair of baggy trousers such as the men of the city wear. I put them on. They were much too long. I rolled them up to my knees.

'They used to belong to a pirate,' she said. 'He won't be needing them now.'

She rummaged around among the debris and produced a single boot. I tried to put it on. It was nearly twice the size of my foot.

She sighed. 'Always the pattern changes. I'm sure it's portentous. Never mind.'

She took the boot from me and threw it aside.

Then she leaned down and kissed me on the forehead. The touch of her lips was so cold it burned.

'Now you are marked by the Sybil, sorcerer, son of sorcerer, and by that mark men will know you. Because you are marked, you may call on me three times, and I shall hear you and reply. But beware. If you ask my favor more than that, I shall own you, like all the things in my house. That is the price I ask of you.'

She gave me a water bottle and a leather bag with food in it – cheese, bread, and dried fish – and told me to put the grave coins in the bag too so I wouldn't lose them.

The bag had a long cord. I slipped it over my neck. I hung the bottle from the loose belt I wore outside my robe.

My forehead was numb where she had kissed me. I reached up and felt the spot. It was cold as ice.

'Now go, sorcerer, son of sorcerer, into the very jaws of the Devourer, of your own will. Go, as the Sybil has prophesied, *right now—*'

She stamped her foot once. I screamed as the floor swung away beneath me like a trapdoor and I was falling endlessly down amid glowing white bones and debris and the Sybil's tumbling lamps. I saw her face once, far above, streaking away in the darkness like a shooting star.

I hit the water hard and sank deep, but somehow reached the surface again, lungs bursting. I started to swim. The sword cut my legs. The bag choked me. I almost threw them both away, but did not, and slowly, clumsily made my way back to where I thought my boat waited. I looked around fearfully for the *evatim*, which surely haunted this place.

Above, the house of the Sybil was silent and dark.

At last my feet touched soft mud and I stood up in the gloom. Faint light filtered between the ten thousand wooden legs of the city.

I waded through thick mud, then into open water and fell in over my head and swam a short distance, struggling toward the light. Then my feet found a sand bank, and I climbed out of the water and rested.

A whole night must have passed then, for I slept through terrible dreams of my father in his sorcerer's robe, stalking back and forth at the water's edge, his face so twisted with rage that he hardly seemed to be my father at all. He would lean over, raise his hand to strike, then pause, startled, even afraid, as if he had seen something in my face he had never seen there before.

I tried to call out to him.

Suddenly I was awake, in total darkness. A footstep splashed nearby. Far away, the birds of the marshes sang to announce the dawn.

And my father's voice spoke.

'Sekenre . . . do you still love me?'

I could not answer. I only sat terribly still, shivering in the cold air, my knees drawn up to my chest, hands clasped tight to my wrists.

Daylight came as a gray blur. I saw a boat nearby, beached on the same sandbank. It was not my own, but a funeral boat, made of bound reeds.

For an instant I thought I understood fully what the Sybil had prophesied and I froze in terror, but I had known so much of terror in my life already that I had grown indifferent to it. I couldn't bring myself to care. I couldn't think coherently.

Like one bewitched, when the body acts of its own accord without the will of the mind, I pushed the boat out into open water, then climbed in and lay still among the scented corpse-wrappings.

I felt only resignation now. So it had been prophesied.

Almost on a whim, I reached into the leather bag and took out the two grave coins. I placed them over my eyes.

Chapter 3: Among the Dead

For a long time I lay still and listened to the water lapping against the side of the boat. Then even that sound faded, and I felt, very distinctly, the boat reverse direction, and I knew I was drifting with the black current now, out of the world of the living, into the land of the dead. The water was silent, as if the boat were gliding along a river of oil. I could hear the pounding of my own heart.

I lay awake and tried to make sense out of my adventure with the Sybil, reviewing every detail in search of some central thread by which all the parts would be connected, like beads on a necklace, assuming form and meaning. But there was nothing. I had expected as much. It is the way of prophecies: you don't understand them until they're about to come true, and then, suddenly, the whole pattern is revealed.

Even the silence of the river and the thunder of my heart were part of the pattern.

Even my sister's voice.

I thought it was just a ringing in my ears at first, but it formed words, very weak, very far away, at the very threshold of hearing.

'Sekenre,' she said. 'Help me. I'm lost.'

I called back to her, either with my voice or my mind.

'I am coming, little one. Wait for me.'

She sobbed hoarsely, sucking in breath as if she had been crying for a long time.

'It's dark here.'

'It's dark here, too,' I said gently.

She was too brave to say she was afraid.

'Hamakina – is Father with you?'

Something splashed in the water right next to the boat, and my father's voice whispered, inches from my ear.

'Sekenre, if you love me, go back. I command you to go back! Do not come here!'

I let out a yell and sat up. The grave coins fell into my lap. I twisted about, looking all around.

The boat slid past huge black reeds. In the silent darkness, white herons stood in rows along the river's edge, faintly glowing as the Sybil's face had glowed. And in the water, the *evatim* watched me, rank upon rank of them like dead-white, naked men with crocodile heads, lying motionless in the shallows. But there was no sign of Father.

Above me, the sky was dark and clear, and the stars were not the stars of Earth, but fewer, paler, almost gray, arranged in the constellations of the dead, which are described in the Books of the Dead: the Hand, the Harp, the Jar of Forgetting, the Eye of Surat-Kemad.

Very carefully, I picked up the grave coins and put them back in my bag. I was thirsty and drank a sip from the water bottle. I could not drink river water here, for only the dead may drink of the water of the dead, and only the dead may eat the fruits of the land of the dead. That too is written in the Books of the Dead.

And so I gazed with mortal, uncovered eyes into the darkness that never ends. Far behind me, along the way I had come, there was a faint suggestion of light, a mere paling of the sky, as if way back there was an opening through which I had already passed. The living world drew farther and farther away with each fading instant.

The white herons rose as one and for a moment the air was filled with the utterly silent passage of their wings. Then they were gone. They too, like the *evatim*, were messengers of the God of the Dark River.

But for me there was no message.

I began to see ghosts among the reeds, sitting up in the mud as I passed, beseeching me to take them aboard my funeral boat so they might go properly into the final land. They were no more than wisps of smoke, suggestions of shapes glimpsed from the corner of the eye. When I looked directly at any one of them, I could not see it.

Some called out in languages I had never heard before. Only

a few spoke of places and people I had known. I was afraid
of these few. I did not want them to recognize me. I lay back
down in the bottom of my boat and put the coins back over
my eyes. I slept fitfully after a while and dreamed of my father.
He paced back and forth on the surface of the black water, his
trailing robe sending ripples as he walked, his face contorted
with rage. Once he stopped and seemed to shake me furiously,
saying, 'No, my son, no. This is not what I wanted for you. I
command you. I forbid you. ... because I love you still. Go
back to Reedland. Go!'

But, in my dream, I only answered, 'Father, I will go if you
let me take Hamakina back with me.'

He made no answer but continued to rage and pace, too
furious even to ask if I loved him.

I awoke from my dream to the faint sound of singing like
many voices carried on the wind from far away. I sat up once
more, put the coins in my bag, and saw a vast trireme bearing
down on me, its sail bellied full, its oars thrashing the water
into foam.

Yet it was an insubstantial thing like the ghosts in the reeds,
a shape of smoke. The voices of the oarsmen were muted, the
throbbing of the pace-setter's drum like the failing thunder of
a distant, dying storm. The stars shone through the hull and
sail, and the foam of the oars was a phantom thing, the water
around me still black and smooth and silent.

This was a wonder, but no mystery, for the Great River
co-exists with the River of the Dead, for all that they flow
in different directions. Sometimes the rivermen fleetingly
glimpse the traffic of the dark current, faint shapes in the
night. When they do, they reckon it a bad omen and make
sacrifices to soothe the anger of whatever god might have
been offended.

Now I, on the River of the Dead, saw the living as phantoms.
The trireme loomed up, and then my boat passed through it.
For a moment I was among the oarsmen and I could smell the
reek of their laborings. Then a richly-furnished cabin swam
around me. A great lord feasted, surrounded by his followers.
I think it was the Satrap of Reedland himself. One lady of his
company paused, cup in hand. Our eyes met. She looked more

startled than afraid. She poured out a little of her wine, as if to make a libation to me.

Then the trireme was gone, and I lay back again, the coins on my eyes, my father's sword clutched against my chest.

I slept once more and dreamt once more, but my dream was only a confusion, shapes in the darkness, and sounds I could not make out. I awoke parched and famished, and took another sip from my water bottle, and ate a little of the food in the leather bag.

It was as I ate that I realized that the river was no longer flowing. The boat lay absolutely motionless in the middle of a black, endless, dead marsh beneath the gray stars. Even the *evatim* and the ghosts were gone.

I was truly afraid. I thought I would be left there forever. No, somehow I was *certain* of it. Somehow the Devouring God had tricked me, and the Land of the Dead would not accept me while I yet lived.

I forced down one last bite of bread, then closed the bag and called out, half sobbing: *'Sybil! Help me! I've lost my way!'*

And the sky began to lighten. I saw not merely reeds, but huge trees rising out of the marsh, stark and barren like ruined stone pillars.

Some of the stars began to fade. I thought the Moon was rising – how strange that I should be able to see the Moon here! – but instead the face of the Sybil drifted into the sky, pale and round and huge as the full Moon. She gazed down on me for a time in silence and I was afraid to speak to her. Then her face rippled, as a reflection does when a pebble is dropped into a still pool, and she was gone, but her voice came rattling through the reeds.

'Sorcerer, son of sorcerer, you have called on me foolishly and have wasted one summoning. You are near to your goal and could have found your own way. Nevertheless, if you think you need a guide, reach down into the water and draw one up.'

'Into the *water?*' I said. For an instant I was terrified that I had wasted a second summoning with that question. But the Sybil did not reply.

I reached down into the frigid water, wary of lurking *evatim*. I groped around, swinging my arm from side to side, my fingers outstretched. For an instant I lay there, half out of the boat, wondering if this were another of the Sybil's riddles. Then the water suddenly stirred, as if something were rising, and my fingers closed on something stringy and slippery like an underwater weed, and I pulled.

A hand broke the surface, then another. I let go of what I had been holding and scrambled back. The hands caught hold of the side of the boat and the boat rocked beneath the weight of that which climbed aboard. There was a sudden, overwelming stench of decay, or rotted flesh. Long, muddy hair fell across a face that was more bone than anything else.

I screamed then, and kept on screaming when the thing opened its eyes and began to speak and I knew that it was my mother.

'Sekenre—'

I covered my face with my hands and merely sobbed, trying to remember her as she had been once, so very long ago.

'Sekenre –' She took hold of my wrists and gently drew my hands away from my face. Her touch was as cold as the Sybil's kiss.

I turned from her.

'Mother, I did not expect –' I could not say more, and broke into tears again.

'Son, I did not expect to see you in this place either. Truly, it is a terrible thing.'

She pulled me forward and I did not resist, until I lay with my face in her lap, my cheek against her wet, muddy gown, while she gently stroked my forehead with a bony finger. I told her all that had happened then, of Father's own death, and his return for Hamakina.

'I am your father's sin, returning to him at last,' she said.

'Did he—?'

'Murder me? Yes, he did. But that is the least part of his offense. He has sinned more against you, Sekenre, and also against the gods.'

'I don't think he meant to do wrong,' I said. 'He says he loves me still.'

'He probably does. Nevertheless, he has done great wrong.'

'Mother, what shall I do?'

Her cold, sharp finger drew a circle around the mark on my forehead.

'It is time for us to resume our journey. The boat has served its purpose now. You must leave it.'

I looked at the black water with ever-increasing dread.

'I don't understand. Are we to . . . *swim?*'

'No, beloved son. We are to walk. Get out of the boat now, and walk.'

I slipped one leg over the side, one foot into the icy water. I looked back at her uncertainly.

'Go on. Do you doubt this one small miracle, after all you have seen?'

'Mother, I—'

'*Go on.*'

I obeyed her and stood upon the water. It felt like cold glass beneath my feet. Then she stood next to me, and the boat drifted slowly away. I turned to watch it go, but she took me by the hand and led me in a different direction.

Her touch was like the Sybil's, a touch of living, frigid iron.

The channel widened, and the *evatim* were waiting for us. Here the water flowed almost swiftly, making silent waves and eddies and whirlpools behind the dead trees. Many ghosts waded in the shallows, but they did not call out to us. They merely stood there, turning as we passed. One of them was a man in full, gleaming armor, holding his severed head in his hands.

Then there were other boats around us, black and solid and silent, not phantoms of the living, but other funeral boats. We came alongside a long, sleek barge, its pointed ends rising high above the water, a lantern flickering inside its square cabin. The *evatim* crawled into this cabin and the barge rocked. I could hear them thrashing in there.

At last something huge and dark loomed before us, like a mountain, blotting out the stars. On every side I saw drifting funeral boats following our course, some of them twisting and turning among reeds. One caught on something, or else the *evatim* tipped it over. A mummy slipped into the water and drifted by, bandages trailing, so close I could have reached out and touched it.

The darkness closed around us very suddenly, shutting out the stars. I heard water rushing, and boats creaking and banging against one another.

'Mother!' I whispered. I reached forward and tugged at her gown. A piece of it came away in my hand. 'Is this it? Is this the mouth of Surat-Kemad?'

'No, child,' she said softly. 'We have been in the belly of the beast for some time now.'

And that, somehow, was even more terrifying.

Chapter 4: Everybody and Nobody

Nothing was clear anymore, the whole adventure no more than an endless continuity of dream and waking, stark images and featureless mist, pain and terror and dull discomfort.

I had been on the river I knew not how long – hours, days, weeks – and at times it seemed I was inexpressibly weary, and at others that I was back home in my bed, asleep, that all of this was some crazed nightmare. But then I reached out, turning and stretching as one does when awakening – and I touched my mother's cold, wet, ruined body.

And the stench of decay was gone from her, and she smelled only of the river mud, like some long-sunken bundle of sticks and rags.

Sometimes there were herons all around us, glowing dimly in the utter darkness like smouldering embers, their faces those of men and women, all of them whispering to us, imploring, speaking names – and their voices blended together like a gentle, indistinguishable rustle of wind.

Mostly, we just walked in the darkness, alone. I felt the cold surface of the river beneath my feet, but there was no sense of motion, for all that my legs moved endlessly.

Mother spoke. Her voice was soft, coming from the darkness like something remembered in a dream.

I don't think she was even addressing me. She was merely talking, her memories, her whole life rising into words like sluggish bubbles: scraps of unfinished conversations from her childhood, and, too, much about my father, and me, and Hamakina. For what might have been a very long time or only a few minutes, she sang a lullaby, as if rocking me – or perhaps Hamakina – to sleep.

Then she was silent. I reached out to assure myself that she was still there, and her bony hand found mine and squeezed

41

gently. I asked her what she had learned about the Land of the Dead since she had come here, and she replied softly, 'I have learned that I am forever an exile, without a place prepared for me, since I have come unprepared and unannounced into Surat-Kemad's domain. My place of exile is the river, along which I must wander until the gods die and the worlds are unmade.'

I wept for her then, and asked if this was Father's doing, and she said that it was.

Then she asked me suddenly, 'Sekenre, do you hate him?'

I had been so confident just then that I did, but I could not find an answer.

'I don't think he meant to do any harm—'

'My son, you must sort out your feelings toward him. That is where you have lost your way, not on the river.'

Again we walked for a long time, still in utter darkness, and all the while I thought of my father and remembered my mother as she had once been. What I wanted, more than anything else, was merely for everything to be restored – Father, Mother, Hamakina, and myself, in our house by the edge of the City of Reeds, as all had been when I was small. Yet, if I had learned any lesson in life thus far, it was that you can't go back, that our days flow on as relentlessly as the Great River, and what is lost is never restored. I was not wise. I understood very little. But I knew that much.

The Father I longed for was merely gone. Perhaps he, too, longed to be restored. I wondered if he knew it was impossible.

I tried to hate him.

The darkness and the silence of the river gave a sense of being in a tunnel, far underground, but were we not more than underground, deep in the belly of Surat-Kemad? We passed from darkness into darkness, always beginning, as if through countless anterooms without ever finding the main hall.

So with our days. So with our strivings, I thought. Whatever we seek to understand yields only a glimmer, and a vast mystery.

So with my father—

Very suddenly, Mother took both my hands in hers and

said, 'I may only guide you a little way, my son, and we have come that little way. I cannot go where an exile is not welcome, where there is no place prepared—'

'What? I don't understand.'

'I am not permitted into the god's house. I must leave you at the doorstep.'

'But you said—'

'That we have been deep within his belly for some time. Yet we are at the doorstep of his house—'

She let go of me. I groped frantically for her, then found her again.

'Mother!'

She kissed both my hands very gently, and her lips, like the Sybil's, were so cold they burned.

'But you are a hero, my son, and you may take the next step, and the next. That is what it is to be brave, you know, merely to take the next step. I have always known that you were brave.'

'Mother, I—'

Then she sank down into the water. I clung to her. I tried to hold her up, but she sank like a thing of stone, and I lost my grip. At the very last I found myself crawling absurdly about on the cold surface of the river, sliding my hands from side to side like a blind child who has lost marbles on a smooth floor.

I stood up, suddenly shivering, rubbing my arms with my hands.

She was wrong, I told myself. I wasn't a hero. I wasn't brave. I merely had no choice. The Sybil had seen that much.

Yet I never once thought of turning back. The road behind me was impassable, in more ways than one.

I wanted to call on the Sybil again, to tell her I had once more lost my way. In the darkness, without any point of reference except the sensation in my feet to tell me which way was down, I couldn't even tell if I wore facing the way I was supposed to be going, or the way I had come.

In the end, it did not matter. I don't think direction is a physical thing in the belly of a god. Instead, it is a matter of degree.

Things began to happen swiftly once more. Lights rose around me, like lanterns drifting up from the surface of the water, then above me like stars. The water itself rippled, frigid, oily waves washing over my feet.

I started to run, afraid that whatever magic had held me up was leaving me, now that Mother had. Nothing, it seemed, could be more horrible than to be immersed in that river, here, in the belly of Surat-Kemad.

I ran, and the points of light moved with me, turning as I turned, swirling about me like burning motes on the wind. There was a sound. I thought it was indeed the wind, but then I realized that it was *breathing*, spittle hissing through teeth, and the lights were *eyes*, not reflecting light as a dog's will by a campfire, but actually glowing, like living coals.

The darkness lessened and I saw that I had indeed emerged from a tunnel. Jagged, fissured cliffs loomed on either side of the river, towering to unknowable heights. Far above, the gray stars of the deadlands shone once more.

And the *evatim* stood around me by the thousands, on the river, scrambling up the cliffs, some of them just standing at the water's edge, staring. By the light of their eyes and by the pale stars, I could see that I had come at last to the place where the Great River ended and truly began, a vast lake where the white-bodied, crocodile-headed ones paced back and forth, ankle-deep in thick gray mist, their long jaws bobbing up and down.

The *evatim* bore long hooks on poles, like boathooks, and as I watched one of them would occasionally pause, then reach down with his hook and draw up a human corpse, heave it onto his shoulder and depart, or just stand there, holding the dead in a lover's embrace.

I realized to my horror that I was standing on a vast sea of corpses. I looked down and I could make them out dimly beneath the water's surface, inches below my feet: faces, arms, bobbing chests and backs and buttocks jostling slowly in the black water like numberless fish in a net. I jumped back in revulsion, but there was nowhere to jump to.

I started to run again. Somehow, miraculously, the *evatim* seemed too busy with their tasks to notice me.

For the first time my footfalls made a sound, a heavy splashing and sucking, as if I were running through mud.

Truly this was the place I had read of in the Books of the Dead that Velachronos and I had copied, where the bodies and souls of the dead and the unborn are sorted out by the *evatim*, who are the thoughts and servants of the terrible god, and each person is judged, and carried to his rightful place, or cast out, or devoured.

I despaired then, for I knew that if Hamakina were *here*, I would surely never find her.

Yet I took the next step, and the next, and the next, slowing to a fast walk. If that is what it is to be brave, then I was. I continued. The mist swirled around my shins.

I seemed to be nearing the shallows. Reeds rose around me like bare iron rods. I passed one sunken funeral boat, then another, then a long stretch of boards and debris but no corpses or *evatim*.

A beach spread before me like a pale band on the horizon, like a white sunrise. The *evatim* struggled across it in an endless procession, dragging their burdens from the water.

I stood among the reeds and watched them for a time. Then I took a step forward, and cold water splashed around my knees. I gasped involuntarily at the sudden shock of no longer walking *on* the water, but in it. There was mud and sand beneath my feet.

I neared the beach and crouched down, trying to conceal myself among the last of the reeds. Gradually I could make out three huge doorways in the cliff-face beyond the end of the white sand. The crocodile-headed ones labored toward them, bearing their burdens through the doorways.

I didn't doubt that each doorway led to a different place, and that here the final judgement of the god was made. Yes, I was on Surat-Kemad's doorstep, in the anteroom of his great hall, forever beginning my quest.

But I didn't know which of the three doors to go through. Surely my Father waited beyond . . . one of them.

I took the next step, and the next, freely mingling with the *evatim*, who took no notice of me. We crowded toward one of the doors. I was hemmed in by cold, hard bodies. I let the movement of the great mass of them determine my direction.

The empty face of an old woman bobbed in front of my face, her corpse slung over the shoulder of her bearer, her open mouth black, frozen as if perpetually about to shout or kiss or devour.

Once more the cliffs rose around me. Once more some of the *evatim* scrambled up the jagged stones, their glowing eyes seeming to rise into the sky like stars. Those who had climbed, I saw, set their burdens down on ledges and began to feast.

I turned away quickly and stared at the ground, and at the almost luminously pale feet and legs of the *evatim.*

The sides of the great doorway were carven smooth, its iron gates flung wide. The gates resembled, more than anything else, enormous, gaping jaws.

I tried to peer ahead again, but I could not see over the mass of the *evatim.* I jumped up. I turned and looked back, but only masses of crocodile-faces stared back at me, like a swirling shifting cloud filled with burning eyes.

'Stop! You are not of the brotherhood of the *evatim!*'

I whirled around again. A pallid, black-bearded face hovered before me, its red eyes unblinking. It rose on the body of a snake, only stiff as a tree trunk and covered with glistening silver scales the size of my outstretched hand. As I watched, another face rose from the ground on such a glittering stalk, and another, bursting out of the sand, out of the stone of the cliff face until a forest of them blocked my way. The *evatim* drew aside.

'*You may not pass!*' one of them said.

'*Blasphemer, you may not enter our master's domain.*'

I got out my leather bag and struggled desperately with the drawstring, then poured the two grave coins into my hand.

'Wait,' I said. 'Here. These are for you.'

The foremost of the man-headed serpent-things leaned forward and took the coins into its mouth. Its lips, like the Sybil's, like my mother's, were searingly cold.

But the coins burst into flame in the creature's mouth and it spat them out at my feet.

'*You are still alive!*'

46

Then all of them shouted in unison, '*This one is still alive!*'

And the *evatim* came writhing through the scaled, shrieking forest, free of their burdens, on all fours now, their great jaws gaping. I drew my father's sword and struck one of them, and another, and another, but one caught me on the right leg and yanked me to my knees. I slashed at the thing again and again. One of the glowing eyes burst, hissed, and went out.

Another reared up, closed its jaws on my back and chest, and pulled me over backward. That was the end of the struggle. The great mass of them swarmed over me, while still the serpent-things shouted and screamed and babbled, and their voices were like thunder.

Teeth like knives raked me all over, tearing, and I still held the sword, but it seemed very far away and I couldn't move it—

A crocodilian mouth closed over my head, over my shoulders and I called out, my voice muffled, shouting down the very throat of the monster, 'Sybil! Come to me again—!'

I cannot say what actually happened after that. I saw her face again, glowing like a distant lantern in the darkness below me, but rising, racing upward, while the *evatim* tore at me and crushed me slowly in their jaws.

Then I distinctly felt myself splash into water, and the viscous blackness closed around me and the *evatim* were gone. I sank slowly in the cold and the dark, while the Sybil's face floated before me and grew brighter until the darkness was dispelled and my eyes were dazzled.

'This time, you did well to call on me,' she said.

I awoke on a bed. As soon as I realized that it was a bed, I lay still with my eyes closed, deliberately dismissing from my mind any thought that this was my familiar bed back home, that my adventures had been no more than a prolonged, horrible dream.

I knew it was not so, and my body knew it, from the many wounds where the *evatim* had held me. And I was nearly naked, my clothing in tatters.

But I still held my father's sword. I moved my right arm stiffly, and scraped the blade along hard wood.

This bed was not my bed. It was made of rough boards and covered not with sheets but with sand.

I started to sit up, eyes still closed, and gentle hands took me by the bare shoulders. The hands were soft and warm.

I was dizzy then. The sword slipped from my grasp. I opened my eyes, but couldn't focus. There was only a blur.

Warm water was being poured over my back. My wounds stung. I let out a cry and fell forward and found myself awkwardly embracing some unknown person, my chin on his shoulder.

I could see, then, that I was in a room stranger than any I had ever imagined, a place once richly furnished but now a wreck, turned on its side like a huge box rolled over, its contents spilled everywhere. Stained glass windows hung open above me, dangling, ornately worked with designs of glowing fishes. Books and bottles lay in heaps amid fallen beams, plaster, and bricks. There was a splintered staircase that coiled out and ended in midair. An image of Surat-Kemad had been fixed to the floor and remained fixed, but now it stuck out horizontally into space. A lantern dangled sideways from the gray-green snout.

My host pushed me gently back onto the bed and I was staring into the face of a gray-bearded man. He squinted in the half-light, his face wrinkling. For a moment the look on his face was one of ineffable joy, but it faded into doubt, then bitter disappointment.

'No,' he said. 'It is not so. Not yet . . .'

I reached up to touch him, to be sure he was real and alive, but he took my hand in his and pressed it down on my chest. Then he gave me my father's sword, closing my fingers around the grip, and I lay there, the cold blade against my bare skin.

Then he said something completely astonishing.

'I thought you were my son.'

I sat up and this time sat steadily. I saw that I was indeed almost naked, my clothing completely shredded, and I was smeared with blood. Suddenly I felt weak again, but I caught hold of a bedpost with my free hand and remained upright.

I blurted, 'But you are not my father—'

'Then we are agreed,' he said.

'I don't understand.'

Wind roared outside. The room swayed and creaked, the walls visibly shifting. More plaster, wood, and a sudden deluge of human bones clattered around us, filling the air with dust. Tiles rained over my shoulders and back. The window overhead clacked back and forth.

I thought of the Sybil's house. I looked to my companion with growing dread, but he merely shrugged.

'It'll pass. Don't worry.'

When all was once again still, I said, 'I am Sekenre, son of Vashtem the sorcerer.'

He hissed and drew back.

'Then I fear you!'

'No,' I said. 'I'm not a sorcerer myself.' I started to explain, but he waved his hand, bidding me to cease.

'You are a powerful sorcerer indeed. I can tell! I can tell!'

I concluded that the man was mad. What could be more natural, after all I had been through, than to meet someone who was mad? If he thought I was a sorcerer, there was no sense dissuading him.

I placed my father's sword across my legs, then folded my arms across my chest, and directed toward him what I hoped was a stern gaze.

'Very well. I, a sorcerer, command you to explain yourself.'

He spread his hands and looked helpless. 'Sorcerer, I don't know where to begin—'

'Why did you think I was your son?'

He moved over to the broken statue of a bird and sat on the flat space where the head had once been. He did not answer my question, but sat still for several minutes. I thought he had forgotten me and had fallen into some sort of reverie. I stared up at the dangling window, then toyed with the sword in my lap.

At last he sighed and said, 'What do you know of where you are, sorcerer and son of sorcerer?'

I told him something of my history, and he only sighed again and said that I was a mighty sorcerer for all I was yet an ignorant one.

'Then teach me,' I said.

'When your mother left you,' he said, 'that was because she could not pass beyond *Leshé*, the realm of dreams. Because she had never been prepared for burial, she could not truly enter the land of the dead. There are four realms; you must understand this. Earth is the realm of *Eshé*, the world of living men. But our dreams arise from the mists of the river, from *Leshé*, where the country of sleep borders the country of death. We see unquiet ghosts in our dreams because they linger in *Leshé*, as your mother does. Beyond is *Tashé*, the true domain of the dead, where all dwell in the places the god has appointed for them.'

'And the fourth realm?'

'That is *Akimshé* – holiness. At the heart of the god, in the mind of the god, among the fiery fountains where even gods and worlds and the stars are born – that is *Akimshé*, holiness, which may not be described. Not even the greatest of the prophets, not even the sorcerers, not even the very gods may look on the final mystery of *Akimshé*.'

'But it's still inside Surat-Kemad,' I said. 'I don't see how—'

'It is well that you do not understand. Not even Surat-Kemad understands. Not even he may look on it.'

I said very quickly, 'I have to continue on my way. I have to find my father.'

And my companion said one more surprising thing.

'Yes, of course. I know him. He is a mighty lord here.'

'You – you – *know* him –?' I couldn't say anything more. My thoughts were all a jumble.

'He dwells here in peculiar honor because he is a sorcerer,' the old man said, 'but he must remain here, unique among the servants of Surat-Kemad, but a servant nonetheless.'

I got to my feet unsteadily. The remains of my trousers dangled. I wrapped them around my belt, trying to make myself at least decent, but there wasn't much to work with. I slid the sword under the belt.

I stood there, breathing hard from the exertion, wincing as the effort stretched my lacerated sides.

'You must take me to my father,' I said.

'I can only show you the way.' He shook his head sadly.
'Where?'

He pointed up, to the open window.

'There?'

'Yes,' he said. 'That way.'

'But—' I walked across the room to a door now sideways
in the wall, and opened it, lowering the door against the wall.
I stared through at a dense sideways forest, the forest floor
rising vertically to one side, the trees horizontal. There was
a glowing mist among the trees, like fog at sunrise before
it melts away. Brilliantly-plumed birds cawed and fluttered
in the branches. Warm, damp air blew against my face
and chest.

The gray-bearded man put his hand on my shoulder and
led me away.

'No,' he said. 'You will never find your father through that
door.' He pointed to the ceiling again. *'That* way.'

I started to climb, clumsily, my muscles aching. My right
palm was numb where the guardian-serpent's lips had touched
me.

I caught hold of the image of the god, hooking an arm over
it. Then pulled myself up and sat there astride Surat-Kemad,
my feet dangling.

'You never answered my question. Why did you think I was
your son?'

'It is a very old sorrow.'

I didn't command him. 'Can you . . . tell me?'

He sat down on the edge of the bed and gazed up at me. 'I
was called Aukin, son of Nevat. I dwelt far beyond any land
you ever knew, beyond the mouth of the Great River and
across the sea among the people you would call barbarians.
I had a wife. I loved her very much. Is that a surprising thing,
even for a barbarian? No, it is not. When she died bearing
my first son, and my son too was dead in her womb, my
grief was without bounds. The gods of my homeland could
not comfort me, for they are harsh spirits of the forest and
of the hills, and they do not deal in comfort. Therefore I
came into your country, first to the City of the Delta, where
I prayed long before the image of Bel-Kemad and gave the

priests much gold. But he did not answer me, and when I ran out of money, the priests sent me away. So I wandered all along the Great River, in the forests, on the plains, among the marshes. I tarried with holy men in the high mountains. From them I learned to dream. They thought they were teaching me contentment, but no, I clung to my bold scheme. It was this: I would be the mightiest dreamer of all and travel beyond *Leshé* to the lake of *Tashé* and farther, and I would find my son who had tried but failed to enter the world, and I would bring him back with me. The dead have been truly reclaimed by the Devouring God, so there is no hope for my wife, but the *unborn*, I thought – I still think – perhaps will not be missed. So far I have succeeded only with the first part of my plan. I am here. But I have not found my son. When I saw you, *alive,* here, I had hope again, just briefly.'

'This is the Sybil's doing,' I said.

'Yes, I can tell that it is, by the mark on you.'

'The mark on me?'

He got up, rummaged among the debris, and handed me a broken piece of mirrored glass.

'Didn't you know?' he said softly.

I looked at my reflection. The spot on my forehead where the Sybil had kissed me was glowing as brightly as had the eyes of the *evatim.*

I handed the glass back to him, and it was then that I noticed that my hands, too, gave off a faint light where my mother had touched them at the very end. Where the guardian-serpent's lips had touched me when it took the coins, the skin was seared and healed into a smooth white scar.

I sat still, staring at my hands.

'If I really am a sorcerer,' I said, 'I'll try to help you. You don't have to be afraid of me.'

He offered me a cup. 'Here, drink this.'

'But I can't. If I drink anything here, I'll—'

The old man sighed. 'You are still an ignorant sorcerer. *This* water is from *Leshé,* from the river where it is filled with dreams. It will give you many visions. It will truly open your eyes, but it will not bind you to the dead. The waters of *Tashé* will do that, but not those of *Leshé.*'

'Do I need to see visions?'

'I think you do, to get where you're going.'

'This is the Sybil's doing again,' I said.

'Yes, it is. Drink.'

I drank. The water was very cold and, surprisingly, sweet. My whole body trembled with it. Only in the aftertaste was it bitter.

'Now go,' said Aukin, son of Nevat, who had lost his own son.

I stood up, balancing myself precariously on the image of the god, and caught hold of the window-ledge, then heaved myself up. For a moment I dangled there, looking down at the old man. He waved me on. I heaved again and felt a blast of hot wind against my face and chest, and sand stung me, as if I had crawled out into a sandstorm.

Then I was falling, not back into the room, but *down*, away from the window as directions somehow reversed. The window receded above me and was gone as I tumbled head over heels through hot, blinding, blowing sand.

Then visions came to me:

As I fell, I saw the whole of *Tashé* spread out before me. I saw that each dead person there dwelt in a little space formed out of some memory from life, either a pleasant one, or, if some guilty memory tormented him, an endless terror. So the domain of *Tashé* was an incongruous tangle, a jumbled mass like the inside of the Sybil's house.

And as I fell, I was in many places at once. I walked on soft moss to the edge of a pool, deep in a forest suffused with golden light. Three young girls sat by the pool, washing their hair. A young man, scarcely older than myself, sat by them, strumming on a lyre. All around them, the forest seemed to go on forever. Pale white fishes drifted through the air among the trees.

Then I took one step back from the pool, and the forest was gone.

I ran beneath the pale stars over an endless expanse of bricks so hot that they burned my feet. Bricks stretched glowing to the black horizon. I wept with the pain and began to stagger. It was all I could do not to sit down. Smoke and flame hissed out of fissures. Still I ran on, gasping for breath, streaked with soot and sweat, until I came to a window set horizontally in the ground, in the bricks as if in a wall. The window was open. A curtain blew straight up at me on a searing gust. Still, somehow, I had to look.

I swayed dangerously, then dropped to my hands and knees, screaming aloud at the new pain. I crept to the edge, peered in, and beheld a king and his courtiers below me, all sitting solemnly at a banquet table. Yet there was no feast before them, and each face was contorted in unimaginable agony. Their bodies and clothing were transparent, and I could see that the hearts of these men and women were white hot, like iron in a forge.

And again, I saw a girl in a pleasantly lit room, singing and spinning forever. A man sat at her feet, carving a piece of ivory into a form that was somehow infinitely ornate and beautiful but never complete.

And I lay, naked as I was, in a stream so cold it burned, more subtly, but as painfully as any fire. My body faded to numbness. I was drifting away, a little at a time.

And crowds babbled in a marketplace; and I was alone in endless, silent halls thick with dust; and I walked on water to a ruined tower where men in white robes and silver masks awaited my coming; and a resplendent pirate paced back and forth endlessly on a single deck suspended in the middle of the air. He looked up, startled, as I plummeted by.

And I saw into memories, into the lives of all who dwelt in that land of *Tashé,* and I knew what it meant to be a king, and a slave, and in love, and a murderer, and I knew what it was to be old and remember all these things vaguely, as in a fading dream.

And I found my sister, Hamakina.

I fell amid swirling, stinging sand, and suddenly the sand became millions of birds, flapping their soft wings against me to hold me up. All these birds had my sister's face, and they spoke with my sister's voice.

'Sekenre, I am here.'

'Where?'

'Brother, you have come for me.'

'Yes, I have.'

'Brother, it is too late.'

I wasn't falling anymore, but lay choking in a heap of cold, soft ashes. I sat up, spitting out ash, trying to wipe ash from my eyes.

In time, tears and spittle gave me enough moisture to clean my face, and I could see. I was in a garden of ash. Fading into the distance in all directions, white, bare trees stood in neat rows, leafless, yet heavy with round, white fruit. Ash rained from the sky, the ash, the sky, and the earth all featureless gray, until I could not tell where earth and sky met.

I stood up amid dead flowers with stalks like winter reeds – huge, yet delicately preserved in every colorless detail.

The ash fell heavily enough that I could feel it striking my shoulders in clumps. I was coated with it, until I too seemed a part of this place. I held my hands over my face, struggling to breathe and to see, while making my way along a path amid sticks that might have been the remains of hedges, the ash cool and soft and knee-deep.

The overwhelming smell in the air, the odor of the ash, was intensely sweet, unpleasantly so, strong enough that I felt faint. But I knew I could not stop here, could not rest, and I took one step, and the next, and the next . . .

In an open place, which might have been the center of the garden, a wooden shelter stood half-buried amid drifts, a domed roof atop squat pillars. The roof was shaped into a wide-mouthed, staring face, the mouth already clogged as if the thing were vomiting gray powder.

Hamakina sat waiting for me there, on a bench beneath that strange roof. She too was barefoot and in rags, plastered with ash. But her cheeks were newly streaked with tears.

'Sekenre . . .'

'I've come to take you back,' I said gently.

'I can't go. Father . . . tricked me. He told me to eat the fruit, and I—'

I waved a hand toward one of the white trees.

'This?'

'It didn't look like this then. The trees were green. The fruit was wonderful. It smelled wonderful. The colors were

... *shining,* changing all the time, like oil on water when the sun touches it. Father told me to, and he was angry, and I was afraid, so I ate ... and it tasted dead, and then suddenly everything was like you see it now.'

'*Father* did this?'

'He said it was part of his plan all along. I didn't understand a lot of what he said.'

'*Where is he?*'

I drew my sword, clutching it tightly, furious and at the same time aware of how ridiculous and helpless I must have seemed. But it was *my* sword now, no longer my father's, given to me by the Sybil for a specific purpose—

'Sekenre, what will you do?'

'Something. Whatever I have to.'

She took me by the hand. Her touch was cold. 'Come on.'

I don't know how long we walked through the ash garden. There was no way to measure time or distance or direction. But Hamakina seemed to know for certain where we were going.

Then the garden was gone and it seemed I was back in the cramped, swaying darkness of the Sybil's house again. I looked around for her luminous face, expectant, but my sister led me without any hesitation across a rope bridge above an abyss, while vast leviathans with idiot, human faces swam up out of a sea of guttering stars, splashing pale foam, each creature opening its mouth to display rotting teeth and a mirrored ball held between them. I gazed down through the swinging, twisting ropes and saw myself reflected there on the curving glass.

Somehow Hamakina was no longer with me, but far away, down below, inside each mirrored sphere, and I saw her running ahead of me across featureless sand beneath a sand-colored sky. Then each monster sank down in turn and she vanished, and another rose, its jaws agape, and I saw her again.

There were black stars in the sky above Hamakina now, and she ran across the sand beneath them, a gray speck against the dead sky, receding into the black points which were the stars.

And each leviathan sank down and another rose to give me

a glimpse of her, and from out of the abyss I caught snatches
of a song she sang as she ran. Her voice was still her own,
but older, filled with pain, and a little mad.

> *'When I am in the darkness gone,*
> *and you're still in the light,*
> *come lie each day upon my grave;*
> *I'll lie with you each night.*
> *Come bring me gifts of fruit and wine.*
> *Bring them from the meadow.*
> *I'll bring dust and ash and clay;*
> *I'll bring gifts of shadow.'*

Without any transition I could sense, I was suddenly on that
endless expanse of sand beneath the black stars, and I followed
her voice over the low dunes toward the horizon and a black
shape that huddled there.

At first I thought it was one of the stars fallen from the sky,
but as we neared it the thing resolved itself, and I slowed to a
terrified walk when I saw the pointed roofs and the windows
like eyes and the familiar dock beneath the house, now resting
on the sand.

My father's house – no, *my* house – stood on its stilts like
a huge, frozen spider. There was no river, no Reedland at all,
as if the whole world had been wiped clean but for this one
jumble of ancient wood.

When I reached the dock, Hamakina was waiting for me at
the base of the ladder.

She turned her head upward.

'He is there.'

'Why did he do all this to you and to Mother?' I said. I held
onto the sword and onto the ladder, gripping hard, trembling
more with sorrow than with fear or even anger.

Her reply startled me far more than anything the dreamer
Aukin had said. Once more her voice was older, almost
harsh.

'Why did he do all this to *you*, Sekenre?'

I shook my head and started climbing. As I did the ladder
shivered, as if it were alive and felt my touch.

And my father's voice called out from the house, thundering:

'Sekenre, I ask you again. Do you still love me?'

I said nothing and kept on climbing. The trapdoor at the top was barred from the inside.

'I want you to love me still,' he said. 'I only wanted what was best for you. Now I want you to go back. After all you have done against my wishes, it is still possible. Go back. Remember me as I was. Live your life. That is all.'

I pounded on the trapdoor with the pommel of my sword. Now the whole house shivered and suddenly burst into white, colorless flame, washing over me, blinding me, roaring in my ears.

I let out a yell and jumped, barely clearing the dock below, landing face-down in the sand.

I sat up, sputtering, still clutching the sword. The house was not harmed by the fire, but the ladder smouldered and fell as I watched.

I slid the sword under my belt again and started climbing one of the wooden stilts. Once more the white flames washed over me, but they gave no heat, and I ignored them.

'Father,' I said. 'I am coming. Let me in.'

I reached the porch outside my own room. I was standing in front of the very window through which Hamakina had been carried away.

All the windows and doors were barred against me, and flickering with white flames.

I thought of calling on the Sybil. It would be my third and last opportunity. Then, if I ever did so again – what? Somehow she would claim me.

No, it was not time for that.

'Father,' I said, 'if you love me as much as you say, open up.'

'You are a disobedient son.'

'I shall have to disobey you further.'

And once more I began to weep as I stood there, as I closed my hands together and opened them again. Father had beaten me once for attempting this act. *Then* I had gotten no results. *Now* I did, and it was as easy as breathing.

Cold blue flames danced on my outstretched palms. I reached up with my burning hands and parted the white fire like a curtain. It flickered and went out. I pressed my palms against the shuttered window. Blue flames streamed from between my fingers. The wood smoked, blackened, and fell inward, giving way so suddenly that I stumbled forward, almost falling into the room.

I climbed over the windowsill and stood there, amazed. The most fantastic thing of all was that I was truly in the house where I had grown up, in the room Mother, Hamakina, and I had shared, and in which I had remained alone for half a night at the very end waiting desperately for the dawn. I saw where I had once carved the first two characters of my name into the back of a chair. My clothes lay heaped over the edge of an open trunk. My books were on a shelf in the far corner, and a page of papyrus, one of my own illumination projects, was still in place on the desk, with pens and brushes and bottles of ink and paint all where I had left them. Hamakina's doll lay on the floor at the foot of the bed. One of Mother's *hevats,* a golden bird, hung from the ceiling, silent and motionless.

More than anything else I wanted to just lie down in that bed, then rise in the morning, get dressed, and resume work at my desk, as if nothing had ever happened.

I think that was my father's last offer to me. He was shaping my thoughts.

I walked out of the room, the floorboards creaking. I knocked on his workroom door. It, too, was locked.

Father spoke from within. He sounded weary.

'Sekenre, what do you want?'

It was a completely astonishing question. All I could say was, 'I want in.'

'No,' he said after a long pause. 'What do you truly want, as my son, for yourself?'

'I don't know anymore.' I drew my sword once more, and pounded on the door with the pommel.

'I think you do. You want to grow to be an ordinary man, to live in the city, to have a wife and family, to be free of ghosts and shadows and sorcery – on this we are agreed. I want that for you, too. It is very important.'

'Father, I am not sure of anything. I don't know how I feel.'

I kept on pounding.

'Then why are you still here?' he said.

'Because I have to be.'

'To become a sorcerer is a terrible thing,' he said. 'It is worse than a disease, worse than any terror, like opening a door into nightmare that can never be closed again. You seek to know. You peer into darkness. There is a certain allure, what seems like unlimited power at first, then glory, then, if you truly delude yourself, vast wisdom. To become a sorcerer is to learn the secrets of all the worlds and of the gods. But sorcery burns you. It disfigures, changes, and the man who becomes a sorcerer is no longer the man he was before he became a sorcerer. He is hated and feared by all. He has countless enemies.'

'And you, Father? Do you have countless enemies?'

'My son, I have killed many people in my time, thousands—'

That, once more, astonished me into helplessness. I could only say, 'But *why?*'

'A sorcerer must have knowledge, not merely to ward off his enemies, but to *live*. He hungers for more dark spells, more powers. You can only get so much from books. You *need* more. To truly become a sorcerer, one must kill another sorcerer, and another, and another, each time stealing what that other sorcerer possesses, which he, in turn, has stolen by murder. There would be few sorcerers left were it not for the temptations, which recruit new ones. Sorcery goes on and on, devouring.'

'Surely some magic can be used for good, Father.'

I stopped pounding. I looked down at my hands, where they had been marked, where the flames had arisen so effortlessly.

'Sorcery is not magic. Do not confuse the two. Magic comes from the gods. The magician is merely the instrument. Magic passes through him like breath through a reed pipe. Magic can heal. It can satisfy. It is like a candle in the darkness. Sorcery, however, resides in the sorcerer. It is like a blazing sun.'

'I don't want to be a sorcerer, Father. Truly. I have ...
other plans.'

Now, I think, there was genuine sadness in his voice.

'Beloved Sekenre, my only son, you have looked upon the
evatim and been marked by them. Throughout your life you
will be scarred from their touch. You have conversed with the
Sybil and you bear her mark also. You have journeyed among
the ghosts, in the company of a corpse, through the realm of
Leshé, the place of dreams. You have drunk of the waters of
vision and have seen all that is in *Tashé,* the land of death.
And, at the last, you burned your way into this house with
flames summoned from your hands. Now I ask you ... are
these the deeds of a *calligrapher?*'

'No,' I said weakly, sobbing. All my resolve drained away.
I let the sword drop to the floor and I slid down, my back to
the door, and sat there. 'No,' I whispered. 'I just wanted to get
Hamakina back.'

'Then you are a disappointment to me, son. You are a fool,'
he said with sudden sharpness. 'She does not matter.'

'But *she is your child too.* Didn't you love her also? No, you
never did. Why? You owe me that much, Father. You have to
tell me why ... about a lot of things.'

He stirred within the room. Metal clinked. But he did not
come to the door or touch the bolt. There was a long silence.
I could see my mother's *hevat,* the golden bird, through the
open doorway of my own room, and I stared at it with a kind
of distracted intensity, as if I could discern all the answers to
all my questions in the intricacies of its design.

I felt cold. I clutched my shoulders hard, shivering. The
slashes the *evatim* had made in my sides and back pained
me again.

After a while, Father resumed speaking.

'Sekenre, how old do you think I was when I married your
mother?'

'I – I—'

'I was three hundred and forty-nine years old, my son. I
had been a sorcerer for a long time by then. I had wandered
through many lands, fleeing death, consumed by the contagion
of sorcery, slaughtering my enemies, raging in my madness

61

against the gods, whom I considered to be at best my equals. But I had a lucid interval. I remembered what I had been, long before. I had been . . . a man. So I pretended I was one again. I married your mother. I saw in you . . . all my hopes for what I had once been. In you, that ordinary man lived again. If I could cling to that hope, I too, in a small way, would remain human. So *you* were special. I loved *you.*'

'But *Hamakina*—'

'—is mere baggage, a receptacle and nothing more. When I felt the weight of my death on me at last, when I could no longer hold off my enemies, I planted the seed of Hamakina in her mother's womb, and I raised her as a prize specimen, for a specific purpose. I brought her here *to contain my death.* The seed of her was something wrought in my laboratory. I placed her inside her mother with a metal tube, while her mother lay in a drugged sleep. So, you see, her life did *not* come from the River, from the dreams of Surat-Kemad, but from *me.* I offered this new life to the Devouring God in exchange for my own. It is a bottle, filled with my own death. So I am still a sorcerer, and a great lord in the land of the dead, because I am neither truly living nor truly dead. I am not the slave of Surat-Kemad, but his ally. And so, my son, your father has outwitted all his enemies, evaded all dangers. He alone is not wholly consumed by sorcery. He *continues.* There is a certain beauty to the scheme, you must admit—'

I rose to my feet, numb beyond all sorrow now. I picked up the sword.

'Sekenre,' Father said, 'now that I have explained everything – you were right; I did owe you an explanation – you must go away. Save yourself. Be what I wanted to be. You are a good boy. When I was your age, I too was good. I only wanted to do what was right. But I changed. If you go now, you can remain as you are—'

'No, Father. I, too, have changed.'

He screamed then, not out of fear, but despair. I stood before the door, sword under one arm while I folded my hands together, then opened them.

Once more, it was as easy as breathing.

The flames leapt from my hands, red and orange this time.

They touched the door, spreading over it. I heard the metal bolt on the inside fall to the floor. The door swung open.

At first my eyes could not focus. There was only darkness. Then faint stars appeared, then an endless black plain of swirling sand. I saw hundreds of naked men and women dangling from the sky on metal chains, turning slowly in the wind, mutilated, their faces contorted with the idiocy of hate.

The darkness faded. The stars were gone. Father's room was as it had been before the priests had cleaned it out. All the books were there, the bottles, the shelves of jars, the charts, the strange shapes muttering in jars.

He lay on his couch dressed in his sorcerer's robe, as I had last seen him, his eyes gouged out, sockets covered with golden coins.

He sat up. The coins fell into his lap. Fire burned within his eye-sockets, white-hot, like molten iron.

And he said to me, 'This is your last warning, Sekenre. Your very last.'

'If you are so powerful, Father, where is your power now? You have not resisted me, not really. You only give me . . . warnings.'

'What would I have to do then, my son?' he said.

'You would have to kill me. It is too late for anything else.'

His voice began to fade, to become garbled, to disintegrate into a series of hisses and grunts. I could barely make out his words.

'Now all my preparations are undone. You disobeyed me to the last. You did not heed my many warnings, sorcerer, son of sorcerer—'

He slid off the couch onto the floor, wriggling toward me on all fours, his whole body swaying from side to side, his terrible eyes blazing.

I almost called on the Sybil then. I wanted to ask simply, *What do I do now? What now?*

But I didn't. In the end, I alone had to decide what was right, the correct action. Anything I did would please the Sybil. She would weave it into the pattern. Surat-Kemad did not care—

'My son . . .' The words seemed to come from deep within him, like a wind from out of a tunnel. 'To the very end I have loved you, and it has not been enough.'

He opened his huge, hideously elongated mouth. His teeth were like little knives.

At that final moment, I did not fear him, nor hate him, nor did I sorrow. I felt only a hollow, grinding sense of duty.

'No, it was not enough, Father.'

I struck him with the sword. His head came off with a single blow. My arm completed the motion almost before I was aware of it.

It was as easy as breathing.

Blood like molten iron spread at my feet. I stepped back. The floorboards burned.

'You are not my father.' I said softly. 'You cannot *have been* my father.'

But I knew that he had been, all the way to the end.

I knelt beside him, then put my arms around his shoulders and lay with my head on his rough, malformed back. I wept long and hard and bitterly.

And as I did, dreams came to me, thoughts, visions, flashes of memories which were not my own, and terrible understanding, the culmination of long study and of longer experience. My mind filled. I knew a thousand deaths and how they had been inflicted, how a single gem of knowledge or power was wrested from each. I knew what every instrument in this room was for, the contents of all the books and charts, and what was in each of those jars and how it could be compelled to speak.

For I had killed a sorcerer, and if you kill a sorcerer you become all that he was.

This was my inheritance from my father.

In the dawn, Hamakina and I buried our father in the sand beneath the house. The black stars were gone. The sky was dark, but it was the familiar sky of *Eshé*, the Earth of the living. Yet the world was still empty, and we dug in the sand with our hands. When we had made a shallow grave, we rolled him into it, placing his head between his feet in the way a sorcerer must be buried if he is to be buried at all, so that he will not rise again. For a time, Mother was with us. She crawled into the grave with him and we covered them both up.

The sky lightened into purple, then azure. Then water flowed beneath the dock and I watched the first birds rise from among the reeds. Hamakina stood among the reeds for a little while, gazing back at me. Then she was gone.

Suddenly I began to shake almost uncontrollably, but merely from cold this time. Though it was early summer, the night's chill lingered, and I was almost naked. I climbed up into the house by means of a rope ladder I'd dropped through the trapdoor and put on trousers, a heavy shirt, and a cloak.

Later, when I came down again with a jug to get water for washing, I saw a man in a white robe and a silver mask walking toward me across the water. I stood up and waited. He stopped a distance off, but I could hear what he said clearly enough.

At first he spoke with my father's voice.

'I wanted to tell you the rest of the story of the Heron Boy. There is no ending to it, I fear. It just ... continues. He was not a heron and he was not a boy either, but he looked like a boy. So he dwelt among men pretending to be one of them, yet confiding his secret to those who loved him. Still, he did not belong. He never could. He lived out his days as an impostor. But he had help, because those he confided in did love him. Let me confide in you, then. Sekenre, when a boy becomes a man his father gives him a new name which is known only between the two of them, until the son gives it to his own son in turn. Therefore take the name your father had, which is *Heron.*'

And he spoke with the voice of the Sybil.

'Sekenre, you are marked with my mark because you are my instrument. All men know that out of the tangle of the world I divine the secrets of their lives. But do they also know that out of the tangle of their lives I divine the secrets of the world? That I cast them about like bones, like marbles, and read the patterns as they fall? I think not.'

And, finally, he spoke with the voice of Surat-Kemad, god of death and of the river, and the thunder was his voice; and he took off the mask and revealed his terrible face, and his jaws gaped wide; and the numberless, fading stars were his teeth and the sky and the earth were his mouth, and the river disgorged itself from his belly; and his great ribs were the pillars of the world.

He spoke to me in the language of the gods, of *Akimshé,* the burning holiness at the heart of the universe, and he named the gods yet unborn, and he spoke of kings and of nations and of worlds, of things past and things which are to come.

Then he was gone. The city spread before me now. I saw the foreign ships at anchor in the river, and the bright banners waving in the morning breeze.

I took off the robe and sat on the dock, washing. A boatman drifted by and waved, but then he realized who I was, made a sign against evil, and paddled away frantically.

His fear was so trivial it was somehow incredibly funny.

I fell back on the deck, hysterical with laughter, then lay there. Sunlight slanted under the house. The air was warm and felt good.

And I heard my father whisper from his grave, gently, 'My son, if you can become *more* than a sorcerer, I will not fear for you.'

'Yes, Father. I shall.'

Then I folded my hands, and slowly opened them, and the fire that I held cupped there was perfect and pale and still, like a candle's flame on a breezeless summer night.

Chapter 5: Sorcerer, Son of Sorcerer

What now, sorcerer Sekenre, son of sorcerer Vashtem, you who promised to be more?

What . . . ? I was like a swimmer in a raging current, who has seized hold of a bit of flotsam after a long and arduous struggle. I hoped to be allowed a moment of rest.

But I could not deny what I had become, not any longer. Father was right. Mine were not the deeds of a mere calligrapher.

So . . . ?

I began writing this account of my adventures, my purpose being, I thought, to distance myself from them, to hold them up into the light as a carver does some strange and intricate woodwork he has just finished. He scrutinizes it closely, remembering how he created every detail of its form; but he only grasps it in his fingers. It is a separate thing, not part of his hand.

I sat for whole days on the various porches of our house – no, *my* house now – scribbling away in the morning dampness, as the mists burned away; in the hot afternoon sun; only driven inside when the shadows deepened and the mosquitoes rose out of the marsh in clouds. I wrote steadily, a rough draft on anything available, almost without pause, until, at the end of each day I would put my pen aside and regard the sun setting among the reeds, always searching for any sign or omen that might be revealed in the infinite variety of shades and colors. But there was nothing. The coming darkness. Mosquitoes. And, even for me, the peril of the *evatim*.

This was a hungry time. No one brought food to the door and I did not even think of venturing into town. Fishing lines perpetually trailed from the dock, and sometimes I caught something, but otherwise survival was a matter of what meager stores remained within the house: stale bread, a little smoked meat that tasted like an old leather belt, dried fruit. I began to fancy myself a ghost like the rest of my family; mind elsewhere, body inconsequential.

Often I forgot to eat at all, and would rise from my work vaguely befuddled that my body did not obey me, that I seemed to have become a hollow figure of paper, swaying from side to side, barely able to keep myself from blowing away in the wind. I could only cling to the railing and wait for the fit to pass.

By the end of the summer I had completed the rough version of my tale, and had begun work recopying it carefully onto the finest reed-paper, drawing the initial letters with infinite care. If I sat very still and did not get up suddenly, I could rely on a steady hand. That was enough. As I worked, I was not discontent, for the text seemed to tell of someone else, some imagined Sekenre I had perhaps met a long time ago. But I was not he. I was not the hero of the story, but merely the calligrapher.

Lies, all lies. Sorcerer Sekenre, did you believe a word of that, even as you wrote it?

No, not really. Sometimes my terror would break out uncontrollably and I could only shut my eyes hard and try to drive it back within the little cage I'd made for it in my mind. I fell down and wept. I pounded my fists on porch railing or wall or floor, but I wasn't fooling anyone, least of all myself.

Nothing, truly, had been resolved. Vashtem's legacy was upon me like a cloak of stone.

They say that no sorcerer is ever quite dead. He merely becomes less animate, less visible to the eye. But he is still there, in the periphery of the mind's vision, in the shadows. He slips between the floorboards and the bolted shutters, through the keyhole in the locked door. You open a book, and he is on the page, resting among the painted letters like a tiny serpent in a bouquet of flowers. He survives, if only in dreams, his unquiet spirit returning again and again from mist-bound *Leshé*. Not even Surat-Kemad can swallow him entirely.

And magic, too, never completely fades. It diminishes infinitely, like an echo in a cave, but if the ear is sensitive enough, the ancient reverberation may still be heard.

Thus:

The house creaked and shifted in the night like a ship resting at anchor. Often I would lie awake, listening to its secret voices: what might have been footsteps or whispers or just wood settling in the soft river mud. Sometimes I got up and wandered from room to room. Shapes vanished from sight around corners.

And one morning I encountered an old woman in the pantry. She sang softly to herself, preoccupied with some task, as if kneading invisible dough.

I spoke to her. She did not look up as I approached, nor did she pause in her work. I touched her shoulder, and for an instant felt something even less substantial than a spiderweb, but definitely there. Then, nothing. I never found out who she was.

On the evening of the same day, one of the corpse-things I had so feared in childhood, one of Father's summoned visitors I had seen only through cracks in the bedroom door – one of *those* crawled up out of the river, onto the porch, and leaned in a window where I sat reading.

'*Vashtem . . .*' it said, with a voice like a cold winter wind come alive.

I looked up and slowly closed my book, showing neither fear nor amazement.

'I am not he.'

'*Nothing is forgiven, Vashtem. Your new guise will not conceal you from the eyes that seek.*'

The thing leaned in further. River mud and black slime dripped onto the cover of the book. Calmly, I wiped it clean with my sleeve and set the volume aside. This creature was little more than a skeleton shrouded in rags – it stank more of stagnant water than of rotting flesh – and I was not at all sure it had ever been human. Its face extended forward into a snout, like a dog's.

'I am not Vashtem. I am Sekenre. I am not responsible for whatever Vashtem did to you or those who sent you.'

'Nothing is forgiven, Vashtem, while yet the sun burns; nothing erased while yet the darkness pours from Surat-Kemad's belly; nothing changed because you put on a new mask of flesh.'

'I say again, I am not Vashtem.'

'I call you liar.' The thing snatched at my face with a malformed, four-fingered claw. I jerked back.

'Call me what you will,' I said. 'That changes nothing.' I noticed that the house was otherwise totally silent. All creaking and shifting had stopped, as if the structure itself had paused to listen.

'I call you Vashtem, then, and before Vashtem, I call you Orkanre, and Talno, and Balredon, and Tannivar. I call you by many names. All are the same. Your evil is like a spear hurled down the centuries, impaling one heart, then another, then another—'

'And who are you?' I sat, still forcing myself to be calm, gripping the sides of my desk with both hands, confronting this apparition in a way that, indeed, no mere calligrapher ever would.

'A messenger.'

'Oh? Are you one of the evatim, then? I did not think that the Most Holy One would employ a person so shabby—'

The thing hissed through broken, dog-like teeth. 'It is useless to mock, Vashtem.'

'When you see Vashtem, you tell him that—'

'I behold him now.'

'I could – I could kill you.' My voice broke into a ridiculous squeak. I could barely restrain my fear. I was making impossible threats. But if I turned and ran, the thing would be on my back in an instant. So I'd kill it instead. I had no idea how. Even though it was so obviously already dead. I glanced around and realized that Father's silver sword was upstairs in a chest.

'Just as useless. I am nothing. There are countless more like me.'

'What then?'

'Vashtem, those whom you have destroyed, those whom you have betrayed, those do not lie at rest. They will return to you, all of them, in their own time.'

'Then why did they send you to warn me?'

'Because it amused them.'

I shouted, not words, just inarticulate rage, simultaneously incredulous that I should *be* enraged at a time like this, and I did something to which my rational self was only an even more incredulous spectator: I rose from my seat, seized the monstrosity by the muzzle and top of the head, and gave a sharp twist. It was as if someone else acted. I looked out through someone else's eyes. Someone else wrenched the head around in a full half circle, then seized the creature's shoulders – cold, wet, crumbling, like a mass of rusted metal rods long buried in river mud – and heaved it back out the window.

An instant later there was a splash, as my unwelcome visitor tumbled over or under the porch railing.

But I did not dare look out after it. Instantly, I pulled the shutters closed and fastened them, and ran frantically throughout the house, bolting every window and door I could find, even many of the inner ones, and hatchways to numerous, discontinuous crawlspaces. Only when I was done, only when I was in the far reaches of the attic among old trunks and apparatus and discarded pieces of my mother's carvings did I truly come into myself and shake, almost sick with the realization of what I had done. I couldn't stand. I sat on the edge of a trunk and slid backward into it, resting on a heap of my mother's gowns. I clutched at the musty cloth.

Somehow, just then, I could not weep. I occurred to me that sorcery and the presence of uncanny things dry up tears. A genuine sorcerer cannot weep. That is reserved for human beings. So, at least, I had read somewhere, or heard in a story or as a whispered rumor or a revelation in a dream.

Was it true? I didn't know. I lay back in the trunk filled with my mother's clothes and, very gingerly, reached up to feel my face for tears, my heart racing in anticipation of what I might find.

My face was slick with sweat. My fingers reeked of mud and rotten flesh. I gagged, then wiped my fingers on the front of my shirt, not on the gowns, which somehow would have been a desecration.

As I lay there, the house was alive again with its little noises. I fancied it a huge animal, muttering in its sleep.

Eventually it was I who slept, and Father came to me in a dream. I knew it was a dream, then, for I had slain him, and part of me was glad of it, even as at least part of him had commanded me to do so. His soul, too, was infinitely divided, like mine. Now he was but a fraction within me, along with Orkanre and Talno, Balredon and Tannivar and all the rest, my ancestors in sorcery and murder.

Father rose out of my sleeping mind like steam from a teapot, darkened, took shape, and began to pace back and forth in the cramped attic room. In my dream I raised my head and looked at him, feeling an odd mixture of love and hatred, fascination, repugnance, sorrow, and a desperate anticipation as I waited for him to speak.

But he kept on pacing, utterly silent, without footfalls. It was only as the first gray light seeped in through the shutters that he paused and looked down on me where I lay, his lip trembling, his face showing the same confusion of feelings I had toward him.

He placed something in my hands, folding my limp fingers around it: something hard and square, which smelled of leather, wax, ink, and several odors I could not identify.

I tried to speak, in my dream. I think I wanted to curse him and beg his forgiveness simultaneously. Then somehow I knew that I must greet him politely, as if he were an ambassador from a far land. My dream demanded tact and reserve. I should not press him, but wait for him to state his purpose in his own way. I had no idea why.

I made to pronounce his name, but in my dream I could not, and my voice was the whisper of the morning wind; my words were the waves lapping faintly against the pilings beneath the house.

Sunlight shone through him, and he was gone. I awoke then, startled to find that I clutched a square, wooden object to my chest. I first thought it a box, but discovered a latch, opened it, and beheld pages of what appeared to be a sorcery text written in a strange and distorted hand, in equally distorted language – though the words were Reedlandish, and I could puzzle most of them out. The pages were some kind of tanned hide rather than reed-paper or parchment.

The author's name caught my attention immediately: Tannivar the Parricide.

I snapped the book closed, trying to deny what I had seen, holding it tightly in both hands. But after a while, I opened it once more, and the name was still there. This Tannivar was, in a sense, myself. In that sense, I had written this book. Likewise, I was guilty of the same crime Tannivar proclaimed so boldly on his title page.

My immediate impulse was to throw the thing away, into the river, but instead I merely opened a window to let more light in, and sat down in that attic room, amid the relics of my parents' lives, and read the volume cover to cover.

Poor Tannivar had slain his father too, and yes, he was foolishly proud of it, thinking he had brought to an end the successive generations of sorcery. He was older than I, a grown man in his later twenties when he did the deed, and over thirty when he wrote his book – which he cast, oddly, as a fictional tale, about someone else named Tannivar – but his powers of denial were greater than mine. All this while he was troubled by dreams, by memories which were not his own, and, yes, by nocturnal visitants like my own of the previous evening; but somehow he convinced himself that these were the fading *remnants* of sorcery. *Like smoke that lingers when the fire is put out,* was how he put it. And so on. Sometimes he stopped his narrative and reflected that the smoke simply would not disperse. He feared for his sanity. I think he wrote in a final attempt at self-exorcism. Yet he would not admit the obvious truth. To what ultimate and wretched end he came, the book did not say. The narration ended abruptly, almost in mid-sentence—

—almost as if, I thought wryly, his father had come back, snatched him away from his writing desk, and carried him off into the belly of Surat-Kemad.

Now *my* father had given me this book, perhaps only as a warning, perhaps because it contained some greater secret. I skimmed through it again, searching. There was much I didn't understand. I think that was the true message, that I was like this book, to be deciphered slowly.

All I needed to know was *within* me, but it did me no good. I was a receptacle made full, containing as many disparate souls as did a demon-possessed lunatic. Yet they slept within me, and I, Sekenre, the waking mind, still knew remarkably little of sorcery. I could not *use* what I possessed. Think of a king who forms a council of the wisest and most powerful men in the land, and then discovers that somehow, inexplicably, he does not know their language.

Only in my case, if any of the advisers were truly wise, he would have avoided joining that particular company. They were powerful, yes, and some of them at least – quite unlike Tannivar the Parricide, who was a victim despite his crime – were truly wicked. But wise? No.

I feared them. Yet I realized, too, that I needed them. Within me, some obscure destiny was being worked out; the ending of Tannivar's story yet to be acted, told, and written.

Through *me* then, I decided, then and there. Not some other after me. Enough was enough. Tannivar the Parricide had lived when Sestobast was lord of the Middle River, before the first of the Great Kings had established the Hegemony of the Delta and parcelled out the land to his satraps. And that was five hundred years ago. The story had been going on for a long, long time. Even Tannivar could not glimpse the beginning. He was fully as ignorant of it as I.

Yet now the story would come to an end. Somehow. Through me.

Despite which, I continued to delude myself, to deny everything. One minute, brave thoughts, brave words formed in those thoughts, and then—

Here is what happened:

I carried the book downstairs, into my father's old workroom.

There, particularly, the house spoke with many voices: creaks, chirps, sighs, groans. As I sat in shadows that never could be dispelled no matter how bright the sun or how wide I threw open the shutters, my father's presence seemed more than just a dream. This remained *his* place. The priests with their incense and exorcisms had not changed that, even though holy images were now nailed to the walls – an ikon of Surat-Kemad, another of Shedelvendra the Mother of Waters, a third of Bel-Kemad, the forgiving god – and feather-and-reed charms dangled from the ceiling. It was all so much rubbish, the huge circles and stars and lines the priests had carved into the walls, the crudely-painted and deliberately broken figure of the serpent swallowing its tail which was supposed to indicate immortality interrupted, eternity brought to an end.

A blackened chamber pot by the door had once held incense.

It didn't matter. The priests had swept the shelves clean of books and bottles and strange devices, yet, particularly as evening came on and the shadows deepened, those shelves seemed full again. Details were hard to make out, like things glimpsed out of the corner of the eye, but it was all there.

I concentrated very hard on what I was doing, reached out, and caught hold of a bottle.

The bottle was solid enough. I held it in my hand and peered through the black glass at something pale and shapeless within, like a raw egg yolk – no, it scurried about clumsily, like a soft spider with too many limbs. A thought came to me unbidden: I knew this man's name. This captive had been a *man*. I could question him or torment him as I chose.

Quickly I put the bottle back on the shelf. It faded among the others. I sank down into my father's chair, before his workdesk.

I understood something else, too. No doubt this was Vashtem's mind working within mine, his thoughts rising out of the darkness like bubbles from the bottom of a still pool. He was telling me that in the house of a sorcerer *time* is not what it otherwise might be, that past and future are drawn together, intertwining like delicately colored lines in an intricately illuminated initial letter. The room was changeless, unaffected by time or events, much less by the priests' futile efforts. The longer I remained, the more it would reveal itself as it had always been. The books and bottles I had seen dumped in the river would reappear on the shelves.

And more—

'Sekenre, hurry. We'll be late for our lessons . . .'

My sister Hamakina stood in the doorway, not as a ghost, but truly her, alive, dressed in a plain smock, her hair carefully braided, her kit of papers and brushes and pens under her arm.

I didn't know what to say.

'Hurry! Velachronos is waiting!'

It was too good to be true, but I wanted it so badly that I did not question how I had returned to those comfortable days when the two of us studied calligraphy and classics with Velachronos the sage. I merely rose from where I sat.

'I'm coming.'

She took me by the hand. Her touch was warm and firm. She dragged me impatiently to our bedroom. I searched around for my school things, able to forget all else as I assembled pens and ink bottles and my latest, incomplete project. Then I regarded how I was dressed, in an old shirt smeared with mud and slime. I changed into better clothes: a plain blue tunic which was too large and came down to my knees, loose white trousers, a broad belt with pouches.

I was still barefoot. Yet I was a man now. The Sybil had initiated me into the rites of manhood. I should be wearing shoes. But the present absurdity was that, for all my adventures, I didn't own a pair.

I looked at Hamakina, embarrassed.

'Come *on!*'

I followed her, and in that instant it seemed only proper that I didn't have shoes. I was able, just so briefly, to convince myself that the past few months had never happened. Therefore, I was still a boy.

We opened the trapdoor and climbed down onto the dock below the house. My boat was gone. Part of me knew that I had last seen it moored to the underside of the Sybil's dwelling and that it had doubtless been incorporated by now into her vast and talismanic collection. But that was another Sekenre, some hero of a story, who had gone there. Yet I mourned for the loss of that boat, trivial as it was, for it was something I had owned as long as I could remember, and it was another link to childhood torn away from me. That part of me which wanted to remain a child, to slide backward into the safe years, couldn't understand what had happened to the boat at all.

'Come *on!*' Hamakina said, tugging on my hand.

Back up the ladder we went, into the house. I thought I heard my mother humming in the kitchen. Fresh bread was baking. Someone paced back and forth in the workroom—

Hamakina and I hurried out the front door, onto the porch and then along the walkway which connected our house to the city. Many planks had been pulled up or hacked apart. It wasn't storm damage, but something done deliberately by the neighbors.

Why? part of me wondered. There was no answer, even as we climbed precariously along a single beam where the rest of the planking and supports had been cut away.

My ability to ignore the obvious was amazing, even as I set foot in the town I had not entered for many months and Hamakina's hand became insubstantial in my own. I was holding an empty glove, then a feather, then smoke, then nothing at all.

Alone I continued through the tangled byways of the City of Reeds. No one recognized me. No one cried out as I passed. Perhaps it was because I had starved myself to gauntness and my hair now fell in a tangle below my shoulders; perhaps because I had merely been forgotten. I walked unnoticed among foreign sailors, along streets lined with booths, past temples where two or three worshippers made offerings to a miscellany of lesser gods. Then I reached the familiar district of better houses, where some dwellings were built on stone pilings and even made of stone themselves. I passed the great, central temple of Surat-Kemad where the priests lived, but even there no one challenged me.

And I stood, emaciated and ungroomed and barefoot, but neatly dressed in clean clothes, eagerly holding my satchel of school things, before a certain door within a certain courtyard. I knocked, then ran my fingers lovingly over the familiar carven birds that decorated the doorway.

The door opened, and wide-eyed Velachronos the scholar was there. *He* knew me. The look of terror and pain on his face struck me like a blow, and I staggered back, suddenly ashamed and confused.

'I – I—'

'*You!*' He spat on the doorstep and made a sign against evil.

Again, I denied it all, even to myself, pushed past the astonished man into the house, and sat down at my usual writing desk. I got out pens and ink, and spread a parchment before me.

Velachronos gasped, sputtered, struggled to find words. 'You're out of your mind, boy . . . you can't j-j-ust go on with your lessons as if *nothing* had happened—'

'Please,' I said desperately. Again I was divided within myself, part of me clinging to this bright, impossible hope, part turning away in shame and despair.

The old man had no pity for me. His amazement gave way to fear and revulsion, even a trace of anger, but I searched very hard in his words, his expression, in his eyes, and there was no gentleness, no forgiveness.

'*Why* are you *really* here?' he demanded. 'Is this part of some malevolent scheme of yours, some magical *plot,* some conjuration of devils—?'

'I just want you to help me,' I said, sobbing. (A sorcerer cannot weep, they say, not a complete and genuine one. Is that true?) 'Make things good again—'

Now he looked at me strangely. I could not read him at all. He was as inscrutable to me as a blank stone. 'You stink of blackest sorcery, Sekenre. You are forever stained. It doesn't take a practiced eye to see that much. I could suggest that you surrender yourself to the priests, but they would burn you. *That* might cleanse your soul. It might be the only possible answer—'

'*No,*' I said, firmly now. 'There is another.' I pointed to the chair beside my own.

Somehow the gesture cowed him. Obediently, he sat down, and in the hours that followed we two together created the beginnings of a vast and beautiful illumination, our text being *Three Brothers of the Air,* one of the sacred stories from the beginning of time.

And for a brief while, all was as it had been, and time ceased, here in this room, all terrible memories banished outside. I wondered where Hamakina was. She had always loved this kind of work.

Slowly the shadows of afternoon shifted.

Yet my teacher was not at ease. Often he started and looked up, as if something had moved suddenly in the room. I looked too, but didn't see anything. He trembled. Sweat gathered on his brow, though the air was cool.

His hand shook. I spent half an hour scraping to clean up where he had blotted the page and almost ruined a fine initial letter shaped like a winged serpent. I did not even reflect on how incredible it was that I should be correcting my master's mistake.

'I beg you, tell me. What do you *really* want?' he whispered, as if terrified that someone else might overhear.

The house creaked and shifted slightly. Odd, for it was set on stone.

I did not speak for a long time, but went on, following a gracefully curving line with gold paint. Here, I thought. Now. I wanted to freeze the two of us here and now, like insects in amber.

'Let me stay with you,' I said. 'Let me live in your house and be your apprentice, and succeed you when you die. I don't want to leave this place, ever.'

Now it was his turn to be silent. I paid him little heed and went on with my work. Velachronos seemed to be watching something in the air around us. I didn't see anything.

How beautiful the page was turning out. How proud he would be of me.

'I see,' he said at last. 'You must excuse me for a minute.'

I shrugged and started coloring the little blue and green leaves around the edge of the page. Velachronos rose from his chair and left the room. He did not return. At least another hour passed. I was beginning to feel hungry and thirsty, but labored on, determined to have at least the beginnings of something worthy to show my teacher.

It was only as the light began to fade that I stopped, sat back, and stretched. My neck and shoulders were stiff. Both legs had gone to sleep from sitting so long. The first page of the tale of the *Three Brothers of the Air* was almost done, but I could not continue without candles.

I called for Velachronos, but got no reply. I stood up unsteadily, legs tingling, and began to rummage through desks and cabinets for candles or a lamp.

Eventually I went into the next room, and found old Velachronos dead on the floor. He had cut his own throat with a small knife and died silently, apparently so afraid of the prospect of spending the rest of his life with me at his side that he had hurled himself headlong into the jaws of Surat-Kemad.

I just stood there. I covered my face with my hands. I tried to weep and made a coughing sound. And then I did weep; and my whole body shook with my sobbing as I knelt beside him and took his hand in both of mine and begged him to forgive me. He was right, I said. I had been completely mad to come here. I was a sorcerer and could not deny it, leaving the question of sorcerers and tears unsettled for the time being. I performed such funeral rites for him as I could. I found candles in the kitchen, and came back and placed them in a circle around the corpse, lighting them with the touch of my own hands. Then I sat with him all night while the candles burned down, and sorcerous flames danced on my open palms, and the *evatim* scratched at the doors and windows, hungering for my beloved teacher. I did not sleep, even for an instant. I did not relinquish my guard.

In the morning I, his murderer, stole away, my satchel of pens and papers held tightly under my arm.

Chapter 6: The Arrows of King Neoc

I didn't go home. I was afraid of my father's house, with its ghosts and, to use my teacher's phrase, its stench of sorcery. Yet I loved it too, as the only home I had ever known. All my memories were there. I, Sekenre who walked in the flesh, was no more than the physical extension of the mind of Sekenre, which existed in the house as echo, as resonating dream from within the confines of those walls.

Maybe that was it. I was afraid the house would swallow me up. Or perhaps it already had.

Liar, Sekenre, always ready to turn a pretty metaphor. No, what I feared I bore within myself.

I wandered the streets for hours, throughout the morning, taking comfort in my continued anonymity, pressing through the crowds of local wives and serving women come out to haggle, mingling with tradesmen, foreign sailors, and slaves. Once I felt a tug and turned in time to see a boy my own age run off. He had snatched one of the pouches from my belt. I didn't cry out. There was no money in the pouch. If it contained anything at all, it exuded the vapor of sorcery, and the thief would regret the taking.

In the narrow, twisting street of the idol-carvers, I paused before the images of the gods. Here, without paying a temple fee, one could contemplate Bel-Kemad and Shedelvendra and the rest, for the carvers were less quick than other merchants to hurry idlers away. Sometimes a god spoke to a customer slowly over the course of hours; then there would be a great flurry of activity and the carver's business would prosper for days. Statues shaped from direct revelation or in the afterglow of a miracle found eager buyers.

I passed many booths devoted to different commodities, to various gods and rites. Out of one, incense poured, thick as smoke, filling the street until a break in the storefronts let in the wind to clear the air. From the back of another, behind a drape, came the slow, steady beating of a drum.

It's said that merely going into these little pavilions is a form of divination. Your choice determines and reveals much.

I didn't particularly want my future or any deep secrets revealed just then, but still I felt that I must make a choice. There are times when you can feel the Sybil's fingers, threading the course of your life.

I shrugged and opened a wooden door at random, ignoring whatever was carved on it.

For a minute I thought I'd made a mistake and perhaps discovered a privy or else the entrance to some very poor dwelling. I stood in a narrow, smelly corridor. At the far end was another door.

But this had been my choice. I closed the first door behind me and waited for my eyes to adjust to the gloom, then made my way slowly, outstretched fingers touching both walls. Boards creaked. The river sighed, just below the floor.

I opened the second door and descended a short flight of rotting, soggy stairs.

Someone lit a lamp, and I saw that my selection had been a strange one. The uncertain light revealed bundles of thorn-branches dangling from pegs along walls which were themselves carved in relief to represent leafless branches, thorns, and wilted flowers; the whole place was a mass of dark, dead vegetation emanating from the central wooden figure of a gaunt, naked youth impaled on thorns, his arms and legs outstretched, painted blood pouring from his many wounds. The expression on his contorted face particularly terrified me: not the glazed look of a torture victim who has suffered for so long that further degrees of pain are meaningless, but of utter bewilderment, as if the wooden boy had suddenly awakened into this dreadful predicament with no idea how he got there.

Then the light shifted and he seemed to be laughing.

I swallowed hard and turned to leave, then turned back at the sound of a footstep. More lamps descended from the ceiling on rattling chains, settling in a circle around the feet of the wooden image as shadows writhed among the branches and thorns as if to suggest a thicket at sunset, sunlight filtering through, the evening breeze rattling the undergrowth.

Two dancers appeared, children, in swirling gauze, one in black with the wings and mask of an eagle, the other in white, with a mask like polished, featureless pearl; the two of them rotating in slow circles around a point between them, their hands locked together, the eagle's eyes gazing into the enigmatic void of the other. Somewhere in the darkness, cymbals shivered. There was no other sound but the shuffling footsteps of the dancers, whose motion, I thought, represented a struggle of some kind.

Finally, the two fell face-down before the hanging statue, then hurried away, covering their faces with their hands. The masks remained on the floor, side by side, face up.

Someone touched me on the arm. I jumped back, startled. An old woman held a small lamp up to my face. Her own face was subtly deformed or distorted in a manner I could not define.

'These are the rites of the Thorn Child,' she said, 'of immemorial antiquity. No one knows what they actually mean. Perhaps you do, young sir, for you were drawn to them.'

I glanced up at the silent, shrieking face among the thorns and considered the obvious, trite conclusion that the image was, in some inexplicable and sinister way, myself. But the statue depicted no distinct individual at all. It was a mere type and, I thought, of poor workmanship.

'I don't know.'

I tried to draw away. She clung to me.

'Perhaps you will know. Perhaps it will come to you.' She trembled, shaking me. I could tell that this information was inexpressibly important to her. 'In the end, when you are done with everything, it will be clear to you.'

'Please,' I said, fumbling in my bag. 'I don't have any money. I have to go—'

'You chose this place.'

'It was an accident. Random chance.'

She shook her head slowly, as if saying, *Don't be ridiculous, my boy.*

I broke away from her and ran, up the stairs, down the corridor, and through the outer door, into the street. No one followed. I leaned against the wall for a moment, breathing hard, squinting in the bright sunlight.

I continued along the street, gazing up at the kindly wooden faces of the divinities, pausing here, there, being jostled by the crowd; sometimes turning away, coughing, my eyes streaming from the incense and cook-fire smoke that filled the shops and gathered beneath the low, sweeping roofs. Priests went by in bands, banging on little metal drums, blowing horns, rattling cups for alms, swirling holy ecstasy. The noise, the smoke, my own exhaustion all blended together until the world seemed to murmur and heave like the sea.

I sat down on a bench and fell asleep, leaning forward to rest my head on the carved feet of Bel-Kemad, the forgiving god, the Lord of Flowers.

My dream was a muddle of images and sounds. I knew even as I dreamed it that this was not from the god, but out of my own mind. I spoke to myself. In my mind, Velachronos confronted me, afraid, angry, wronged, streaming impossible quantities of blood from a thousand wounds, his mouth spewing blood as he tried to speak, until it seemed the whole city was submerged beneath a brackish, red-brown sea. I paddled my boat among the rooftops, while the sun glared through reddish haze. People clung to the roofs, to debris, to walls, to the masts of sunken ships. They cried out for me to save them, but I could not. Some cursed me. I didn't know what to reply.

I paddled on, and my father was walking beside me on the surface of this bloody world-ocean, wearing his sorcerer's robe and a battered, metal mask that might once have had the face of a bird. He whispered to me, in worried, urgent tones. I couldn't make out anything he said.

More persons thus clad joined us, until my little boat was in the midst of a vast procession of anonymous sorcerers, each of them struggling to tell me something, to make me understand; simultaneously, I was certain, threatening me and begging me to release them from pain.

Hamakina appeared, laughing as if at play, her face and

hands so pale they seemed to glow, flashing and blinking like lanterns as she weaved through the crowd of sorcerers, vanishing, returning, calling my name. Of all those present, she alone was unstained with blood. The rest of us were gradually drenched with it, from the red mist that rose like steam all around.

Absolute darkness descended like a suddenly dropped cloak. Desperate for light, I folded my hands together. They stuck, greasy with stinking, half-congealed blood. I parted them, and a tiny white flame arose, then burst in a roar and a blinding flash as if the mist and sea were oil, and the air itself inflammable. Sorcerers screamed and writhed and floated away like scraps of burning leaves. I sat very still in my boat, paddle in my lap, gazing upon myself as I too burned. But there was no pain as my flesh bubbled away, as I became no more than a charred husk collapsing in on myself.

At the very last I saw a common heron wading through the flames and blood, dipping its head again and again, as if feeding in shallow water.

And I awoke with a shout, then sat silently, one hand over my mouth, eyes wide, heart thumping, as I realized that a crowd had gathered. I gazed into awed, amused, hopeful, greedy, occasionally frightened faces. A crippled woman lay at my feet. She reached up, imploring me by the look in her eyes, by the unspoken words her lips formed and lost, by the grotesque calligraphy of her twisted limbs and back, to cure her of whatever had made her this way.

She grabbed my ankles and nearly pulled me from my seat. A startled murmur went up from the crowd, but I jerked away, and sat there, defensively clutching my bag of pens and school things.

She wept. I looked on her with helpless embarrassment. Many of the crowd made signs with their hands or even fell to their knees.

The keeper of this particular shop forced a cheap image of Bel-Kemad into my grasp.

'Speak to them,' he said, leaning over me, 'of the revelation that came to you.'

'There was . . . nothing.'

'Surely the god spoke to you. The signs were obvious. I've seen it before. I can *tell.*'

'I didn't understand it—'

The shopkeeper stood up and turned to the crowd, arms raised. 'A miracle! A mystery! A new oracle! Not for the merely curious, no, not for the vulgar, no, but something ineffable, for the truly holy to ponder in their devotions, for those who seek the gods, for those who bear with them the images of the gods—'

The kneeling spectators rose to their feet. Everyone spoke at once, not to me but to the shopkeeper's assistants, who appeared with trays of wooden statuettes. Coins clinked; statuettes were passed over the heads of the crowd into eager hands; and I heard again and again the shouted promise that with *this* particular image, bought here on this miraculous day, all religious mysteries would become clear, surely, or the buyer could have his money back.

I regarded my own little carven god: raw wood, not even finished or polished. I almost tossed it aside, but put it in my school-bag instead.

Someone touched me on the shoulder. 'Master, do not forget this wretched one.'

I looked up, startled. One of the crippled woman's attendants had spoken. Two of them now held her in a litter, level with my knees.

I leaned forward. No one was watching. Everyone else was buying or selling statues.

Smiling broadly, almost terrified with anticipation, the attendants brought the litter nearer, so that I could reach out and touch the woman's face without rising from my seat. I stroked her cheeks and eyelids. I laid my marked palms upon her. I opened my hands outward, so the attendants could see the white, oblong scars where my dead mother had kissed me.

The attendants set the litter down, making holy signs. The deformed woman heaved up, gasped, and fell back again.

'I shall remember you,' I said. 'Be comforted in that.' All the while, as I spoke, as I did these things, it was like a continuation of my dream. Someone else acted out the role of healer, of miracle-worker, not I. One of the slain sorcerers within me had perhaps yearned for such a thing once, and now had a chance to play the part. But I, Sekenre, felt polluted and ashamed from the fraud. Her affliction might have been an accident of birth, the result of witchcraft, or even the curse of an angry god, but I couldn't help her. My words were cruel deceit. This was work for some holy man or sage, some thaumaturge who has no magic within himself but is a conduit for the divine mercy. It had all been a blunder, an accident. I was merely in the wrong place. If I'd fallen asleep in a refuse heap and had the same dream, there would be no awe-stricken admirers; the last thing I deserved. I was to be feared, shunned. I stank of blackest sorcery.

Before I realized what he was doing, the attendant was pressing silver coins into my hand. When I didn't take them, he put them in my bag.

I broke away, clutching the bag, and ran from that place. No one called after me.

'A miracle!' the shopkeeper exhorted the crowd behind me. 'A revelation! And yet, because I am a reasonable and compassionate man, I charge you only two and a half royals—'

After a while, I slowed to a walk, then leaned over a railing, gazing down into the river as I caught my breath, while behind me crowds of hawkers, laborers, and sight-seers parted to make way for a great procession of bizarrely-garbed foreigners.

I turned to watch: first came men in wonderfully articulated, golden armor, arms folded, gazing sternly ahead, curved scabbards clattering against their thighs; then women in diaphanous white, naked underneath, ringing little silver bells, dancing as one, like a wriggling serpent; and finally a black-clad, toad-faced dwarf who bore on his back the four-armed, golden, jewel-encrusted image of an archer who used one arm to draw arrows from his quiver, two to work his bow, and the remaining one to hold a war-trumpet to his lips.

While the foreign rite, the symbolism of the costumes and

the dwarf were all lost on me, I recognized the god. He is well enough known in Reedland, although usually in a less ornate form and made out of wood.

It was a likeness of King Neoc, or more formally, Neoc-Kemad, the warrior who alone among all mortal men rose again after his death, not in the belly of Surat-Kemad, but on the sunlit bank of the Great River, as the battle in which he had been slain still continued. The gods needed him in their struggle against the Night Serpent, that Nightmare of Desolation which rose from the troubled sleep of the Devouring God and would have swallowed up the Earth, Sun, and Moon. Neoc, the bravest of men, freed from death, fortified against all fear by his resurrection, defeated the Night Serpent at last. But he could not kill it, instead shutting it up in a stone at the core of the world. Then Shedelvendra bore him into the Sun in her arms, where the fires purified him and made him immortal.

He is the father of soldiers, the just and righteous avenger whose searing visage no one may behold, whose fiery arrows seek out the wicked wherever they hide. He is a protector, an intercessor. You see his image in courts of justice, and, more terribly, in places of execution.

Now I was certain that none of my encounters had been chance ones, that they formed a long, inscrutable sentence leading up to this: King Neoc would let fly his arrow. King Neoc had come to avenge poor Velachronos and rid the world of Sekenre, who was Vashtem the black sorcerer, who was Orkanre and Talno and Tannivar, many times parricide.

Why then didn't I just climb into a roof, stare into the rising sun and say, as my eyes melted, *Here I am, Avenger* and let him shoot? Because even to the most wretched, life is unaccountably precious. Even the slave does not want to die.

Or was it because Vashtem my father and Tannivar, who slew his own father, and all the rest of them within me would not allow it? Surely if I – if *we* – were killed *by a god,* by the slayer who could not be slain, the contagion would not continue. That would be the end.

Or, *would it?* The most terrifying prospect of all might be that a sorcerer could somehow become a god, or a god a sorcerer, and fill the world with fire and blood and chaos.

So I hung back against my railing and let the procession pass. King Neoc did not turn and shoot, not then.

I must have stood there for almost an hour afterward in a kind of daze. Then I realized suddenly how terribly hungry I was. I took out one of the silver coins, bought a fish and some bread from vendors, and went into a cookshop to have the fish prepared in spicy sauce. I ate there, trying to look inconspicuous, sitting at the common table in the smoky cookshop, amid sailors who told bawdy stories and spoke of the wind and the river and cargoes, who remembered their wives and distant homes, who broke into uproarious songs in languages I didn't understand; all of this as if no sorcerer existed anywhere in the world, as if Surat-Kemad did not send the *evatim* into the streets of this very city each night to claim his due.

I wanted to linger there and listen longer, but when I had finished eating, and got a look from the man at the counter which clearly meant, *Buy something else or get out,* I left.

Toward the end of the day – somehow I knew this was my very last day of liberty, the last day of my old life among my own people in my native city, the day in which the ordinary child I had once been caught his ultimate, fleeting glimpse of the adult world he would never grow into – I wandered among bookstalls and listened to poets declaiming from atop crates; and then, as the sun began to set and traffic thinned, I came to an alley of leather-working shops, where belts and bags and waterproof capes hung on display.

The first shop on the right was a cobbler's.

I broke out of my reveries, and regarded the shop and myself. My feet were grubby from walking all day. That didn't bother me. I'd gone barefoot all my life. But I was a *man* now, initiated into the rites of adulthood by no less than the Sybil. I wore trousers, not a child's loose robe, and it was proper that a man should wear shoes. Only beggars did not. I was a man of substance. I owned a house. I had coins in my bag.

Amid all my troubles, with my teacher dead but a few hours, this point still seemed absurdly important.

I entered the shop. A bell jangled.

The cobbler looked up from his workbench. I froze in the doorway as our eyes met.

'Sekenre . . . ?'

'Nahmekh?'

He made no reply, but I knew it was Nahmekh. He was two or three years older than me and had been my friend once, one of the very last to desert me after the other boys did. I remembered vividly how the two of us had paddled in my boat beneath the city in the autumn twilight, the both of us more afraid of what our parents would say than of the *evatim* lurking in the darkness. But we pressed on through the endless maze of stumps and pillars and pilings until we found the Wooden Sage, a gigantic, sculpted head half-buried in the mud, whose other names have long since been forgotten; and like so many generations of boys before us, we clambered over his rotting features and carved our names into his rippling beard, while he gazed on us with vacuous eyes. It had been a brave and a foolish thing to do, but then I had felt safe as long as Nahmekh was with me, and he, no doubt was just as certain that my dubious magic would protect him.

But that seemed a lifetime ago. Four years? Only three?

'What do you want, Sekenre?' he said without any trace of friendliness in his voice. He rose from where he sat, wiping his huge hands on his leather apron. He had grown very tall. Traces of a black beard shadowed his long jaw.

'I—?'

'Sekenre, I never expected to see you again.'

'But I – but my father's house – but I only live a short distance away.'

'I never expected to see you, nor did I hope to. What do you want?'

I looked around the dingy shop. He was clearly master of this place now. When I had known him, he had been his father's apprentice. Perhaps his father had died and left him the business.

He walked toward me, his heavy boots clumping on the floorboards. I gazed up into his eyes. I could not read his impassive face. He had grown *so* tall.

'I ask you again. What do you want?'

His voice was that of an exorcist, droning a ritual. I shrugged, tried to laugh, tried to pretend we were boys together again and this was some kind of joke with which I'd grown vaguely impatient. I looked down. I wiggled my toes.

'Isn't that obvious, fool? Shoes. This *is* a shoe store, isn't it? Or are all those' – I waved my hand to indicate the stock on his shelves – 'some kind of fancy bird-feeder?'

He cracked a mirthless, hostile smile.

'Nahmekh?' It was a female voice. Nahmekh turned. His expression changed suddenly, to one of unconcealed dread. A girl about my own age came into the shop from one of the back rooms. She was visibly great with child. Nahmekh hurried over to her, placed his hands on her shoulders, and whispered urgently. She glanced at me, wide-eyed. I clasped my hands together and stared at the wall, avoiding her gaze. She nodded and was gone.

'Your wife?'

'You wanted shoes,' said Nahmekh.

'I'd like to meet her. We could be friends . . .'

'Come, let me measure your feet.'

I pointed to the shoes on the shelves. 'Couldn't I just try some on?'

'Your *first* pair has to be made specially. This is your first, isn't it, Sekenre?'

As embarrassed as if I were a small child caught at mischief by an adult, I looked down at my dirty feet and said, 'Yes.'

He backed away, motioning me to come further into the shop, then to sit on a stool. He measured my feet with a notched, wooden rod.

'Are you a man yet, Sekenre?'

Perhaps I should have taken offense. It is a common taunt of the youth of the city to yell, *Are you a man?* When gangs fight, the winners steal shoes from the losers and whoop triumphantly, *Are you a man?*

But I only said softly, 'Yes, I am.'

Nahmekh returned to his bench behind the counter. When I rose to join him back there, he held up his hand and said, 'No. Wait where you are.' I sat down again. The silence between us was painful. I tried to fill it with a babbled and feebly imagined tale of how I'd been properly initiated into manhood by my father, but he'd forgotten about the shoes, or else had been hiding a pair for me which got lost when the house was cleaned out.

'Is that so?' was all my friend said.

Again silence as he worked with leather, all but his head hidden from my view behind the counter. Once or twice he bent low, out of sight entirely. I heard the tapping of a small hammer.

It was growing dark. Nahmekh lit a candle near where he sat, but offered no light to me.

I couldn't stand it any longer. 'Nahmekh. I'm your friend. Why don't you talk to me?'

He drew breath sharply, and indeed he began to talk, but to himself, as if merely thinking aloud.

'I had a friend named Sekenre once. He's dead. His father killed him, people say, and filled his body with the spirit of the Night Serpent, that monster King Neoc overcame in the old days. Sekenre's father was the most evil sorcerer who ever lived, and he found a way to let the Night Serpent out of its prison—'

'No, it isn't true—'

But Nahmekh went on with his tale with such intensity that I knew I must be silent and listen carefully, that this, like so many things that had happened this day, was some kind of revelation, a piece of a larger puzzle. The gods, or fate, or the Sybil – someone spoke through my friend here. He wasn't the sort who made up stories. When we had been children together, it was *I* who told the stories, he who listened enraptured.

'—and this Serpent who *killed* and *ate* Sekenre stole his *shape* and is still *there*, haunting the old house. It killed and ate the *father* too. He deserved worse. For a time we dared to *hope* that the evil was *gone*. But the signs are clear now. It's obvious. The Night Serpent still sends us evil, curses, disease. It will kill us all and damn us to endless torment unless someone can kill it first. So we pray that King Neoc will return and save us—'

I jumped up. 'No! You can't believe that! It's all lies!' I ran to the counter. It was chest-high to me. I caught hold of the edge and heaved myself up in a frenzy, and paused there, on all fours, breathing hard, looking down at Nahmekh. I saw that he hadn't been working on shoes at all, but on a crude leather image of a serpent-headed demon with oversized, very human-looking, bare feet. He'd carved it out of a flat piece of leather, nailing it to a board, driving in studs for eyes, nose, and mouth.

He sat with a dagger in his hand, poised to strike the image. But when he saw me on the counter top, he stood up, seeming to grow even taller as he did. I scrambled back, fell off the counter in a painful heap. He vaulted over and lunged at me, breathing hard, wordless. I rolled. The dagger sank into the floor. I screamed. He caught hold of my ankle and I kicked him in the face with my other foot as hard as I could. My schoolbag somehow became entangled in his grasp, and in the madness of the moment it didn't seem crazy that I should refuse to abandon it, that I should fight to the death tugging at a bag containing ink and brushes, a manuscript, an idol, and a few coins.

He slashed at me again, slitting open my left trouser leg, cutting deep into my thigh. Almost without knowing what I was doing I reached out for the hand which held the dagger. I thought of fire. Fire hissed out of the scar in my hand and it was Nahmekh who was screaming now. He let go of the dagger and crawled away, too startled to realize the flames were cold and he hadn't been burnt.

'Unholy bastard! You'll die soon anyway. We had hoped that *you* were dead, all the way dead. Then I thought *I* could rid the world of you. But my wife had a better idea. She told me to keep you busy here while she went for the priests and the soldiers—'

I stood up, painfully slid the dagger out of my leg and let it drop, and limped toward the door, clutching my bag.

'I was your friend—'

'Haven't you learned *anything*, Sekenre? *Anything?* Sorcerers can't have friends.'

'I'm sorry. I'll go now. Try to remember that I was your friend once.'

'My friend is dead.'

I had reached the door. Hot blood streamed down my leg. The pain was worse now. I looked fearfully along the street, but there was no sign of any soldiers. Possibly Nahmekh's wife had experienced difficulty convincing the authorities that the one and authentic monster was waiting in her husband's shop. Perhaps there was a reward for such information, and as a result the priests heard stories like that every day.

I tried to run, staggered, and managed a kind of half-run, half-hop. Nahmekh came to the door and shouted after me.

'Don't think you can get away! Everybody knows where you are!'

Indeed they did, but no one stopped me. Already evening twilight deepened. The streets filled with shadows and beggars climbed onto rooftops. Householders barred windows and doors. High in the tower of the temple of Surat-Kemad, the priests rang bells and sang out prayers, that the city might be preserved one more night from the maw of death.

I turned a corner amid a row of battered boats on racks awaiting repair, and there came face to face with one of the naked *evatim* wheezing as it climbed a ladder up from a dock below. It opened its crocodile jaws wide. For an instant I thought I saw the night sky, the stars, and the burning Moon all in miniature within the creature's mouth, but this particular *evat* only hissed at me and made no attempt to follow as I hurried on.

The pain in my leg was worse. My left foot was wet with blood. I sat on a barrel, tore a strip from my ruined trousers, and bound the wound as best I could.

At last I came to the ruin of the final wharf which connected my house to the rest of the city, and desperately, precariously, I made my way across the shattered boards while the dark water below me seemed to swarm with bodies.

When I reached the porch, I lay there for an instant, clinging to the familiar railing with relief. But something dark and smelling of mud and rotting flesh stirred toward me. I heaved up, caught hold of the doorknob, spoke the secret word which undid the lock, and stumbled inside, relocking the door with that same word spoken backward, then sliding the heavy bar into place.

I cannot account for my state of mind after this. I took no sensible precautions. Perhaps loss of blood had made me stupid.

I leaned against the door and slid slowly down to the floor, shaking with fear and grief and exhaustion, clutching my schoolbag as if my life depended on it. I think I slept for a time, for it must have been a dream when the room filled with angry, stern-faced men who paced back and forth, scolding and arguing; sorcerers, all of them, and their names were Tannivar and Orkanre and Talno and Balredon; and my father Vashtem was there too, as I had last seen him in life, haggard, swaying from side to side, moving as if his legs and spine were strangely malformed.

Then I opened my eyes in the darkness, in the empty hallway. My leg hurt terribly. I explored gently with my fingers. The bleeding seemed to have nearly stopped. If I kept the leg outstretched, the pain was less.

All around me, the house creaked and shifted and spoke with its many voices. Once, I thought I heard Mother singing upstairs as she rocked Hamakina to sleep. Again, Father's workroom called to me, the trapped victims in the bottles screaming and pleading and babbling ever so faintly, like marsh-crickets chirping.

I even thought I saw my younger self, clad in a child's loose robe, schoolbag under one arm, venturing one puzzled glance in my direction before hurrying away. The trapdoor opened. The ladder creaked as someone descended to the dock below.

Shortly before dawn, Mother's *hevat* appeared, the wooden man-crocodile with luminous scales, the very image of Surat-Kemad himself. It swam through the air, winding its endless tail in and out of every room in the house; and the huge, idiot's face of the god hovered above me, whispering the names of my interior selves.

Pale sunlight seeped through the slats in the shutters.

Outside, the birds of the river sang in a great chorus to herald the dawn. A human voice interrupted them, someone shouting. Another answered, and then a third. Far away, a horn blew.

As Nahmekh had said, everyone knew where I was. And I thought of running away, but that was impossible. More than impossible, meaningless. Here, this house, here was the center of my world, the only safe place I had ever known. Here, despite all its ghosts. Where could I go? I could no more flee this house than I could shed my own skin.

Outside, a crowd was gathering.

As I said, my behavior from this point is hard to account for. Perhaps I was more than a little bit mad. Perhaps all the sorcerers within me exerted their wills at once, resulting in a paralyzing babble of thought.

I dragged myself to my feet and hopped into my own bedroom, trying not to put any weight on my injured leg. Here I would be safe. Here I could shut out the rest of the world and get on with my work.

Yes, the blood-loss must have made me stupid. I opened the window, throwing the shutters back. I wanted light.

'There he is!' someone on the dock opposite shouted. A roar went up from many voices.

But it was only background noise to me, like the wind. I set up my desk there by the window, where I could enjoy the morning sun.

'Murderer! Will you kill us all?'

I fumbled with my bag, dropping it to the floor, leaning over painfully to retrieve it. Nothing seemed more important. How great was my relief when I found that after everything the ink bottles remained unbroken and my book was not ruined.

I fastened a sheet to the desk with a clamp and continued the project I had begun at my teacher's house, illuminating the tale of *Three Brothers of the Air,* meditating on the deeds and sorrows of the three, who awoke in a single room which alone remained after the dissolution of their world, even as I sat in this one after the dissolution of mine.

But each of the brothers left the room in his turn, to meet his own fate. I wasn't about to.

Something rattled against the wall outside. I thought, vaguely, that neighboring children had thrown a handful of pebbles, as sometimes they dared one another to do, playing games of Tease the Sorcerer.

I lost myself in the beautiful swirls and curving letters, certain that the secret of my own happiness could be found there, that all the truths of the universe lay hidden in these tiny, convoluted lines. Only as I performed this act, as I created this beautiful, miniature cosmos on the page, could I banish pain and fear and grief. I was completely alone now, locked in my own illuminations, safe there.

Something whizzed by my ear. Irritably, I waved it away with my hand. Then came more knocking; rattling sounds against the side of the house; a deep crash like distant thunder. The floor shook. A bottle of golden ink hopped off the desktop and spilled. I looked down at it dumbly.

I smelled smoke, but couldn't bring my mind to focus on what it meant. Then, as I tried to continue with my work, I discovered to my dull amazement that I could not lift my right hand. My fingers still held the delicate brush, but my wrist was pinned to the table by a quivering arrow. Blood spurted freely onto the manuscript page.

Outside, the crowd shouted in triumph, voices blending with horns, bells, and drums in a rising wave of noise.

More arrows whizzed in through the window. Several stuck in the bed and the opposite wall.

Smoke seeped up through the cracks in the floor. The house was on fire. But only when an arrow struck the bookshelf with a loud *thunk!* and scattered the meager volumes I'd owned as a child that I was able to rise. Somehow that shook me out of my stupor.

I shrieked aloud as the arrow impaling my wrist tore free. The desk fell. I tripped over it, lurched to my feet and reached toward the window. Five or six more arrows came through at once. One went up my right sleeve and through my upper arm. Another caught me in the right side, between the ribs. I felt like I had been punched. The force spun me in a crazy dance.

More crashes, now above me. The room was thick with smoke. I knew I was dying then. I dropped to my knees, gasping, then sobbing as the wound in my leg tore open. Somehow I managed to crawl to the window and hang on the windowsill.

The whole city seemed to have turned out for my execution. Nahmekh's wife had been convincing after all. A squadron of the Satrap's archers lined the dock, loosing wave after wave of arrows, some flaming, some not. Priests chanted, beat on drums, and blew trumpets. They held aloft ikons of the gods. The common people howled and threw whatever was at hand, stones, boards, spears, torches.

Then the crowds parted and the soldiers wheeled some huge engine to the edge of the dock. I caught only a glimpse of it before an arrow caught me in the cheek, jamming into my upper jaw. I went down, spitting blood and a couple of teeth. But I caught hold of the windowsill again and made a feeble effort to close the shutter.

It was out of reach. No matter. No shutter could have stopped the monstrous, burning shaft which hurtled through, inches above my head. The whole house shook as it flattened my bed and came to rest, half of it jammed through the floor into the room below. This was an arrow longer than my whole body, as thick as my leg, the arrow of a giant, of a god, *the avenging missile of King Neoc,* I thought.

Here I am, Avenger. Here.

Flames roared around me, the heat growing ever more intense. I could only huddle against the wall. The house trembled again and again as the enormous missiles crashed into it.

It was time to die. Time for Vashtem and Tannivar and the rest to meet their end. Perhaps it was for the best. Perhaps this was the only way.

But I couldn't accept that. Or else *they* couldn't, and drove me. I wept. I screamed in my agony, wriggling along the floor, through the flames. My trousers were on fire. I tried to swat the fire out, but my right hand wouldn't obey me.

The voice of the city became a song, of victory and jubilation.

I reached the threshold of Father's workshop, but could go no further. The arrow in my side caught against the doorway.

I pulled it out, fainted momentarily from the effort and seemed to be floating in red haze. My trousers were only smoldering now, but my shirt was all wet. I was drowning, choking in blood. The arrow still protruding from my face flapped like a tongue. I thought of the Sybil. I thought I would call out to her and say, *Well, what about this? So I don't get three times after all, do I? Did you tire of weaving my life and just throw your work into the fire? Is THAT IT?*

But I did not call out to the Sybil. I called to Vashtem the Sorcerer, my father.

And he came to me. He was there, kneeling over me amid the flames. He seemed to take me under the arms and drag me into the workshop. How could he do that, a ghost, a projection of my own mind? I don't know. I screamed at the pain as he heaved me up onto his couch.

I waited for him to put coins on my eyes, to bind my hands and feet and make me ready for the river.

Instead he spoke to me urgently, and behind him in the swirling smoke the others gesticulated wildly.

'You shall not die here and now,' Father said, and his words were a command rather than mere reassurance.

And he whispered to me of the dholes, and bade me raise my hands, however painful that might be with an arrow through my wrist and another in my arm; and I formed the Voorish sign, invoking the five angles the eye cannot see, speaking the secret names of the gods; and the very gods cried out in horror that such as I should know their secret. I heard them, their voices like drums, like cymbals, like trumpets shouting. The sky was blasted. The house leapt and heaved like a frail boat on a stormy ocean. Lightning dazzled my eyes; wind whirled inside the workroom, strewing books and bottles and apparatus like leaves.

Everything I was doing came to me as *memory*, as a procedure I had been through many times before and could complete without thinking, as easily as breathing.

Easier. It was hard to breathe. I coughed. Blood splattered down my chin.

Silence. The shouts of the gods were still. The vengeful voice of Reedland spoke not. The flames, too, paused, motionless in the air like sheets of diaphanous gold.

I tried to sit up to behold the wonder of this, but all my strength was gone. The arrow in my side had pierced a lung. I coughed again, mouth closed. Blood spewed from both nostrils.

Father continued to speak to me. I think he was only a memory then. I think I was alone in the room and he was merely a part of my mind. But he said to me, 'Sekenre, a sorcerer lives outside of time. It touches him but lightly. He wears it like a garment, and when he chooses, he goes naked. Do you understand? This is why the sorcerer does not age. For you a single moment may linger for centuries, for all eternity, and the very stars might fade from the sky before the fires around you burn to consummation. A sorcerer is not bound by space either, and to him anywhere is everywhere. It may be that your house walks through both time and space like a great spider on wooden legs, wading in the shallow water. Or perhaps it does not move at all, but causes the world to reform itself again and again, until the City of Reeds is far away, and you are come into strange lands where your name and the dread of your name are not known.'

In that moment, the house was an extension of my own body, many times wounded, haunted with a multitude of voices, wracked with pain; and I forced the parts of it to move, to hobble, to crawl, the log pilings and stilts creaking. Slowly, unsteadily, in utmost agony, the house *walked* away from its peril, wading along the river's edge as days and nights flickered by in the blinking of an eye.

'Father, I'm hurt. I'm hurt.'

Once more he commanded me to raise my hands, seizing me by the wrists when I could not. I gritted my teeth at the sudden pain. The arrow in my face fell out and blood poured down my throat. Once more I gagged, spitting blood in my Father's face. But he was not stained with it. It did not touch him.

I closed my hands together. It was all I could do to concentrate on this one act. I clasped them hard, forcing outraged muscles and tendons to work together. Fire hissed between my palms, but I did not release it, instead forcing it inward, into my body. I felt it burning through me. I watched in sick amazement, my mind drifting, my last strength ebbing away, as reddish-orange flames burst out of my side and wrist, as the arrow in my upper arm was burnt to ash and fell away, as flames covered my legs, first red, then yellow, then white, then an almost invisible blue. Finally, fire poured from my mouth, out of the hole in my cheek, so bright that I had to shut my eyes.

It was cold, burning cold.

All this was an abstract, far away thing: my tears sizzling. Or was it blood? What's this about sorcerers being unable to weep?

'Truly you are filled with magic,' my father said, 'and you burn with it; you seethe, and magic heals you; you are transformed, and the very flesh of your body is magic, the very blood in your veins utterly, utterly magical.'

Still I wept. No sorcerer can do that, I reminded myself.

'Father, I—'

Sobs.

He was gone.

I must have fainted then. Much later, I awoke in semi-darkness, gazing at the motionless flames which glowed like luminous gold.

My whole body was numb. I seemed to be floating. I thought for a moment that I was on the river, in my funeral boat.

But I was alone in the silent house. I slept and dreamt once more of a heron wading slowly among reeds.

Three Brothers of the Air

(orthodox version, from the notebooks of Sekenre the Illuminator)

Three brothers awoke in darkness, on a cold, smooth floor of stone. Nearby, coals glowed in a copper bowl. For an instant, each brother had a fleeting vision of far more: the thunder of battles, great flashes of fire, terrible conjurings and the howls of spirits, and the very skies ringing with the cries of the dying. Then, the three of them in their final exhaustion, their magics spent, their armor and weapons tarnished and battered, gathered here, lying down in silence to await the end.

But that faded swiftly, like a dream. There were only the darkened room, the copper bowl, and the three brothers lying motionless on the floor.

They did not speak at first. Somehow, as if some faint trace of the dream remained, they shared one another's thoughts. Images flowed between their minds like the sea splashing into tidal pools one after another, spraying, gone.

The three sat up in the darkness, without any wounds, without armor or weapons. All were very young, little more than boys, but they were also older than any counting, their minds searching for the echoing ghosts of past years and lives.

And when that searching ceased, when but the barest trace of whatever had once been remained, the eldest – for so they all knew him to be – rose and walked to a balcony. He took up a wine glass he somehow expected to be waiting there, drank, and hurled the glass into the black void. It fell forever, silently, and did not break.

Then the second brother blew on the coals in the copper bowl and flames leaped up, revealing the three of them: smooth-limbed, wide-eyed, beardless, pale, clad in white.

'Let us tell a story,' he said, 'against fear and the night.'

The youngest stirred. He was less haunted by memories than the other two, his mind all but empty of them. If he had ever awakened like this before, it was only once.

He spoke in a soft voice, gently.

'I shall begin, and fill up the emptiness with my telling.'

'No, I shall tell it,' said the eldest, 'as is my right.'

'You shall act in it,' said the youngest. 'You shall perform mighty deeds.'

The middle brother merely nodded, and the eldest sat with them around the fire in silence. Their shadows loomed on bare walls. A draught blew, and the flames and the shadows of the three brothers flickered.

And the youngest began his story, telling how the eldest climbed onto the railing of the balcony at the edge of the room and paused for a moment with arms raised, his white robe suddenly golden from the light of the fire behind him. Then he dove into the abyss, as smoothly and skillfully as a cliff-diver, who knows that a single false motion will mean his irretrievable doom.

Down he fell, through starless spaces, until he was no longer aware of motion. He did not come to rest, for there was nothing to rest upon. Yet he apprehended a vast bulk in the darkness before him, the shape and presence of Death, whose form is the crocodile that lies in the darkness ready to devour all things.

Perhaps Death already had feasted, until only Death remained, and the three brothers, and their room. The teller did not know. Perhaps the telling would make these things clear.

The tale continued: the eldest brother ventured into the very maw of Death, among the great teeth, wading ankle-deep in the frigid spittle of the monster. He recalled that he had been a hero once, that he had come to perform mighty deeds once more, that nothing less was expected of him. Therefore he strode deeper into the open mouth, until he heard the slow drumbeat of the creature's heart, as Death lay in uneasy sleep.

A glimmer caught his eye. He reached down and picked up a gold coin which glowed of its own light. He turned it over in his hand and saw that the image on it was of himself, only scowling and fiercely armed.

Soon he found another gold coin, and another. He followed a trail of them deep into the crocodile's belly, until he came to a room not unlike that where his brothers waited even yet.

Flames flickered in a copper bowl. Behind it, an armored figure sat on a throne, far back in the shadows, with a great sword across its knees.

He recognized this figure, and the armor, and the sword, from the image on the coin. But as he drew near, he saw that the figure itself was a dried-out husk, little more than a skeleton.

He reached for the sword, and the seated one slid out of the throne with a rattle of bones and metal, settling into a heap on the floor. Dust rose gently.

So the eldest brother, the hero, put on the armor and took up the sword. He gathered as many of the coins as he could find into a bag and said, 'Truly, these things were meant for me, not this other.' He shouted and raised his sword, afraid of nothing.

Then Death stirred, dreaming, and the eldest brother grew silent. He stole out of the monster's mouth and found his way into the sky, up through the darkness, sometimes swimming, sometimes climbing invisible stairs, sometimes rising like smoke. He thought only to show his brothers the treasure he had won.

But Death suddenly *awoke* and opened his baleful eyes. The fleeing brother dared not look back, but then Death whispered a secret name, and all volition was gone from him. He turned and beheld that awful gaze. The two eyes were like sullen moons half-sunken in mud.

Death spoke once more, and the brother screamed. He threw the coins away, scattering them across the sky until the heavens gleamed with them. He struggled to remove his armor, but could not, and it burst into flame. In an instant, nothing remained of his flesh, and he was clad in unquenchable fire.

'So the tale ends,' said the youngest brother.

The two of them turned, and saw that the eldest brother was gone. They sat beneath the dark sky, gazing up at the gleaming specks scattered there. Then the black void faded into a featureless blue, and a great light shone somewhere far below, blazing through the railing of the balcony.

'That is not the end of the tale,' said the middle brother. 'It offers no comfort against fear.'

After a pause, the youngest brother said, 'Yes, there is more,' and he told how the middle brother searched through the sky for the great sword the eldest had thrown away in his agony. But he did not find it. Once more, Death stirred, and transfixed him with his terrible gaze.

And laughing, Death struck the second brother with a flourish of a claw, and all the flesh was torn from him, and his bones were scattered. His bare skull went tumbling.

'That is the end,' the teller said, and when he looked up, he was alone. He sat still for a long time, his hands clasped about his knees, watching the smoke from the copper bowl drift upward. He realized that he was still afraid, that his tale had given no comfort. Therefore he spoke to the empty room, to the smoke and to the copper bowl, and told how he went to the railing and looked down, and wept for his two brothers.

And he knew the true ending of the tale, and he told it: how he too stepped off into the abyss, and the room vanished like a burst bubble as soon as he left it.

Down through the sky he plunged, as true as a hurled spear, through the bright spaces, into the ultimate darkness below, which no light can ever penetrate, where Death lies sleeping in black mud. There he found the great sword his brother had lost.

He took it in hand and marched into the open mouth of Death, past teeth as tall as mountains, into the ultimate darkness, until he stood before the cold, sluggish heart of the beast.

He raised the sword and shouted a challenge. As if in answer, memories came rushing to him, and he knew that when Death has devoured all things, when the very world itself is gone, then the last surviving life must be given, not lost, that time and the world might begin again.

Therefore he slit open his own belly, and hot blood and organs spurted out. With his last strength, he drove the sword hilt-deep into the frozen heart of Death.

And the monster awoke, roaring, disgorging a great gout of blood; and all the lands of Earth poured out again, warmed and made alive by the blood of the third brother. A great river formed in the mud before the crocodile's mouth. Humankind stirred and groped in the mud by the river's bank, and the gods, too, awakened, and rose into the sky all at once like a flock of startled birds.

Now it is time to name them, for the tale is truly done. This is the oldest of all stories, the story of Death, who is Surat-Kemad, the crocodile that waits in the mud. He is called the Devouring One, the Eater of Years, and the Father of Dread.

The first brother, who burns, is Kadem-Hidel, the mighty Sun, whose own pain gives him strength. He warms the day and drives the wind and is the father of courage, and of vanities. His lost coins are the stars.

Maena-Illakun, whose skull tumbles, is the pale Moon we see in the daytime. How sad his face is, how terrified.

And the third brother is Timsha, the Sacrifice, the One Who is Not Afraid, the Giver of Life, whose blood flows through the flesh of the Earth.

He is the father of us all.

Chapter 7: The Language of Corpses

I awoke in a kind of twilight that I instinctively knew was neither evening nor dawn, but some timeless interval between the passing of the hours. I still lay on the couch in my father's workroom. All around me, books and papers and shattered bottles littered the floor. Something small and dark heaved feebly, squeaking like an injured mouse.

Smoke hung motionless in the air like gauze. Jagged, equally motionless flames fringed the doorway like tatters of glowing metal.

I listened for a while. The thing on the floor shuffled through papers, then was still. I was certain it had died. But this death did not matter, since any useful information had long since been tortured out of it.

A hidden part of my mind told me that, one of the others, whispering to Sekenre.

Otherwise, the house was utterly silent. For the first time in my life, I did not hear even the river. I and the house seemed to be floating in empty space as the Three Brothers of the Air had, before the new world was created. This fragment alone remained of the old, the prior world, a raft adrift on the current of nothingness.

I sat up cautiously, expecting pain, but found I was merely numb in every place I had been injured. I put my hand to my face, feeling the spot on my right cheek where the arrow had gone in. My tongue told me that I had lost two teeth on my upper jaw.

I wondered: do sorcerers regenerate, as serpents do when their tails break off?

I wriggled the fingers of my right hand, flexing the wrist. The muscles and tendons worked as they should. Where the arrow had pierced me was yet another white scar, utterly without sensation when I touched it, as if it were a part of something else not quite alive. There was no pain in my right arm. I stretched carefully, then pulled up my sleeve and found, as I now expected, a jagged scar from the entry wound and a little knob of flesh near the shoulder from the exit.

Then I examined my side and found another scar amid my ribs.

That one should have killed me.

Fascinated, I got up and rummaged through drawers in a nearby cabinet until I found a long, delicate needle. I pushed the needle into the mark on the top of my wrist, feeling nothing at all save a slight scraping when the point struck bone. Then the needle slid to one side and broke through the skin on the bottom. I held up my arm, examining this, and suddenly felt faint. I sat down on the couch, gritted my teeth, and pulled the needle out, still expecting pain but feeling none. A single drop of blood remained on either side of the wrist, where the point had gone in and come out.

I lay down on the couch again, sideways, grasping my wrist, trying to make sense of what was happening to me. It was as Father had explained. I was becoming magical, bit by bit. I knew the stories of sorcerers who slowly transformed themselves into beasts, into metal automatons, into weirdly malformed shapes no words can adequately describe. Somehow I wasn't even afraid of such a fate, not now, not this instant. I felt I should be. I should be terrified, but my mind, like my body, was partially numb. Perhaps the sorcery had healed me there too.

I just wondered if my transformation would continue until I could no longer pass for human even in a dim light. Perhaps that would be more honest, I thought. Sekenre still looked like an ordinary Reedlandish boy. In many situations, admittedly, that would be useful.

I was thinking like a sorcerer.

But then I remembered my precious book, my diary and autobiography and school project bound into one. I got up from the couch and hurried into my bedroom. All was as I had last seen it, a chaotic mess of broken boards and fallen books;

the huge arrow thrust through bed and floor; the toppled desk, pens, paper, bottles scattered.

Carefully I gathered up what I could and put it back in my bag. I leafed through the manuscript itself, sadly, thinking it ruined, for the edges of several pages were stained with gold and black inks, and the page I had been working on now had a diagonal rivulet of dried blood from upper right to lower left. I wondered if I should just scrape the page clean, or even throw it out and start over; but then I understood that everything I did, everything I wrote, was part of the overall design. Even the bloodstain, which formed, not a rivulet at all, but a tree from which I might hang illuminated letters – even this, even by the positioning and selection of those letters – all this would help bring forth the true meaning of the document.

Even as every aspect of our lives, no matter how trivial it appears, is the Sybil's weaving and part of her intended pattern. It remains only for us to see the whole, to figure out what the pattern is.

I was thinking like a sorcerer who is also a calligrapher.

I righted my desk and laid the bag on it carefully, then went to the window and looked out. For all the inside of the house was dark, as if no light could truly penetrate there, the sky outside was still blue, just beginning to fade into red and gold as what must have been a late autumn sunset. The air was cold. I shivered in my thin, summer clothes. I looked around for something heavier to wear, but didn't see anything; so, still shivering, I climbed out the window, onto the porch, and stood there, hugging my shoulders.

I could see now that the house stood in the shallows at the water's edge, along some broad stretch of river I didn't recognize. There was no trace of any other habitation. Wind rustled in reeds. A flock of geese flew over, honking. Then, after I had been there for a while and was beginning to think that I would, indeed, go back inside to find something warm to put on, a great barge slid by, far away, a blunt, black blade knifing through golden water, silhouetted against the fading sun. I wondered if the crew could see me. Did they look up in astonishment at this odd, tumbledown house in the middle of nowhere? Or was I closed off in a little world of my own, merely peering out into theirs as if through the glass of a bottle?

I started walking, first to keep warm, then to take stock of the damage. A brief tour revealed eight of the huge, flaming shafts thrust into the sides and roof of the house, like harpoons in the body of some great leviathan, each streaming smoke and fire which neither drifted nor burned, frozen timelessly like all else.

Back inside, I struggled frantically to remove the missile which had destroyed my bed. A kind of frenzy came over with me; my one secret, safe place had been violated; *I* had been violated; but if only I could wrench the gigantic arrow loose or break it off, then all would be well, all restored.

But I couldn't move it. I thought I'd have to find an axe or a saw. Meanwhile, I sat down on the floor, exhausted, idly fingering what remained of the bedclothes. Gradually I realized that my shirt was wet, sticking to me, cold in the cooling air. For an instant I was afraid the exertion had opened my wounds, but it was only sweat.

Then I got up again and went back outside, through the front door this time, onto the porch. I found some comfort in gathering up the torches which had fallen there. As I tossed each out over the river, it came to life, burning in the gathering darkness for a brief arc, then sizzling as it hit the water. I kicked away other debris, rocks, boards, a couple of skulls, one rotting mass of cloth and bones.

Up above me, the walls and shutters of the house bristled with arrows, like the spines of a porcupine. There were so many around my bedroom window that the window seemed a mouth and the arrows a beard.

None of these, not even the huge shafts as thick as my leg, were truly the arrows of King Neoc, I knew, but the common-place work of the Satrap's archers and siege-engineers. The idea had simply been to burn me and all my sorcerous workings together. Had I emerged, arrows, spears, or even swords would have finished me off while priests held aloft ikons to ward off any baleful spells I might hurl.

It should have worked too; it would have worked, but for Father. He had saved me, setting me in the sorcerer's domain. I was utterly alone now, in the sorcerer's solitude. It remained only for me to explore my little kingdom, as a sorcerer should.

I was feeling light-headed again, from exhaustion, from the cold, from pain, perhaps from sorcery itself. I should have gone back into the house, wrapped myself in a warm blanket, and left the exploration till morning; but instead I climbed down to the surface of the river and stepped out onto the water. The surface was smooth and cold and subtly yielding, less like ice beneath my feet than, I thought, dead flesh. I imagined myself some tiny vermin walking in the cold corpse of a dead giant.

I breathed the sorcerer's flame out of my mouth. I shaped a ball of fire with my hands and set it adrift in the air before me, then catching it on my fingertip and holding it aloft like a lantern.

And I walked throughout the evening among the reeds, as the sun sank beyond the riverbank and the sky faded from orange to red to deep, rich purple, as the stars gleamed above me on the cloak of night; I walked among the swaying reeds and out onto the open water, silent among sleeping ducks which drifted in the darkness like puffs of cotton; once encountering a heron wading, greeting it as a brother, remarking that my name, too, was *Heron*. The bird opened its beak but made no sound. It waved its wide wings, rose soundlessly into the air, and was gone.

I glanced back once at the house where it crouched at the water's edge like a great, dark beast about to drink, the frozen flames its numerous glowing eyes. I wasn't afraid of this monster. To me it was familiar, benevolent.

After a while, I no longer felt the cold.

Once a long, low, sleek boat slid by, oarsmen along its whole length chanting softly as they walked the boat – rivermen call it that when the oarsmen stand and thrust their oars straight down, rather than rowing from benches, the oars slanted down from the horizontal; walking the boat on its many legs while paper-covered lanterns shone softly in the raised stern. This, too, seemed a kind of creature, receding from me backward into the night, its lantern eyes regarding me. I called out. I raised my fingertip light. Someone held up a lantern to see better, but there was no reply.

Later, an old Moon rose, horns thrusting up out of the black water, streaking the river with silver and white and pale gold. The Moon is many things and many persons, among them a goddess, some say an aspect of Shedelvendra, or perhaps another, who is called only the Mother of Stars; her birth and decline and disappearance reflect the mysteries of age and death; her rebirth shows us eternity.

But I saw the Sybil's face there. I knew her as she rose above the dark water. She opened her eyes suddenly, and spoke. I jumped back, startled.

'Heron,' she said.

'I did not summon you.'

'Heron.'

'Is my story tangled enough to keep your interest? Is it entertaining?' I had to be light-headed or a little bit mad to speak to the Sybil thus.

'Yes, Heron. It is.'

'I am so pleased, then.'

She closed her eyes and her face was once more just the Moon.

I walked on, neither awake nor asleep, in a kind of dream, but knowing I was dreaming, aware somehow that I was in two places at once, in my own private world of sorcery and in the real world; or perhaps I stood on a threshold, and could go either way I chose.

I found a ruined castle awash in the river's meandering, and wandered among its stones, listening to its weeping ghosts.

For a long time I traversed the shallows, where white and yellow fish streaked away from my every step, just beneath the surface. The shallows gave way to a mudflat, and as soon as I touched the earth, the water-walking magic dissipated, and I sank down ankle-deep in cold mud, my feet making sucking sounds each time I raised them. The light on my fingertip went out. I felt the night air again, and hugged my sides, shivering in my thin shirt.

Up ahead of me, a hovel stood at the water's edge, where the mud jutted out into the river and formed a little peninsula.

And inside the hovel, someone was screaming.

More intrigued than alarmed, I neared the place. I crossed an inlet of water, wading knee-deep. I slipped once and landed on all fours, now thoroughly soaked.

I could have deliberately assumed my uncanny aspect, drawing a great, deep breath of magic and exhaling fire, then stepping onto the surface of the water again, in properly sorcerous style, but I didn't think to.

Someone was screaming louder, in pain and in utmost terror.

I hurried on. The hovel was a badly assembled mass of reeds and driftwood and mud. The whole thing shuddered, ready to collapse. Suddenly a blanket-door was flung aside and a woman burst out. I glimpsed no more than a blur of a face, a white gown, dark hair. She ran to the water's edge, then saw me and paused. She was young, scarcely older than myself, a little taller. She stared at me, eyes wide, and raised her hand.

I opened my hand and showed her a tiny flame.

She made a sign to ward off evil. I shrugged. She lowered her hand.

Inside the hut, another woman screamed, and the girl before me turned back in that direction, then to me. Tears streamed down her face. She spoke to me rapidly in a tongue I didn't know.

Sekenre the sorcerer stood on the threshold between the magical and the human. He took a step, into the human world.

The woman inside the hut let out another long, trilling shriek. The girl screamed too, at me, pleading, imploring me to help, having overcome whatever fright she might have had at my arrival. I was less fearsome to her than—

The woman inside screamed once more, then was cut off. The girl and I stood in silence, staring into each other's eyes.

I bounded along the mudflat to the hovel, and she was following me. I got there first and tore aside the blanket which covered the entrance.

A woman lay there, weeping, trembling, half-covered by something dark and glistening. I momentarily staggered back

115

from the overwhelming stench of filth and decay, then leaned forward, my hand over my nose, as the woman whimpered softly and the thing that lay over her lurched up.

The girl behind me screamed again. I glanced back and saw that she had fallen to her knees, yanking at her long, bedraggled hair.

I backed away from the doorway. The dark thing rose and followed me, outside where the moonlight revealed the naked, badly rotted corpse of a man, jerking toward me on unsteady, wasted legs, the grasp of its outstretched arms, I was certain, more than humanly strong. I had seen so many like this before, the apparitions my father had summoned, the messengers his enemies sent to taunt him.

But this one was different. For all it lunged toward me again and again as I dodged its grasp, the look on its face and in its darkened eyes was of the most wretched despair imaginable.

I spoke in the immemorial language of the dead, the speech of that unmapped land inside Surat-Kemad's belly, where all men of all nations come together and share a common tongue.

'Stop!'

'Why should I not rend thee limb from limb?'

I clapped my hands, throwing a spark. The dead man hesitated, sensing magic, but then resumed chasing me around the mudflat, splashing into shallow water and out again, the two of us locked in a frantic, scrambling dance that would end whenever I lost my footing and the corpse dropped down on top of me.

'Leave us!' I said. 'Be gone forever!'

'Not until I claim what is mine . . .'

'I promise aid. I know the way—'

'. . . forever . . .'

The woman inside the hut cried out and this shocked the younger – her daughter? – into motion. The younger ran inside and then emerged, holding up the other. I saw in an instant that the older – though not old – could have indeed been the mother; both had the same thin face, the same long, black hair.

At the sight of them, the dead man lost all interest in me. He approached them slowly, as if certain they could not escape, and they only stood there in the moonlight, waiting for him, as if they knew that this was the case. The older woman wept. The younger called out to the corpse, speaking rapidly, desperately.

I ran around in front of the dead man, blocking his path, but a back-handed swipe sent me sprawling. I got up again, avoided the swinging arm, and shouted in the archaic and formal corpse-speech.

'Stop! Lost One, I know the way to the dark land. Truly, I have been to *Tashé*, where the dead reside. Truly, I can show thee the way.'

At the mention of *Tashé*, the dead man paused once more. I held my burning palm up to the decayed face, dazzling the black, oily eyes.

The thing gazed at me as if uncertain, then continued toward the two women, but slowly.

'Father!' the girl shouted. That word I recognized. It is the same in many languages of the River. It was I who paused now, startled. I stared at the dead, pain-filled face and began to understand.

Once more the arm like a swinging iron bar swatted me aside, but I got up again, fire rising from muddy hands.

'I shall light thy way to the Black River,' I said in the intricate convolutions of the death-speech, almost chanting the words, 'for behold, I am sent to thee by the gods, by Surat-Kemad himself, by the god, the devouring god, the masterful, merciful god, to summon thee home. I come as a friend, as a messenger of final peace. Fear not. Listen. Obey. I will ease thy pain.' I spoke to it as gently, as tenderly as I would to my own father, and the thing stood where it was, swaying. The two women took this opportunity to run past us and up onto the river bank.

Hours must have passed. While I talked to the corpse, the sky began to lighten. The dead man's eyes gleamed in the first light of dawn. Perhaps he even wept. He swayed and staggered, seemingly about to fall to pieces, but at last he hissed to me sharply, 'I shall return for what is *mine*. Do not oppose me,' then waded swiftly into the river and sank out of sight.

I stood there for a long time at the water's edge, watching the spreading ripples where he had disappeared.

Only after several more minutes was I aware that the two women stood beside me. The younger one put her hand on my shoulder. I turned. She embraced me, chattering more words I didn't know, obviously all but delirious with gratitude.

I didn't know what to say, even if I *could* say something they'd understand. I was still stunned by the suddenness of all that had happened.

Then one within me – was it Balredon, was it *Vashtem?* – whispered inside my mind, *Sekenre, there is a certain game, known to sorcerers. It is called* tanal madt, *the scattering bones. You don't toss literal bones as a diviner would. No, inside yourself, you toss yourself. You fling your life onto the playing-board of Destiny, then step outside into the street or walk along a country path or sail across a sea; and whoever you meet, whatever occurs, that is the scattering of your bones, your random casting which is not random at all, which seems to suddenly shift the course of your life but is, you will come to understand, merely a part of some larger design, now suddenly revealed. Sekenre, I think you have been playing* tanal madt *this night—*

And I started to dream of a face sinking down into mud, disappearing before I could tell who it was; and the girl was shaking me by the shoulder, babbling strange words, clearly alarmed. I didn't have to know her language to comprehend that she was saying, *What's wrong with you? Are you all right?*

I shook my head, suddenly aware of my surroundings again.

The mother said something sadly, bitterly. The daughter let go and looked into my eyes, as if imploring me to deny what the mother had said.

I could only shake my head again and say, 'Reedlander.'

'Arnatese?' the younger woman said.

Arnatisphon – or sometimes just Arnat, I knew, was the name for the City of Reeds in trade-speech. Those who dealt with foreigners, the hostelers, merchants, shopkeepers, the police, all must know the river-talk as well as their own language. But I had only a few words.

'Arnatese. I am Sekenre.'

The younger one, the girl – now I saw she was no more than a year or two my senior – curtsied as if to a great lord. Her gown was sadly torn and muddy. 'I am Kanratica.' Several words I didn't know followed. 'Tica.'

I wiped my muddy hands on my pants, and made to shake her hand, then thought better of it. I drew back, slightly embarrassed.

'I greet you, Tica.'

'I greet you, Sekenre.' Several more strange words. She turned to the older woman. 'My mother, Hapsenecuit. You ...' several more words ... 'call her Necu. I call her Mother.' The girl laughed nervously, as if this were some sort of joke, or she merely needed to laugh to drive away the horror of what she had been through. For just a moment, I thought that she was going to faint.

I turned to the older woman, bowing slightly. 'Necu, I greet you.'

'You ... a magic ...?'

I could only make out a few of her words.

'Yes,' I said.

'You help us.'

'Yes. If I can.'

'It is not good. I shall die here.'

Tica's barely controlled nervousness gave way to sobs. Mother and daughter fell into one another's arms, weeping, conversing rapidly in their own tongue. I wondered then why I had been able to understand the corpse clearly, but not these two. Knowledge of the corpse-speech was simply *there* when I needed it, perhaps placed in my consciousness by my father or one of the others.

But, further, why had I had no translation problem when I was actually in the underworld, *before* I became a sorcerer? The plaintive cries of the ghosts along the river, as my boat drifted into *Leshé,* had been perfectly intelligible. Perhaps the speech of the dead is ultimately no speech at all, but something more universal, like a dream, which one hears in one's own language.

In any case, I was now fluent in the secret language of corpses, as befits a sorcerer.

My thoughts began to drift into something bordering on whimsy. I speculated on the possible literature of the dead, whole libraries of books written by scholarly cadavers in their own spectral script which would remain illegible to living eyes, except, perhaps, to mine. It was an intriguing notion.

But then Tica took me by the hand and the two women, their attitude toward me an uneasy mixture of gratitude and fear, made breakfast for me on the ground outside the hut, mixing a bit of meal and fish in a surprisingly expensive bowl – porcelain inlaid with silver, not at all the sort of tableware you expect in a wretched hovel. Then, as I observed them closer, I saw that their clothing had been fine once, before wear and grime had ruined it, and both women wore several golden rings. Tica had finely-tooled, leather boots, though her mother was barefoot. These were not peasants, but wealthy people, maybe even nobility, who had fallen into misfortune, all of which, I was certain, related to the circumstance of the dead man who plagued them.

We ate and spoke as the day brightened, communicating with a mixture of words and gestures. Tica seemed uneasily fascinated as she saw that the whole right side of my tunic was stained in blood, but I didn't appear to be injured. She watched me closely, but didn't say anything. Her mother remained too caught up in her own thoughts and troubles to notice.

Gradually I drew their story from them, mostly from Tica, whose trade-speech was far more fluent than her mother's, or mine. She did most of the talking.

They were from Radisphon, the famous City of the Delta, where dwells the King of Kings, the lord of all the lands of the Great River. They had been, as I surmised, attached to the royal court, but Tica's father, Necu's husband, had been murdered by his enemies, his body heaved into the river without any funeral rite at all and somehow cursed so that he did not find his way even to the edge of *Leshé*, the borderland of death. Instead, this former high lord – his name was Ptadomir – returned to his wife each night as a lover. At first, she did not realize that he was dead, and she rejoiced, thinking he had miraculously escaped. But even then, the foulness of his breath and the chill of his touch troubled her. It was not until they undressed, and she saw his gaping, bloodless wounds, that she appreciated the true horror of her situation. Yet she was a strong, brave, great lady, so her daughter said, and she did not descend into shrieking madness that first night. She lay with him, as a wife should, and in silence.

But each night thereafter Ptadomir returned, and the secret could not be kept. Necu and Tica were banished from the city, for Ptadomir's enemies had gained favor with the king and the priests; and they fled upriver, never very long evading the attentions of the decaying husband and father. He was relentless and terrible, for all that he suffered endlessly with the knowledge of what he was doing and what he had become. It was certain that before his body dissolved totally, the curse would compel him to slay his wife, Necu, or to carry her off into the dark lands. There was not much time left.

'I'll try to help,' I said, all the while wondering if I really could. I thought back to the crippled woman I had pretended to heal that day in the street of the idol-carvers. I had been ashamed to lie to her, but unable to withdraw the scant comfort of that lie.

Tica reached out and took my right hand. She hesitated for an instant, eyeing the pale scars, but then she held my hand firmly and looked into my eyes and said, 'I know you will, because you are good.'

I was so amazed at being described this way, at being regarded as anything other than a universal enemy and monster, that I didn't know what to say.

But Necu only said, 'I shall die soon.' When we tried to share the food with her, she would not eat. One who is about to die doesn't need food, she insisted, and would not be dissuaded. The only thing I could do was prove her wrong.

When I rose to my feet and nearly fell face-down into the mud, I realized how exhausted I truly was. I had been up all night, sustained only by magic. I had suffered much pain, lost a lot of blood, and was healed only by magic. I hadn't eaten since – I had no idea when – and now the little bit of fish and meal lay heavily in my stomach. Now my body would not, *could not,* go on and it was all I could do to make my way up the muddy peninsula to the river's permanent bank, and find a warm, dry spot where higher, sandy ground curved beneath an overhang of grass. There I slept throughout the day, and of course I dreamed, for when so many souls are crowded into a single body it is impossible not to. Those others, banished, imprisoned within, clamor to be heard in dreams.

In my dream, I lay in darkness, in a dry, close place, amid dust and stones and scorpions, as I had lain for centuries. Suddenly a searing light dazzled me as my world was torn apart. Stones, plaster, bricks, sand all rained down, and sunlight touched my face for the first time in numberless years. I could see again, for the first time in so long that the sense itself was strange, disorienting . . . but it only lasted for an almost imperceptible instant before my eyes burned away – before my face boiled and my body crumbled into dust and ash – and I saw another face gazing into mine with an amazed, almost reverent expression: *Vashtem,* younger than Sekenre ever knew him, a Vashtem with a dark, smooth face and curling beard, clad in the silver armor of the Knights Inquisitor, his visor raised, his features distorted with hatred and lust, his sword drawn and ready to strike. . . . I was called Lekkanut-Na. I was a witch of the Delta, who lay entombed by her own devising, whose spirit rose from the dry earth every night to wander the world and work my magic . . . until Vashtem of the silver armor slew me, not with his sword, but merely by opening my grave, exposing me to the sun's touch . . . and I became part of him. I was the first. I was there to welcome Tannivar the Parricide, Orkanre, Talno, and all the rest. . . . Vashtem had joined the Knights in an attempt to deny what he was, to battle righteously against wild things, against sorcerers, dream-demons, and the Shadow Titans from whom all sorcery springs. But he had already felt the temptation of dark magic, and yielded to it. The poison had already stung him. His sojourn among the Knights Inquisitor was a charade. It could only delay the inevitable, which came that day when Vashtem, like Sekenre much later, slew a sorcerer for the first time and thus became the very thing he had hoped to avoid becoming. It began with Lekkanut-Na. With her, Vashtem graduated from apprentice sorcerer to journeyman, and there was no going back.

Vashtem remembered this now, in his pain and sorrow. Others, Tannivar, Orkanre, and several more Sekenre couldn't identify were like listeners in the shadows, leaning forward into the firelight, eager for the tale. And Sekenre ... I was Lekkanut-Na remembering what it was like to be Sekenre, for all Lekkanut-Na had never been Sekenre; Lekkanut-Na awakening in the evening on the sand beneath the overhanging ledge of grass; Lekkanut-Na running her hands over a slender body, astonished at the sensation of being so young, so tiny, and male ... while Sekenre dreamed, similarly astonished at discovering himself an old, enormously fat woman, immobile in darkness for centuries without end.

Lekkanut-Na rose unsteadily to her new-found feet, lost her balance, tumbled down the embankment onto the mudflat, and lay there, face in the mud, trying to control the unfamiliar hands and arms to raise herself up ... how very strange, she thought, one of the wrists numb, with a huge, white scar.

A little way away, two women crouched by the door of a hut. The younger ran toward Lekkanut-Na, her boots sucking mud as she came. Slowly Lekkanut-Na heaved herself up on stick-thin arms, marvelling at the lightness of this body, at the sensation of mud oozing between such impossibly small fingers.

'Sekenre!' the booted girl yelled, followed by a rapid string of words in trade-speech I couldn't make out.

'Tica,' the other woman, still sitting in the doorway of the hut, called after her in the tongue of the Delta, 'It's no good. He's just a boy magician. He doubtless has exaggerated ideas of his own powers, which will just as doubtless get him killed. Send him away.'

At one instant, I was a prisoner in my own body, able only to observe while Lekkanut-Na struggled so awkwardly to rise; but in the next, as Tica called my name, as Necu referred to me as a boy, I remembered who I was, and awoke from my dream. Lekkanut-Na receded, and I was Sekenre once more.

Yet the Delta-speech, Lekkanut-Na's native language, remained in my mind, like a scum left behind on the sand by the receding river. Radimeki, as it is called, was now as easy for me as Reedlandish, and in Radimeki I said to Tica, 'We'll have to take the shack apart and build a funeral boat. For your father.'

She came to a stop before me and stood, wide-eyed, one hand over her mouth.

'You really *are* a magician, aren't you? Did you travel to the Delta in your sleep, live there for many years, learn our language, and return all in a couple of hours I've heard stories—'

I stood up, shrugged, and held out my muddy hands. 'Something like that.'

'Oh.'

'But we have work to do,' I said. 'We don't have much time before the sun goes down.'

It was a poor vessel we made for Ptadomir. Along this stretch of the river, the bank was high and grassy almost to the water's edge. Only little rushes grew there, nothing sufficient to build a boat with, nor were there any vines to tie the bundled reeds together. Yet for some hours Tica and I labored, her mother joining in only at the end, and then in such a dispirited fashion that she rendered us little assistance.

Necu was giving up. She sat lost in her despair most of the time, hands around her knees, rocking gently back and forth, either silent or muttering softly under her breath. Sometimes she gazed out into the distance. Sometimes she stared at her feet.

'You *must* help her,' Tica whispered.

'I can only *try,*' I said, and at once regretted the utterance. It seemed my constant role to destroy other people's hopes. 'No,' I said after a minute or so, 'I know what has to be done. I will help you.'

'I pray to the gods you will.'

We tore the hovel apart, but lacking hammers, nails, or even rope, could construct little more than a raft out of some of the larger pieces, binding it together with Tica's one spare gown, which we carefully tore into strips.

'I need something sharp,' I said. Tica seemed puzzled. I pointed to the raft. 'To carve on it.'

She searched about in the rubble of the hut and among her mother's remaining luggage, and finally offered me a comb, the handle of which came to a metal-tipped point. I scraped the tip across the weathered wood of our raft. Splinters flew. The metal piece shot off to one side.

She looked at me helplessly, opened a small bag and got out an ivory fork.

Suddenly Necu stirred and said, 'No, here. I have something.' She pulled up her gown and revealed a dagger tied to her leg with a strip of lace. I took the dagger from her gingerly, uncertainly. 'You must return it when you are done,' she said, 'for if you fail in what you're about to do, I'll need it to kill myself.'

'Mother, no!' Tica said.

Necu took her by the hand and spoke gently. 'You must resign yourself, child. It is my fate, written by the gods in the Book of Lives. There is no erasing it, no help for what is truly written. In the end, I shall die with dignity, as befits one of our lineage and station.'

'But Sekenre – he can save us.'

'The boy is sent to us by the gods. I don't doubt that.' She squeezed her daughter's hand and smiled slyly. 'Let us hope that he's a sign that there's a little more yet to be written about me in that book. All right, then?'

'All right, Mother.'

'Then let us get on with it, shall we?'

Tica and I finished our construction, while Necu fussed over the knots, pulling this one tighter, examining that one critically. But she made little difference. I think she was doing it for the appearance of hope, for her daughter's sake.

With the dagger I carefully carved the sign of the *Ouroboros,* the serpent swallowing its tail, on the center of the raft. To this I added, on what was to be the front end, two open eyes, so the vessel could see its way into the next world, and at the rear, two closed eyes, signifying that the dead man looks no more on the lands where he lived his life.

I began working on an inscription of the lawfully-written names of Surat-Kemad.

'We're almost out of time,' Tica said.

I glanced up. She was correct. As I gazed south, upstream, the sun was sinking below distant dunes, far across the plain to my right. Shadows blackened the water like oil pouring from the bank, obliterating waves and the last gleam of reflected sunlight.

I continued carving. Calligraphy with a knife on rotten wood is far more difficult than with a pen on paper.

'I'm going to need two coins,' I said.

Tica let out a little gasp of surprise, as if she thought I was demanding to be *paid* for my services, and in advance.

'No, child,' Necu said. 'They are for your father's eyes.' She reached down the front of her gown, drew out a little purse, and gave me two silver coins. 'These are the last we have.'

I took it as a favorable sign that both coins depicted Bel-Kemad on their reverse sides. The front images were of some king or other of the Delta and hardly mattered, but there on the backs of both was the Forgiving God, with birds of spring resting on his shoulders.

Suddenly Tica stifled a scream and pointed. Something splashed at the water's edge. I turned and saw the corpse of Ptadomir standing there, dripping slime from the river's bottom. As he lumbered toward us, I could make out the darkening sky through his ribs. His eyes were gone. His face was no more than a bare skull with occasional patches of rotting flesh and scraggly hair. I had no doubt that the end Hapsenecuit had spoken of was upon us. This would be her husband's final visit.

I rose to my feet, as did both women. I gave Necu the dagger back, and she did not put it away, but held it in her hand.

'Help us, please!' Tica said softly. She was the one who seemed to have lost all hope now. She was the one who fell to her knees and wept. Her mother faced whatever was to come with the utmost dignity.

And I knew what I had to do. I don't think it was because some other sorcerer inside me told me, but because I was growing into sorcery myself, learning as a young bird learns to fly. The actions, suddenly, are just *right*. However clumsily, the bird flies. The rest is mere refinement.

I put the two coins in the one remaining, otherwise

empty pouch that hung from my belt. I would need both hands free.

As I stooped for a stick of wood, the corpse lunged forward, hissing. But Lady Hapsenecuit – Necu – held up her hand, they curtsied, and spoke in the language of the Delta.

'My Lord Husband, you have returned.'

Ptadomir replied in the same, 'I shall not leave you again until the Great River flows no more.'

'I do not fear you,' said Necu. Yet her voice quavered. I could tell that she indeed feared him. But she went on, and spoke to him of former times, of their life together. The corpse paused to listen, and those few moments were enough for the magic to swell up within me. I closed my hands together over the stick – a foot-long splinter torn from the shed – and my own sorcerer's fire burned along it. I held it aloft like a taper.

'Sir,' I said in the language of corpses. 'Come with me now. Thy journey has been too long delayed.'

The dead man replied in kind. 'What art thou that stands between Ptadomir and his just desires?'

Even as he spoke, I positioned myself directly between husband and wife, legs spread out, digging into the mud with my toes. Necu remained very still, the dagger clutched to her chest, point downward.

'I am no one of consequence, Sir, but I am a friend, who knows the way into *Tashé*, having journeyed there.'

'Then thou art dead like myself and have no power over me.'

I made the Voorish sign, which binds the dead, and replied, 'But I have *returned* from that place.'

The corpse hissed and lunged at me once more, as if to grab my neck with both hands. I held up the burning stick and spoke the holy and secret name of the Devouring God. Ptadomir froze where he was, lowered his arms, and stood meekly.

I realized that I could only hold him momentarily. To Lady Necu I whispered, in trade-speech, hoping that Ptadomir wouldn't understand, 'Quick! What's his true name?'

'Why . . . Ptadomir . . .'

I almost turned to her. The corpse jerked forward as my

concentration faltered. I thrust the taper inches from the ruined face.

'No! His soul-name. The secret name.'

'But, I—'

'Tell it to me *now!*'

'His name is Sennet-Ta. It means Hawk of the Morning Light.'

To the corpse I spoke, in the language of the dead, 'Sennet-Ta, Hawk of the Morning Light, turn from the morning light, turn from the dawn, turn from the day and the light; spread thy wings nightward, toward the darkness, for in the darkness must thou reside now, in the belly of Surat-Kemad, who is lord and devourer of all things. Behold, a funeral boat has been made ready. All things are made ready.'

The corpse leaned forward, then back, then forward again, uncertain, perhaps merely about to fall apart as the spell animating it began to fade at last. It turned toward Lady Hapsenecuit and reached out with one hand, the gesture suggesting, not hatred or lust, but longing. Possibly a farewell. She backed away, clutching the dagger.

I could not *force* the dead man to obey me. I wasn't strong enough, nor skilled enough; or rather, the curse and passion that drove him were stronger than I.

I could only delay him. I could only attempt to persuade.

'Sir, Illustrious Ptadomir,' I said in corpse-speech, 'thou art a great man, a scholar and a lord. Therefore let us walk a while and discourse as scholars on life and death.'

This worked. Somehow I knew it would. The corpse staggered after me as I began to walk along the water's edge. I held the taper between us and asked Ptadomir many questions about the City of the Delta, about its King of Kings, about the intrigues of the court. He spoke at length, without bitterness, even when telling how his enemies used a reed flute to train a tiny serpent to crawl into his ear while he slept at his wife's side and sting him in the brain; even when he told how Necu woke up screaming and screamed again, later, when his body was stolen out of his own bed and heaved into the river without any rite or ceremony.

'The workings of men are great,' he said, lapsing from

corpse-speech into the common language of the Delta, 'as are the lusts of men; they are like furious summer storms, rising without warning; and the yearning for power is as inexorable as a tide. Gold too, and glory of wide renown, these too make men mad, make them destroy one another . . . but to one who is dead, none of this matters. It is merely gone, like yesterday's dew once the sun has burned it off.'

I told him of the land of the dead and of my journey there. Ptadomir, whose soul-name was Sennet-Ta, asked me many questions then, and I think he drew comfort from my answers, from the certainty I gave him as I told him of the kingdom of Surat-Kemad, or the residences of the dead, and of the *evatim*.

'They are the messengers of the god,' I said, 'but also the lice that dwell on his body. They are the vermin that devour the scraps that fall from his mouth. They are more than human beings, and far less, half-divine and bestial. I don't think anyone knows their true nature, not even they.'

The dead man touched me. I allowed him to place his hand on my shoulder. The stench of his decay was very strong now, but I bore it calmly. He touched me as a father would when counselling his son, and he reverted once more to the formal corpse-speech, uttering a solemn pronouncement or prophecy, 'Sekenre, thou alone among the sorcerers shall increase in wisdom. To thee alone the true understanding shall come, after a long time, after many hardships, but it shall come. I, Sennet-Ta, who am dead, see this clearly.'

Thereafter his words became slurred, disjointed, and he rambled on about the dreams he dreamed while lying in the mud at the river's bottom, about scenes from his childhood, of family things that must have meant something to Necu and Tica but were beyond my understanding. He tried to recite the words to an old song. So many things had slipped away. He said he could glimpse both worlds, life and death, but dimly; both of them are far away and hidden in mist.

Once more he became completely lucid when he said, 'Sekenre, I want to weep, but I have no tears. Can you forgive me?'

'What's there to forgive?'

He told how he was compelled to haunt his wife and drive her into madness, even to her own death, for all he still loved her, for all he wished her no harm; as if he were a helpless captive in his own body while some malevolent spirit animated him and he could only watch.

My heart was racing then. I was afraid. I was moved with great sorrow for Ptadomir. 'We are very much alike,' I said. 'I understand completely.'

'Can anyone forgive me for what I have done?'

'Yes, certainly. They can weep for you.'

'Do not pity me. I shall be released soon.'

'Yes,' I said. 'Very soon.'

Then his reason left him once more, and he babbled, like a man talking in his sleep, scarcely aware of me, following the taper as mindlessly as a moth drawn to a light. So we walked throughout the night. I sensed that dawn was not far off. Once I glimpsed the Summer Hand low in the sky, but I could hardly stop and study the stars.

'Only a little while longer,' I whispered to him. 'Be brave, be patient for a little while longer.'

His head turned all the way around on his shoulders. He gazed down his back at me.

'I would have carried my beloved wife into the darkness with me. I would have drowned her in my arms. We two would have haunted this spot forever – but I did not want to – I—'

In that impossible position, he turned to his wife, who stood nearby. She dropped the dagger into the mud as he spoke to her in the language of the Delta, his voice fading, fading more, like the last rustling of leaves when the wind rests. 'I dreamed of you. I remembered – I wanted only—'

His jaw fell to the ground, followed by his skull, which rolled off his shoulders. I jumped back, startled. The effect was almost comic as his body walked on a few steps more. An arm fell, then the other, and his whole torso folded up, ribs scattering as he tumbled into a heap of random bones.

Lady Hapsenecuit stood over him and sobbed softly.

I saw that the dawn was indeed upon us. The river was too wide here to see the other side through the low, morning mist, but the eastern sky had begun to lighten. The water softened from black to brown to a metal-gray.

'Hurry now,' I said, waving to Tica. She had spent the entire night kneeling nearby, watching, entirely left out of our little drama but unwilling to desert her mother. Now she, Necu, and I gathered up the bones of Ptadomir, whose true name was Sennet-Ta, and laid them out on the raft we had prepared. It was needful to bind his limbs, as the limbs of any corpse should be bound, and in this case his whole body had to be bundled, lest his bones roll off from the motion of the river. There was nothing left to tie him with, so I took off my bloody, scorched tunic and the three of us tore it up carefully, making do with that. I placed the still burning taper in the dead man's hands, and the two silver coins in the cavities where his eyes had been, the images of the Forgiving God upward.

Then, as I had for my own father, I recited what I knew of the service for the dead, and bade the Hawk of the Morning Light the journey hence, to regard the daylight no longer, but to turn instead, and forever, into the darkness.

Tica, Necu, and I dragged the raft out into the water, and as soon as it floated, I told the two women to return to shore. I waded with it until I stood chest-deep, trembling, I hoped, only from the cold.

Now, for the first time, I saw the *evatim* all around me, waiting; and I sensed other presences. Inside my mind, as if in a flash of a vision, I glimpsed a man in fantastic garb – naked to the waist, a necklace of golden squares around his neck, a golden band like a series of cut-out eagles around his bald head, a skirt of golden cloth about his loins – standing in the middle of a black marble floor inside a circle of oil-lamps. He drew figures in the air with a glowing wand. I felt the tug of his magic, some final, malevolent spell directed at Ptadomir and incidentally at myself; and I knew that I could not merely set this dead man adrift as I had my father. He had to be protected. I would have to accompany him at least part of the way on his final voyage.

So I struggled with the raft, dragging it upstream, against the current, and the *evatim* parted for me and did not touch me. In time I noticed that the water was even colder than before, somehow *thicker,* and that the dawn had faded from the sky. Darkness returned. The stars were not those of Earth. Something stirred out of the mud beneath my feet, rose up, brushed my legs and nearly knocked me over. But I clung to the raft, floated for a minute, then found my footing once more and continued on. By taper-light I saw the surface ripple. Again and again crocodile heads rose, jaws gaping wide, bare white human shoulders beneath them, the *evatim* forever watching, keeping pace with our progress.

Now I was wading among hard, unyielding reeds that felt like rods of iron as I brushed against them. Ghosts sat up in the shallows and called to me in the language of the dead, begging for me to take them along on Ptadomir's boat.

I could scarcely breathe. My legs were so numb it was hard to keep my balance or even tell where my feet were. I clung to the boat desperately, submerged to my shoulders. All was like an endless dream, one step after another as all sensation faded from my body and my awareness drifted like a sorcerer's light inches above the dark surface.

The *evatim* hissed and drew nearer. I thought of the Sybil and of my father and of all the dead sorcerers imprisoned within me, and I could not believe that my life was to end here. I could hardly believe, either, that the *evatim* had come to devour Ptadomir. There wasn't enough left of him. It was a puzzle, a problem of arcane lore of me to work out as my mind became ever more detached from my distant body. I tried to think like a sorcerer. But I was so cold, so afraid, so exhausted that I could hardly think at all.

At last the dead man spoke. His bones stirred.

'I thank thee, friend Sekenre, for this kindness to one who remains but a stranger to thee. Had I known thee in life, we would have been true friends. Now, I leave thee forever. Here we part. Thou hast delivered me beyond the reach of mine enemies, beyond their magics and their curses. Thine is an infinite kindness, which I shall contemplate for all eternity. Now, Sekenre, thy final task. Push me out into the deep water, far from the river's shore, where thou canst not follow. For this last I thank thee, Sekenre, whose soul-name I have not been worthy to know.'

'Sennet-Ta, Hawk of the Morning Light, my name is *Heron*. I bid thee farewell.'

I pushed him out into the deep water beyond the reeds, until I stood neck-deep in the frigid water. I let go of the raft and watched as the *black current* caught him and bore him away, upstream, against the natural flow of the living river. Soon the taper was a speck in the distance, like the last star fading.

The sky began to lighten once more. The *evatim* lingered near me for a time, silent, glaring, but they did not harm me. This I took for a sign that the Sybil's weaving of my life was far from complete. She would want a more interesting conclusion.

But I was too exhausted for more thought of magic or destiny or the gods, or anything but rest. I struggled through the reeds, gasping in the cold, as ghosts caressed me and whispered to me of their sufferings and their garbled, fading memories, a babble of inconsequential details, and then there was just the wind in the reeds.

Only after I had been walking for a while was I even aware that I had reached the bank. I wanted to lie down, but I was too cold to rest. I staggered on, arms crossed over my naked chest, hands too stiff to grasp, until at last I heard, not whispering ghosts or the winds of *Leshé,* but common birds singing with the delight of the morning. The sky overhead was bright blue and the sun wonderfully warm, as were the sand and stones beneath my feet.

Walking thus, basking in the glorious sunlight, my eyes almost closed, I came upon Necu and Tica once more. They ran up from the mudflat to meet me, and both had their arms around me and I was sure they were going to crush me or pull me apart; while we three did a crazy, delirious dance, shouting and laughing and sobbing all at once. I, Sekenre the Sorcerer, found myself moved beyond my ability to put my feelings into words by the amazing circumstance that someone should greet me fondly, that my arrival should, for once and at long last, bring cries of joy rather than horror.

Chapter 8: The Great River

Some days later, as evening drew on, as we three sat around a fire eating the fish we'd managed to catch with reed spears, Tica asked me, 'What will you do now, Sekenre? Will you travel with us?'

Her mother, I noted, was eyeing me intently. She tried to hide it. She turned away from my gaze and went on eating, then coughed and spat out a fishbone; but she was measuring my response very carefully.

'I suppose so,' I said. I shrugged, then shivered and leaned nearer to the fire. These autumn days were still warm, but the nights grew ever colder, and, though I never would have made such a remark aloud, my immediate problem was that Ptadomir was still wearing my tunic.

'Do you ... live around here?' Tica asked.

'My house is –' My teeth were chattering. I rubbed my shoulders for warmth. 'I don't want to go back just now. I'm from the City of Reeds, actually. I grew up there.'

'But you will eventually return to your own country, then?'

This was the first hint I had that we were not in the Satrapy of Reedland at all, but possibly downriver, nearer the Delta.

'Not right away.' In truth, I didn't quite know what my plans were. I was playing *tanal madt*. I would follow the throw and see how it turned out.

Lady Necu coughed on another fishbone, then reached her fingers into her mouth and drew the bone out. She turned her back to me quickly, embarrassed, I supposed, at some breach of Deltan etiquette. When she was done she turned around again, laughed softly, and said, 'Great magicians are always evasive, aren't they?'

I said to her very plainly, 'Yes, we are.'

I could tell this intrigued her. She would assume I was

135

joking, and wonder whether sorcerers are any more capable of laughter than they are allegedly capable of tears. The betrayal of one or the other might make her think she did not possess the genuine article. And possession was what she had in mind. She thought of me as a tool, a thing to be used.

Her puzzlement was but a flicker across her face, which was otherwise a mask I could not see through. Her mind was turning, always turning, now that the fright of her initial predicament had passed. Now that I had gotten rid of Ptadomir.

Did she suspect the actual truth, that I was a very young sorcerer, half-formed, who still might have a lot of human traits? Did this make her think that she'd do best to abandon me and find someone else? Or did she think, ah, here was someone she could use, who might not have a strong will of his own?

My own reaction surprised me. I wanted to stay with these two. I felt affection for Tica, even for Necu, for all that I knew I was but the whip in her hand; so starved was I for any acceptance, any kindness at all, even the status of a pet dog. After all, a dog isn't abused, but fed, cared for, comforted when lonely or sick – and who would do as much for Sekenre?

Do not be maudlin, Sekenre. Father stirred within me. His voice spoke inside my mind. *Travel with these two if you like, but keep a distance. Retain your own secrets.*

'Sekenre?' Tica was nudging my shoulder. I shook my head. Father was silent. But he was still there, still listening.

I returned to the here-and-now.

'Uh?'

Necu was still watching me closely. Here was someone who could set any feelings aside, I realized, even her own goodness, toward some greater end. Maybe she was more suited to sorcery than I.

I turned to Tica quickly. 'What are *your* plans now?'

'We hope to return to the capital,' she said. 'We have friends there, who will aid us. When we regain our former state, we'll all live in the palace. I think you'll like that.'

'I think I will,' I replied. Indeed, a part of me did *not* want to return to my father's house. He was strongest there. As long as he haunted the place, I could not think of it as my own. It was too filled with memories and ghosts. There, Sekenre was still a child, subservient to Vashtem. Here? Vashtem still remained, inside my mind, but who was the master? I did not know. It seemed incredible that I could have so easily walked out of my former life. A little stroll down the river, and all my terrors were left behind, the burden of sorcery and my father's legacy tossed aside like a discarded garment. It was too good to be true. The one thing I truly feared was that I would lose my good fortune *because I could not believe in it*.

But I couldn't go back, not just yet, not even for a few minutes to pick up warmer clothing. To go back would be to revert to what I had been.

No, this was my *tanal madt*, working itself out.

I had but one regret: the loss of my schoolbag, with the book I was working on. Somehow, I would recover it, perhaps when I knew more of magic and could return safely – or send a spirit to fetch the bag. For this reason I would travel with these two women, not merely because they were the only people in the world who weren't afraid of me, but because I was sure I could learn much from the magicians of the Delta.

But first, the immediate problem. I sat as close to the fire as I could, leaning over until the flames almost touched my bare chest. The night wind up my back was *cold* and I trembled violently.

Lady Hapsenecuit finished eating and, looking around for a napkin and finding none, wiped her fingers on the sides of her ruined gown. Then she rummaged among what remained of her luggage and came up with a white cloth, a thin blanket or sheet perhaps, but it looked more like a tablecloth.

'You must understand,' she said, 'that we had to leave our vessel suddenly. We lost almost everything.'

I glanced toward Tica, puzzled.

'They threw us off the boat,' Tica said. 'We were sailing up the river – going to your city, in fact – when somehow, as he always did . . . *Father* found us. You can imagine how it was. Father on the deck, like that, in front of everyone, people screaming, pushing to get away. I think an old man died of fright. The crewmen tried to push Father overboard with their oars, but he grabbed the oars and broke them like twigs. And Father . . . *came into Mother's cabin –*' She paused, controlling herself, then forced herself to go on with the story. 'I had to stay on deck with everyone else. I was so afraid the sailors would kill me. The called me a witch and wouldn't go near me. In the morning, when Father was gone, they grabbed us and heaved us over the side.'

'Fortunately we were in the shallows,' said Necu. 'Still, we lost almost everything we had. So I'm afraid we can offer you no more than this.' She held up the cloth, then got to her feet, came over to me, knelt down beside me, and tied the corners of the cloth around my neck so I could wear it like a cloak. She paused then, and ran her hand down my side, not quite touching me, as if counting my ribs. I was suddenly terribly self-conscious about how thin I was. Her finger paused on the white arrow-scar. She said nothing, but I was certain she was wondering how I had survived such a wound.

In the days that followed, we walked along the river's bank, going north, with the river's flow, toward the Delta. By day, the air was comfortably warm, the earth beneath our feet mostly soft dust. I could wear the cloth tied around my waist.

To either side, the flat landscape stretched out to distant mountains, the empty country a mixture of sand and scraggly grass. Once a herd of hoofed and horned creatures scattered at the first sight of us. *Bamnets,* Tica called them in the Deltan tongue. Hawks wheeled overhead. Several times a day ships passed, far out on the ever-widening river, but we did not hail them. Once Tica pointed out a vessel far grander than any I had ever seen, with a raised stern and an iron-studded prow shaped like an eagle's head. Three banks of oars drove it, and two black sails flapped from its single mast, decorated with the double device of the eagle and the crocodile. This was one of the Great King's war-galleys, she told me, the means by which he extended his power all the way up the river to its source and controlled much of the Crescent Sea besides.

I told her I had never seen such a ship in Reedland.

'Oh, you would,' she said, 'if there was a rebellion. But the people are content and don't give the Satrap any trouble, so the King doesn't have to show his hand.'

I didn't ask her how she knew so much about conditions in a place she had never visited, but merely said, 'We must be near the Delta, then.'

'Not that close,' Necu said, 'but we are within the boundary of the old kingdom, where the kings ruled even before Radisphon conquered the whole of Riverland.'

Later that day we reached the ancient tombs of the conqueror-kings of the Delta, vast, sleeping figures of stone lying in rows, guarded by brick lions larger than houses, who gazed alternately at the river and out into the desert, vigilant in all directions.

But the wind had erased the eyes of the lions, and weeds grew among the sleeping kings.

We paused among them to rest for a while. It was supper-time, but we had nothing to eat, and so just sat, staring up at the pillars where processions of tiny figures paraded up and around. Black birds nested at the top, oblivious to us, the kings, and the lions. Shadows lengthened.

Necu stretched out on the sand, then Tica did the same. I gave Tica the cloth to use as a pillow. After a few minutes, while the ladies still lay in the shade of the tombs, I got up and started to explore. All of this was doubtless boring and familiar to Tica and Necu, but I was a provincial Reedlander, and to me it was a great wonder.

I walked among the stone images, running my hands over the marvelously detailed carvings, the folds in stone robes, the stone jewels set in stone crowns; details so delicate that the giants seemed merely asleep there.

I climbed onto one and stood astride his neck, leaning over onto his face to touch his eyelashes of black stone, which were still sharp as daggers after what must have been centuries.

Yet others were all but faceless, their features worn smooth by the desert. I imagined these ones angry, shouting in wordless wrath at the fleeing centuries that stole their faces away – but the fancy did not hold, and they seemed merely forlorn.

There were more kings than I had initially thought. I walked through their midst for easily half an hour, then came to a hollow of ground – perhaps it had been excavated; now it was nearly filled in again by time – and there, among broken pillars and part of a wall, in what must have once been a temple courtyard, I discovered another reclining figure, not a king at all, but an almost skeletal abstraction in green, smooth stone; huge, fully a hundred feet long, all but buried in a mound of sand, its exposed parts so worn and featureless that I couldn't tell if the nude form was supposed to be male or female.

I climbed up three or four feet to where the navel should have been and stood there, looking one way, then the other in a fascination I could not account for, as if some memory stirred within me at the sight.

The figure was all arms and legs, the chest narrow, sunken, the sunken spaces between the ribs filled with sand. I jumped from rib to rib, toward what remained of the face, paused at the collarbone and gazed into the soft and round features, into the wide, blank eyes.

Somehow I knew that this stone one was far older than any of the kings, that it had been ancient long before the first lord of the Delta came to rest here; but just as certainly I felt it to be *alive,* stirring beneath my feet after countless centuries, aware of my presence.

I slid down off the figure, stepped back, then let out a cry more out of surprise than pain when a hard, dry hand clasped my sunburned shoulder.

I broke away, whirled about, and found myself confronting another ancient, naked figure, this one an awesomely gnarled man, bald and almost beardless, his whole body so blackened, twisted, and polished by the elements that he looked like a thing of carven wood. He leaned on a stick and moved in such a trembling, jerky manner that I thought him a badly-made puppet rather than a living man.

He seemed just as surprised to see me, and stared with white, watery eyes – the only part of him that seemed really human.

He held out one unsteady hand, either for me to take it, or to point, or just at random. I didn't know. I stepped back and stood still, beyond his reach, arms folded, fingers digging into my own ribs, uncertain of what to do.

He spoke in a coarse whisper, like the sound of two sheets of dry parchment being rubbed together. I didn't know the language. I delved into myself, inquiring of Vashtem and Tannivar, and most especially of Balredon, who was widely-travelled and very learned – but none of them knew either.

I replied in the speech of the dead.

'Father, Elder, I greet thee with good signs and pray that I have not given offense.'

The old man's response was startling. He whooped. His shriek was not words at all, but like the long, shrill cry of a marsh bird. He jumped into the air with an agility I would never have imagined him capable of, whirling in a kind of dance, waving his cane.

I backed away, amazed and a little bit afraid.

He fell to his knees, weeping, his hands over his face, and he too spoke in the secret language of corpses. 'Surely thou art the Holy One, the Returning One, come to release me at last. Oh Sir, Divine Messenger, have I fulfilled my commission well?'

'I . . . know not,' was all I could say.

His hand shot out, quick as a striking serpent. He caught me by the wrist and yanked me forward, then caught my other wrist and held me by both, sobbing, leaning his head against my thigh.

'But I *touch thy flesh*. I am *visible to thine eye*. I, who am neither living nor dead, I who guard the Sleeping One until he ariseth—'

He looked up into my face, and nodded his head to indicate the huge green figure I had discovered.

As I regarded the pain in his eyes, as I felt his desperate need, whatever it was; as he knelt there imploring me to work some miracle, to utter some secret formula I did not know, I thought back to that day in the street of the idol-makers, the woman on the litter equally desperate for a cure I could not provide. Was she more wretched than ever now that she knew my comforting promises had been cruel lies? Did she curse the gods on my account?

I shook my head. 'Perhaps I am but a prefigurement of one who is to follow after.'

The old man bowed his head, resigned, and let go of my wrists. 'Perhaps that is so.'

I paused, listening to the wind stirring among the tombs, and a bird cawing from the top of a palm tree. I cleared my throat and said, 'When the sleeper awakens, what shall come to pass?'

The old man sobbed once more. He shook his head, as if to deny to himself that he had heard what I said. 'Why? *Why* am I still tested after so long, Great One? But if it so pleases thee, I say again that the Resurrected Master shall be like a god, deathless, neither young nor old, an equal to the gods, for he has dwelt among them all this time his body has slept in the earth. When he returns, the earth and the heavens shall be remade. He shall set all men to righteousness. That is my faith, Holy Sir. Am I found fitting to my task?'

I could only think to comfort him, lies or no. I took him by both shoulders and raised him to his feet.

'Yes,' I said, 'thou hast been found right and correct and ever worthy, as hast thou been since the beginning, as thou shalt remain yet, for what little while remains until thy task is complete.'

'A little while? Great One, I have been waiting since before the kings, since before there were even cities, since the gods themselves walked the Earth in their unmasked forms and men who looked on them were blinded or changed into beasts—'

'I know these things,' I said, for all that I had no idea what he was talking about. I had begun to fear him, for he seemed more than merely sun-mad. 'Thou shalt be rewarded. The time is shortly at hand.'

He smiled then, his face wrinkling fantastically, and, incongruously, his aspect was no longer that of an old man, but of a beatifically contented child. I could not explain it, even to myself.

'Sekenre!' Tica called from somewhere behind me. I turned. She ran toward me from between a pair of tombs, gasping for breath as she waved the white cloth Necu had given me. 'Sekenre. Mother and I. Wondered what had become of you.' She handed me the cloth. 'Thought you might need this.'

I wrapped the cloth around myself.

'I—' I forgot myself and spoke the word in the corpse-tongue, *tche-a*. Tica looked puzzled. I turned from her and saw that the old man had disappeared as if he had never been there, without leaving footprints. But he had been more than a ghost, I knew. He had been solid to my touch, as I was solid to his.

Now by some trick of light and deepening shadow, the green figure seemed much more lifelike than ever, an emaciated stone child asleep in the sand, dreaming some unknowable dream from the beginning of time.

'Sekenre?' Tica said. 'What is it?' She stood beside me, regarding the mound, the face, the protruding stone knees and ribs.

I shrugged. 'I don't know. Have you ever heard anything about a One Who Is To Return, the Resurrected One, something like that?'

She climbed up and brushed the sand clear from where the child's genitals would have been, revealing smooth stone. Then she drew away, a little nervously, rubbing her hands together as if to cleanse them of every grain of sand.

She made a quick sign to ward off bad luck. 'No,' she said. 'But there are so many stories about these places that nobody knows them all.'

I wasn't sure she was telling the truth, but said nothing.

She tugged me by the arm. 'Come on. Mother is waiting.'

I went with her until we came upon Lady Necu, who had fallen asleep behind the huge throne of a very recent figure; he alone sat, leaning forward intently where the other kings reclined; his stone face, with its high cheeks, hooked nose, pursed mouth, and small chin gave the impression of a grim hawk.

Necu awoke at the sound of Tica's bootsteps.

'Oh,' she said. 'Sekenre, I had a dream. Perhaps you can interpret its meaning for me.'

'I'll try.'

'I saw an old, naked man standing over me. He put a crown

on my head, but not one of gold or silver. It was a circlet of black stone, like this' – she ran her hand over the smooth throne-back – 'and it was so heavy that I could not get up. So I lay here, awake, for what must have been a thousand years, just watching the sun move across the sky and the stars turn in their courses. Then I heard Tica coming, and I awoke. The sensation was like ... like coming back from a very long way away.'

'I don't know what it means,' I said. 'I'm not a dream-reader, really. In my city there are lots of them. They have stalls by the waterfront.'

'But –' She was obviously disappointed in my answer, and a little puzzled. Tica put her hand on her mother's arm. Necu said no more.

We camped that night among the tombs, but no one dreamed. In the morning, we walked on. It was a hungry time. Once or twice I found edible roots in the mud by the river's bank. Once Tica found a clam. But the water was wide and muddy, and there were no fish to spear. Birds fled from us into the tops of palm trees, where their nests and eggs remained out of reach.

A hungry time. Tica or I carried the single cloth bag which she had managed to snatch up when she and her mother had been flung into the river. Necu was delirious much of the time, her feet swollen and bloody. We held her up between us. Surely she wasn't used to walking long distances without shoes, but she couldn't wear Tica's boots. Her feet were larger.

Much of the time Necu talked about food, fantastic banquets the likes of which I, at least, had never known. I looked to Tica for any reaction, but her face betrayed nothing. For once I was glad I was so thin. I could get by on very little. These two high-born city people were much softer than I.

But at other times, especially after she had rested, Necu remained alert. It was she who raised her hand one afternoon and bade us to stop talking. The three of us stood still. She listened to something I at least could not make out at first.

A quick shove and a hissed command sent Tica and me scrambling into the river, and all of us lay half-submerged among reeds while hoofbeats grew louder and a company of wild-looking, black-skinned men in turbans and flowing robes galloped to the water's edge. Some of them spread out, swords and spears gleaming in the sun, scouting, then standing guard while others paused to fill their bottles and water their horses. All but a few who seemed to be servants were heavily armed, most with mail or plate armor beneath their robes, many sporting complicated jewelry, necklaces, armlets, earrings of spun metal thread. More disconcertingly, their teeth were filed to points and capped with brass or silver.

Both women were motionless with fear, but I had never seen such folk, and I raised my head for a better look.

Necu grabbed me by the hair and yanked me down. 'They'll make you a slave,' she whispered, 'or worse!'

'Worse?'

'They rape boys, then impale them because they're no longer pure.'

The horsemen thundered away, passing to either side of us, splashing. I thought we were going to be trampled. It was only after they had been gone for several minutes that Necu let go of my hair. We sat up.

'Who were they?'

'Zargati raiders,' Necu said. 'I am surprised to see them so far east this time of year. There must be a famine in their own country.'

'I thought the Great King ruled this land.'

She glanced out over the water. 'The *river* he rules absolutely. The shore, less securely. The hinterlands, even less.'

We travelled in silence for a while. Necu limped. I let her lean on my shoulder.

I began to ask about the customs of the City of the Delta. It was, Necu said, the center of all civilization, filled with wondrous sights, with the temples of the gods, with – and I tried to get her to admit she exaggerated, but she said it was the plain truth – ten thousand gigantic marble statues of heroes, kings, illustrious benefactors of all kinds, poets, magicians, prophets, even obscure personages no one remembered anymore.

'That's not counting the city prefects,' Tica said. 'They're life-sized. You can find them in all the city parks and gardens, like an army of white stone men. Hundreds of them.'

'Does anyone remember all of *them?*'

'Whether they are remembered or not,' Necu said, 'every spring on a special day, each one of these statues is draped with a floral wreath, and people stand and talk to them, as if to honored guests.'

'Do they ever . . . reply?'

Necu smiled wryly. Her eyes met mine, looking for the joke. I didn't get it. 'Yes,' she said. 'Sometimes they do.'

'But whenever a statue speaks,' Tica said, taking me by the hand, 'it's always something gloomy and portentous. Wars, the deaths of kings, plagues, famines . . . so what you do on the Feast of Statues is talk incessantly, so the statues can't get a word in edgewise.'

I looked at her, bewildered. She smirked and turned away.

Very seriously, Necu said to me, 'Sekenre, do you know how to smile?'

I forced a smile.

'That's not good enough. It doesn't answer my question.'

'We great magicians must remain mysterious,' I said.

Tica laughed hysterically at that, bent over, staggering, all but consumed with hilarity, not because I'd said anything particularly funny, I don't think, but out of exhaustion and delirium and the released tension of her previous terror of the Zargati horsemen.

So another day passed. We rested many times, but had nothing to eat. Once we found a dead animal at the water's edge – some kind of monkey; it must have fallen from a ship or drifted a very long way indeed – and Necu stood staring at it, as if she were desperate enough to consider carrion, but Tica took her by the arm and led her away.

Tica made a sound of disgust and said nothing more.

Now that we had seen the raiders, Necu forbade us to build fires at night. We slept by the water's edge, in one another's arms for warmth, shivering.

The next morning, I caught a large fish that had become stranded in a shallow pool. We piled up palm fronds and twigs. I twirled a stick until my palms were raw before I

146

got any result, but it was real fire at last, not the sorcerer's cold illusion. We cooked the fish quickly, then ate it as we walked, so we would be a good distance away before anyone could come to investigate the source of the smoke.

In the middle of another night, when Necu had gone a short way off to relieve herself, Tica stirred beside me. She lay with her head raised, her chin in her hand, gazing down on me in the moonlight. She gently pulled aside the cloth Necu had given me. I stared at her, puzzled, but not afraid. She touched me on the cheek, then ran her hand down my bare chest and stomach, and, giggling softly, walked her fingers toward my groin.

'What are you doing?'

She leaned over and kissed me softly, once on the lips, again on the chest. I tensed.

'You're blushing,' she said. 'Even in this light, I can see it. You may be a mighty sorcerer, Sekenre, but I don't think you know very much about some things.'

'Like what?'

'Like –' She ran her hand across my chest again. I felt ticklish, but kept still. 'Like, girls.'

She kissed me again, on the shoulder, on the cheek, on the lips, and then her mother came back, saw us, and laughed. Almost angrily I covered myself and rolled over, my back to Tica. But long after the two of them had gone back to sleep, I lay awake, puzzling out what had happened. When I finally did sleep, I dreamed, as I often did, of a single white heron wading among reeds.

By mid-morning of the following day, we reached the edge of cultivated fields. The tracts seemed to me immense, row upon row of stubbled crops interspersed between muddy channels. Once we saw a dozen people far away, bent to some task, but did not hail them. Otherwise the fields were deserted. We walked along what was now a road by the river's bank, sometimes on just trodden earth, sometimes on pressed stone.

Necu and Tica were more at ease now, as if here we would be safe from the raiders, or possibly because this was a familiar place, near to home. I half expected the vast City of the Delta to loom before us around the next turning.

Even the Great River seemed, somehow, more familiar, friendlier here, its wide, lazy expanse thick with reeds and grasses along the edges. Boats and barges passed frequently, some quite close, but no one hailed us. Two women and a boy walking along the bank drew no one's attention.

Toward noon, we beheld two of the King's triremes resting in the middle of the water, their sails furled, their oars drawn in, like two monsters of the river pausing to converse.

And, in the later afternoon, we discovered a walled town of mud and white stone, quite unlike anything I had ever seen before, since, of course, the only town I knew was Arnatisphon, the City of Reeds, which is built of wood and stands on stilts in the river itself like an enormous, wading beast. We camped by the side of the road, within sight of this strangely *solid* construction which seemed more like a natural feature – an oddly-shaped hill, perhaps – than a work of mankind. Necu built a fire quite fearlessly while Tica and I made reed-spears and went wading into the river for our supper.

After an hour of trying, we produced one large frog.

'A delicacy in these parts, I understand,' Necu said. I could tell she was bracing herself against the prospect of actually eating a frog. When it was done, Tica and I each had a leg, and Necu picked at the rest. I refrained from mentioning that we Reedlanders ate frogs regularly and that this one was of middling quality.

Both of them thought me strange enough already. And a sorcerer must have his little secrets.

When we were done, Necu rummaged through the carrying bag and took out something small, wrapped in leaves and string.

'I had been saving this for the end,' she said, 'so that, if my daughter and I were to starve to death, she would have the strength to build a funeral boat for us and perform the rites. But now we don't need it. We'll be fine once we get to town. This is for you, Sekenre.'

I took the thing and unwrapped it, discovering a lump of an

odd, whitish substance, soft to the touch, crumbly like cake, but perforated with holes.

'Eat it,' Necu said.

The taste was completely unfamiliar. I made a face.

Necu chuckled. 'Haven't you ever encountered *cheese* before?'

'I guess not.'

'I see.' She looked at me *shrewdly*. I can only call it that; as if she had discerned some great intelligence by this trivial admission. She paused, licking her lower lip slowly.

I stood up and stretched, then suddenly felt dizzy with the effort and nearly fell over. I sat down again, my head spinning. I was more exhausted and starved than I'd realized. Then, slowly, carefully, I got to my feet once more. The makeshift cape fell off. But since the air was still warm, I only tied the cloth around my waist and said, 'Shouldn't we get going?' I was eager to see the town.

Tica looked startled, Necu incredulous, as if I'd just made some awesome magical pronouncement, it seemed. No, that wasn't it. As if I had said something so absurd any child should have known better. Necu laughed aloud, reached up, caught me by the wrist, and pulled me down beside her.

'My boy,' she said, and that was the first time she had ever called me a boy, let alone hers, as if my ignorance of *cheese* had convinced her I was truly young and helpless, not some ancient and possibly maleficent sorcerer who had merely assumed a youthful guise. 'You may be a great magician and I don't doubt that you are, but you must learn to pay attention to appearances.'

I felt very awkward. I said slowly, 'What do you mean?'

She laughed again and poked me in the chest with one finger, then ran her hand through my hair, got caught in the tangles, and yanked. I cried out.

'Well, *look* at you!' she said. 'A few tattoos, a bone in your nose, and you're the perfect savage! You can't go into town like *that!*'

I drew away and wrapped myself in the soiled cloth.

Necu shook her head. 'You'll have to do a lot better. But never mind.' She got to her feet and took Tica aside, whispering. I couldn't hear what they were saying.

Tica got a brush out of the bag and brushed her own hair first, then brushed her clothing as best she could. Necu fussed over her, talking all the while. At the very last, she gave Tica a ring off her finger, and mother and daughter parted, Tica toward the town.

Necu stood over me. 'She'll be back soon with everything we need. Come with me.'

Before I could rise, she reached down, caught me under one arm, and hauled me up. Her strength surprised me. I couldn't believe it was the frog meat which had revived her. More likely, it was having an immediate prospect, some plan to be carried out.

She led me to the river, followed the bank for a while until we found a shallow pool.

'Perfect,' she said, and before I realized what she was doing, she had taken the cloth from me and tossed it aside. She tugged at my trousers. 'Now these.'

'*What?*'

Not even laughter now. She was all business. She shoved me down by the edge of the pool and pulled my trousers off, then held them with her hand up one of the legs. She wiggled her fingers through the ripped knee. Without a word she waded out, and threw the trousers as far as she could. I watched forlornly as they floated away.

She undid my loincloth, holding it at arm's length while pinching her nose, and heaved that after the trousers. Before I could even demand she explain why she wanted me to go into town naked, she had me by both shoulders and plunged me into the pool. I thrashed. I thought she was trying to drown me. She held my head under while she scraped my scalp vigorously with her fingers.

I struggled free and sat up, sputtering. She pushed me back under again, then let me come up for air, rubbed me down with sand, then dunked me once more to wash the sand off.

When she finally released me, she sighed and said, 'That's a lot better.' She pointed to a flat rock. 'Now go over there and let the sun dry you.'

I obeyed, stretching out on the rock. The sun was still warm. The air was pleasant. All the while Necu sat, crouched down on the opposite side of the pool, her chin in her hand, regarding me, her true thoughts hidden as if she were still measuring me for some future use, as if, on some level, I were merely an *instrument* to be honed and cleaned and made ready. That disturbed me, but still the mere novelty that another human being should tolerate my company was such a powerful lure that the very consideration of it almost brought to my eyes those tears no sorcerer is supposed to have. We are not solitary creatures, we humans. Companionship is a craving. It rules us.

Neither happy nor sad, but a little bit of both, unable to sort out my feelings, I lay in the late afternoon sun, turning every once in a while as Necu sat across from me. I nearly dozed off. I remember some geese honking and splashing on the river.

'Mother—'

Tica had returned. I sat up suddenly, searched around for the cloth, didn't find it, and made a feeble attempt to cover myself with my hands. Necu crouched beside me. She put her hand on my shoulder and said, 'Don't worry. Tica knows what boys look like.'

I was blushing again, but neither of them paid any heed. Tica knelt by her mother and opened a new cloth bag. Necu looked inside. 'Just right,' she said. Tica counted out seven silver coins into Necu's palm.

'Sekenre,' Necu said, 'I have just sold my bridal ring to purchase necessaries, for you mostly.'

Now I was flustered by more than my nakedness. 'But, *why?*'

'I have my reasons.' Once more she took me firmly by the arm. Tica drew a strip of cloth out of the bag: scented linen, absolutely new. The two of them wrapped it around my middle, handling me as if I were a small child, ignoring protests. They dressed me further, in loose white trousers held tight at the ankles with embroidered bands, quite unlike the Reedlander style, which is simply loose. There was a scarlet shirt with long, open sleeves and more embroidery, done with stiff, golden thread. I ran my fingers over the designs, marvelling. Then came a kind of jacket, light, loose, and long and perhaps a little too large. It stretched below my knees. And worn over everything, a necklace of beaten brass serpents, linked head to tail. All the while I was the object of these attentions, the women tugging and adjusting, I thought of Hamakina at home, playing with a doll, decking it out in fantastic costume.

They even trimmed my fingernails with tiny scissors.

What Tica got out of the bag next left me speechless. New shoes. I could only stare.

Tica looked at me, puzzled, then to her mother, as if to say, *Reedlanders DO know what shoes are, don't they?*

Necu laughed softly. 'I think I understand,' she said, but she didn't explain.

I sat on the rock as they worked over me. Every sensation was strange, the clothing softer, filmier than anything I had ever worn before. I supposed you could find such materials in the marketplaces of Reedland, and presumably I had seen rich foreigners so clad, but I'd never had any money while I was growing up, and even if I had, I wouldn't have thought to spend it that way anyway. Necu said I would have to learn to pay attention to my appearance. Previously, I had never given it any thought.

It would make a good joke: *What is your favorite style of clothing, Sekenre?*

Covering.

The shoes were made of soft, flexible hide, a little thicker in the soles than elsewhere, somehow laced through with leader strings which Tica wrapped around my ankles, then tied. When I tried to stand up and walk, the sensation was very odd, as if someone were tugging at my ankles. I nearly lost balance and fell. But I managed to stand still, my arms outstretched, the breeze from the river flapping my new clothes, while the ladies regarded their handiwork.

'His hair's a horror, Mother,' Tica said.

'Gods, yes.'

They sat me down again and puttered about my head for the longest time, pulling, brushing, ignoring yelps, swatting my hands away, until my hair was straight and silky and hung down over my shoulders.

'It still looks barbaric,' Tica said. 'If he's going to wear it long—'

'Yes.'

More tugging. They wove my hair into a heavy braid and bound it with a silver thread.

'Now, Sekenre,' Necu said. 'Go look at yourself. You won't know who it is.'

I crouched by the pool and regarded my reflection. I saw a stranger there, who might have been some immaculate young gentleman of the City of the Delta come to pay a call on the Satrap himself.

It was such a strange thing, that someone would go to such trouble or even care what I looked like, that I found myself close to tears. I wiped my eyes and forced an uneasy smile.

'You like it?' Necu said.

'Why have you done this for me?'

'Well, you *did* save me from a terrible fate. Or have you forgotten?'

'But – I—'

I stood up.

'It's time to go,' Tica said.

'Yes, it finally is,' Necu said.

They'd spent all their money on me. The only things remaining in the bag were a pair of plain leather sandals for the footsore Necu, and a kind of musical instrument I had never seen before, a curved wooden stick fitted with tiny bells and jangling metal disks. I was sure this was for a purpose. It wasn't a toy.

Not quite time to go. Now the two women groomed one another, straightening their hair, until they looked at least minimally respectable. I wondered if they planned to pass me off as a prince and play the role of my servants.

'One final thing,' said Lady Hapsenecuit. 'We should pray to the gods, both in thanksgiving for our deliverance, and in hope of future success.'

So we three knelt on the stone by the water's edge and prayed to the River, which flows from Surat-Kemad and is both the highway of death and the source of all life, and to Shedelvendra the Mother of Waters, and to King Neoc in his aspect as the Invincible Sun, even as that sun was now setting; and to the coming darkness we prayed, calling out the names of the first stars as they appeared.

I felt a certain unease when I recognized among those first stars that of Malevendra, the Goddess of Pain and Murderous Vengeance. Lady Necu, especially, prayed to Malevendra. For this particular prayer, I remained silent, telling myself that a sorcerer can no more pray than he can weep – *Oh really, Sekenre, why do you keep saying this when you know it isn't true?* – and that a sorcerer may fear the gods, or steal from them, or even command them, but he does not pray. He does not beg what he knows will not be given.

Yet I prayed. I had prayed even to King Neoc. I trembled.

Tica put her hand on my arm. 'Are you still cold?'

The town was called Thadistaphon, Tica told me, meaning the Place of the Sleeping King. I was sure there was a story behind the name. I would learn it someday perhaps.

But we had more immediate concerns—

Above the gate shone the relief of the solitary royal eagle, the emblem of the Old Kingdom, never updated with the additional crocodile of the Hegemony, but carefully maintained, painted gold and silver, the outspread wings almost orange in the fading sunlight.

As we approached, guards lit lanterns along the walls one by one. From within the town, a chorus of horns sounded, like a long, deep sigh. The gate was already closed by the time we got there. All along either side of the road, caravans and single travellers had made camp to wait for admission in the morning. Out on the river, a wide-bellied ship lay at anchor.

I could only crane my neck back and gaze up in amazement at the stone walls, the endless jumble of rooftops beyond. I imagine that the mountains to the far south, where the River is born, must be something like that, looming one behind another to the horizon.

Twin towers loomed over the gate itself, lined with slits for archers. Stone beasts crouched at vital points, ready to vomit red-hot sand and stones on foes. There were quite a lot of soldiers on the walls, some standing watch, some marching back and forth to barked orders.

Perhaps the people of Thadistaphon had good reason to lock their doors and fear the night – the Zargati, even *evatim* crawling up out of the river – but then, I considered, the caravaneers showed no special alarm. They merely made their fires, cooked their suppers, and tended their animals.

But Lady Necu wasn't about to wait till morning. She snatched a piece of firewood from an astonished camper, pounded on the gate, and shouted, 'By all the gods above, let us in!'

Caravaneers hooted derisively.

She pounded again. The three of us stood there, waiting, Tica holding the two bags, I standing a little further back straining in the dim light to make out the intricate beasts formed of colored tiles on either side of the gate: eagles and crocodiles fighting together against a variety of half-human monsters.

Necu glanced over her shoulder at me. 'No, that'll never do,' she said. She hauled me forward. 'Here. Stand with your arms folded. Try to look imperious.'

I tried.

A panel in the gate slid open with a loud snap. Necu argued with someone inside. It snapped shut again.

She poked it with her stick.

'Hey! Have some respect. I bring to your city the great magician *Sekenre,* who deigns to set foot within your walls.'

The panel snapped open.

Tica whispered in my ear, 'Do something magical.'

'But it doesn't work like—'

She stepped on my foot. '*Something. Now.*'

'. . . a mighty thaumaturge,' Necu was saying, 'renowned for his miracles . . .'

The guard within mumbled something. A second voice, loud and firm, said, 'Madame, our orders are that no one is to be admitted until sunrise. You'll have to wait with the others—'

I think it was the strangeness of the place that drew the magic out of me, the expectation of wonders within. The city whispered in a thousand echoes: shouts far away, music, a shutter banging, horns. I wondered if some festival were taking place.

Across the river, the Moon rose, The wide water rippled golden. The tile beasts seemed to come alive as moonlight touched them.

I made a fist with my right hand, then opened it. A little flame danced on my palm, the color of moonlight.

The two within the gate were arguing. Then the loud voice said, 'Ha! We've seen that trick before. A little alcohol on the skin and—'

'What did he light it with?' Tica called out. 'Where did he get the fire? You were watching us all the time, weren't you?'

I turned my hand over. Flames flickered silently between my fingers. Necu turned toward me. Her eyes met mine. She was very pleased with me.

Metal snapped. A wooden bar was being slid aside. A smaller door set in the gate opened part way. Lady Necu stepped through first, completely self-assured, as if entry had been her unquestionable right. Tica followed. I went last. The two guards in leather armor, one of them tall, young, and long-faced, the other a grizzled barrel of a man, refused to meet my glance. I held up my hand to show I hadn't been burnt. Necu slipped the grizzled one a coin. They hurried to close the door and replace the bolt and lock. I walked on, hands in my pockets, as if nothing extraordinary had happened.

Tica stopped, put the bags down, and pulled my hands out of my pockets.

'No. Act dignified.'

We followed an arched pathway which sloped gently upwards. This opened out into a court where a few peddlers still sat with their wares outspread on cloth or displayed from the backs of wagons, for all that the gate was closed and there couldn't be much more prospective business this night.

Necu paused. She took me by the right hand, touching where the fire had been.

'That was good enough for the time being,' she said.

'I'm surprised there was anything at all. Magic comes from deep within—'

She released my hand. 'But you shall have to tame it for your own convenience. Or else what good is it, eh?'

I didn't know what to say to her. She spoke more truth than she could possibly have known.

'Don't look so downcast, Sekenre,' she said. 'You did well. By morning those two louts will be telling the whole town that a mighty magician came right *through* the gate juggling balls of fire and breathing lightning.'

Tica laughed. 'They'll have to make the story good or they'll be whipped for breaking the rules.'

Necu sent her off to hire a strange sort of conveyance: a chair with a roof over it, closed by curtains, borne by two burly men who gripped handles fore and aft.

I wondered at this extravagance, considering how little money we had left, but I assumed Lady Necu was merely too exhausted to walk further. I couldn't really blame her.

I opened the door for her to get in.

'Oh, no,' she said. 'It's for you, Sekenre. Just get in. You don't have to do any more tricks for a while yet. This will make enough of an impression all by itself.'

I climbed aboard. Tica handed me the two bags she carried. The bearers started off. The chair swayed gently with their strides like a boat on the river. All the while Necu ran before us and shouted, 'Make way! Make way for the great magician! Make way for Sekenre of Reedland!'

To my right, Tica shook the musical hook-thing and did a whirling dance.

Certainly we made an impression. As the street widened, then opened out into a great square filled with people, I caught a momentary glimpse of, indeed, a festival of some sort, booths, a juggler with flaming batons, someone walking on stilts clad in enormous, gossamer wings, the huge image of a god being wheeled either into or out of a temple – but then the crowd closed in around us. Tica and Necu both danced on either side of me now, racing back and forth to prevent the people from getting too close as we eased our way slowly along. I could hear Necu gasping for breath. I watched through a crack in the curtains, careful not to show myself. I was sure Necu wanted to keep me mysterious as she continued to shout the news of my advent, to promise signs and miracles.

I wondered what I had gotten myself into. My casting of *tanal madt* had taken a strange turn indeed. I was a little bit afraid, and at the same time both amused and amazed that after all her privations Lady Necu should remain so resourceful and tirelessly leather-lunged.

The bearers set the chair down before an inn. Tica hustled me inside before the crowd could get close. The servants of the place scattered. Necu slammed the door shut behind us and leaned against it. She looked tired, dark under the eyes. But then the servants returned with the landlord, his wife, and more attendants. All of them regarded us with undisguised awe. Even the landlord's wife touched her forehead and nodded to me, a sign of abasement. When the landlord spoke, it was with the utmost deference. 'Would the great one like this?' 'Would the great one be pleased to accept my humble fare?'

We were served the finest – and largest – meal I had ever attempted to eat, course after course of meats in strange sauces, vegetables I couldn't identify, heavy, sweet pastries, and a lot of wine.

When I looked around for a fork, didn't find one, and started to use my fingers, Lady Necu unobtrusively caught my wrist.

'No. Magicians can't be barbarians, even if they're from Reedland.'

Tica tried to teach me the art of picking up one's food with two sharpened sticks, one half the length of the other. I kept dropping things, staining my new clothes. The landlord offered me a device like a long, thin, double-bladed knife with the handle in the middle, one of the blades rounded into a spoon at the end. I made do with that.

Necu seemed to regain her energy almost at once. She was graceful, endlessly polite, as if putting on a carefully considered performance for the benefit of the host and his staff, but when no one was looking she nudged me and said, 'Now, isn't this much better than spitted frog?'

Tica laughed, then covered her mouth and smirked from behind her napkin.

All the food was making me sleepy. I leaned on Necu's shoulder. She put her arm around me. I glanced up once, noting how awed the landlord was that this lady could be so intimate with a magician. I was sure it was yet another deliberate effect. I didn't care.

'Much better,' Necu said. 'I almost feel civilized again.'

After dinner, the landlord and his servants led us by lamplight up a winding stair, and I was shown through a semi-circular doorway into a low-ceilinged room. When the servants had gone, I stood in complete darkness for a minute or so while Necu spoke with the others in the corridor. I scraped the wall with my fingernail. Little grains rattled to the floor. Everything was strange here, even the stuff they made houses of.

I was too exhausted to stand. My knees bumped into the edge of a bed. I fell face down across it and lay there, my outstretched arms dangling into space.

Almost at once Necu came in, carrying a clay lamp shaped like a bird. She shook me by the shoulder, hard. I rolled over. She placed the lantern on a table, then opened the room's single, shuttered window.

'Get up. You can't sleep yet, Sekenre. We have work to do.'

'Can't we wait till morning? Don't you want to sleep too?'

She sat down beside me on the bed and hauled me upright. She opened something I first thought to be a book, two mirrors set in wood, hinged together, and set this device on the table.

'What I want doesn't matter. There are more important things to think about than our immediate comfort. There's quite a mob outside. You're a magician. Everybody knows magic is best done at night.'

I stared into the mirrors and saw only myself, bleary-eyed, staring back. I wasn't sure about magic, or night-time, or anything. I was truly fog-brained. I wondered if the food had been drugged. But hadn't she eaten it herself? I couldn't work that out.

'What's this for –?' I reached for the mirrors, knocked them over, but she caught them before they fell.

'Careful. Just sit still, with your hands in your lap. When a *client* enters, you capture that person's reflection in the mirror, study it, and divine that person's nature.'

'But this is crazy – I don't know how to do that—'

'You *are* a magician, aren't you, Sekenre? Or am I misled?'

Even then I realized how extraordinary it was that Lady Hapsenecuit, who seemed to know everything about the regular world, could be so ignorant of magic and magicians ... and criminal, murderous sorcerers. But I did not argue with her. I merely sighed and said, 'Yes, I am.'

'It's settled, then.' She took my hand in hers and squeezed affectionately. 'Thank you, Sekenre. Think of it as another step toward our goal, toward the City of the Delta. That's all. Right now, quite bluntly, we need the money.' She took hold of me, straightened me up. 'Don't slouch, Sekenre. Don't put your hands in your pockets. Act dignified, as formidable as you can manage. And don't worry about what you see in the mirrors. Just make it sound good.'

She left the lamp on the table and withdrew to the far side of the room, into the shadows. I halfway expected the lantern's form to be that of a heron. But it was a duck, the wick hanging out of its bill.

Tica admitted one townsperson at a time, allowing each about five minutes. The customer sat on a stool while Necu introduced me, then repeated the customer's questions in a trailing, sonorous voice. I suppose my drowsiness must have added to the effect, making me seem to be in a trance.

It was all common stuff, advice about marriages, crops, fortunes, and trade. Each time the customer took the mirrors, gazed into them, closed them, then handed them to me. I pretended to study the reflection captured in the glass – but I only saw myself, and the lamplight – and mumbled prophecies. I guessed as well as I could. The clients went away silently, often shaking their heads.

Necu whispered for a pause. Tica held up the next customer.

'Sekenre!' Necu said. 'You're going to have to do better. Look *within* yourself. You contain many secrets. I know.'

Again she spoke more truthfully than she could have

known. From her, it was an amazing, almost alarming comment. I stared at her. Her face and eyes betrayed nothing.

A young girl, no more than thirteen, came in and sat down.

I looked within myself. I drew magic forth. What followed was very strange. The memory of it became garbled almost before the event ended.

I was listening to some other, faraway voice. At first I thought it someone else entirely, in a room down the hall perhaps, but very slowly I realized that it was *I* whose mouth formed the words, whose breath projected them. It must have been one of my other selves who spoke, come to the fore as Sekenre drowsed; someone who actually knew the art of mirror-reading, and whose accent was Deltan rather than Reedlandish.

The mirror actually caught and held the girl's reflection. The image glowed sufficiently to illuminate the bed I sat on and the wall behind. I – or someone – studied the reflection for several minutes, watching the girl's face change very slightly, then suddenly darken and bloat, at last withering away until she was no more than a skull with tatters of flesh. The meaning was clear. She would be dead within the year. All her questions about the youth she loved and her fortune and how many children she would have were cruelly in vain.

I spoke to her in the formal language of corpses, in my own voice now, trying to comfort her, to give her guidance for her journey into the belly of Surat-Kemad, which she would embark upon soon. I told her of my own adventures in the dark land. She understood me, and replied in like speech, and asked many questions. Then she rose silently and departed, more like a figure of smoke than of flesh.

I closed the mirror-book and laid it flat on the table. The room seemed utterly dark for a minute. I tried to focus my eyes on the lamp's wick, but it was like a single, tiny star, far away in an endless, empty sky.

The next thing I knew Necu had me in her arms, raising me up from the bed again. She shook me firmly. She held me under the chin and stared into my eyes, but said nothing.

A man of about twenty entered the room. Necu retreated to

her far corner, and we continued. The man stank of sweat and of animals. As I studied his reflection, he said to me, 'Magician, I dare entrust only you with this secret. If the prefect knew, he'd have me in a dungeon, and they'd sell me to the Satrap and send me to my death. I am the descendant of a prince, who was cast from his throne unjustly. My forebears ruled this place long before any king of the Delta. When each male child of my family comes of age, his father tells him of his true inheritance and passes to him the secret regalia of the ancient princes of Thadistaphon. Now say to me, Seer, how I may reclaim what is mine, so that I might rule and my son rule after me.'

The *other* stirred within me once more. He asked a few questions in faultless Deltan.

The mirror showed that the smelly man was the son of a butcher who was in turn the son of a butcher begotten by a rogue who seduced a maiden, then deserted her, leaving her to work herself to an early death as a drudge so that the boy, the present customer's grandfather, could be set up in the butchering business. The story was nothing but lies and delusions. The would-be prince had told it many times before, in taverns, on streetcorners, to anyone who would listen. The city prefect already knew, and regarded the fellow as harmless, if a bit mad. But the garrulous butcher would tell his tale once too often, too insistently, and in front of the wrong people. He would find his death here, in Thadistaphon, chained to a platform in the public square while passers-by laughed at his babblings. His princely regalia had never consisted of anything more than an old leather cloak, a stick, and the skull of a cat wrapped in wire.

I folded the mirror between my hands. The prophetic *other* left me. I think I spoke as myself now. But I am not sure. It was all I could do not to fall asleep right there, my head on the tabletop.

I think it was Sekenre who told him the story of *The Boy in the Cage*:

In the old times (I began), a boy was born inside a cage, without any apparent mother or father. A magician found him among the reeds by the river's edge, an infant floating in a wicker cage such as you might transport a dog or cat in.

The magician found him and hung the cage in a tree. Then he went away.

Ghosts tended the boy, rising up out of *Leshé,* whispering to him things of the past and future, of the living and the dead. He cried lustily, content with his lot, for he knew no other. The spirits fed him on moonlight and spider silk and the river's shadow.

He grew, not large or strong, but he grew, and the cage grew with him. He would go to sleep one night, cramped in small quarters, and awaken to find his cage enlarged, whole new sections added, until his cage became a treehouse of many rooms, filled with furniture and strange apparatus and stranger books. But the windows and doors were always barred. The boy could not get out. He had not yet encountered any other human being, for the spirits who tended him were like living shadows, like smoke, or else completely invisible. Most of the time he only heard them in the darkness or felt the faint touch of their hands.

Still he grew a little larger, though in truth his growth was stunted, leaving him reed-thin, almost a dwarf. He played games in the darkness, conversing with the spirits, puzzling over what he found in his house, and still he was content, for he knew nothing else.

Yet, inevitably, the world outside the cage began to intrude. He heard voices in the distance, a few at first, then many, then laughter, and horns blowing.

Once a brilliantly-plumed bird alighted between the bars of his window. Marvelling, the boy reached for this new thing, but it flew away, out of reach. He stood still for a long time, his face pressed against the bars, his arms hanging out, gazing into the sky where the bird had gone.

He looked out on the greater world then. He watched the river as it passed, as it changed with every wave and ripple, subtly, infinitely. He saw great vessels filled with people, far away, as unreachable as the bird. Nearer at hand, he saw other children playing on the bank. He called out to them, but they thought it was just the wind rattling the leaves of a tree. He had never learned the speech of children, only of ghosts.

He commanded the spirits to let him out, but they would not obey him.

He wept.

Now he studied the books he had with great deliberation, and, though unable to sort out sober history from extravagant tale or prophecy from confession, he learned much of the world. Or he thought he did. Everything was a jumble.

In time he came to believe himself to be a prince, the wronged heir of an ancient and noble line, who had been exiled and imprisoned by magic.

Now he wept every night as he lay in his bed, thinking on this.

Then one night he forgot to put his candle out. Wind blew it over. Fire devoured the floor of his chamber. But he fell harmlessly to the ground. Then rain extinguished the fire, so the rest of the house was not consumed. Perhaps some god showed mercy on him in this manner. Perhaps it was no mercy at all.

The boy ventured but a few steps into the world. Then he turned back, saying, 'Oh, I have forgotten something.' He climbed back into the cage and recovered his shoes, which he would need for walking.

He came among the people of the land, speaking only the language of ghosts. No one recognized him as a prince. They thought him a ragged, malnourished, mad boy.

He returned to his cage, saying, 'I have forgotten something else, which will distinguish me as a prince.'

He recovered a fine cloak and a lantern. He entered a town, expecting the people to marvel. But they did not.

Again, he returned to his cage. 'I forgot my throne,' he said. He carried a wicker chair away with him and sat on it by the crossroads, looking, he thought, princely and magnificent in his bright cloak, with the lantern in his hand.

A few people took him for a beggar, and dropped coins at his feet.

'I have forgotten my palace,' he said, at last. 'That's it.'

He took apart the entire treehouse, laboring for many days,

until he had reconstructed part of it as a throne room set on the back of a wagon, which he pulled with his own hands.

Still, no one knelt down to him. No one bowed. Children asked to play with him, but he said, in the language of ghosts, 'I cannot. I am a prince.' They didn't understand him and just ran away.

Once a woman offered him food, if only he would come into her house and share it with her. He said, in the language of ghosts, 'A prince must dine in his palace.' He sat in his wicker throne-room, she in her house, shaking her head sadly. She left a few scraps out for him when she was done.

At last a sage came to him and said, in the language of ghosts, which he spoke fluently, 'Foolish boy, you are still imprisoned because you're dragging your cage everywhere you go. Let go of it and be free.'

The boy only lamented, 'I cannot. It's part of me now. The bars grow out of me like quills on a porcupine's back!'

And this was so, for in the long journeys, in the many rains, the wicker cage had come alive and begun to grow again, binding the boy's hands to the handles by which he pulled the wagon. Now the prisoner and the prison were of a single flesh.

'What kind of rubbish is this?' said my malodorous client. 'If I want a silly story, I'll go to the bazaar.'

I folded the mirror in my lap.

'Did you understand your fortune as I told it?'

He spat on the floor. 'No. Did you?' He left without another word, stamping his boots heavily on the stairs outside.

There was only one more customer after him, an ancient woman who did not sit, but leaned forward on her cane and said, 'Your eyes, child. What is it about your eyes?'

'What do you mean?'

She all but screamed. 'You're on fire inside! Burning!'

I held up the mirror to catch my own reflection, but at first I saw only the flickering lamp-flame. Then there were two points of light, and they did indeed suggest eyes. A face formed in the mirror, my father's. He seemed to be walking toward me up a steep slope, laboring but determined, one step after another.

His gaze met mine. I cried out and dropped the mirror onto the floor. Necu came over to me and I clung to her, and after that I can only remember the old woman shouting and Necu calling for Tica, and all three of them prying me loose. Then the old lady was gone and Necu and Tica eased me down onto the bed, lifting my legs up, slipping my shoes off.

That night I dreamed that my father came to me up a long slope and stood by the bed, stinking of death. He wore a tarnished silver mask which he left on the table in exchange for the hinged mirror.

'My son,' he said to me, 'for the dead there is no time, so you cannot delay them. For the dead there is no distance, so you cannot run away. An instant and a century are the same, as are a single footstep and the entire length of the Great River. These things are true for the dead, and for the sorcerer also.'

Chapter 9: The City of the Delta

I awoke gasping, in absolute darkness. I thought I was dying. The dream wouldn't *end* and still I dreamed that my father knelt on my chest, his huge hands around my neck, choking me as he leaned close to my face, his breath foul with corruption, while he rocked back and forth and crooned, 'I am with you forever, son, forever, forever—'

'No! Don't—!'

I rolled onto the floor, wheezing, unable to cry out more, my lungs burning as I thrashed against the table, knocking it aside. Something metallic crashed. I rolled, tried to rise, fell again as the sheet from the bed clung to me like a shroud. Somehow I couldn't get my legs free and had only my hands to drag myself across the room, to heave myself up and catch the window ledge. Fortunately the shutters weren't locked. I banged my head against them and leaned out, clinging precariously to the ledge, gulping in the cool morning air.

In a courtyard below, a woman sang softly to herself as she drew water from a well. My first instinct was to slide back into the room so she wouldn't see me; but she did see me, and only smiled, nodded, and went on with her work and her singing.

When she was gone I rolled over and lay across the ledge, gazing up at the indefinable blue-gray sky that comes just at dawn. Around me, pigeons stirred under the eaves, babbling softly. Nearby, a baby cried. Someone shouted something. A few streets away, a peddler bellowed a song. I couldn't make out any words, but the tone was unmistakable.

These were the many voices of Thadistaphon as the city shrugged itself into wakefulness.

I must have lain there in that awkward position for half an hour as the sky brightened. When I finally let go and slid back into the room, I could see the interior well enough to confirm that I was, indeed, alone, that the table by the bed had been knocked over. I sat there for a moment on the floor, below the window, then freed myself of the sheet and crawled across the floor.

I found what I expected to, my father's silver mask on the floor by the overturned table. The folding mirror was gone.

The air still reeked of mud and decay, but I could breathe freely now. I picked the mask up, cradling it in my lap, gazing into its blind eyes; I think I was waiting for it to speak to me in its own voice, not that of any wearer, and promise me that somehow I could make Father leave me once and for all. That was what I wanted most of all. I wanted to be someone else, of different parentage entirely.

In haste, before the household was roused, I put on my shoes, struggling to tie the unfamiliar laces properly, and slipped quietly downstairs with the mask under my arm.

I encountered one servant in the common room below, a woman wiping the tables with a cloth. She glanced up, then turned away quickly.

Outside, the sun touched the mask and made it glow a brilliant silver. I held it up in front of me at arm's length, and almost put it to my face, but did not dare. Instead, I raced through the streets, letting the light guide me. Where the mask glowed, I turned; where it dulled, I turned away; tricks of sunlight and shadow, yes, but also deeper signs to show me the way.

I found myself in the great square I had seen on the previous evening. It was empty now, but for a few vendors setting up booths, a cluster of ragged children scampering from one trash heap to the next like a flock of starlings, three or four drunken revellers sleeping on benches, and a single soldier ambling toward the city gate, his spear over his shoulder like a fishing rod. In the center of the square, water splashed in a great fountain, a stone man clad in stone leaves standing ankle-deep in a pool, holding aloft two gaping-mouthed stone fishes from which twin streams fell.

With arms crossed, the mask against my chest, I walked slowly along the periphery of the square, startled at first when my shuffling footsteps echoed back at me. I made my way to the temple at the far side, the house of Bel-Kemad, the Gentle God, who brings peace and forgiveness and the winter rains. Great flocks of birds rested on the temple steps, the messengers of the god. I waded gently among them, trying not to frighten them. They parted silently but did not rise.

As I hesitated before the huge bronze doors, a tall, thin man was suddenly at my side. I had not noticed his approach. Now I turned and saw a strangely smooth and puffy face above a white gown flecked blood-red; he wore it loose and without a belt, flapping in the morning breeze like a sail that hasn't yet caught the wind.

His voice was soft and high, almost like a woman's.

'My boy, you can't go inside. Not for another hour yet.'

I held up the silver mask. His eyes widened and he let out a distinctly girlish yelp.

'*Where* did you get that?' he whispered.

'My father wore it in a dream. He left it for me.'

The other made a sign with his hand, then took out a key and opened the temple doors for me, pushing the left one ajar just enough for one person to slip through. He motioned that I should go in, and when I did, he did not follow. I think he stood in the doorway peering after me, but I never looked back to see.

My first impression was of vast, indefinably benign gloom, of a peaceful, silent cavern, then of the sun rising somewhere, slowly and gently from the depths. But that was a trick of the light. As my eyes adjusted, I made out, first, the circular opening at the top of the temple's dome, and directly below that the slightly bowed, massive head of the god, and then his hunched shoulders covered with sleeping birds. Behind him were bronze shutters, which would be opened later in the morning to let the birds out. For now, Bel-Kemad wore them, his only raiment, birds of many species draped over his marble shoulders, on his knees, gathered at his feet.

I shuffled slowly across the polished floor amid thousands of silent birds and knelt at his feet, where a single votive candle flickered. I laid the mask down on the floor for Bel-Kemad to examine.

And I spoke to him for a long while, not praying in any

formal sense, just telling him about the things that had happened to me, as I would to the sort of human confidant I'd never really had. I told him that I didn't understand what Father wanted or why he kept coming back to me. I explained that I both loved and hated my father, who had murdered my mother and my sister, but who had tried to reach out to me at the last, to save me from becoming precisely what he made me into, as if that conclusion were more a defeat for him than a victory.

Finally, I asked Bel-Kemad to forgive my father, and give him rest somehow.

But the god did not speak, not to me anyway. The dome slowly brightened, and when the sun's rays touched the image itself, there came a muted grinding, groaning sound which seemed to pass down through Bel-Kemad until the whole temple resonated and the floor beneath me vibrated gently.

Several loud, sharp snaps followed, and the clank of heavy chains rattling off a winch. I looked up, startled, as the shutters in the dome slid open, flooding the whole room with brilliant daylight. The birds rose all as one, and the air was filled with whirring wings and a shrieking cacophony that blended into a wordless song. Birds swarmed about the god's head like bees, then passed out of the windows and the skylight and were gone.

And I sat down, very still, in the renewed silence while feathers settled around me, holding the silver mask in my lap, ready to offer it to Bel-Kemad if he would only reach down and take it. Only after a long while was I aware that both doors behind me were open, and that people crowded the doorway, pointing and whispering, held back by more beardless men in red-speckled, white robes. I supposed they were priests.

I left the silver mask there on the floor for the god's future contemplation, then rose and walked toward the doors. People in the back jumped up to see me. But others drew away, a little fearfully. The crowd parted as I emerged onto the temple steps. A great murmur arose, like a surging tide, for the square was filled with people, come to go about their daily business, but now gathered in excited clumps as word doubtless spread about the new prodigy. More and more drew toward the temple, many gazing up at me with intense expectation. Some of the nearer ones fell to their knees.

One of the soft-voiced priests stood beside me and said, 'Magister, what sign do you have for us?'

I couldn't tell him the truth, that I was no holy thaumaturge or visionary at all, but a black, criminal sorcerer, of the sort shunned by all but employed by the powerful and therefore never efficiently exterminated; and the gods do not hear the prayers of sorcerers.

'Tell them all will be well,' I said.

'Magister, you bore the mask of the Faceless King, the Weigher of Souls, Surat-Kemad's appointed judge. There must be more.'

'Yes ... but ... I cannot reveal it now.'

I walked down the steps, into the crowd, trying to keep my own face as expressionless as my father's mask. A hush spread over the square, and the great tide of humanity parted for me. Tica met me at the far side of the square. There were a few outcries as she broke free of the mass and approached me, but no one stopped her. She ran and clasped my outstretched hand.

'What happened?' she said as we walked, the crowd following at a distance, squeezing into the narrow streets.

'I had a dream. My father came to me again. He often does that. I don't know what he wanted.'

'Oh.'

'Your mother must have been surprised to discover me gone.'

'When we found your room empty, and the window open and the air smelled like—'

'You thought I was dead.'

She lowered her eyes and nodded. At last she said, 'Worse ... We thought that you had been *dead all along*, like Father.'

I pulled her to a stop. 'Whose? Mine or yours?'

We left Thadistaphon by boat that afternoon, first riding to the river's edge in two litters, Lady Hapsenecuit in the first, resplendent in a fine gown and many jewels, and a golden, radiate crown in her hair. She sat utterly still, rocking gently with the motion of her litter like a divine image.

But I was the one the people had turned out to see. I think they were expecting a miracle or some sign, though nothing was forthcoming. Tica and I rode in a second, curtained litter. More of the white-robed priests walked on either side of us, to keep the crowd away.

When I considered all this, I whispered to Tica, 'We couldn't have taken in *that* much last night!'

She sat back in the shadows, dressed in her old clothes. 'Mother arranged things.'

Suddenly a hand thrust into the litter. The curtains parted, and an old woman was there, straining to keep pace. I clasped her hand. Our eyes met. She seemed afraid at first, then immeasurably grateful. The priests hauled her away as the crowd shouted.

I pulled the curtains closed and held them.

'What did your mother *do?*'

'She told everyone that you were a prophet and a healer, that you'd worked a lot of miracles in Reedland, and that this morning the god called you into his temple because he wanted to talk to you, like an old friend who was passing through. You are on very familiar terms with the gods, we are led to believe . . .'

'But those are *lies.*'

Tica smirked. 'Useful, though.'

'Then the people gave her money? What for?'

She seemed exasperated, almost angry with me. 'Sekenre, you're so naïve. What do you *think?* It's good to be seen as one of earliest supporters of a new holy man, especially if he's a friend of a noble lady who once was very powerful and soon will be again.'

There was a lot of Necu in her daughter Tica. It was very obvious then. Even naïve Sekenre could discern the same hardness, the same withdrawal behind the mask of an assumed role. Here was someone capable of not merely telling a lie but living one, forever if necessary. I didn't like her much then, and drew away from her, to the opposite end of the litter.

* * *

But afterward, on the river, she came to me. We drifted downstream on a vast barge. Sails flapped slowly from the numerous masts like palm fronds in the listless air. It was twilight, almost dark. Here the Great River turned sideways, as it does so often just above the delta, and broadened out so that the sun seemed to be setting into the water itself, for all that the river flows south to north.

I sat with my face against the railing, my legs sticking through, bare feet dangling in space. Though there were more than a hundred other passengers, nobles returning to the capital, wealthy merchants, famous men from towns all long the river, I was very much alone. A section of the stern had been fenced off with wooden blinds. It suited Lady Hapsenecuit's purpose to keep me hidden for the time being.

Tica sat down behind me. She touched me on the shoulder. I didn't turn around. Neither of us said anything for a few minutes. Forward, there was music and laughter. I gazed into the setting sun and the infinitely receding water.

'Do sorcerers always like to be alone, Sekenre?'

I leaned forward, pressing my face against the smoothly carved rungs of the railing. 'I don't know.'

She slid in beside me and watched the river. Ours was a profound solitude just then. I fancied that we had spewed forth from Surat-Kemad's mouth at the beginning of time, just Tica, myself, and a lot of dark water.

'Mother cannot figure you out, Sekenre.'

'So? Aren't I supposed to be mysterious? Isn't that the whole idea—?'

She took my hand in hers. 'Please, don't be angry with us.'

'I'm not.'

She smiled. 'It's just that—'

I turned to her, my face still pressed against the railing. 'I'm not what you expected in a sorcerer, am I?'

'Sometimes you *are*. Last night when you spoke in that *other* voice, you lost your accent. Did you realize that, Sekenre? Most of the time I can hear Reedland in every word you say. You name the gods *Kemad*. In the delta, we use the after-name *Hemad*. But last night, you spoke as one of us. And then there was the time by the River, when we first met you, and you couldn't speak our language at all until you went to sleep – was that what you did? – and woke up again. Then you knew the words, but Sekenre used them as a Reedlander would. Last night, you were not Sekenre.'

'Then I must be a proper sorcerer. I can do tricks. Is that what you prefer?'

She put an arm around me. 'That is what Mother prefers, yes. She needs a sorcerer like that. But I can also see a little boy who's lonely and afraid.'

I broke away from her. She was being either devious or patronizing. I was in no mood for either.

So we sat in silence once more. By now it was completely dark, and reflected stars rippled in the ink-black water. Once a great owl came swooping low in our wake, as if trying to catch up with the barge, its round face like a tiny moon. But then it turned aside sharply.

Behind us, more music and laughter. I glanced back once and saw strings of paper lanterns swaying between the masts. One of the rich lords must have been entertaining. People clapped in time with the music.

'Sekenre?'

'What?'

'What do you do for yourself, when you're not doing whatever it is sorcerers do most of the time?'

'I don't know.'

She leaned over and began to stroke my cheek gently with her finger. I tensed, but did not move away. 'There must be something.'

'Well, I like to . . . illuminate things.'

She was puzzled. 'You mean with light?'

'No.' I turned toward her and motioned with my hands as if unrolling a piece of paper and writing on it with a brush. 'I draw things. I mean . . . letters. Calligraphy. I was working on a book before—'

'That's all? You sit alone in some room and make marks on a piece of paper? Is that what you want to do with your life?'

'Yes,' I said dreamily. 'Very much. It can be quite beautiful.'

She sighed and gazed out over the water again. 'There's more to living than that. Don't you know?'

'I'm not sure.'

She was behaving oddly. I didn't see where this questioning was going.

'Do you have any friends, Sekenre? Any at all?'

I thought about it very carefully, and finally said, 'No,' in a soft voice.

She paused as if startled, then took me by the hand again. 'Is it *impossible*, then, for a sorcerer to have friends?'

'Yes, I think so.'

She drew me to her and kissed me softly on the cheek. 'I am not entirely convinced.'

I didn't know what to say and so said nothing. We sat in silence for a long time. After a while I realized I was sweating. I felt sticky under the arms. Behind us, beyond the screens, the laughter, clapping, and dancing had given way to a chorus of horns and heavy, solemn drums. I didn't bother to find out what was going on.

In the darkness, in our wake, everything I had ever known in the world, my whole life, receded inexorably. I remembered a great deal then, games, people I'd met, words spoken, but most especially my father's butterfly, the one he'd made out of wood and wire and brought to life by magic when I was small; how beautiful and delicate it had been, and how I'd cried when it died and the light in its wings went out.

Reaching through the railing, I closed my hands together carefully, then opened them, and there on the palm of my hand was a tiny butterfly made of fire, gold and white and veined through with a brilliant red.

Tica looked at it, wide-eyed, her mouth a wordless 'O.'

'For you,' I said.

She reached for it.

'No. Let it come to you.'

It rose into the air tentatively, drifted a little ways out into the darkness, then darted back and circled Tica's head several times, finally alighting on her forearm.

'Oh! It's warm.'

'But it won't burn you.'

So we sat, the butterfly opening and closing its wings. After a while I drew my legs in through the railing and we two huddled together, Tica asleep with her head in my lap as I watched the butterfly resting now on her cheek. I sat up through the night, and in the morning twilight the butterfly faded and disappeared.

Our progress from this point on seems to have been a carefully orchestrated tour of the Lower or Inner Hegemony, with pauses for days or even a week in the great cities between Thadistaphon and the delta: Akhnosiphon, Goradas, Morakisphon, Der-as-Irrad, and several more. Lady Hapsenecuit held court as if she were a queen, and at times privileged favorites were allowed into my presence. I told fortunes. I read the meanings of omens described to me, or even sensed the secrets of small objects I could hold in my hand: a broken tooth, a piece of wood, an intricately inlaid dagger. How much was prophecy, how much fraud, how much magic worked by my other selves, I cannot say.

Once, a nobleman's daughter was brought to me, possessed, I was told, by a demon shaped like a serpent but with the face of a man. It had passed into her as she bathed in the river.

Confronted with such a case, Sekenre was lost. But Balredon knew how to deal with it; old Balredon who once dwelt in a curious city of stone high up in the mountains near the river's mouth, where men worshipped Ragun-Kemad, the Eagle God. I yielded to Balredon's certain experience and the rest was a dream to me. It was Balredon, who had not touched flesh in six hundred years, who laid hands on the girl, who entered into her, who found the evil thing coiled around her heart. I could only watch and listen as he and the demon conversed for long hours, sometimes more cordially than I liked. I feared the two would strike up an alliance, that they would emerge together, Balredon wearing my body like a new suit of clothes and the demon wearing Balredon; but in the end they quarrelled, and at last I awoke, sweating and weak on the floor by the girl's bed, and the demon was no more than a smoking stain by my outstretched hand.

Balredon was gone. I think it was the jealousy of Tannivar

and Lekkanut-Na and Orkanre and my father and the rest – all those who dwelt within me, even those I did not yet know – which saved me. They would not let Balredon have what they were denied. I heard them whispering, 'He shall not possess the body. He shall not.' That was what I was to them, the body, the receptacle, a thing to be used. For that purpose Father had intended my sister Hamakina. Nothing more than that.

Necu could not have been more pleased at this authentic miracle. Word of it spread. She made sure. Now I was 'Lady Hapsenecuit's wizard' in the common parlance. In each town, I was the object of wonder, and of fearsome stories.

Our retinue grew: scholars, philosophers, soldiers, officials, great numbers of wealthy curiosity-seekers, many others who courted the favor, or even, if they dared, the hand of this great lady. We took over the barge entirely when we were on the river, and the vessel was crowded, as all manner of pavilions and tents were pitched on the deck. Soon a smaller barge accompanied us, then three low, swift ships with triangular sails, and at last a warship, low and long with a single bank of oars, its raised prow and stern both fashioned into the heads of fierce river-hawks.

I dwelt on deck at the stern of the original barge, behind the wooden curtain as before, either out in the open if I wanted, or in a tent barely large enough for me to lie down in. A cordon of armored guards ensured my 'privacy.' I felt like a prized bird, fed, cared for, but kept apart, brought out only when needed.

Yet still Tica found time and the means to come to me at night, and I took comfort in her nearness. She told me about the City of the Delta and what wonders I might expect there. She tried to teach me to play a stringed instrument called the *tsat,* and we sat together for hours in the darkness, plucking away, making up snatches of songs, whispering.

'Mother intends to be queen,' Tica told me one night.

'I know.'

'Ah, yes. A wizard should know things.'

'A while ago you said I was naïve. But it's obvious, isn't it?'

Tica shrugged. 'Yes, I suppose so. People are afraid. The

old king will die soon. The satraps grow restless and overly independent, but the Zargati raiders threaten them all. Either they must unite, or each city must fend for itself and many of them will fall. So it's an obvious chance—'

'The *old* king?' I said. 'I don't remember him being that old.'

'Blessed Wenamon the Fourth has reigned as Great King of all the Hegemony for forty-seven years, and the gods protect him.'

'But . . . but I was born in the tenth year of his reign and—'

She shook her head, a little frightened at my bewilderment. 'That would make you *thirty-seven.* I don't know much about you Sekenre, but I am *sure* you are not thirty-seven.'

'I don't understand,' I said.

'I don't either. Possibly you Arnatese miscounted.'

I couldn't resolve the matter. Was it possible that Father had moved our house *twenty-two* years into the future? Had I been gone from the City of Reeds for twenty-two *years,* when it seemed a matter of a couple of months? Would my friends of childhood all be grown men now, with sons my own age? Would they have, perhaps, mercifully, forgotten me?

Tica soon changed the subject.

Much later, we lay together in the darkness. She hummed softly to herself, then began to slide her hands under my clothing. Her touch was warm, soft, but I found myself ticklish. I had never been touched that way before.

'You're definitely not thirty-seven,' she whispered.

Later still, she was asleep in my arms and I gazed out over the water. To right and left, boats drifted, their sails furled, lanterns swaying from their sides.

A light appeared in the middle of the water. I thought of a huge lantern being raised from the river's bottom. I observed what followed without alarm, as if it were a dream, but it was not a dream, for all no one else on any of the other vessels saw anything; or if they did they did not cry out.

Only inches beneath the surface, a naked giantess floated on her back, as if asleep, so close to the edge of the barge that I could have reached down and touched her. Her skin glowed strangely, mottled like a mass of coals. I gradually perceived that her shape was stranger still: legless, a serpent from the waist down, and her hands were webbed.

She spoke, not aloud, I think, but in my mind. *Sekenre, I shall come to know thee in the centuries to come, when thou art awakened into thy true self, when I too have awakened from the sleep of my birth.*

Then she sank down into the dark water.

Shortly before dawn, I could see the souls of the newly dead walking on the water, upstream, into the mouth of Surat-Kemad. I heard their moans like a faint wind, and I knew there was a great disturbance in the land.

South of Ronatisphon, the river turns far to the east, so that, in more secure times, it would have been the custom of travellers to disembark, form a caravan, and take the Royal Road across the range of hills known as the Hump, and so save several days' travel. So many writers mention their first view of the City of the Delta from those heights, and the Crescent Sea beyond it, gleaming in the sun like an enormous, polished shield.

But we remained on the river, our little flotilla drifting into the rising sun. In the morning, Lady Necu held what seemed to be a council of war with her followers. I was not invited. I sat alone on a folding chair in my little enclosure, peering between the wooden blinds at the lords as they argued and frequently pointed in my direction. Lady Necu sat above them all on a raised throne, with Tica at her feet. The great lords bowed before them, one by one.

After the meeting was over, Necu made a great show of joining me on the after-deck. First a gang of servants slipped into the enclosure, clearing my little tent away, then fussing over me, combing my hair, lacing up my shoes. Tables and chairs were set up, and the lords, ladies, and I ate a fine banquet, while the wordless servants fetched and poured.

Then Necu, Tica and I moved to another table, set apart, and a servant brought a folding board. Lady Hapsenecuit made another obvious display of playing a kind of game with me and Tica, an affair of dice and pegs and cards. I protested I had no skill.

'Never mind,' Necu hissed. 'Just pretend you know what you're doing. It's supposed to bring us luck and good fortune.'

So we played. I had no idea who was winning or losing, or if indeed one was supposed to do either.

'Sekenre,' she said, rattling three dice in a cup. At that moment she looked very hard, her lips pursed, her face thin and drawn and old, her hands bony claws. 'Sekenre, I swear you are the strangest child. Your eyes. You never blink. You stare at me like a fish.'

I folded my hands and leaned forward. 'I am a sorcerer, Lady. Could I not be a thousand years old and no child at all?'

'From what my daughter tells me—'

I looked at Tica sharply. She turned away.

'Never mind,' Lady Necu went on. 'Sekenre, I have made promises to you, and I intend to keep them. You do what I want, and I shall reward you. You'll live in the palace. Your every want shall be attended. Tica tells me –' again her daughter averted her gaze, pained – 'that you're interested in . . . calligraphy. Whether it's part of your magic or just a hobby, you can have a whole damned scriptorium to yourself.'

Suddenly there were shouts from the front of the barge. Necu and Tica looked up.

'What is it, Mother?'

Lady Necu waved impatiently for a servant, and sent him scrambling. I turned my chair around to see forward.

Black smoke stained the sky. Slowly we drifted around a bend in the river and beheld on the western bank the charred ruin of a city, its walls breached in a dozen places. The inner keep was still burning fiercely.

People on the barge cried out in dismay. Lady Necu made a sign to ward off evil.

I noticed the stakes in a long line at the river's edge. Some of the dark masses atop them writhed.

'Gods! Merciful gods!' Tica said.

Lady Necu shouted orders. The barge moved farther out into the middle of the river and the other vessels followed. The warship slid between us and the murdered city.

'That was Ran-Ys-Te,' she said. 'It was to be our last stop before the capital ... I had never imagined the Zargati would come this far.'

'Perhaps the old king is dead,' Tica said.

'We'll find out soon enough. Who knows? Even this may serve our purpose, regrettable as it is.' She reached out and took my hand in hers, her grip hard and dry, like living wood. 'I am going to need your help, Sekenre,' she said. 'I really am. In fact, everything may depend on you.'

I continued to stare at her, unblinking, like a fish.

We rounded the Hump, sailed for five more days, and so it was that I first beheld the City of the Delta on the sixth morning, not as a white-domed mass in the lap of the Crescent Sea, but through the mists of the first, warm winter rains, the houses and walls and towers rising like a many-sculpted mountain of white and gray stone.

But we did not enter the city immediately. I was impatient. I gaped, Tica said, like any back-country peasant. I should be more dignified. I should act like a sorcerer, the ally of a great lady. I should wait until the proper time, for the proper entrance.

So we lay at anchor while the sun burned through the mist and one boatload after another of emissaries came to confer with Lady Necu. She had built a huge pavilion for herself in the middle of the barge, and she greeted them there, standing in all her finery, her crown and jewels gleaming in the brilliant midday light, surrounded by guards, attendants, and the robed priests, looking very much, it seemed to me who had never seen one, like the mightiest queen in the world. One by one the men from the city knelt before her, then kissed her outstretched hand and rose as she bade them. To some, she spoke only a few words. With others, she walked and talked for a long time.

I wanted to see more, but the guards surrounded my enclosure and politely but firmly refused to let me pass. I glared at them. They avoided my gaze, but still obeyed what were obviously the Queen's orders.

The Queen. I was already thinking of her that way. So too were many others. That was the whole purpose of everything we had done. Even naïve Sekenre could figure out that much.

Shortly after noon, Tica brought me a basket of bread and cheese and some sort of fruit I didn't recognize. We sat down on the deck and ate, far from the others.

'What is happening?' I asked. 'Why are we still waiting?'

'It's not quite safe yet. Mother – we – have enemies who must be dealt with. The old king is indeed dying, and the factions are trying to position themselves. You can imagine their surprise – and embarrassment. They never expected to see us again—'

'So what do we do now?'

'We wait, and maybe we pray to the gods, unless you can provide a miracle, Sekenre.'

I could have assumed my guise of Mysterious and Terrible Sorcerer then, but it was hard to pretend in front of Tica. I shrugged and said, 'How long will it take?'

'A few hours more, I imagine, until Mother settles things. She's very good at it, you know. She has turned everything that happened to our advantage.'

'*Everything?*'

Tica spoke with difficulty, swallowing hard. 'Yes. Absolutely everything. Like pieces on a game board. We must make do with what we have. Even . . . my father. Because what they did to him was an abomination, because it would incriminate the doers, our opponents cannot acknowledge that it happened. Therefore they can't say that Mother was lawfully banished, or that she is . . . polluted . . . by a corpse . . . which would certainly disqualify her from being queen.'

'I see.'

'Do you really, Sekenre?' Then, after a pause, she said, 'Yes, I think you do.'

Tica went away. I wanted her to stay with me. I took her by the hand and tried to hold her, but she broke free and merely said that she was needed.

The political situation was clear enough, but I didn't understand my own feelings. I missed Tica whenever she was gone. I thought about her all the time. I tried to imagine what it would be like for the two of us together, when this was all over. In my mind, I had already been rehearsing what to say to her, how to please her.

But she had to go now and wear finery like her mother's and sit beside Lady Hapsenecuit, nodding sagely, interviewing notables from the city, making vague promises, hinting that this or that reward might be extended to supporters in the course of things.

So I had one more evening alone on the river, sitting with my feet dangling through the railing. For a time I watched the boats as they passed or as they gathered around us like an expectant flock. A great trireme with the king's eagle and the serpent on its mainsail drew near, then furled sails, dropped anchor, and waited, oars drawn in, its deck swarming with marines.

Inside the city, trumpets blew, one or two at first, then a lot of them, like a distant storm. Lanterns and torches flickered from the walls and rooftops.

As I gazed up at the city and the darkening sky, I felt magic stirring within me once more. I raised cold flames with my hands, and bore them like delicate glass sculptures into my tent, where I sat, gazing into what I had created.

A voice spoke from within me, one I did not recognize.

Tanal madt. Sekenre. Tanal madt. The casting of stones and bones and sticks. Randomness that is not random. Not for your amusement, these wanderings, these castings. We are playing them out for our own benefit, and in the end, Sekenre, you shall come to our intended conclusion.

'No,' I said aloud. Angrily I crushed the flames with my closed fists.

Sekenre, do you know what the fire is for, what it can do?

Without saying anything, I called the flames back into my cupped hands and shaped them, barely aware of what I was doing at first, following some obscure impulse as I made a rectangle of cold, white fire which floated shimmering in the darkness. Then the design became deliberate, mine;

translucent, gleaming, every detail there in perfect miniature: desk, ink bottles, brushes, pens, and the manuscript I had been working on as the townspeople attacked.

More fire poured out of me, and it seemed that I was *there*, inside my old room as it had been before it was desecrated. I gazed out the window at the insubstantial City of Reeds; not the true city but a thing of smoke and phantom fire like an aurora sculpted by a god.

My room was complete in every detail, books, trunks, discarded clothing draped over the end of the bed.

Everything. The house spoke to me in its remembered vocabulary of secret sounds.

Someone was at the door. The latch clicked.

'Father?' There was no reply. 'Hamakina?' Still nothing. After a long time, I swallowed hard, my heart racing, and rose to my feet. *'Mother . . . ?'*

It was Tica, transfigured in flame, dressed as a queen in golden robes with a diadem on her head. She reached out for me, bending over as she did, stooping down. I didn't understand why she was hunched over so.

For an instant she must have seen what I saw. She let out a gasp of amazement. Then the room and the flames went out like snuffed candlelight and she was merely stooping down into my tent. I crawled out onto the deck and stood up.

'Sekenre,' she said. 'You must come with me now. It's time to go into the city.'

Chapter 10: The Murder of the Great King

If ever they treated me like a thing, like a girl's doll to be dressed and combed and preened, it was that evening, as Tica and a small army of women I didn't know – servants, presumably – surrounded me in my enclosure on the barge and fussed endlessly, washing, rubbing, oiling; yanking my hair until it hurt, oblivious to my yelps as they tied it into a long braid down the back and two little ones behind the ears. No one listened when I said this looked ridiculous. Tica was all business, a commander snapping orders to her troops. Before she was done, I wore a brilliant red mantle draped over everything else, rings on virtually every finger, and enough bands and sashes that I felt trussed up like so much dockside produce. Finally she held up a heavy necklace of linked, golden rectangles, with a sun-faced pendant hanging down the front.

This Tica lowered onto my shoulders carefully, even ceremoniously, as the other women paused to watch.

'It is an emblem of the court,' she explained. 'It means you are noble and illustrious.'

'What—?'

'Somebody important, Sekenre.'

'Am I?'

'Yes, you are,' she said, a little impatiently. 'Right now, you're very important indeed.' She seized me by both shoulders and held me at arm's length. 'And reasonably presentable. Yes, I think that will do. Mother wanted me to paint your face, but—'

'No!'

'It *is* the custom. The highest of the high-born, the chief priests, members of the royal family itself; they all paint their faces on ceremonial occasions.'

185

'No. I don't want it.'

Tica laughed. 'I convinced her that it wouldn't be a good idea, you'll be relieved to learn. Just *too* pretentious. Every time you speak, Sekenre, you reveal that you are a foreigner, and for a foreigner to paint his face like a prince of the Delta might give great offense—'

'I'm not going to paint my face—!'

She leaned over and whispered into my ear, 'You see, we're in agreement already on a major point of policy.'

She took me by the hand and led the way out of the screen enclosure and onto the center of the barge, where two rows of soldiers cleared a path for us, holding back a great crowd of people. Overhead, strings of paper lanterns swung in the breeze.

'What is going to become of us, Tica?' I said.

'As Mother told you. We're going to live in the palace.'

'I didn't mean that.'

She looked at me strangely. 'What did you mean then, Sekenre?'

I felt myself blushing. I couldn't make any answer. She turned from me, raising her hands as a great cheer went up from the assembled throng.

So we joined Lady Necu in a vast litter which seemed more like a ship's cabin on the inside, a luxurious chamber of pillows and silks and canopies, which swayed gently like a boat on calm water when twenty men before us and twenty behind carried us off the barge, up a gangway and onto the bank.

The Lady who would soon be Queen sat in front, in all her finery, revealed like a votive image behind thin curtains, while Tica and I huddled behind, out of sight. I wanted to lean out and gape like any country child come into the city for the first time, but I knew what was expected of me, so I could only peer out through layers of cloth, and my impressions were fleeting ones.

The bearers themselves, enormous, nearly naked, shaven-headed, were smeared with some oil that gave them a slightly bluish complexion. Each wore a silver collar. I was certain they were slaves, but expensive ones, chosen for size, matched like a team of race horses. They stared straight ahead, never turning, walking in step, the rhythmical tramping of their heavy sandals audible above the noise of the crowd, though not above the periodic trumpets heralding our arrival.

The gateway itself, numbing in its sheer hugeness gleamed in the sunset like the mouth of a god about to swallow the world, like Surat-Kemad emerged from the darkness, transfigured in fire.

And the walls and towers, like sculpted mountains, seemed too vast to be the work of men.

Once we entered in a long enclosed passage, far darker, far more smothering than the narrowest spaces I had ever explored beneath the City of Reeds. I felt distinctly uncomfortable, half afraid that we were indeed sliding inexorably down the gullet of the world-swallowing divinity whose mouth was the Deltan gate. Endless friezes of carven serpents drifted by, illuminated by torchlight.

Then, where a side-street opened into a court: enormous, gray teeth showed through a series of darkened windows, and two storeys above, a pair of eyes like silver moons; as if a giant wore a house for a mask and lay there amid the city, watching as we passed.

Far ahead, drums thundered in time, like a supernal heartbeat. More trumpets pealed. On every side, banners and wind-filled paper serpents on poles; holy ikons held aloft; the spears of soldiers rippling above their helmets like a field of reeds in the wind.

Hundreds of soldiers joined us, displacing other marchers, until the armor and oval shields seemed to form the scales and hide of a single, monstrous creature, now turning, scraping, relentlessly invading the City of the Delta, its power manifest in the spears of its spiny back, its mind and its ferocious heart hidden inscrutably behind the powdered face and jewel-laden robes of Lady Hapsenecuit. I thought of my mother's enchanted crocodile *hevat* writhing through our house, brought to life by the ominous wind.

Further in, no tumultuous crowds greeted us. I came to realize that the mass of people around us were all of our own party. We were a parade without spectators. The city itself seemed oddly stricken, stunned into empty silence.

And once I caught a glimpse of the reason why. An avenue opened into a broad square. Before we turned sharply away, I saw men loading corpses into wagons. Beyond them, what might have been a temple or other public building smoldered, burnt to a shell, its white pillars smeared black.

Our soldiers, I noted, wore red ribbons on their arms or around their necks. Most of the corpses wore green.

So the Queen's work had been done while we waited on the raft.

But I couldn't think of that. I grew bolder and leaned out. The enormity of the City of the Delta dwarfed all human endeavors: tier upon tier of marble and brick and a polished black stone I had never seen before, terraces of trees high above, as if some god had created a forest for his pleasure, halfway up to heaven; and among the trees, along the rooftops, gazing down from countless pillars, thousands of statues, larger than life, congregating in the open spaces as if the city were truly their habitation, and we who walked there only fleet vermin scampering at their feet.

Tica yanked me back inside and said nothing. She took my hand once more. I leaned over, face against the curtain, still peering out.

Priests joined us: some beardless and dressed in loose, red-speckled white robes like those I had seen before, others, bearded, faces painted half blue, half white, wearing silver caps adorned with serpents, their robes shoulderless and bright red. Then came young nobles on horseback, dressed as I was, only with even more elaborate finery, a riot of colors and clanking jewelry, many of them with white-painted faces or wearing shouting, contorted, laughing masks that made them look more like demons than men. Unlike the silent soldiers or the grim-faced priests or the bearers who moved like a single, carefully co-ordinated machine, these nobles laughed and shouted to one another jauntily, waving fans and swords and palm-fronds, racing ahead of us, then turning back, crashing into one another like drunken wastrels on a night's frolic. But the Queen did not acknowledge them. She merely sat perfectly still, regarding all.

I looked down another side street and saw women in black,

flowing gowns dancing before a stone god I didn't recognize, a cat-headed figure with arms upraised.

Once more, evidence of fighting: a smashed door, arrows sticking around a window like whiskers around a mouth; a single corpse hanged by the neck, dangling from a high window. The dead man wore a green cloak with a white eagle on it.

I had no sense of a transition between outdoors and in. The sky itself darkened, no swifter than from sunset. The quality of sound changed, the boisterous nobles falling behind, then gone, the footsteps of the bearers and soldiers echoing as if in a vast cave, the single throbbing drumbeat far ahead, muted; the rustling of robes and armor blending together into a murmur like the voice of the Great River passing among the wooden posts beneath the City of Reeds.

The litter tilted slightly as we began to ascend a stairwell, past alcove after alcove from which the gigantic stone faces of kings stared back at us, candles flickering in their hollow eyes.

Tica pulled me back from the curtain.

'We're almost there,' she whispered.

'Where?'

'Before the Great King.'

My heart jumped. I squeezed Tica's hand. She turned to me.

'Are you afraid?'

I didn't know what to say. Somehow, going before the king was more fantastic than beholding a god. As for gods, miracles sometimes happen near to home. But to a Reedlander, the king is a distant force in a distant city, as remote as a star. One might see the Satrap on public occasions, but the King of the Delta, never.

Yes, I, Sekenre, who had invaded the very domain of Surat-Kemad himself, who had returned from the belly of Death; I was in complete and utter awe at the prospect of actually seeing with my own eyes the Great King of the River, Celestial and Elevated Wenamon the Fourth, Holder of the Satrapies, Father of Civilized Mankind, Most Favored of Bel-Kemad—

And I was certain I was here to do more than just look.

I kept my silence, trying to figure out for myself how I fit into the scheme of things. Even naïve Sekenre knew that it would hardly suffice for Lady Hapsenecuit to just announce, 'I'm Queen now', then point and say, 'That boy is a powerful sorcerer. Fear him and obey me.'

There had to be more to it. We were all pieces on a playing board, and I was not the master of the game.

The litter came to a halt, sank down, and rested. Again I thought of a boat, gently drifting aground.

'Well,' Lady Necu whispered, not turning around, but speaking for the first time since we'd left the river, 'now we risk all.'

'Mother, it will be well,' Tica said.

'You're a good daughter, Kanratica.'

We three alighted, assisted by smothering crowds of attendants. Once more I was overwhelmed by vastness, and could only stand there gazing up into dizzy heights, slowly exclaiming, 'Oh . . .' We were inside a hall vaster than any mountain, its ceiling painted with stars and moons that seemed as distant as those in the real sky. This had to be the work of the gods, I told myself, something they created for themselves on the first day of the world, and had inexplicably vacated long before human beings were bold enough to move in.

In every direction, as far as I could see, pillars carven into kings and birds and strange, elongated beasts rose to join arches which criss-crossed above me, holding up the painted firmament. The scale was such that a tall man, were he able to climb onto the pedestals, would still be unable to touch the ankles of these colossi.

Everywhere, torches and braziers gave off uncertain light. Shadows passed like dark clouds.

Tica nudged me. 'Come on,' she whispered. 'Act like you're used to it.'

That was the hard part, the pretending amid such grandeur. Next to this, my native city was just a jumble of stray boards and crates. I thought my legs would fold up.

Necu, Tica, and I stepped forward, accompanied by only a few dozen soldiers and priests. The rest parted before us, like a sea. We made our way in near darkness for what seemed an endless time across a black stone floor so smooth I had to walk carefully just to remain on my feet. If I glanced down, I saw a distant, pale Sekenre staring up at me from depths as dizzying as the heights above.

Every once in a while we crossed stone of a different color, like a stream running through the floor; forming, perhaps, some huge pattern that a god hovering near the ceiling might be able to make out.

A line of about a dozen priests in the speckled robes stood before us, turned as we approached, and marched before us, their soft voices murmuring like pigeons. Some held little lamps. One rang a tiny silver bell slowly, constantly. It seemed to me then that these puffy-faced, beardless creatures were not men at all, but fantastically aged children.

I tugged Tica's sleeve. She turned to me as if to say, *By all the gods, not now.* But I whispered, 'Who *are* they?'

She whispered back, 'Eunuchs.'

'I don't understand.'

'You know how you sometimes ... geld an animal, a horse—'

'We don't have horses in Reedland.'

'Chop off its balls. Emasculate. So it is with eunuchs. Thousands in the palace. They're the government.'

I felt suddenly queasy.

'But why? That's horrible.'

One of the eunuchs looked back at me, sternly and unafraid, as if even a dread sorcerer would not be allowed to offend propriety in such a place.

Tica turned away. I said nothing more.

At last a light appeared far ahead, like a campfire seen at a distance at night. We drew nearer, the light resolving into a circle of braziers and lamps, and within them, a canopied throne on a dais. The priests held their hands in stiff, ritual gestures; their step assumed practiced time, becoming almost a dance. The silver bell was suddenly muffled.

Then everyone stood frozen in the august presence, at the very feet of the throne of the Great King himself, Wenamon the Fourth.

The eunuchs dropped to their knees and prostrated themselves, touching their heads to the floor. Nobles and priests lowered themselves to one knee. Soldiers remained standing.

Necu and Tica led me through the crowd to the very front, then knelt quickly – both knees – and rose without being bidden to rise. I made to do the same, but Necu whispered, 'No. A sorcerer does not.'

I remained standing.

I could see the Great King very clearly. I could have bounded up the three or four steps before his throne and touched him.

As Tica had told me a few days before and I had refused to believe, Wenamon was very, very, old. He sat propped on his throne with pillows, leaning against a metal canopy like a huge shell ornamented with reliefs of serpents, crocodiles, birds, and beast-headed men. I didn't think he would have the strength to rise. His jewel-laden arms were thin as reeds.

He seemed lost amid the splendor around him, buried in his own regalia: silver-embroidered kilt and slippers, serpent-shaped greaves coiling up his shins, a complicated mass of necklaces and medallions around his neck, with the emblem of the serpent biting its tail, *ouroboros*, dangling in front, signifying eternity. But, though he wore a golden cloak, his shirt was so thin it was almost gauze, leaving his sunken chest clearly visible, skin pale, blotchy, his ribs protruding. I could tell he was having trouble breathing.

I couldn't see his face at first. He leaned forward, as if the weight of the beehive-shaped crown were too much for him. One of the eunuchs by his side reached gently forward and raised the king's chin. Half of Wenamon's shrivelled face was already dead, distorting his mouth into a grimace. He drooled from the dead side, smearing his white face-paint. The eunuch wiped him with a napkin.

Only Wenamon's eyes were alive. Within the wreck of his body, he was fully alert, his dark gaze piercing. He looked to Lady Hapsenecuit and said something I couldn't hear. I don't think she could hear it either.

She suddenly raised both hands as if saluting a god, and said, so loud that her voice echoed back, 'Great and Heavenly

King, Master of All Lands, if you will deign to hear what services have been rendered your eternal glory, know that this day I have rid the city of your traitorous enemies!'

The King leaned forward. I thought he was going to fall out of the throne, but the eunuchs didn't move to catch him. Wenamon worked his lips as if fumbling with some unfamiliar mechanism, struggling to form words. Then he gained control and spoke slowly and deliberately through the side of his mouth, hissing somewhat, spittle flying. 'Traitors all, yes. Including, I understand, my own son.'

'Great King, your enemies have fallen!'

The King nodded, then sat back. 'So, they are traitors now that they are dead. That makes political allegiance . . . so much simpler.' His mouth twitched. He raised a spotted hand. His fingers were like twigs. A eunuch brushed the hand away and applied the napkin.

'Mighty One, I seek only to perpetuate your endless glory,' Lady Hapsenecuit said. 'Great King, live forever!'

All those around us took up the cry, 'Great King, live forever!' Even I shouted it.

'Or at least for a few more days,' the King said when we were silent once more. 'Until things are settled.' His gaze fell on me. I stood petrified. 'And this is the famous young miracle-worker from . . . where?'

He was waiting for me to reply. Now it was I who struggled to form words. The eunuch by my side nudged me and gave me an angry look.

'From Reedland, Great King. From Arnatisphon.'

'Speak slowly, boy. Your words are clouded. Yes, I hear Reedland in your voice. I visited Arnatisphon once, when I was still a prince, about your age. Did you know that?'

I stared at the floor. 'No, Lord.'

'Look at me,' he said. I looked up. Despite his condition, he was master of the situation. I sensed he had weighed me in the balance and been unimpressed at the result. 'If you are a genuine sorcerer, you need not grovel before a mere king . . . eh? Isn't that so?'

I swallowed hard and forced myself to say, 'Yes, it is so.'

Now Wenamon's gaze was more intent than any I have

ever known. The hall was utterly silent. No one else even dared breathe.

'Well, then, *what are you, child?*'

I searched inside my mind: *Father? Balredon? Lekkanut-Na? What do I do now?* But all of them remained silent, their interest unaroused, the present situation irrelevant to their own plans. I was on my own.

I glanced to Necu and Tica. Their faces were inscrutable as masks. The whole world seemed paused to listen to what I would say next, as if the fate of all things was poised. I think it really was. I didn't understand why Lady Necu hadn't rehearsed me for this interview. It didn't make sense. Perhaps she truly believed that I was a mighty sorcerer who only pretended to be an inexperienced boy despite all evidence to the contrary; as more than a human being, I would be expected to know the proper course. Was this what she'd meant when she said, 'Now we risk all'?

Now the only thing I could do was play the part, put on the mask of the sorcerer.

'Lord King,' I said, 'I am Sekenre of Reedland, sorcerer and son of Vashtem the sorcerer, of whom you have no doubt heard.'

'Yes,' said Wenamon. 'Your father was widely feared. But he is also dead.'

I considered my reply very carefully. I was sick with dread, but I knew what my next words had to be.

'He was feared above *all others,* Lord, but he is dead only because I slew him. Therefore *I* am to be feared above all others.'

Gasps went up from the crowd, followed by a brief flurry of astonished whispers.

'You murdered your own father,' the King said, a statement, not a question.

Tica looked at me, as if she had never actually seen me before and didn't like what she saw. And in that awful moment I caught my breath and could not speak. I was near to panic, afraid that I would break into tears or faint or run away. Under my splendid clothing, I was soaked with sweat.

There were just no words. I folded my hands together

and opened them again. Tiny white flames danced on my palms.

The King showed no surprise. 'Come and sit before me.'

I shuffled forward.

'There,' he said. A eunuch placed a pillow on the top step, by the king's feet.

Unsteadily, I climbed the steps and sat, my hands half-open in my lap, the flames flickering between my curled fingers.

'Now tell me, Sekenre, son of Vashtem, what you know of the ways of the gods?'

Why didn't he ask a priest? Surely he knew that the gods shun sorcerers. He was playing his game. I had to play along with him, as if it were mine. It was one more casting of *tanal madt,* randomness which assumes a pattern, but only in retrospect. I could only wait and hope to discern the meaning later.

'Great King,' I said, 'I have journeyed into the land of the dead. And returned. From the domain of Surat-Kemad.'

'*He*mad, boy. Here in the Delta we say *He*mad when naming the gods. It is Surat-*He*mad.'

I looked up at him, amazed that for an instant he sounded like a pedantic schoolteacher. The living side of his mouth smiled faintly.

I swallowed, paused, and went on. 'I had a mission there, among the houses of our ancestors ... and I learned many things.'

The king tensed, as a fisherman does when he feels the first, firm tug on the line.

So this was what he was after.

'*Did you discover the secret of eternal life?* Is it true that sorcerers can live forever?'

I closed my hands into fists and put the fires out. 'I don't think they can live *forever*, Lord King. The Devouring God will catch all of us in the end. But I can tell you that my father was more than three hundred years old before I did ... what I had to do.'

'Sorcerers and kings are alike, Sekenre. Both must do what would be reprehensible on the part of anyone else.'

'I suppose so, Lord King.'

Now Wenamon trembled, his arms and legs in the throes of some great spasm, his head rolling, terrifying to behold. I thought he was going to fall apart right then and there, and come tumbling down from his throne in a heap of bones and dust. The eunuchs caught hold of him and held him still. For a time he sat there, head down, wheezing and coughing. Then he forced himself to speak once more.

'*Sekenre, can you make me a sorcerer?*'

'No, Lord. I could not even make myself one. Rather, sorcery chose me.'

Wenamon sank back. 'I had feared it was so.'

'Great King, I know the way into the Dark Kingdom, and I speak the language of its inhabitants fluently, but I cannot divert the soul from the journey it must eventually take.'

'Then what *can* you do? What good is sorcery?'

'At times, even I do not know. It is like a storm within me. When it rages, I do many things.'

'Is that so?'

At this moment I chanced to glance out at the assembled audience. The nobles still knelt. The eunuchs remained on all fours, but they had raised their heads. Necu and Tica watched me and the King intently.

And, approaching this crowd, out of the darkness and distance, from somewhere among the pillars off to my left, came a most extraordinary figure. I thought at first that the Moon had descended from the sky to inhabit the Great King's basilica, for I saw a glowing face like a crescent moon, a visage distorted as if by a mad sculptor until the brow rose to a curving point and the chin too curved enormously outward, these deformities rendering the overall head twice normal size. The newcomer's skin truly glowed, like a thing of paper lit from within. The eyes were intensely dark.

This being drifted rather than walked across the floor, in absolute silence, without any visible movement of legs, the Moon-face mounted on a body shrouded in a robe as black as night and flecked with stars – not mere dark cloth with gems sewn into it, but as if, truly, a piece of the heavens had been torn away and fashioned into a garment. These stars flickered as he drew nearer. One of them streaked down his front to its death.

I let out a startled cry, but the King only nodded. Amazingly, no one else seemed to observe the stranger, even as he passed among the mass of kneeling, crouching people. Then he raised his arms – invisible, the sleeves apparently empty – and suddenly we three were alone in the empty hall, myself, the King, and the living Moon.

The huge face split with a malevolent smile, revealing a black mouth and darkened teeth.

'Ah, Sekenre, son of Vashtem, I understand, I have waited a long time to meet so illustrious a sorcerer as yourself.' The voice was shrill and high and sounded as if it were coming from much farther away.

I rose to my feet.

'Who are you?' I asked. My own voice echoed back and forth with startling effect. When the other spoke, his did not.

'Surely, Sekenre, mighty sorcerer that you are –' Moon laughed softly, raising an invisible hand to his mouth in feigned politeness – 'you mean only to test my humble wit, since no sorcerer or even common magician gives out his true name freely. You may call me by whatever obvious name you wish, such as, for instance, Moon.'

I watched him, fascinated. 'So be it. Moon.'

'So be it, Sekenre, son of Vashtem, and, I am led to believe, quite a few other people, whose true name is—'

I held up my hand. 'Stop! Be silent!'

'Very *good!* A true sorcerer must learn to command. But I will not be silent, not entirely, for all I do not *choose* to let you know whether I know your secret name or not.'

Magic awoke within me, not my other selves but the force itself, more powerful, fiercer than I had ever known it. For an instant I felt merely sick, as if a fist within me shook my whole body like an empty sack. Then came an uneasy tingling, a lightness as if my skin were thinner than paper, something woven of cobwebs, trying to contain smoke.

I held up my hand to my face and saw that I was aglow with magical fire. When I flexed my fingers, the light sparkled.

Moon broke once more into his black-toothed smile. 'I see

that you contain the true power, Sekenre. Yes, I knew that already. But have you any understanding of what it is *for?*'

'Yes.'

He stroked his long chin with invisible fingers.

'Ah.'

Once more he raised his arms and water poured out of his empty sleeves, soundlessly splashing on the floor, pooling, lapping against the bottom step of the throne platform, impossible quantities filling the whole enormous audience hall as far as I could see. Torches and lanterns reflected off the rippling surface. Still there was no sound at all, and Moon stood before me, his outstretched arms like twin fountains. The king's throne had become an island. Slowly the tide rose up over the first step, then the second, then the third, to where I stood.

The Moon-faced sorcerer floated up, standing on the surface of the water.

I retreated to the top of the dais, but the water soon splashed over my shoes and filled them, then rose above my ankles, intensely cold, extinguishing the fire in my flesh wherever it touched.

I looked to the King, but he was gone too. We two remained on opposite sides of the throne, Moon elevated as the water rose, myself knee-deep.

I was certain that Moon was my enemy now, that he had come to kill me when he was done toying with me.

But he merely crouched so that our faces were level, and said, 'Take off your shoes, Sekenre. Flesh must touch. You know that. Otherwise I must conclude you are a hedge-trickster from the provinces who has wasted my time. Surely this impression is incorrect, is it not?'

I reached down into the water. The fire in my hands was extinguished.

'Go on.'

I untied my shoes, kicked them off, then caught hold of the throne and climbed up onto the seat, standing where the King had been sitting a moment before.

'Ah,' said Moon, smiling yet again. He stood up.

Cautiously I stepped out onto the water, just as the throne-seat was awash, and the surface held me.

Moon lowered his arms. The water ceased to flow.

'I wondered how long that was going to take,' he said. 'Come.'

He turned, motioning me to follow, and the two of us walked in silence through endless flooded corridors for what seemed many hours, until I was greatly weary. But Moon never slackened his pace. I kept up with him. When we passed near a lantern or window, I could see that his own invisible feet sent ripples across the black water, as did my own footsteps. In the dark I could make out my own reflection, a pale ghost-image gazing up at me – or down, from its own perspective – from some vast distance.

'Sekenre, do you see that door?'

'What door?' At once I knew I'd given the wrong reply, that I had merely exposed my own limitations.

But Moon made no sign. After a few more steps he paused. I stood by his side. He raised his arms and seemed to part the darkness itself like a pair of curtains. For an instant I had the impression of gray mist, then not even that, a formless void all around. Then images rippled like reflections in a pool and settled into a high-ceilinged, brightly-lit room filled with shelves and cabinets, cluttered with familiar books and bottles.

We stood on a dry floor, the stones gritty and slightly warm beneath my bare feet. I wondered if there might be a furnace below us.

And in front of me lay a great pile of charred human bones, and beyond them, blackened skulls in neat rows on a tabletop.

Moon drifted to a cabinet and opened it just a crack. 'Welcome to my humble workshop, master sorcerer. Now look here as I reveal my greatest treasure.'

He swung the cabinet door wide, revealing two empty shelves.

'Do you see it?'

I had to pretend.

'Yes, of course.'

Quick as a striking serpent, his invisible hand seized me by the front of my jacket and swung me like a load of laundry toward the table, scattering bones. Only the briefest struggle ensued. White fire rose from my hands. He breathed blue flames on me and extinguished the white. I thought of a sword. It broke over his invisible stone. I leapt into the air, a shrieking heron, wings stretched wide, but an eagle with a crocodile's head caught my feet in its mouth and dragged me down.

Moon slammed me onto the tabletop, holding me effortlessly with his left hand as I thrashed. Skulls toppled to the floor. A curved golden dagger materialized where his right hand should have been, like a lunar crescent coming from behind a cloud.

He tweaked my nose with it. 'You can see *this* well enough, can't you, murderous brat? Yes, yes, I think it will be the last thing you ever see, because I fancy taking your eyes out first, then your tongue, then your manhood, while I bleed you of life and magic. Sekenre, you have truly seen my greatest treasure, which is the emptiness of your own ignorance. Put everything you know about sorcery in that cabinet and it's still empty. Yes! Yes!' He slashed my face with the dagger point, little nicks below the eyes. 'Sekenre, you are a weakling child who guards a vast, nay, an *inestimable* treasure which you inherited from your father, and you are completely helpless to prevent the first person who comes along from ripping it out of your hands. The King promised me I could do that. Yes, I serve Wenamon, not that bitch-whore Hapsenecuit. When she finds her precious sorcerer gone, you can well imagine—'

He cut me under the chin. I twisted around, got my knee up, then kicked as hard as I could where his groin should have been. But my foot seemed to pass *through* his body, as if his robe were filled with dried leaves or ashes.

The robe tore away, and his impossible head hovered above me, the dagger floating before my face, two moons in the dark sky, the rest of him completely invisible, his grip as strong as ever.

'How disappointingly *physical* of you, Sekenre. I don't think you know any offensive magic at all. Isn't that *incredible?* You have this huge library of knowledge, and you haven't bothered to open a single book. You haven't even found the key to the library door. *Unbelievable*. Within you is the greatest repository of sorcery ever accumulated, the work of centuries – yes, I know much of your history. Vashtem was quite, quite celebrated at the College of Shadows.'

'The College of Shadows . . . ?' I managed to gasp.

He cut my broad sash in two, flipped the buttons off my jacket, slit open my shirt, and drew a red line down my chest. I controlled myself. I did not cry out.

'That fellowship to which all true sorcerers belong,' he said, 'where each of us is trained, where we rise from apprentice to journeyman to master of murder; for our degrees are in death, the artful demise of our fellows. To graduate, you must kill your teacher, or else he kills you. That is the final exercise.'

The knife was under my eyes again.

'Where is this college?'

He laughed, stuck the knife up my left nostril, and jerked hard. I screamed. Blood and tears poured down my face.

'If you were anything but a fraud, Sekenre, you wouldn't have to ask. You would *see*. But you *are* a fraud, and as such you have brought to me the greatest of all rewards – for I confess that even I could never have bested your late father, but you, my boy, are another matter – and when I have finished with you, after I've killed you by slow and imaginative degrees, then everything Vashtem and Balredon and Tannivar and all the others possessed will be mine. I'll even possess Sekenre inside myself, as a curio. Unlike Sekenre, I'll know what to *do* with my inheritance.'

I tried to call out to the Sybil, but before I could Moon's knife flashed through the air before my face and around either side of my head. The blade never touched me, but he cut *something* and suddenly my face was numb. I could not speak. He worked the knife around my entire body. I lay paralyzed on the tabletop. He no longer had to hold me there with his invisible hand. I was like an illustration cut from a book with a few strokes of a razor, a mutilated nothing.

He held up my right hand where I could see it. The arrow wound through the wrist had opened up. My sleeve was soaked in blood.

'How very convenient,' he said. 'You seem determined to save me every trouble.'

The wound in my side had opened too. I couldn't breathe. Blood from the punctured lung filled my mouth. When I tried to speak, bloody spittle spewed down the side of my face.

Still I thought of the Sybil, reaching out to her with my thoughts. I filled my mind with the memory of her face. But I could not reach her. I could not make her hear.

It seemed that the sorcerer Moon opened my chest like a bag and reached in to take out my still beating heart, which he held up for me to see as he spoke a word and the heart burst into blue flame. Darkness followed. I don't know for how long. But when I awoke he stood over me as before. My shirt was cut open, but my chest was only scratched, for all that my whole side was wet with blood.

I slipped into a kind of delirium, a half-dream in which my father's house had filled up with *evatim*. The crocodile-headed messengers of the God of Death came to my bedside and commanded me to rise, dress myself, and follow them into their own country, where Surat-Kemad, whose mouth is the night sky, whose teeth are the stars, from whose belly the Great River spews forth, awaited me as he awaits even sorcerers in the end.

Waking and dreaming together, I saw Hamakina and my mother beside me, both of them weeping. Mother took hold of my bloody hand. She spoke to me in the language of the dead, and I replied to her, conversing pleasantly about earlier, happier times.

Orkanre wore the body. It was not Sekenre who acted now, any more than it was Vashtem or Tannivar or Lekkanut-Na. This Orkanre had dwelt in the City of the Delta in the reign of King Sestobast the Conqueror, when the Hegemony of the River was newly established. But Orkanre was older than even that; a tall, gray, reed-thin man aged more than a thousand years, who remembered the battles and heroes and earth-walking gods of the Earth's beginning; ancient, all-wise Orkanre, advisor to King Sestobast as he slew dragons and drove the dark forces hence. Was it by some inscrutable scheme then, something he devised, then allowed to run its course, that an enemy slew Orkanre, another enemy slew the first, a third slew the second, and so on, until the river of Orkanre's death merged with the murderous lineage of Vashtem, and ultimately became Sekenre?

Here he was, infinitely patient Orkanre, in the lair of his enemy who did not suspect him.

He sat up on the tabletop, grinning.

Moon let out a cry of amazement. 'Sekenre! How have you done this?'

'Leave the child alone,' Orkanre said. 'The quarrel is not his. Rather, it is between you and me, Moon, whose true name is *Dekac-Natae-Tsah,* which means, appropriately enough, wriggling lizard or something like that.'

'You are not Sekenre!'

'I've already told you as much. Come, discover who I am—!'

Moon hurled a flaming spear, but Orkanre did not even raise his hand, let alone form a shield out of his own body's fire. That would be – the notion filtered into my fading consciousness, as if Orkanre whispered to Sekenre in a dream – childish, an apprentice's trick, beneath the dignity of a true sorcerer of the College of Shadows. His mind was his shield. He formed an impenetrable mesh of *thought,* as if he had gathered thousands of iron bars into existence and woven them into place with the force of his will, all in less than a second.

The fire-spear slid between the first few bars, then was lost in a maze. It fell to the ground, fading to dull red, gone.

Moon retreated, possibly waving his invisible arms before his face. I couldn't tell. Orkanre did not bother to say. Slowly Moon's hands became visible, floating in space before his face, skeletal traceries of living glass.

Still sitting on the table's edge, Orkanre reached out with a spoken word and snapped those glass hands off. Moon screamed, but he did not bleed. He fell to his invisible knees, staring forlornly at where the hands had been.

Orkanre slid off the table and found his footing unsteadily, momentarily amazed at the lightness of the body, and the shortness of the limbs. He took one step, and another; then his knees buckled and he fell back against the table, clinging to the edge, fingers unable to grip.

Moon looked up, hopeful. A criss-cross of blazing white lines slashed the air in front of him, the whole formation turning, whirling as it grew ever larger.

Orkanre waved his right hand. The whirling light vanished. Blood arched, splattering Moon's face. Orkanre hesitated, puzzled; then understood that the blood was his own, from the body's wrist. The sleeve was dripping, the whole side of Sekenre's shirt hot and wet with blood, which had begun to seep through his jacket.

Orkanre coughed, and spat blood. For an instant, nausea overwhelmed him. I screamed, inside his mind, to rouse him, then struggled very hard to focus my thoughts, to tell Orkanre how I had received these various wounds, to plead with him to do something before I – we – bled to death.

He smote Moon once more with a backhanded flourish of his mind. The other sobbed and lay still. Then Orkanre summoned fire from within the body, until cold flames hissed from his mouth, his wrist burned like a torch, and his whole side was covered in brilliant light. Sekenre's clothing billowed from the fire bursting out of him. He felt no pain.

This fire sustained us both, as Orkanre strode across the room, almost leaping from the unaccustomed lightness of a body so different from the one he had worn in life, blazing, streaked with blood. Moon gazed up in abject terror. Orkanre reached down, a little clumsily, with that burning hand. He caught Moon under the chin and hauled him up. The defeated sorcerer was hot and dry to the touch, and weighed about as much as a melon. I had the distinct impression that only the malformed head now remained.

'Come with me. Let us finish what we began long ago.' Orkanre's voice squeaked and broke in his wrath and excitement. He was unused to speaking with a boy's lungs and throat.

Moon whimpered. 'Who *are* you?'

Orkanre's voice steadied, his accent one Sekenre did not recognize.

'Don't you know?'

Moon rolled his eyes and pleaded. '*No!* You know my

name. You brush me aside as if I were nothing, but I do not recognize you.'

'That is because you *are* nothing. Had you not arranged for me to be murdered simultaneously by several of your betters, had my soul not been scattered among them – but for this, you would *always* have been nothing. I could have squashed you like a bug. But those betters, whom *you* could never overcome, were murdered one by one by Vashtem of Reedland. And so I am reconstituted and have found my way back to you.'

'No! No! I do not know you!' Moon's face was mad with terror. I, Sekenre, thought he had truly lost his mind, but Orkanre was merely amused and knew better.

Moon struggled to use one final advantage. I had been wrong on a significant point. His invisible body was still there. He *stood up,* so much taller than the boy Sekenre that Sekenre's hand could not even reach his chin. For an instant he was free.

Orkanre laughed, and passed a foot where Moon's knees should have been, meeting no resistance. The invisible body collapsed. Orkanre caught the glowing head as it fell, hefting it in his hand, pretending to throw it, while his enemy wheezed, 'I ... don't ... know ... you ...'

Orkanre pitched the head into the air, caught it, then held it until their noses almost touched. Sekenre's nose was still bleeding from where it had been slit. Orkanre had only tended to major wounds. As he spoke, blood flecked Moon's face.

He stared into the other's eyes. 'You must have gone soft. You called me Old Beanpole when you were a boy, for I was already old then, older than you could ever dream of being. *Remember?* When you grew up, you called me things far worse. But the insults could not hurt me, any more than your pathetic spells could. *Remember?* So you lured me into the Vaults of the Dead beneath the city, where you successfully betrayed me. *Remember?*

'Merciful gods! It cannot be! Oh Surat-Hemad, take me into thy kingdom from which I have tarried too long—'

Orkanre pressed his thumbs into Moon's cheek, crushing the face impossibly. The tongue protruded. The eyes bulged out.

Orkanre gave a sharp twist, turning the forehead one way, the chin the other. Moon hissed between his teeth.

'I am Orkanre, you fool, ancient Orkanre returned to settle old scores. You shall have to tarry just a bit longer, until I am done with you. Now, come, it is time for a return journey to the Vaults of the Dead. We have so much to discuss, you and I. I have waited so long for this opportunity, and I don't care to wait any longer.'

Orkanre carried his enemy Moon into the Vaults of the Dead. To Sekenre it was all a muddle, walking for hours through low, damp tunnels, emerging into great halls lined with statues, descending frigid stairs of black stone deep beneath the palace, past grottoes where unfamiliar idols crouched alone and untended. The flames of the body did not illuminate, the wound on the wrist fading to a glowing scar.

They encountered no other person. Whatever spell Moon had wrought in the audience chamber was still in effect. We remained alone in our private, empty world. Sekenre wondered if it had involved a manipulation of time, like Father had done with the house. Had all this taken place in a few real-world seconds, too fast for the non-sorcerous eye to see?

Indeed, Sekenre observed, the flames in the mouths of the idols stood absolutely motionless. He fancied that to anyone else, his invisible passing would be like a sudden and mysterious draught.

Yes, child, like that, Orkanre thought. *Exactly.*

Sekenre wanted to ask more, but Orkanre had no time for idle chatter. He had so much to discuss with his defeated foe. Fragments of Orkanre's memory filtered up. I was a mere passenger in his mind now, and all I could do was experience snatches: a flash of bright sky, a peaceful day fishing on the river; pages of books he'd read; a particularly hideous doom he'd meted out to one of the most deadly foes of King Sestobast. There was even a nostalgic yearning for a time when Orkanre thought himself reconciled with Moon, when they had almost been friends. Then a flash of anger, recalling how he'd let his guard down and Moon had trapped him.

Orkanre knew what he was about to do. He felt a touch of sorrow, but only a touch.

Now Orkanre stood in the perpetual darkness below the City of the Delta, where dragons once nested in the first days of the world, and, later, dragons died at the hands of demigods and heroes. There chambers had been cut from the living stone by the breath of dragons; there the swords of heroes carved more out of the bodies of the dragons. The glow of Moon's face revealed white pillars, rising into impenetrable gloom. These were the dragons' teeth. Enormous white arches curved overhead, ribs of butchered monsters; and round, flat stones gleamed along the walls, the scales of the long-dead beasts.

Only sorcerers knew how to find this place. Magic closed it off from normal eyes.

The select dead lingered here, exiled from the River for a brief time, which might be several centuries by human measurement, but the mere blinking of the eye of Surat-Kemad.

Orkanre used Moon's head as a lantern, groping his way amid stone sarcophagi and painted mummy-cases, ankle-deep in the dust of dragons' flesh.

For Sekenre, the experience was like being in a locked room at the top of a house, eavesdropping on bits of conversations from the rooms below; but Orkanre heard the ghosts of the imprisoned dead clearly as they pleaded for release or cursed him or merely babbled. With some, Orkanre held long conversations.

Here was the secret known only to sorcerers of the Delta, a repository of minds, of fallen sorcerers, kings, and philosophers; wicked men and women mostly, but useful, so very useful to the sorcerers of subsequent ages.

We surprised a company of ghouls who had toppled a mummy-case and torn it open. They scattered at the first gleam of light, naked, gaunt creatures with fish-belly white skins and enormous golden eyes like grave-coins. Orkanre lowered Moon into the case and saw that the ghouls had devoured the corpse's eyes. He leaned over and blew fire out of his mouth – my mouth – until the corpse was entirely burned away. Not even bones remained. I, Sekenre, looked around for the ghost, thinking to tell it the way to the River and the death-lands, but it had already fled. Orkanre shrugged and went on.

Again we walked for a long time, but the body's fire held off any weariness. Moon sobbed softly. Sometimes he made sucking sounds with his lips. But he no longer spoke. I think his mind had failed him at last with the realization that he had been reduced to a gibbering lunatic. Orkanre laughed aloud at the implied pun.

At last we stopped before a mummy case somewhat larger than most and ornately painted, still bright and new after what Orkanre knew were many centuries. Up and down its sides, relief-images of snakes writhed, yellowish-green against the black wood.

Orkanre held Moon up to the visage carved on the front of the case: an old man, eyes closed, beaked nose lightly tilted back.

'Was this not your crowning achievement, old friend?'

Moon drooled, but made no reply.

Now the serpents stirred slowly to life, wriggling along the sides of the mummy-case, to Sekenre's eyes their motion like a series of time-lapses, as if over the centuries or even millennia the original carvings had worn away and the black surface was planed smooth, then festooned with new reliefs. All the while the case itself shrank, diminishing inward as it was worn and planed and recarven, as if a million years were confined here and were unravelling themselves like wrappings crumbling from an ancient corpse.

Orkanre understood the process to be the operation of a locking mechanism. Slowly, as time peeled away, the case would open.

He named the centuries, one by one, commanding them. The serpents weaved their way up and down. At last something inside the case snapped. Orkanre shifted Moon to his left hand, then eased the lid open with his right. The mummy-case vibrated gently as he touched it.

Orkanre stood back as black smoke poured out of the case, filling the chamber with swirling vapor. But there was no odor to it. We did not choke. The smoke was not smoke at all, merely *darkness*.

Only Orkanre truly saw what came after, using some sorcerer's sight beyond the body's eyes. To Sekenre, it was something glimpsed fleetingly in an evil vision.

Living, gleaming serpents coiled around the corpse of a man, as if he had been wrapped in serpents rather than bandages and left standing there, his ankles bound together, his arms tied across his chest, his head thrown back in an endless, silent scream, his *living* eyes wide and glassy with pain and what had to be madness. For centuries he had suffered thus, the serpents devouring but never consuming, his agony beyond all imagination.

Orkanre held up Moon. 'Unworthy son, behold your father, my loyal friend. *Remember?*'

Moon shrieked as Orkanre tossed the glowing head into the mummy-case like so much trash. With an abrupt jerk, the crossed arms broke free of their bonds. Skeletal hands caught Moon and held him fast while hundreds of serpents wriggled over the glowing face. Moon found his voice again. He screamed and screamed until the vaults seemed to shiver, but the mummy only *laughed,* its own voice deep and thunderous and infinitely terrible.

It was only much later, perhaps after centuries of subjective time, that silence returned. I looked out through my own eyes. Orkanre still wore the body; I remained but a passenger within; but I could see.

He raised a flame from the palm of my hand, then stood there, thinking thoughts I could not fathom, his anger and his sense of triumph fading, that faint sorrow lingering to trouble him.

He reached into the case, the light revealing the ruined, near-skeleton of the corpse. The serpents had gone. Moon's head lay at the bottom of the case, dark and flattened like an empty bag.

Orkanre breathed fire into the case, destroying what remained.

Moon, whose true name was *Dekac-Natae-Tsah,* whom

we had slain and thus absorbed, awoke screaming in my mind. Orkanre flourished a thought, suppressing him for the time being.

I felt the mummy's ghost passing. I tried to call out in the speech of the dead, to guide him to the River and the Dark Lands, but Orkanre spoke within my mind, *Don't worry, Sekenre. He knows the way. He has contemplated it for a long time.*

Then I noticed that while Moon's head and the mummy were completely incinerated, the mummy's *hands* remained, floating in air where they had held the screaming face. The fingers flexed, like the working of some intricate machine made of metal rods.

Orkanre had expected this. I understood that the *hands* were the product of sorcery rather than nature, and that the departed one had been, like everyone else involved in this affair, a sorcerer who had been maimed and transformed by his sorcery. Now only the hands were left.

'There is but one task remaining,' Orkanre said aloud, whether to me or to the hands, I could not be sure.

We turned away and walked in utter darkness, Orkanre guided by some sight beyond sight. We passed along the bank of the River of the Dead, I am certain. I heard the waves lapping, the spirits whispering among the reeds, and Surat-Kemad's heartbeat, far away but unmistakable.

When I could see again, I thought my eyes deceived me: a long hall lined on either side with squat pillars like enormous spools. A common lantern shone at the far end.

Only then did I realize that the hands were still with us, floating before us in the air, fingers outstretched forward.

A while later, at the top of a staircase, I wept at the sight of the risen Moon in the sky – the real one, called the Goddess's Mirror – the pale light streaming through a tall window.

My face was caked in blood. My nose hurt terribly.

The hands gleamed before us, reflecting the moonlight. The fingers opened and closed, clutching the air.

'Only a little way more,' Orkanre said.

We walked through the empty palace now, on dry floors, down long corridors illuminated by motionless flames. Once or twice I caught a glimpse of another human being, a soldier raising his spear to attention, an official in a sweeping blue robe turning from us, flickering, blurred, as insubstantial as the flashes you get before your eyes in absolute darkness.

Moon's time-spell was wearing off by degrees. I sensed that Orkanre was calculating that it would last just long enough.

'A little way more.'

The skeletal hands opened a door and we entered the throne room. Barefoot, I walked over the smooth, cold floor amid semi-transparent eunuchs, guards, and courtiers. I saw the Ladies Necu and Tica clearly, but frozen in place, transparent as ghosts.

We climbed the stairs up to the throne of the Great King, Wenamon the Fourth. He looked up, startled, heaving his heavy crown back. *He* could see us. His eyes showed alarm. The living side of his face tried to form words, but only managed a wet gurgle before the floating hands closed around his throat. He leaned forward, eyes popping out, tongue stuck between his teeth. One living, spotted hand clutched feebly at the mechanical ones.

'My Lord King,' said Orkanre, 'I am a stranger to you, but your great-grandfather knew me, and your grandfather also. Since your dynasty has given aid and comfort to my direst enemies, know that the vengeance of past wrongs is visited upon you.'

The King's head exploded, blood spewing from mouth, nose, ears, from ruptured eyes. Then the head was off completely; and, almost too quickly for the eye to follow, the two murderous hands buried themselves inside his neck like burrowing spiders. His body swayed from side to side, fountaining blood, too amazed to know that it was dead. Scrawny arms flapped. Incredibly, the headless king *rose to his feet* before his chest burst open in a shower of blood and bones and shredded flesh.

The body crumpled. The hands remained floating in air, holding the King's heart aloft. They paused for a second. Orkanre nodded.

The hands swooped down the steps and across the floor, trailing royal gore into the distance.

Sekenre, Orkanre said within my mind, *I am returning the body to you now, for I am satisfied and want to rest. I wish you no harm, and am even grateful that you have provided the opportunity for my vengeance. But be warned. Others would not relinquish possession as I have done. You have been extraordinarily fortunate thus far. Learn your craft, boy, or you will not survive another such encounter.*

I felt him sinking back into my thoughts, and then people were screaming all around me and I felt very sick and weak and filled with pain. I tripped over the King's ruined corpse and rolled down the steps, huddling on the floor, soaked in blood, clutching my nose, certain I was dying, that all my wounds had opened up again.

Someone seized me under the arms and hauled me off. Everyone was running, shouting. Metal clanged on metal. More screams. At the very last I heard a trumpet blast, and the distant voice of a herald shouting, 'The King is dead! Long live his grandson King Wenamon the Fifth! Long live the divine Hapsenecuit, Queen Regent, favored of the gods!'

'Favored of the gods!' many voices returned.

Chapter 11: The Engima of the Sorcerer

Her face hovered above me in the slowly fading darkness, her skin whiter than paper, her hair like an old woman's for all she was young; her eyes so impossibly, alarmingly blue. I thought she was a ghost.

And the other was a beautiful demoness, delicately featured, but black as a Zargati raider, her eyes gleaming, her pupils darker than her skin.

Someone touched my forehead with a damp cloth. A cup was pressed to my lips. I sipped, coughed, then swallowed. The drink was warm and sweet.

'What is it?' I said in Arnatese.

The two paused, glancing at one another. 'Only cider,' the pale one said, in the tongue of the Delta.

My face seemed encased in plaster. I started to explore with my fingers. The supposed demoness lifted my hand away.

'Don't touch,' she said. 'The doctor sewed you up very nicely.' She smiled broadly. 'He says your nose will only have a little mark.'

'Oh.'

I was fully awake now. I lay back in a bed beneath a vaulted ceiling. Sunlight streamed in through windows of colored glass, brilliantly illuminating figures of serpents and maidens and warriors embedded in the glass by some mysterious art.

I touched the bandage on my face quickly and remembered. Yes. There'd been a knife up my nose. What puzzled me more was that both my feet were raised on pillows and heavily dressed in gauze. Only after I'd wiggled my toes and been rewarded with sharp pain could I piece together how I had become a heron and my opponent a crocodile-headed hawk which seized my feet in its jaws.

The two women whispered to one another excitedly, possibly in a language I didn't know. I couldn't make out any words. But now I saw that they were merely women, not ghosts or demonesses at all, dressed in identical smocks, wearing identical bone jewelry in their hair and around their necks. Slaves, I concluded, fashionably mismatched to emphasize their diversity. The dark one could well have been Zargati, or of any of the southern peoples. The other must have come from beyond the sea, from a race type I'd never seen before. Now that I studied her, I saw that her hair wasn't *white* like an old person's, but a very pale yellow. Her skin was almost pink. I didn't see how she could go out in the sun much. I wondered if her homeland was some haunted place of mist and eternal darkness near the top of the world, such as we hear about in stories, but I did not ask.

I tried to sit up, but the two of them gently eased me down into the soft bedding.

Didn't they know who I was? Hadn't someone told them I was a terrible sorcerer who had lately ripped the Great King's living heart out of his body?

Apparently not. It didn't make any sense. But I was amazingly weak, wholly unable to resist them.

More memories returned. I slid a hand under the covers and surreptitiously discovered that, one, I was naked, and two, all my wounds had closed. There was no trace of blood. I was clean and slightly scented.

I swallowed and tried to speak again. The black woman raised my head in her hands. The pale one gave me more cider.

Suddenly there came a heavy tramping from outside the room. Armor clattered. Double doors burst open and four soldiers paraded in, positioning themselves on either side, thumping their spears smartly to attention. I noted the serpent emblems on their shields and their red armbands.

Next a herald entered, proclaiming much louder than he had to, 'The Princess Royal approaches!'

The two slave women withdrew out of sight behind the head of the bed as the doorway filled with a familiar figure in a plumed headdress and a sleeveless gown of brilliant

red, embroidered with gold. Golden serpents encircled her
bare arms.

'Tica!'

I forgot myself and heaved up. The sheet fell down,
uncovering me to the waist. Then I gasped an involuntary
'Oh,' tried to cover myself, and fell back, almost in a faint.
The slave women reached down from behind the headboard,
straightening and covering. I drew my bandaged feet under
the bedclothes.

Tica entered the room stiffly, looking neither to left nor
to right, never acknowledging the existence of any of the
others, her face so expressionless that at first. I thought
she was wearing a waxen mask; then I saw that she was
heavily painted and powdered, with dark shadowing around
her eyes extending back across her temples to give the absurd
impression of two fish plastered to either side of her face.

Her gown rustled. Her endless complexity of golden necklaces rattled.

'Tica?'

'You are ill and a foreigner, so I shall forgive your lapse
of etiquette, Sekenre. Even you must call me 'Highness' or
'Princess' in the company of others.' For the first time she
seemed to acknowledge the presence of the soldiers, herald
and slaves, only to dismiss them with the wave of a hand.
The herald went first. The four soldiers closed the door behind
them, then stamped and thumped to attention outside. The two
women slaves must have left by another door.

She smiled and sat on the edge of the bed, to my right.
'There. That's better.'

I reached out from under the covers and took her hand
in mine. She did not resist, but she turned my hand over to
examine the scar on my wrist.

'You heal quickly, Sekenre. Is that the way of sorcerers?'

I nodded and rolled my eyes, indicating my bandaged nose.
'Not always. I . . . I—'

'Yes, Sekenre?'

I didn't know what to say. A barrier had already come
between us. I couldn't quite leap over it with words.

'Not always.'

'Are you in pain, then?'

'Not much. Not now. But, you know, I don't think I'll ever learn to enjoy being a sorcerer.' It was a joke. I tried to laugh. She didn't respond.

'Mother is startled and . . . alarmed, a little. She didn't expect you to do . . . what you did.'

'She didn't tell me what I was supposed to do.'

'Nevertheless, the circumstances impelled her to move . . . more rapidly and forcefully . . . than she had intended – but of course she is *very* grateful to you, Sekenre, and will keep all her promises to you. She just misjudged you. She didn't think you were capable of—'

'What is going on, Tica?'

She let go of my hand. I drew it back under the covers. 'I had hoped *you* would do the explaining,' she said.

It was time for masks. I put on the mask of the sorcerer, the mask of mystery. 'Perhaps you perceived events differently than I did,' I said tonelessly. 'I would expect that. You did not see as I saw.'

She shuddered, and looked away from me, speaking very deliberately. 'The King's head exploded like a melon. There was blood everywhere. People were showered with it. I felt it raining over me. A piece of his brain landed on the floor in front of me. And *after he was dead,* he stood up and did a horrible dance until an invisible demon tore out his heart and carried it away. *Everyone* saw that, even with the confusion and so many people screaming. An old man died of fright. I was afraid, too, afraid of *you,* Sekenre, because you could do such a thing, even as you murdered your own father. I realized that I didn't know you at all.'

She wept softly. That startled me.

I lay very still and said, 'But your mother got what she wanted in the end, didn't she?'

'Yes. She kept her head when the others panicked and acted like it had all been part of her plan. So our enemies were all arrested or killed while *they* were still too terrified to act. She made it out as the sort of swift and terrible stroke she could visit upon any who dared oppose her. But, inside, I think she was as afraid as anyone else. She didn't show it, though, and was queen within the hour.'

'Then everyone's happy. What's the problem?'

'There is no *problem*, Sekenre. But my mother, the Queen Regent Hapsenecuit, would like to be better informed of what you intend to do in the future, so there will be no more *surprises*.'

'I was surprised too, Tica.' She turned to me sharply. Our eyes met. A long, awkward silence followed. I couldn't read her. The barrier between us was already impossible to cross, as if more than a thousand miles of the Great River lay between where we were now and where we had been together on the barge.

She rose to go.

'Stay with me, Tica. Tell me about the Delta. Everything is strange to me here.'

'I am needed elsewhere,' was all she said. She clapped her hands. The soldiers opened the doors to let her out, then closed them again. I heard their footsteps echoing in the corridor outside for a long time.

There followed an interval of sleeping, waking up, being fed light meals by the two slave women, who would not answer any of my questions. If I spoke to them directly, they covered their faces, or shook their heads, or just looked away fearfully. Then I'd sleep again and dream vague, incoherent dreams filled with fire, thunder, and wind, with a vast shape rising slowly out of an abyss, like a giant rising from sleep.

It must have been at least three days later when two blank-faced men came for me in the earliest hour of the morning; slaves, I had no doubt, not mine but Queen Hapsenecuit's, temporarily assigned to me. One lifted me out of bed and held me upright while another slid a loose black robe over me. I took a careful step on my lacerated feet, and stood swaying, about to fall, when one of the slaves caught hold of me and lifted me up in his arms.

I could tell these two didn't relish the assignment. The one who held me shuddered. The other seemed reluctant even to touch the clothing I had worn on my arrival, which now lay cleaned and neatly folded on a stand by the bed. But he did what he had to, gathering the fancy coat, shirt, sashes – and my shoes – into a bag. He would not meet my gaze.

I reflected that a slave seldom gets to choose what he does with his life. It is merely assigned. How is a sorcerer any different?

Unceremoniously, these two hauled me along a series of corridors, the one with the bag in his hand going before the other, opening doors, parting curtains, perhaps even looking, I fancied, to see if the way was clear. We met no one in the hallways, or even when crossing big, empty rooms with vaulted ceilings and more of the marvelous colored glass in the windows. Alone, we went up stairs, then down stairs, then outside, into the cool morning, traversing a garden filled with fantastic plants shaped like birds, animals, and even people, which turned to watch as we passed. I reached out once, to touch a leafy camel with my hand. It snorted, and drew away. The slaves said nothing.

Once I caught a glimpse of the palace walls, and the rooftops and towers of the city beyond, gleaming beneath a brilliant blue sky as the sun rose.

Then we were in darkness again, travelling through a low wooden tunnel hung with vines. This gave way to stone walls and stone floors, more roughly-fashioned than any I had seen before in the palace complex. The journey seemed endless, exhausting.

At last we stopped before two enormous doors. I reached out again, running my hand over the intricate carvings – birds, beasts, ships on rivers which swirled around stones and islands; a nude, bird-headed woman rising out of flames – finding the wood so polished, so hard, so cold it almost could have been stone.

Both slaves stood impassively for several minutes. At last I stirred in my bearer's arms, looked up at him and said, 'What's the matter? Are we going in or not?'

The other one shaded his eyes as if gazing on a blinding light, and said, more to the floor than to me, 'You must open it for us, Master. You alone have the key now.'

I hesitated, uncertain of what they meant, but pretended to

218

understand fully and to be mysteriously meditating something far more profound.

'Ah, yes,' I said, not to the one who spoke, but to the one who held me. 'Put me down.' He did. I stood still, wincing as I clung to the door. The crocodilian teeth hadn't torn the soles of my feet nearly as much as my ankles. As long as I stood still I was all right, but it was agony to walk, to shift weight.

Unsteadily, I made my way to where the two doors met. Here two wooden hands folded together, an old man's hands, large, long-fingered, and wrinkled, with prominent veins. I placed my own much smaller hands over them as best I could, and willed the door to open.

I felt the wood shifting as if it were alive. When I released my grip, the images were of my own hands, detailed even to the arrow-scar on the right wrist.

The doors swung inward. The slaves caught me before I fell and dragged me forward into a room I knew all too well.

It was Moon's workshop, as I had seen it last, high-ceilinged, oval windows of colored glass, endless shelves of books and bottles, and disordered heaps of charred bones on the gritty warm floor. Perhaps Moon had led me here by other corridors, or else he had transported me by a magic path invisible to the rest of the world, but there was no mistaking where I was. His headless corpse still lay amid the bones, robe stiff with blood, covered with swarming flies. The stench of his death filled the room.

This was to be my domain now, I understood. I had inherited. I was sorcerer-in-residence for the City of the Delta now.

The slaves beheld all this and made signs to ward off evil. I motioned toward a high-backed chair. They sat me down.

'Clear all that away,' I said, waving at the bones and the corpse.

The slave who had carried me looked up fearfully. 'Into . . . the furnace, Master?'

I sighed and slouched back. 'No, no. Give them all decent rites.'

Both slaves tied cloths over their noses, then took up the corpse, under the arms and by the ankles.

* * *

I must have slept. When I awoke, the sunlight flooded the room from the side opposite to where it had previously. The slaves still labored, removing bones. I realized that hundreds of people must have died here, possibly thousands.

The slaves would be busy for hours, and seemed content to ignore me. So I was left to explore on my own. I rummaged through the bag of my clothing and got out my shoes. With the shoes tied tightly over my bandaged ankles, I could walk a little more easily.

I stood up, shuffled to the nearest wall. Still the slaves paid me no heed. I could have commanded them to help me, but decided I'd rather not. So I was the one who found the long metal pole with the hook on the end and used this to open all the windows, to let the smell of death out.

I must have spent hours going through my predecessor's library. Once I was aware that a slave set a tray of food beside me. I ate a little and continued with my reading, poring through volume after volume, stacking to one side those I couldn't open yet because I had not discovered their secrets. Later, as it grew dark, a slave returned with a lamp.

But I couldn't concentrate. The thought, the dread implication kept coming back to me: *the furnace*. The slave had asked if the bodies and bones should go into the furnace, expecting that they would.

I closed the book I was reading and stood up. I felt a little unsteady on my feet still, from pain and exhaustion and loss of blood, but I would have to make do. I picked up the lamp from the library table and made my way back to the main laboratory room.

The bones were gone. Even the black stain of their ashes had been scrubbed from the floor. There was no sign of the slaves. I supposed they had retired for the night. It was just as well. I didn't want them to see what I might find.

Now, where was the furnace? Moon stirred within my mind, half-awake. I concentrated on what I was doing, trying to avoid rousing him. I was not ready to confront him within myself, not yet, not until I knew more of his secrets.

At last I found a trapdoor set in the floor. I knelt down

– my knees could take the strain far better than my ankles could – then set the lamp beside me and took the iron ring in both hands. Heaving with all my strength, I managed to get the door open. It slipped from my grasp and hit the floor opposite with a loud crash.

I hesitated as the echoes faded. No one came, not even the two slaves.

A stairway was revealed. I took the flickering lamp in my hand and descended into semi-darkness. When I reached the floor below, I seemed to be facing into an enormous, glowing mouth, a few yards distant. The furnace. Yes. Coals smoldered amid pungent ash. The room was broad and low, with squat brick pillars and archways. I had the impression of many side chambers leading to this main one, with the furnace the center of all.

With the lamp I lit several torches set in the walls. Long shadows wavered, retreated. I was sick with what I saw.

The place was a massive torture chamber. Here were whips, knives, and metal pinchers hung neatly on pegs, like a carpenter's tools. To my right, a coffin lined with knives. To my left, some sort of stretching engine. Beyond, many other machines I did not understand, for all I had no doubt of their purpose. But worst of all was a contraption of chains and manacles and rollers and gears, by which no doubt live and screaming victims were conveyed into the mouth of the furnace and burnt as quickly or slowly as the operator desired.

I drew nearer, both horrified and, I confess, fascinated. Numerous spouts issued from the side of the furnace, each leading to a stone trough or, in some cases, a glass bottle. Stacked around were various sizes of hammers and tongs and long metal tubes, the implements of a smith, perhaps, or a glassblower. A commonplace leather apron lay draped over a chair.

This was, I was certain, the secret core of my predecessor's magic, this foundry and distillery of pain.

This my enemy had bequeathed to me.

I turned away and staggered back up the stairs. I heaved the trapdoor shut, gasping at the effort, then shoved a trunk over it, and sat on the trunk, my face in my hands, sobbing from revulsion at what I had discovered and from the realization that this Dekac-Natae-Tsah, who had worked down there, was inside me. We were fused together. I had become a little bit like him. I hadn't the power to destroy what he had designed, and there was always the terrifying possibility that one day I would find it *useful*.

For the moment all I could do was keep the trunk on top of the trapdoor and not allow the furnace to be fed. In time it would grow cold.

Lamp in hand, I returned to the library. I felt safer among the books. Still I couldn't concentrate, and soon fell asleep over my reading.

In my dream I called out, *Dekac-Natae-Tsah, what were you truly?*

And the rest of the dream came from within my own mind, from that part of me which incorporated the sorcerer Moon, and the dream was his reply.

I was an old man remembering what it was to be young, but the old man's memory did not extend back to my own age, which was a month or so short of sixteen. So here I was doubly detached, doubly estranged, reaching *back,* so very far back in fading memory to when the old man had been twenty-five or so and a tall, broad-shouldered fellow filled with confidence and arrogant expectations, with his own aspirations which were not Sekenre's.

As this other man, I walked hand-in-hand with someone – I could not see the companion's face in my dream, but the presence was strong – across a landscape quite unlike any I had ever seen in waking life. White-capped mountains ripped the sky. Before me, steep slopes covered with yellow and purple flowers dropped away into valleys dotted with iridescently blue lakes.

I spoke to my companion in a language that I – the waking Sekenre – did not understand, but my dream-self *felt* the meaning as each thought completed itself. Still I did not turn to behold the other, as if the dreamer could not quite conjure up the image of a face.

The reply of my beloved was like the whispering of distant

wind. I knew with absolute certainty in my dream that she was indeed my beloved, whom the young man had loved and the old man so fervently remembered. I nodded and seemed pleased at what was said, though Sekenre, who was eavesdropping, did not understand a single word.

The dream was one of contentment and of a wistful regret that if only everything had remained as it had been that one day on the purple-covered mountainside, then much trouble and suffering might have been averted. The dreamer sat with his beloved on a ledge, looking down on the lakes, at clouds drifting below and casting fleeting shadows across land and water. He stretched his long legs, scraping heavy boots and fur-covered trousers on the stones. Pebbles rattled down into the valley. Far away, some voice of the mountain echoed like the thunder of a fading storm. Above, a flock of white birds circled and cawed shrilly.

His beloved leaned against him, soft and warm on his shoulder. Once more they conversed in that incomprehensible tongue.

But then the sky darkened in a single instant, as if a shutter had been closed over the sun. The young man looked up in angry terror. He shouted defiance. He raised his hand to make a sign.

He cursed the moon, which drifted alone in the starless sky, and as he watched, the moon waned, shrinking into a hideously disfigured face, collapsing in on itself, its black mouth wide with pain.

The young man cast his beloved from him and leapt to his feet, shouting, and the moon *shouted back,* its terrible voice filling the whole world, parodying his own, even as the face of the moon became a monstrous caricature of his own.

He screamed and fell to his knees. The pain was like burning. His face was melted, oozing into a new shape he could not control. Sekenre-within-the-other cried out in Reedlandish, as I-who-was-the-other felt his flesh and bones flowing like wax, forehead and chin extending through fingers helpless to confine them.

He turned to his beloved one last time, pleading, crying out to her – and in an instant in the dream I beheld a beautiful, pale woman with long black hair, her eyes wide, her hands raised up to ward him off, her face distorted with terror and she shrieked and shrieked—

I awoke abruptly, my head slipping from a pile of books, banging on the tabletop. For an instant, in absolute darkness, I didn't know where I was. Then my hands found the lamp, which had gone out, and I remembered the library. I eased myself down from my high stool, found the floor, and stood still for a moment, clinging to the edge of the table, waiting for the blood to flow back into my stiff, tingling legs.

I took up the lamp, hobbled back into the main laboratory, blew into a brazier of coals, and relit the lamp.

The floor beneath my feet was still warm. The furnace had not yet died. The waning but still nearly full moon lit the glass windows, bringing alive the figures there, men and animals and birds flashing blue, green, gold.

Behind me, a footstep scraped on stone.

I whirled. A woman stood in a doorway opposite, clad all in white, beautiful, pale, with long, dark hair.

'Where is my beloved?' she asked in some foreign tongue I was only beginning to understand. The words rose up in my mind like bubbles from the bottom of a still pool. Surely this was the native speech of Moon, whose true name was Dekac-Natae-Tsah, who had dwelt once with this lady in a distant, high, cold country. Now his thoughts and memories mixed with mine, like a new color of paint stirred into a pot. But he was twice-removed. I had not even slain him. Orkanre had done that, wearing Sekenre's body. So Moon-within-Orkanre-within-Sekenre opened himself up to me, very slowly, his native speech drifting into my conscious mind word by word.

'Where is my beloved?' the woman said. 'I have come to him this night and on such nights for many years, and never has he failed to greet me.'

She reached out to me with a shrivelled, skeletal hand, a startling contrast to her perfectly unaged face.

'Lady,' I replied in the formal and ancient language of the dead, for I knew now that this woman was long dead, and returned only when the moon was waning, by the power of her lover's sorcery. 'Lady, he cannot greet thee this night, nor any night hereafter. For he is fled from the living world, as art thou.'

She started, stepped back, and hissed. 'He *is* still here. This place is still filled with the smoke of him.'

'Lady,' I said. 'Let me guide thee now, for I know the pathway into the kingdom of Surat-Kemad, where a place has been prepared for thee, where thou shalt await thy lover's coming. Go there. Go into the dark lands where an instant and a century are as one. Be patient. Thy sojourn shall be as the blinking of an eye.'

She staggered into the center of the room as I backed away from her, holding up my lamp. By lamplight I could see that she wept, that her perfect cheeks glistened as if covered with tiny diamonds.

'What do you know of love, child? Very little, I think. You are over-familiar with death and murder already, but love is strange to you. Therefore you cannot understand why I prefer to return, even as I am, to be with my beloved.' Now she was filled with fury, reaching out with both her clawed hands to tear me apart.

The sorcerer Moon awoke within me. I shook with his pain. He cried out. His sob burst from my throat. His tears ran down my face. His words in his strange language comforted the dead lady for a long time, his speech faster than I could follow.

I fought with him for control of the body, but he yielded without a struggle.

The lady stood before me, a draught gently blowing her hair about. Any trace of menace had faded away. She was merely tired and sad.

'I am bidden to forgive the boy Sekenre, for he is not the murderer of my beloved. I am bidden to accept what has happened, merely because it has happened and therefore has been woven by Fate and cannot be changed. And I am to show you the secret my beloved has left behind.'

I swallowed hard and said, choking, 'I think I have already found it.'

'You have not,' she said. 'Come.'

She turned back through that far doorway. Still holding the

lamp, I followed her into the recesses of what had been her beloved's chambers: first, an ordinary room, with wardrobes and a couch, then a door I had found in my explorations but had not been able to open. It yielded to the lady's touch, swinging inward to reveal a long, low gallery lit by a series of colored-glass windows fashioned like the phases of the moon, now gleaming as real moonlight streamed through, filling the room with a faint, white glow even as the gaps between the windows cast long shadows. In the center, a canopied bed covered with golden cloth seemed to drift like a great ship on a sea of light.

'We two rested here,' said the lady, 'for almost a hundred years.'

Once more the slain sorcerer stirred within me. Once more he wept. I nervously wiped a tear away with my free hand. As the lady and I walked slowly past the colored windows, I saw that the far walls beyond the bed were hung with vast embroideries, some depicting scenes I couldn't quite make out, others intricate, abstract designs of white thread against a dark background. Moon, within me, remembered sewing them, and what they meant, and how the days of his life together with his beloved were preserved there by the magic of his beloved.

He remembered, too, periodically dipping his needle into the bloody wounds of a living victim as he worked, to give the magic potency.

The lady stood gazing at the embroideries for a long time.

'Lady,' I said, in the language of the dead, 'if I could in any way comfort thee—'

'No, no, you could not,' she said. She drifted toward the far end of the chamber. I followed, clumsy on my bandaged feet.

Another door yielded to her. What waited beyond may only be described as a miracle.

At first, only points of light drifted in a black void, but slowly I discerned another low, long room, lit by thousands of tiny glass figurines set on black, velvet-covered pedestals, each figurine glowing from within with magical light: winged horses and dragons and birds, dancing bears and monkeys doing handstands and wriggling serpents, grim soldiers, tumbling clowns, all of them alive with the burning fire in their hearts. In the center of the room an enormous table held a complete replica of the City of the Delta, constructed in impossible and exquisite detail of blown and colored glass, all of it faintly glowing as if some delicately burning vapor had been suffused through it.

I turned this way and that, gaping in open-mouthed amazement. I had never even imagined anything so beautiful. I searched the tabletop city for this very room, where I fully expected to see myself and this sorcerer's lady standing before an even tinier image of the city, in which was yet another room, another Sekenre, another lady, and so on to infinity.

I turned away, afraid of some magical trap which would imprison me there, dazzled, forever. But as I did, I demanded of Moon within me some explanation of all this, some answer, some understanding of the purpose of what I saw.

He told me his secret. This room of inexpressible beauty and the furnace-chamber below were two aspects of the same whole, like the roots and leaves of a tree, one bringing forth the other. I knew then that the glass figurines burned with the light of pain, that after long and indescribable tortures, he reduced each of his victims to what I saw here. It was his art, to use the whip and the glowing iron and the pincers selectively, as Sekenre would apply a brush-stroke to a page, and in the secret calligraphy of pain, by the text revealed on the bodies of dying men, women, and especially children, all mysteries, all revelations were made clear to him. In the very end, he read the future from the cracks in their charred bones.

He had intended to add me to his collection.

I would have transformed you, he said, *into a dancer perhaps, not some dullard sitting at a table with a pen. Sekenre, I would have set you twirling forever to secret music only you and I could have heard. In the end, you might have even thought it worth the pain.*

I *remembered* the creation of each of these. His memories were mine, however removed, however much they were filtered through the memories of Orkanre, who had actually slain him. Orkanre, in Moon's opinion, had no sense of the artistic. He was a mere pedant, a workaday sorcerer who should have been a bricklayer.

I *knew* how Dekac-Natae-Tsah, called Moon, had labored at his art for many, many years, waxing great in sorcery, convinced that because he could still love beautiful things he had retained his essential humanity, even as the years and deeds and struggles with countless foes had transformed him so much that he could scarcely remember the young man he had once been, on that mountainside above the blue lakes so long ago.

The glass figures were part of his memory, a kind of theater where every part reminded him of something, every image brought something back. He could walk through this room, watching, remembering, with infinite care actually picking up and handling these delicate fragments of his own soul.

Now his beloved walked among them, remembering *him,* and as I watched her, she became young again, her hands soft, her hair delicate as spider's silk. She closed her eyes and whirled, dancing to some music I could not hear, moving with impossible grace among the figures and pedestals, never brushing against a single one. Many of them, too, moved in time with her.

'Come to me, my beloved,' she said. 'Rise up and come to me. Here, I know, you can find the strength to conquer even death.'

I caught her by the hand and pulled her to a stop. She jerked clumsily. A glass horse crashed to the floor.

'This must cease,' I said to her in the language of the dead. 'Did he not bid thee accept what has happened? He is dead now, lady, and cannot return. Therefore be guided by me, into the dark land. I know the way.'

'I know it too,' she said. 'I have merely avoided that path for a long time.'

'For such as thee, there is no time.'

'Not anymore,' she said.

Then she turned from me and once more drifted soundlessly across the smooth floor, weaving among the maze of figurines like a thing of smoke. Very carefully, very slowly, I followed, once or twice bumping into pedestals, sending glass creatures to myriad-splintered destruction.

Well before I could catch up, she had opened and stepped

through a third door at the far end of the room. A cold wind blew. The glass figures rattled. A few of them fell. The room seemed to fill with a tangible darkness.

I stood very still, shivering, listening to the sound of water lapping gently on a shore, and to the more distant, almost inaudible cries of ghosts among the reeds along the banks of the River of the Dead. I remembered those sounds, and the dank, muddy wind all too well. And as I listened further, I could make out the deep, muted thunder of the heartbeat of Surat-Kemad, the great crocodile god, who is Death.

Truly the lady knew the way into the dark land. She had gone there on her own. I could only stand on the threshold and recite what fragments I could remember of the prayers for the dead.

Once more Moon, who was Dekac-Natae-Tsah, wept, and I did not wipe his tears from my cheeks, for to have done so would have been a desecration.

But when I was sure that his beloved was truly gone, I went back into the room of the glass figures, broke a leg off a chair, and used it to smash every last one of them. For an instant the air was filled with rushing spirits, with the whispering souls of all those released from their delicately-shaped prisons.

I prayed for them too. When they were gone, I stood alone in a dark room full of broken glass.

When I returned to the laboratory, chair-leg still in hand, I gazed up at the colored-glass windows with revulsion and suspicion. It took me a while to figure out that I had seen such glass all over the palace, and it must be the work of ordinary artisans.

I never entered those inner chambers again. I never slept in my predecessor's bed. In all the time I dwelt in the City of the Delta, I slept on a folding bed in the library.

Nor did I ever again go into the furnace room below.

That morning, as I sat bleary-eyed and half asleep in the high-backed wooden chair in the laboratory, Father appeared to me. He paced back and forth, circling behind the chair where I could not see him.

'What you have done was foolish, Sekenre. Do not throw

away a tool before you have learned its use. The pain-magic of Dekac-Natae-Tsah might have proven the key to your whole problem in the end. Now, you will never know.'

'*Father,*' I said impatiently, a little angrily, 'my *problem* is simply this: *Is it possible to become a sorcerer without also becoming an abomination?* Answer me *that,* Father.'

He laughed. I was furious at him. 'Ah, the young are such moralists,' he said, 'relentlessly certain of so many things which – they discover later on – do not actually matter. Sekenre, your problem is merely to become a sorcerer *at all,* any way you can, to stay alive and master your art before you are mastered by someone else.'

'No, Father. You are wrong.'

'Am I? You'll see.'

'Go away, Father. I don't want to talk anymore.'

He circled behind the chair. When I didn't hear him for a while, I got up and looked, and discovered myself to be alone in the room.

In the half-light of dawn, I wandered outside into a garden filled with sculpted hedges and huge, white, drooping flowers that are called, in Reedland at least, Dead Men's Shrouds. How very appropriate, I thought.

But there was nothing dead here, not the hedges, not the flowers, not the birds in the branches shrilly announcing the arrival of the sun, nor even my two slaves, who lay asleep on stone benches.

I stood there, regarding them, reflecting that while I was supposedly an honored member of the court, an important confidant and friend of Queen Hapsenecuit, these two slaves were in some ways more fortunate, possessing a kind of security I would never know. Yes, they would die under a small burden of years, while I might live for centuries; and they would pass into the belly of Surat-Kemad, as have all ensouled creatures since time's beginning; but that was one more certainty. They were men. They would remain men. What time and circumstance would do to them was simple and clear.

But for me, for the sorcerer, there was only mystery, an

endless labyrinth open before me. Dekac-Natae-Tsah, sitting on that mountainside with his beloved, surely could not have imagined that one day he would reside in the City of the Delta, weirdly disfigured and transformed, feared and hated, then be murdered hideously by an ancient enemy he had himself murdered, at last subsumed utterly into the mind of a Reedlander boy named Sekenre, in the company of numerous other sorcerers. No end was in sight for Dekac-Natae-Tsah, for who knew what would become of Sekenre? The thread of both their destinies was as tangled and confusing as ever.

I hoped the Sybil was finding herself amused by it.

I should mention something at this point:

Moon had a sorcerer's mirror. I discovered it a week later, carefully concealed, yet standing in plain sight in that wardrobe room, just outside the bedroom. Only by a sudden shift in perspective, a sudden turning of the eye, did I recognize it as a mirror at all, not as a shadow, or a dark patch on the wall.

I reached out and the air seemed to ripple in the shifting light of late afternoon. Then my fingers touched glass, which yielded slightly, as if the mirror were not affixed to the wall, but floating in air. I groped around to find its edges.

It was indeed floating on the air, like a heavy plank in water, only vertically, a long oval, slightly higher than I was tall. I pushed it into the laboratory, where the light was better, and eased it against the wall.

A sorcerer's mirror, if used skillfully, can reveal many things, living and dead, near and far, of the past and of the future. But for the time being, I saw only myself.

I began to examine the image, not out of vanity, but as a portraitist might, to observe salient points.

What, then, defined Sekenre?

I saw nothing special: a boy in his middle-teens, very thin, somewhat less than average height, stooped shoulders (I stood up straight at once), a round, smooth face with large, dark eyes; shoulder-length black hair, tied back in an unruly tangle; olive complexion, a little pale for a Reedlander, but unexceptional for an inhabitant of the Delta.

Such an ordinary face would never have attracted attention anywhere along the Great River. The mark on the forehead (where the Sybil had kissed me) might have been a burn. Any blacksmith's apprentice has worse. The curving scar on my cheek ironically reminded me of a tiny crescent moon, but it, and the thin line up the side of my nose, might have been gotten in a street fight.

I reached up to touch my face. Ah, the arrow-wound through the right wrist would raise more of a question if someone noticed it. A diviner might read something of my fate in these traceries I had begun to accumulate. But to the untrained eye, what was there to see?

The boy Sekenre dressed slightly absurdly, in clothes borrowed from a tall man's wardrobe, plain black collarless shirt so long it almost came down to his knees, overlarge trousers rolled up to those same of dirt-stained knees; grubby, bare feet, ankles criss-crossed with newly-healed gashes which might indeed have been the result of a narrow escape from a crocodile. Such things happen all too often. The open shirt front revealed a bony chest, splotched with ink. Baggy sleeves rolled up, ink-stained fingers.

On the street, such a person would hardly have caused heads to turn, a poorer artisan perhaps, not quite scruffy enough to be a beggar.

Yet here, incontestably, was a major sorcerer, who had descended into the belly of Surat-Kemad and returned, defying Death; who spoke with the gods; one singled out and touched by the Sybil. Here was the slayer of sorcerers and of kings, who had disposed of both Wenamon the Fourth and his servant Moon by methods too horrible to be described.

From such a creature, people turn away in dread. Even in Reedland, people knew that this boy, to use an old, dead teacher's phrase, 'stank of sorcery.'

The mystery of him, his *difference,* was not in the mirror, not in his face. Even in the sorcerer's glass, I saw only Sekenre, who was far from home and didn't know where he was going.

And something more:

Sorcery is, as Father warned me, seductive. I plunged into the study of it, not merely from fear of what would happen to me if I didn't, but from an undeniable fascination, an appreciation, as Moon would have put it, of its terrible loveliness. Sorcery is a music only the sorcerer can hear. Indeed, he can never shut it out.

Therefore I spent long days in the library of my predecessor, unlocking his magical books one by one, gorging myself on their secrets, applying my calligraphic skills to make charts, diagrams, figures, and signs which I dare not reproduce here in the book of my life.

Sometimes I felt Orkanre or Lekkanut-Na or one of the others stirring within me. *I know that one,* they whispered. *Let me tell you what happened when I tried it.*

And I would sit, in a kind of a trance, while my inner mind spoke to itself, as the company within me conversed, as they bade my hands turn pages, skipping ahead or returning to some passage one of them knew, but which Sekenre read for the first time.

In this manner I came to know the secret of the Nine Angles, the true meaning of the Voorish Sign, the shadow-litanies of the Dholes, and many things which may not be committed to paper at all, lest potencies be released by the mere formation of the letters.

So weeks passed into months. My injuries had healed. My strength returned. I dwelt alone with my invisible companions, visited only by such spirits as any of us might call forth from time to time. I was only vaguely aware of changing seasons, even as I sometimes noticed it was time to eat or sleep or bathe. If servants attended me, I did not notice them. More often I found that if I went to a certain kitchen late at night, food was left out for me. I would pack a basket and go, glad to be cut off from all human society. If officials of the court, if Queen Hapsenecuit wanted me, I assumed, they would send for me. They did not. I was kept hidden, either as an embarrassment – for no legitimate queen could admit to over-much trafficking with sorcerers – or as a dagger is kept concealed under a pillow, unseen until needed.

I learned the use of the sorcerer's mirror by degrees, first to see beyond my own reflection, into my soul. Thus my father Vashtem appeared to me, along with Tannivar the Parricide and the mountainously fat Deltan witch Lekkanut-Na, and many of the others, whom I had known in dreams and visions, but never actually beheld with my waking eyes.

After some while I could observe *places,* other parts of the palace, clerks scribbling away at desks in a great hall, noble children playing a game with colored sticks, soldiers of the now-dominant Serpent faction drilling in a courtyard draped with red banners, a skeletal ghost in a corridor, ghouls in the crypts below, and even, once, a glimpse of Queen Hapsenecuit and her women in the bath. (I watched her with innocent fascination; then she seemed to turn toward me, and I quickly covered the mirror with a cloth.)

And once, very late at night, as I stood wearily before the mirror – I think on that occasion I had forgotten to eat for several days, and had been without sleep for nearly as long – I beheld, without any conscious summoning on my part, the inside of my father's house, the mirror's point of view shifting through familiar rooms, settling at last on my own bedroom, where the desk was toppled over and the bed smashed and parchments were scattered over the floor. My old school-bag lay on the floor by the window where the arrows had come through. Frozen flames gleamed like beaten gold.

I clung to the mirror unsteadily, my face against the glass, gazing into the black glass for a long time, wanting desperately to reach *through,* not certain I knew how, and in any case afraid to. This was my enigma and my contradiction and my mystery at last: that I wanted to return to my childhood (but no one can do that, sorcerer or not), that I wanted more than anything else to return to my father's house (which would be a trap; I would never be able to leave), that I could not let go of so many familiar things (which had caused me so much pain).

Chapter 12: The Inevitable Abomination

'You have a unique way of denying the obvious, Sekenre. It fascinates me.'

Lekkanut-Na spoke. She shared the body equally with me. For once the others within me were not jealous. I knew perfectly well that if she tried to take over, Vashtem and Tannivar and the rest would overcome her.

This was a harmless indulgence to an old lady who had once been so enormously fat that she lay immobile in a vault for centuries before my father slew her. Now she found it endlessly intriguing to be young and slender ('So tiny, Sekenre! So light! You're a grasshopper!') and, quite possibly, to be male, though she turned evasive on that subject. I think she saw me as only a child, too young to know about such matters.

She luxuriated in the sensation of the sun on her skin that afternoon – my skin, actually – as we stretched out on a polished wooden platform deep within the maze of the palace gardens. I couldn't imagine what the structure was for, except for people to sun themselves on it in late spring and early autumn, when the air was still warm and the sunlight less than searing. The wood, unlike metal or stone, never became too hot.

It was now an unseasonably warm day in mid-autumn, just before the beginning of the winter rains, the sky clear, the heat broken by a pleasant breeze. I lay on the smooth wood, wearing only a thin strip of linen about my loins. Lekkanut-Na asked about that. 'Why do you bother?'

'Foreigners often go naked,' I said, 'but we Reedlanders have a sense of modesty.'

'You're not in Reedland. Here, you are the foreigner.'

'Then you'll have to get used to my foreign ways.'

I lay on my stomach, raised up on my elbows, carefully illuminating an initial letter in the tale of my adventures. I had resumed my memoir, and had reached the sixth chapter, the one filled with arrows and pain. Possibly if Lekkanut-Na read that chapter she would be less eager to possess this body, but she was lost in the immediate feelings, the touch of the warm wood, the sun on my back, the breeze ruffling my hair. She had no patience for my careful, intricate strokes as I rendered the minuscule lines and circles with a single-hair brush, dipping again and again into the tiny cups set along the back of an ivory serpent I'd found among Moon's things. I think the serpent was intended as a candle-holder, but I used it to separate the different colors of paint.

Lekkanut-Na could have addressed me silently, inside my head, and no one would have overheard but the other sorcerers; yet it amused her to speak aloud, using my lungs, throat, and tongue and a voice that was not hers. So Sekenre seemed to be conversing between two halves of himself, sometimes imitating an old woman who sounded vaguely like a bullfrog, then reverting to his ordinary voice to reply.

Once, gardeners came upon us, then hurried quickly away, certain, no doubt, that I was mad.

'Sekenre,' Lekkanut-Na said. 'Your obtuseness I find curious. Perhaps it is because you are so young. Most people do not become sorcerers until they have studied for a long time. I was over sixty myself. The magic froze me at the threshold of old age. Child sorcerers are very rare. You're a kind of freak. I think you know that. Is that why you pretend not to see what you really see?'

I shrugged. A rivulet of sweat trickled down between my shoulders. Lekkanut-Na paused, relishing even that. I reached over to twirl the brush in solvent, then dipped into another color.

'And what do I really see but pretend not to see?'

'That you cannot go on like this, comfortably lolling away your time in the garden making marks on reed-paper, or even in the laboratory reading your predecessor's books—'

'*My* books now, by order of the Queen—'

'Shut up, Sekenre. Let me continue. You must study, that is true, and you must learn to master sorcery before it masters you, before your enemies find out just how weak and ignorant you are and seize the great treasure you bear within you. That is to say, us, myself, your father, and the rest. Undeniably, time moves differently for a sorcerer, and a decade or two might slip away as if it were an hour. You might even leave a project incomplete for a century while attending to other matters – but sorcerers never forget, and they tend to return to what they have started. Therefore you can be certain, Sekenre, that a number of your father's enterprises will find ways of resuming themselves, and the consequences of what he did in the past will also continue. That is the way of sorcery, Sekenre. It goes on and on. Once you begin, it never stops. You cannot hide. That which seeks you will find you, more likely sooner than later, Sekenre. I don't think you have a lot of time.'

'Did – did my father make you to tell me this?'

'No, Sekenre. It is my own conclusion, although I am sure he shares it.'

I carefully placed the brush between two flared horns at the tip of the serpent's tail, then rolled over on my back and stared up at the fleecy clouds drifting across the otherwise spotlessly blue sky. I lay still for a minute or two, hands clasped behind my head, and said nothing.

Lekkanut-Na said nothing either. She let out an ecstatic sigh.

'I think I am like a soldier,' I said, 'who knows the battle is about to start. But the enemy hasn't arrived yet. So he sits on a hillside, repairing his armor, sharpening his sword, and waiting. What else is there to do?'

'Sekenre, you're more like a farm boy sitting there whittling a pointed stick. When the enemy army shows up, you will find out to your sudden grief how little you resemble a genuine soldier.'

I sat up and clasped my knees. With my hands, she explored behind my knees, then felt her way down my legs and slipped fingers between toes.

'What do you suggest?' I said.

'You know already, Sekenre. You must attend the College of Shadows as soon as possible. You know what it is and where it is, that it is everywhere and nowhere, and only a sorcerer may find its door. There the sorcerer comes into his true identity. He finds his strength, or he dies. You take a master, as Moon told you. You and your master study together. In the end, one of you murders the other for the knowledge both have gained. That is the way of sorcery. You must face the many dangers of the college, from perpetual students, from perpetual masters, from those who are gluttons for knowledge and blood. But you know that already, Sekenre, even as you know you cannot delay much longer. Since you know all that, you won't have to ask me any of your curiously obtuse questions, now, will you?'

'But the Queen isn't just going to let me go away.'

Another rivulet of sweat ran down my chest. Lekkanut-Na traced it with my index finger, then raised the finger to my lips. I tasted salt.

'Quite correct, Sekenre. Queen Hapsenecuit is not so much a fool that she keeps you here, fed and attended and luxuriously housed, with your own private bath, dining room, library, and whatever else you might want, with so much of the royal gardens turned over to your exclusive use, without having further plans for you. Indeed, you are her instrument, held in reserve. Don't doubt it.'

Almost as if Lekkanut-Na had just summoned them, a whole procession of men suddenly emerged from an opening in the garden's flowering maze. Pretending to be oblivious to their arrival, I lay back lazily and stretched, my head over the edge of the wooden deck, so that I saw the newcomers upside down to myself. I recognized a thin, silver-haired man in a white and red robe, with a golden band around his head and numerous gaudy rings on every finger. He was Takpetor, one of the Queen's eunuch chamberlains, accompanied by five attendants, also eunuchs.

If he was surprised to find me in such a state and posture, he had no reaction. All the Queen's servants are similarly inscrutable. I don't think anything about me could have ruffled him. He had surely heard all the stories, even those that were true. So I remained likewise inscrutable to him.

'Honored Sekenre,' he said in his high, warbling voice, 'Her Divine Majesty, the Great Queen Hapsenecuit, bids me summon you into her presence. Therefore make yourself ready.'

I rolled over onto my stomach and regarded him right-side-up.

'Oh.'

'Hurry, Honored Sir. The Queen can't be kept waiting!'

I sat up and gathered my things while the attendants clucked and muttered among themselves. Carefully I stoppered each of the little cups on the ivory serpent's back with plugs I'd carved for the purpose. I wrapped my brush in a cloth and placed it in a wooden case, then fixed the still-wet manuscript page in its own carrier, a flat, rectangular box with slats inside to hold the paper firmly by the edges and a lid to prevent anything from touching it.

This done, I slipped into the knee-length, sleeveless tunic – actually one of my predecessor's old undershirts – that I often wore in hot weather.

I dropped down off the wooden deck and stood there, box and brush and paints in hand, gazing at Takpetor and the others. For an instant he seemed at a loss over what to do next. Then he made a curt motion with one hand and some of the others relieved me of manuscript box, paints, and brush. He and one other took me gently but firmly by either arm and led me out of the garden, not into the Queen's chambers, but to my own.

Probably Hapsenecuit had told them of our time on the river. I imagine they all had a hearty, if nervous laugh out of it. Otherwise I could not believe that they would dare treat a prize sorcerer like a small child, as they fussed over me, bathing me and scenting me and combing my hair, pillaging my wardrobe for the finest clothes they could find. Their frustration was comical when they discovered that *nothing fit*. The clothes were all Moon's. He had been nearly two feet taller than me. So the eunuchs settled on a black silk shirt with golden serpents on it. This dropped down below my knees, but there was no help for it. The blue trousers they pinned a little above my ankles. Moon's feet had been over twice as large as mine, which left the rather plain shoes Tica had bought for me back in Thadistaphon, still the only pair I'd ever owned. I hadn't worn them much.

Then came a bewildering array of jewelry, rings, necklaces, bracelets, even silver pins in my hair, and finally the sorcerer's long robe with the moon and stars on it, the dark black cloth like a piece of the night sky itself. I couldn't possibly walk without tripping over it, and they dared not cut or even pin such a garment. This caused quite a dilemma until Takpetor figured out how to drape the excess over my left arm and instructed me to move slowly, with grave and mysterious dignity.

I practised, and smirked. 'I hope there won't be a fire. I'd hate to have to run in this thing.'

'Please, Sir,' squeaked one of the other eunuchs, 'your talisman. Where is it?'

He meant the heavy golden necklace the Queen had given me as we entered the city for the first time, the one which designated me a high member of the court. I hadn't afforded it any thought since. I didn't know where it was. And so, despite whatever dread they might have had at going through a sorcerer's things, the whole gang of them rummaged frantically through trunks, drawers, shelves – how one eunuch squealed when he touched a bottle and it screamed at him! – removing everything, carefully putting it back, but relentless until they finally found what they sought.

Then I was hustled over to the sorcerer's mirror, which Takpetor probably took for ordinary glass, and I beheld myself in all this finery, looking, I thought, a trifle ridiculous, more like a girl than a boy. Boys don't wear silver hairpins and jeweled rings in Reedland. But the girls don't wear the iridescent robes of a Deltan sorcerer either.

I thought I looked like Tica impersonating Sekenre.

I felt a strange sort of pang when I thought of her, a mixture of reluctance, eagerness, and longing. I hadn't forgotten Tica. She had been my friend, and I had always had so few friends. Now, I suspected, I had none at all.

True, my studies occupied most of my time, but when I

tried, I never could get in to visit Tica anymore, ever since she had become the Exalted Kanratica, the Princess Royal. I even resorted to sending her letters, never once receiving a reply.

If I were to go before the Queen now, I was looking forward to it, because Tica might be with her.

Lekkanut-Na, still awake within me, smiled wryly in the mirror.

'That's love you feel, Sekenre,' she said, in a low voice, but definitely aloud. 'I remember it from long ago.'

One of the eunuchs glanced at me, startled. I covered my mouth with my hand and turned away.

For a minute or so, I rehearsed walking back and forth in front of the mirror, hiding my drab shoes behind the hem of Moon's robe.

'I'm ready now,' I said to Takpetor.

Within me, Lekkanut-Na relinquished the body and went to sleep.

I often wondered if the palace might not be a magical thing in itself, a solidified dream or a trick of endless, enchanted mirrors, which could go on and on assuming new shapes without ever once duplicating what it had been before.

Either that or I was unaccustomed to large, complicated buildings and easily got lost in them.

The eunuchs led me along a completely unfamiliar route. We crossed the garden in a kind of procession, one of Takpetor's assistants out in front ringing a little golden bell. Was this to make way for the Queen's favorite or to warn people of the passage of a notorious sorcerer? I didn't bother to speculate.

We wound between hedges and rows of flowers, then through a place filled with trees that looked very much like stone and formed walls, doorways, and battlements to merge imperceptibly with the palace itself. The transition from outdoors to indoors was so subtle that I missed it. In a great hall, where stone lions ringed a fountain, a company of armored guards joined us, marching in step to the eunuch's bell, five of them clattering on either side, five more in front, five bringing up the rear.

Above, the sun made little glass windows burn with their own secret fire, as if some great serpent had coiled near the ceiling, its scales gleaming.

Then we were outside again. The light dazzled me. Beyond a wall, tile rooftops huddled; beyond them, square black towers rose. From among the towers, a thick column of white smoke drifted upward. Far away, crowds shouted and drums beat. Something was going on. I had no idea what. I had been isolated for so long in my rooms and my garden that the gods might have refashioned the entire world and I would have been the last to know.

Next, a covered passage descended into a cold, damp, underground tunnel. Flight after flight of stairs spiraled down into semi-darkness, our way lit by only a few torches. I thought of the vaults of the dead that Orkanre had visited. But these were not they. Water dripped. The air was startlingly cold, almost frigid. I was glad for the warmth of Moon's over-sized robe.

The others kept pace with me rather than urge me to go faster.

Once the guards opened two heavy square doors and a flock of bats burst out upon us, chittering, fluttering around our ears. Some of the eunuchs squealed and swatted bats with their hands, but the soldiers continued steadily and I, the sorcerer, remained impassive. Was I supposed to be used to this sort of thing? I wondered if we came this way for security reasons, or as a kind of a test.

But never mind. I would be tested soon enough.

Now our path rose out of the depths: a winding ramp, giving way to stairs, brought us to a long, low-ceilinged gallery. Here sunlight streamed through narrow, floor-to-ceiling windows which, for once, were simply barred, without glass. I squinted. The tiles on the floor formed some immense mosaic I could not begin to make out. Between each of the windows, a larger-than-life statue of a Deltan king stood in a shadowed alcove, looking down on his own individual altar. I counted twenty as we passed, thirty; then I lost count. The overall effect of the place was of an enormous cage, the alternating light and shadow suggesting bars. The stone kings seemed aware, watching our progress. I felt distinctly uneasy under their scrutiny.

Then I paused in sudden dread, recognizing the glaring, newly polished face of King Wenamon IV.

The soldiers came to a halt. 'We shall wait here in the presence chamber,' said Takpetor, 'until Her Majesty arrives.'

Only then did I notice a throne in the far end of the wall, a stone chair set into its own alcove, facing the dead kings.

Queen Hapsenecuit entered quietly, from this distance a toy figure in elaborate, jewel-encrusted robes, surrounded by eunuchs in white and red, ladies in long gowns, soldiers, and three male counselors in kilts and sandals and an extravagant amount of gold plate.

Takpetor's eunuchs prostrated themselves. He nodded, and made a sign, touching his forehead with the back of his hand. The guards marched forward and stood to attention. Takpetor and I approached the Queen along the corridor of their spears and shields.

Before the throne, Takpetor dropped to his knees. I started to kneel also, but he pushed against my leg and whispered. 'No, not you.'

'Oh, sorry,' I whispered back.

I glanced at the Queen. Her expression was impassive, her face so made up that she seemed to be wearing a mask. I stared fixedly at the floor.

Takpetor crossed his wrists before his chest. He leaned forward three times.

'Dread Lady, my Queen, I have brought to you the sorcerer Sekenre.'

'Sekenre,' said Hapsenecuit, 'Come and sit by me.'

Her voice was so familiar, so at ease, that she didn't seem a queen at all, but the lady I had travelled with on the River.

I looked up. Her gaze met mine. She smiled.

'What?' was all I could say.

She indicated a cushion at her feet. I approached slowly, indeed with singularly solemn and dignified demeanor as

Takpetor had insisted, shuffling to avoid tripping over the sorcerer's robe.

One of the women seated on a cushion nearby turned toward me, her jewelry glittering. It was Tica. Her face, like her mother's, seemed a mask. I couldn't read her eyes. She quickly turned away.

I sat down.

'Ah, now we three are together again, Sekenre,' the Queen said. She waved the other ladies and the counselors a short way off. Tica moved to my side. I took her hand in mine, not concerned about protocol just then. She stiffened, let out a little cry, but held onto me tightly. No one said anything.

'Well, Sekenre,' the Queen said finally, 'what do you think of that?'

I wasn't sure what she was referring to, our being together again or Tica's reaction to my touch.

'I don't know what to say, Majesty.'

'You grow in wisdom, Sekenre. Then be silent until you have something important to say. The best sorcerers are always taciturn. Nobody fears a chatterbox, and a sorcerer must be feared if he is to be effective.'

I nodded and listened carefully as the Queen outlined why I had been called from my seclusion.

'The Zargati have formed an alliance with the Hanatesh, the Arhedi, and several tribes I have never even heard of. They have subjugated dozens more, growing more powerful than anyone in the City of the Delta ever imagined possible. Together this combined horde has overthrown my armies again and again. They've destroyed many cities, impaling thousands as is their custom. You saw some of that on the River, Sekenre. The skies are black with vultures wherever the Zargati pass. Soon they will be coming here. You are my one hope, Sekenre. Otherwise, as you know perfectly well, there will be sharpened stakes for you, for me, and for my daughter. The Zargati do not enslave their captives. They have no use for them. All they want is empty land, so they can graze their flocks amid the ruins of civilization.'

'I don't understand,' I said. 'Your army is the mightiest in the world—'

'They are victorious because of sorcery. Their king – Habu-Ita-Zhad is his name; it means Lion of Blood, I am told, or Lion Who Thirsts For Blood, something like that – has some powerful sorcerer in his employ. I am sure of it. Arrows miss their mark. Generals die alone in their tents, horribly mutilated from no apparent cause. Sand blinds my legions while the enemy rides howling out of the storm with the wind at his back. Sekenre, this is a task for a sorcerer and only a sorcerer. *You* must save us. Afterward, you may have any reward you name.'

'I'll try—'

Now her face was stern and she was all Queen and nothing of the Lady Necu I had once known. 'You will do more than *try*. You will slay the enemy sorcerer. My soldiers can do the rest. I command you, Sekenre. I'm not just asking a favor. You must obey me.'

I let go of Tica's hand. 'Yes, Majesty.'

Queen Hapsenecuit was wrong about one thing: had the city fallen, I would have escaped. She underestimated the sorcerer's ability to make himself invisible or suddenly just *be* somewhere else. We have our tricks.

The sorcerer's mirror is the key. That evening, I touched the glass my predecessor had left me, feeling it tremble slightly as magic awoke beneath its surface. In the silent room, I could make out the almost infinitesimally faint and fading screams of the men and women who had died in the creation of this mirror long ago. Like so many of Moon's artifacts, this one had been fired in a furnace of human flesh and tempered in blood.

I stood in the darkened laboratory, still wearing my oversized robe and ridiculous jewelry, and whispered softly into the mirror. After a few minutes, I could see through it, as if out of a high window on a dark night. I saw the Zargati horde, numerous as locusts, encamped before the City of the Delta.

The viewpoint shifted, and I seemed to be drifting among the tents of the enemy.

I heard their song, for the Zargati are a people of song.

They do not write the epics of their ancestors in books as we do. Instead, they sing. Somewhere, always, there is a Zargati bard singing the endless song which grows with the deeds and conquests of each generation, a song of blood and of death and of predation, which are counted the only glories of the people. When a warrior falls, they say merely that he has become part of the song.

There is only one song of the Zargati. There can be no other.

Now, before the city, were thousands upon thousands of voices upraised in the same, terrible litany, like thunder rumbling beyond the hills before a storm. Silhouetted figures writhed before campfires, priests invoking Surat-Kemad, the only god they worshipped, warriors asking the god for courage, promising great spoil of lives in return, children, old men joining in until the air itself seemed to tremble.

I passed among them, unseen amid women who sharpened their men's swords and spears, among huddled horses, among the dancers, too, so close that their sweat splattered me and I smelled the stench of their bodies.

Only the subject peoples did not sing, the conquered tribes who fought for the Zargati but could never share the communion of song, desert nomads, blacks of many nations who were not Zargati. They huddled like frightened gazelles in a field of lions.

I came to a broad pavilion of outstretched hides. There sat Habu-Ita-Zhad, the Lion of Blood, among his counselors, his back to a fire, his broad frame draped in a lion's skin, his ornaments and plated armor gleaming in the firelight. Once he turned toward me, laughing, and I saw that his teeth were filed into points. His smile gave the impression, not of a lion, but of a crocodile. Here was Death made flesh, a true servant of Surat-Kemad.

I whispered once more, and Habu-Ita-Zhad heard me. His eyes widened with surprise and, I hoped, terror. He gazed into the darkness, but did not find me.

I reached out, touched glass, and the scene vanished. I stood before the mirror in the laboratory.

It was not for any reward, not for any riches the Queen

might offer, that I resolved to save the city, but to keep Tica from falling into the hands of this man.

Once more I ventured into the enemy camp with the aid of the mirror, and when the glass showed only two sullen, yellow eyes in the darkness, I knew I had discovered the Zargati sorcerer, whose name I did not know.

'Sekenre,' he said in Deltan, his voice deep and rasping and strangely accented, as if distorted by wind, 'you have found your death. Come to me, boy.'

'Indeed, I have found death,' I said. *But not my own,* I did not say.

The enemy sorcerer smiled. His teeth, too, were filed. He drooled like a dog.

I banished his image. I wasn't quite ready. He knew it. I knew it. But I would be, very soon.

The glass remained dark, reflecting nothing.

The next morning I bade my servants fetch a litter and had myself carried around the city walls. I wore the sorcerer's robe and, at Takpetor's advice, a silver serpent-mask which fit over my head, lest the city's defenders lose courage from the revelation that the Hapsenecuit's famous sorcerer was little more than a child. It would be acceptable for them to discern merely that he was unusually short. If I never got out of the litter, they might not even see that much.

The view from the battlements was as I had expected: the enemy had crossed onto the eastern bank where the city stood, their camp encircling us, numberless tents extending north, south, and east as far as they eye could see. A mile or so upstream, the river swarmed with Zargati rafts, which the Queen's warships did not pursue, lest they be drawn away from the shelter of the walls.

Cavalrymen raced back and forth outside of arrow range, shouting taunts, the barbarians laughing and gesturing as they raised hundreds of pointed stakes along the Great River's edge and cut down every available tree to make more.

Three widely-spaced columns of smoke smudged the horizon where distant towns still burned.

Back in my rooms, I tossed the mask aside, wriggled out

of the robe, and commanded Takpetor to procure three fresh corpses.

'I don't care whose,' I said, as he looked down into my face, gulping, unable to speak. 'Grown men, with all their parts. Naked. I require them.'

He nodded, trembling, and made a sign to ward off evil as I gave him further instructions.

I wanted to laugh. Considering what Moon had been doing, could my request have been all that shocking? Sorcerers are known to be a grim lot. That they should have sinister uses for a corpse should surprise no one.

No, I think what unnerved him was that no wizened old man said these things, nor a seven-foot-tall deformity like the late Moon, but an undersized boy with a plain face. My apparent innocence must have made me seem all that much more terrible.

My father, Vashtem, stirred awake within me, amused at Takpetor's distress.

'Make a note of it, son. Such details can be very useful.'

The corpses arrived, criminals, I think. They had been hanged, one of them flogged first, their necks broken. One was black, like a Zargati, but his teeth were not filed and his face was covered with an intricate, swirling calligraphy of scars and tattoos I had to admire for its workmanship but did not have the time to decipher.

I spent the whole night lying naked in their midst. Flesh must touch for sorcery to live. I lay on my back on the cold floor, in the center of a circle of heatless blue flame, legs over one corpse, arms embracing the other two.

Spirits stirred in the darkness, sometimes becoming visible for an instant. A man-faced owl spread its wings and fluttered from a bookcase, then vanished. I turned my head to watch a long, white, scaleless snake slide across the floor, approach the burning circle, and vanish, hissing like water tossed into a flame. Something with too many fleshy limbs and no head at all dropped from the ceiling with a wet thud, but I could not sit up to see where it had landed or what it was doing.

I drew the corpses to myself, shivering in the cold, while

twenty or thirty beast-headed men conversed beyond the flames in a language I did not know.

I closed my eyes and concentrated my thoughts, whispering again and again the words of power which may be spoken but never written down. Within me, Vashtem my father and Tannivar and Orkanre and the others waited, alert but silent. I imagined them sitting all around me, glaring at one another, on guard against both external dangers and their own treachery. *I* was the prize no one of them could be allowed to possess without sharing. So they were in balance, locked in place.

For a time I had a vision of Surat-Kemad, the Lord of Death, whose teeth are the stars, whose jaws are the earth and sky. I heard the thunder of his beating heart and I heard the Zargati singing in time with it, for their melody was his own, servant and master united in a single thought, forever.

And the god's frigid, foul breath passed over me. I trembled violently, but clung to the three corpses and made no sound as the god spoke, saying, *'Soon, soon comes the hour of my feasting. Soon, soon.'*

As the stained glass windows of my room glowed with first light, the circle of fire extinguished itself.

I sat up stiffly, teeth chattering from the cold. I let go of the corpses, then knelt among them, still naked.

I made the Voorish sign, binding them to my will. The four of us rose unsteadily to our feet.

All was in readiness now. I left them standing while I dressed, plainly at first, linen strip, one of Moon's long-sleeved pull-over shirts which I could wear as a tunic, and then his enormous sorcerer's robe. I gathered what other things I would need in a satchel, and regarded the three corpses. They could wait. I was weak and exhausted. I took time to heat some broth, chop up a few vegetables, and make a quick breakfast of soup and bread.

Then I draped the robe over my left arm. I commanded the corpses to follow.

Outside, I put on the serpent mask and sat down in the litter in which living men had carried me the day before. Now two unliving men bore me, and a third, a massive, yellow-haired, pale-skinned, thoroughly grotesque-looking brute, followed behind, hefting on his shoulder a huge bundle Takpetor had left precisely where I had told him to.

All three of my new attendants walked stiffly, their heads rolling side-to-side on their broken necks, eyes rolled up, showing only whites.

Thus we left the city that morning by a sally-port. The soldiers who guarded the door turned away and made signs. Some even cried out in fear. But they opened the door when I wished them too, and barred it after my passage, and I could expect no more of them.

We emerged onto the plain east of the city, on the side opposite the river. Behind me, high rooftops gleamed with the new day, but in front of me, on the plain itself, the enemy's campfires flickered like a skyful of evil stars.

We travelled for perhaps a quarter of an hour toward the Zargati encampment. No sound was raised, no challenge uttered. The sky lightened.

An arrow whizzed by. A sentry shouted an alarm in a tongue that sounded like a jackal barking.

Once more I made the Voorish sign and spoke commands, not in the formal language of the dead, for the souls of these three had long since gone to Surat-Kemad, but in the secret tongue of the unclean spirits which inhabited their slowly decaying flesh.

Another arrow pierced the canopy of my litter. Its point dangled in front of my face. Now the enemy had formed a line before me, shields overlapping, spears bristling, while more and more shouting, somewhat puzzled Zargati ran to see what the commotion was.

I ignored them. My bearers set me down. I emerged from the litter, breathing white fire through the mouth of my serpent-mask, pacing slowly back and forth, robe trailing behind me on the ground, while my three attendants erected a pavilion out of the great bundle the fair-haired one had carried.

The enemy stopped shooting. They paused to watch. I stood still, regarding them, flames flickering from my mask. Beneath the dark robe, I dug my toes into the sandy earth to steady myself. Beneath the mask, my face was slick with sweat.

When the pavilion was up and I had no further use for their strength, I positioned my three servants *just so* around the outside, facing the three cardinal directions only a sorcerer may perceive, toward the future, toward the past, and toward death, which is outside of time.

I breathed on their faces, causing their flesh to burn slowly, hair igniting, flames sizzling from their eyes, then spreading slowly downward to consume them. Black smoke rose in snaking columns.

There were no more challenges from the enemy.

Inside the tent, I unpacked my satchel. I sat on a rug embroidered with names of power, and surrounded myself with a circle of ordinary candles. I placed a brass bowl on the ground and filled it with water from a jug.

And one precaution, not in any of the texts. I rolled up my right sleeve and wrapped one of Moon's leather aprons around my forearm, tying it tight.

Then to work. I cut my wrist slightly with a silver knife, squeezing and shaking drops of blood into the water. Folding my hands together, I dipped them into the bowl, parted them, and the water glowed with the sorcerer's fire.

Through the serpent mask, I blew the flames away from the center of the bowl they way you would blow foam, and the circle of water thus cleared became a sorcerer's mirror. Once more, my sight drifted through the enemy camp, as if I were a bird making short flights between tent posts. Once more I spied upon the king, Habu-Ita-Zhad, and his great lords. At last, two eyes floated in darkness. White teeth gleamed, sharp and wet.

'Ah, Sekenre—'

'Be called Dog Face. Be bound by that name.'

The Zargati sorcerer didn't laugh. The teeth vanished as he closed his mouth. I imagined him scowling. Now I had a name for him as he had a name for me. We were evenly matched.

The candles around me went out one by one, although there was no wind.

'Come here and *die,* Sekenre. But let me ravish you first, and as long as you please me, you shall live. Afterward, rise up on high and view the world from atop a sharpened pole. For that, Sekenre, is your inevitable fate.'

I held the silver knife in my right hand. With the leather apron shielding my arm hidden by my baggy sleeve, I reached down into the water, all the way up to the shoulder – though the bowl was only three fingers deep.

With a sudden, upward thrust, I caught my enemy below the cheekbone. I jerked, tried to drive the blade in, but he wriggled away, living up to his name as he howled like a dog in surprise and pain. I smelled his blood bubbling into the bowl.

Yet before I could draw my arm out he grabbed my wrist. His teeth caught my forearm, shredding the sleeve, sinking into the leather apron. I pulled back. He was far stronger. He had me with both hands now and twisted. There was a sudden, intense pain as my wrist broke. I lost the knife. He yanked, clamped his teeth into my upper arm, then tore at my shoulder and before I knew it I was falling into the bloody water while thousands of dog-like faces howled around me. Transformations followed: I was the moon eclipsed by a dark, dead sun; I was the serpent coiled around a lion, crushing its ribs, but the lion became smoke. Rain fell through the smoke. A mountain defied the rain. I was the river, thundering down the mountain's face. He was the of sliding mud, the falling stones, filling the river's course, diverting it into the desert. Fire and steaming water. My father's silver sword striking stone. I, the heron, leaping into the sky, he, a man again, reaching up, his arm stretching like a whip for miles and miles until he caught the heron by the feet and dragged it down.

I landed in darkness with a hard thump and a metallic crash, face down on packed earth, my whole right side in such agony that I was afraid he'd torn the arm from the socket. Gingerly I rolled over and explored with my left hand. My right arm was still there, but the wrist turned at an odd angle and the whole sleeve was soaked with blood. The serpent mask was so mangled I couldn't see out.

'Welcome, Sekenre. Have you begun to suspect that you are not as good at this as you liked to believe?'

I lurched up onto my knees, struggling to maintain balance. I shook the ruined mask off, tasting blood in my mouth. 'I have come to kill you.'

'Have you, now? Sekenre, I think you are like all three brothers in the famous tale – yes, we Zargati know that story too; we are rich in stories. Do you remember it? Yes, the first brother came into the very belly of Death, led astray by his greed, and so he perished. The second, unmanned by his terror, likewise perished. And the third, ah, I think you are more the third than you are the other two – the *third* died in terrible anguish, having wrought his own destruction. Sekenre, I am your ending. I am your terror and your anguish.'

He laughed, deeply and hideously.

I tried to flex my right hand, but there was only pain. All I could do was sit back, fold the injured arm in the remains of my robe and hold it in my lap. I felt very weak, ready to faint, but I knew that if my attention even wavered, Dog Face would have me as a prize within himself. Perhaps, too, he would feast on my remains. I thought he would.

He grinned, regarding me. Yes, he would.

'Sekenre, your final journey has been a sudden one, I fear, without much of the proper comforts. Forgive me. But now apologies are so, so useless.'

I saw him clearly for the first time: a huge, black man, both massively fat and massively muscular, the great mounds of rolling flesh painted with bright zig-zags like lightning rippling over his naked body. He licked my blood from his lips.

Our eyes met, and I was transfixed by his gaze, helpless as my lap grew sodden with blood, my life and my sorcery escaping as if from a spilled glass. I struggled to concentrate, to remember what had to come next. Part of me wanted to just give up, to lie down and rest and be free of pain, but another part of me was angry and afraid and determined all at once, and the voices within me, Vashtem my father and Orkanre and Tannivar and Lekkanut-Na and all the rest cried out in rage. I called them up. I felt them rising within me, gathering like a storm. Father recited words of power. Lekkanut-Na made signs with hands she no longer had. Talno and Balredon, working together, wrote the letters of my enemy's defeat among the stars. Tannivar contributed mere hatred, as mindlessly resonant as a bell, and that gave me strength. And the others spoke and moved, even Moon, awake within me for the first time, and, within him and within the others, more, deeply buried souls I did not know, names and voices strange to me, until we formed a great army, receding, one within the next, downward to infinity, all joined together against a common foe.

The boy Sekenre was just an outer shell. Did Dog Face really know what he had pulled into his lair?

I jerked my head aside, breaking his hold on me.

He snarled and lunged, his body rolling toward me like a toppling idol.

I held out my left hand. It, too, was bloody. 'Look,' I said. 'I have something you've lost. Now I've found it and return it to you.'

He paused, looming over me. His eyes met mine once more, and in that last instant he must have recognized something within me which was far more deadly than just Sekenre. He screamed and clutched his chest.

I held his still-beating heart. I tried to bring my right hand over, to crush the heart between both hands. I couldn't. My right arm wouldn't do anything.

I dug the fingers of my left hand into the heart. Dog Face shrieked and fell to one side, wriggling and heaving, but he did not die. That wasn't good enough. No. Flesh had to touch flesh to complete his death. I had to crush the heart against bare skin. Without a free hand I couldn't even pull up my robe to expose a thigh. I hadn't foreseen this.

My only choice was obvious enough.

I smashed the heart into my own face. It burst, sizzling, burning. I toppled over backward, eyes tightly closed, and lay still, while within me Orkanre began to chant something in a language I didn't know. He used my voice. I spoke the words, spitting out blood.

I lay still, in terrible pain, feeling the blood and strength stream out of me, while far away somewhere Dog Face screamed and barked and howled, then faded to a whine and was still.

I sat up, leaning on my left arm. My enemy lay before me. His chest had no gaping hole in it, of course. His heart was still inside him. I had created a simulacrum out of my *own* blood, not his. What mattered was that he believed it was his heart.

'Now finish what you've started, boy!' Father shouted within me.

'Father, I can't—'

'Finish! Before he realizes—'

Indeed, the Zargati was not dead. He only *thought* himself dead. His soul would mill around in confusion, but it wouldn't be able to depart and eventually he would stir and rise up.

'Finish it!'

An image came to me, of my whole right arm ablaze like a torch with magical fire. But that was a false healing, one more vulnerability. Had Dog Face known my history, he could have merely opened the wound in my side.

I found the silver knife and clumsily cut a strip from the shredded sorcerer's robe, then bound my arm as best I could with left hand and teeth. The worst of the bleeding stopped. I got to my feet unsteadily.

'You know what you have to do. He would have done the same to you. Find what you need!'

I searched among Dog Face's things until I came upon a sharp metal hook such as a butcher would use to hang meat.

'Excellent!'

I felt sick at the thought of what would inevitably follow.

'This is no time to be squeamish! He stirs! He rises!'

I don't know if he did or not. I couldn't see clearly. My face was smeared with blood. My eyes stung.

Still my right hand was useless. Groping with the left, I drove the hook into the flesh beneath the fallen sorcerer's chin, desperately careful not to pierce the great blood-vessels on either side of the neck. I forced it up into his mouth, until I had him like a fish that you dangle over the side of the boat, to keep it alive while you go on fishing.

This was the hard part. *He must not die.* In my sorry condition I wouldn't be able to resist him if his spirit poured into me. He would seize my body and gain the victory even as I slew him.

Father was well aware of this danger. Here was an enormously powerful sorcerer, momentarily stunned by a ruse so elementary he probably had never expected even an incompetent opponent to use it on him; and he was not someone we wanted in our little company, at least not now. His power was too monstrous, too alien to our own.

I tried to drag Dog Face with the hook, but he was too heavy.

Speak the words! Open the door!'

So I spoke them, and Father assumed the body. It was Vashtem who shouted further, who acted, who dragged Dog Face out of his tent. Orkanre, Tannivar, and the rest let him have the body now, for a time. They lent him their strength. Vashtem parted the darkness and emerged into light. He opened a wooden door and hauled Dog Face across a wooden floor.

But it was Sekenre who stood, dizzy from pain and blood loss, in the middle of an all-too-familiar room, not in the Zargati camp, or anywhere in the City of the Delta, but before an open window, looking out over marshlands.

Birds shrilled and circled in the morning air.

I turned from the window, regarding Dog Face on the floor and the shelves, the bottles, the couch in the middle of the room, the time-suspended fire in the doorway like reddish tinsel.

I was in my father's house, in his study.

Dog Face moaned and groped for the hook. I reached down and yanked it hard. He let out a wheezing gasp.

'Continue, son! You dare not pause even an instant!'

I looked around.

'Where is the knife?'

'I lost it!'

'Then find another! Quickly!'

I let go of the hook and ran for the kitchen, where I caught up a handful of cleavers and carving knives. When I returned to the study, Dog Face was sitting up, painfully easing the hook out of his chin. Blood splattered down his front. I barely had time to make the sign of Living Death over him and to lean forward and breathe fire into his eyes.

He screamed and fell back, eyes sizzling, popping, streaming down his cheeks.

And as he lay helpless, I skinned him alive. In his dead-alive state we two were linked. I shared much of his pain. The two of us screamed together and I felt the sharp metal sliding under my own flesh. But Father and the others joined together, relentlessly forcing me to finish what I had started, their own strength combining to push me further than I ever could have gone on my own.

My enemy's blood was everywhere, like a tide washing over me. It burst into flame with the failing power of his sorcery. I burned, but it was only magic. The pain was real enough, yet I was not consumed.

And Dog Face did not actually die. In the end, as I held his dripping hide over my shoulder and he lay before me, a mewling, heaving, almost shapeless mass that had once been a man, he called out to me, in Reedlandish this time, 'Sekenre, by all that is holy and merciful, I beg of you, grant me death.'

'You know I cannot,' I said on my own, without any prompting from those within me.

There was more to do. From Father's collection of bottles I poured out certain agents, acids and solvents onto the outraged ruin of Dog Face of the Zargati. He screamed and prayed and babbled, but I did not pause. Father and the fear of Father drove me, as did the certain knowledge that if I did not finish *now* what I had begun, my own fate would be far worse at the hands of my hideously disfigured, but not yet impotent, foe.

I interrogated him about the secrets of his magic, applying the acid or the cleaver or the flame as needed; and he spoke freely of the deployment of King Habu-Ita-Zhad's armies, of strategy, of his own career and history, those he had slain, what treasures he had hidden in the earth, other things I didn't care about. This Dog Face, whose true-name was

Haryn-Isha, meaning, curiously enough, Soul-of-a-Fish, cursed
and babbled and ultimately lost all words as his flesh shrank
away, as he boiled and melted like a piece of fatty meat on
a hot grill, until in the end, by my various methods, I had
reduced him to a blackened, shrivelled thing like a hairless
monkey no larger than my finger. It squeaked and wriggled
as I picked it up with tweezers and dropped it into a bottle,
which I then stoppered and sealed with hot wax. I peered at the
thing through the dark glass. It flopped around, the ruin of its
face visible briefly before sinking into an amorphous mass.

I put the bottle on a shelf. Father spoke through me, aloud
in my voice.

'We'll continue this interesting discussion some other
time.'

And, within me, he said, *'It is an important principle of
sorcery, my son, that to kill a sorcerer outright is a high
compliment. You honor him by accepting his soul into yourself.
But there are those, like this one, who are too dangerous, too
vile, so that to kill them would be the worst possible folly.'*

I sank down onto Father's couch, the very couch where he
had once lain as the priests prepared him for the underworld.
I only wanted to sleep. I felt weak and sick, from my injuries
and from the sheer horror of what I had done. I leaned over
and vomited up everything I could, until there was only spittle
and my body heaved and heaved.

I shrugged off the sorcerer's robe. It was heavy with blood.
Underneath, I was soaked in blood as if I had bathed in it.

'Get up, Sekenre! You aren't done yet!'

'Father, please—' I only wanted to lie there forever. I had
come home. I wanted to stay here forever and forget about
the City of the Delta. I wanted to sleep here, in the workroom.
I didn't care what was in the bottles on the shelves.

'Get up!'

I think he took over the body again and heaved me up
against my will. That was how it seemed as I staggered
across the room from the couch, stripped off all my clothes,
and put on Haryn-Isha's skin, which shifted and shrank and
closed over me, until I was smothering in the closeness of
the huge Zargati's blood and sweat. Only where my right

arm was bandaged did the black skin fail to close. There was nothing to be done about that.

'Never mind. We only have to be convincing for a short time.'

'What are we doing?'

'You'll see.'

Now I moved slowly, cumbersomely, as if I had become Lekkanut-Na in her elephantine body. But, no, I was Dog Face, the Zargati sorcerer. I wore his skin, which filled out and assumed his likeness. I tried to think. Sekenre knew how this sort of thing was done. Or he did in his more lucid moments. Now, he was merely confused. He followed along, led by Vashtem.

Sekenre touched a door in a certain way – but with a flabby, black hand – and Vashtem spoke a spell, not in Sekenre's voice, but in that of Dog Face – and what seemed to be Haryn-Isha, whose common name was Vishak-Ankri, meaning the Mountain of Death – this avalanche of flesh stumbled out of the house of Sekenre and Vashtem, not over the railing and into the River, but onto the plain before the City of the Delta, into the glare of noon, where the Zargati king Habu-Ita-Zhad walked with his nobles amid a forest of stakes. On every side, chanting barbarians danced in place, waving spears and torches, waiting for the command to attack.

The king turned at my approach, astonished, his copper armor gleaming. The nobles drew away. Some covered their faces. One dropped to his knees.

'Lord of All Men,' I said, my voice deep and rumbling, 'I have come to report a monstrous theft of that which is most dear to your Greatness—'

Habu-Ita-Zhad made a hissing sound, his nostrils flaring. 'How can this be? Who would dare rob *me?* And why do you bring this matter to me *now?*'

I held out my Dog Face's dripping left hand. 'It is your own heart which had been stolen, Master. But here, as you can see, I have recovered it.'

The king screamed. Then blood poured out of his mouth as if spilled from a bucket.

*   *   *

259

That is all I can remember. I assume that when the Zargati saw the sorcerer collapse and shrivel, they believed him slain by the same magic that had killed the king. Anyway, no one ran me through with a spear, as they could have easily done.

I was vaguely aware of a tumult that went on for hours, perhaps days. The hot sun beat down. I was choking on smoke. The ground shook. Voices shouted in many languages. Metal clanged on metal. Men trampled over me. They fell on top of me, some dead, others writhing and screaming. Much later, in darkness, I slid out of the collapsed skin of Dog Face the sorcerer, and lay curled up like a new-born in the cool night air, naked, my skin slick with blood.

Then it was morning. Those around me spoke Deltan now, but no one tried to help me. To the soldiers, one additonal gore-smeared corpse was wholly unremarkable.

Somehow I found a soldier's helmet and let it fill with dripping blood from a dying man's wound, then touched the blood with the fire of my hand, blew on the flames, and once more had a sorcerer's mirror. It was all I could do to focus my mind well enough to remember the bookshelves and tall stained-glass windows of my laboratory. But then I saw it. I reached through the mirror and caught hold of a desk where I had often sat writing. The touch of the familiar wood was enough. I pulled myself through the mirror.

But when I arrived I could only lie naked and helpless on the cold, gritty floor, weeping softly for fear that Tica would somehow find me this way and be repelled forever by what I had done.

Inside me, Vashtem my father only mocked me. *'You asked me a certain question once, Sekenre, whether or not it is possible to become a sorcerer without also becoming an abomination. That, you said, was the whole crux of the matter. Well, what do you think? Do you have the answer now?'*

I croaked faintly, 'No. I don't. Leave me alone.'

Much later, some servants found me, and were at first so horrified that they were afraid to touch me, or else they weren't sure that what they had found was really me. But

Takpetor came and commanded them to carry me to the bath. As I soaked in the cool, soothing water, a physician cleaned and rebandaged my arm. He set my broken wrist between wooden slats. Finally, mercy of mercy, miracle of miracles, I was carried back to my bed in the library and allowed to sleep for a long time while Father and Orkanre and Tannivar and Balredon and all the rest seemed to sit in a circle around me, conversing among themselves in low voices I could not make out.

The Cup of Pain

(from the notebooks of Sekenre the Illuminator, but in another hand.)

Do you think you know the whole, edifying story of the Three Brothers, Sekenre? No, you don't. Your schoolmaster didn't teach you this part:

The gods were glad for the light of Kadem-Hidel's ceaseless agony. Now was the Earth revealed, on the first morning, at the beginning of time, as the eldest brother burned in the sky.

And the gods walked over the bare ground, causing living things to spring up. They opened their hands and filled the sky with birds. They wet their feet in the seas and fish swarmed.

But Kadem-Hidel fell to the horizon, that first sunset a splash of red on the sea, foretelling all the blood of men spilled in future times, the slaughter of nations.

Then the gods were afraid as they saw their own shadows cast long and dark across the world, darkness pouring out of the chaos-void like water into newly opened channels. Such was the terror of the gods: that their own shadows waxed as great as they and stood up on the Earth to defy them.

These were the Shadow Titans, equal and opposite manifestations of the Righteous Gods, rulers of night, kings of discord: the Titans of Desolation and of Earthquakes and of Wrath; and Sedengul, bringer of storms; and Arvadas, the Lord of Lust; and also the most ambiguous Vedatis, the Titan of Dreams, the wildest and fiercest of all, who invades the very minds of the gods, either to bring them strange and beautiful visions, or nightmares, as the whim suits him.

So the gods welcomed, too, the fate of Maena-Illakun, he of the tumbling skull, that whimpering little coward who feared the darkness and the titans and the Devourer most of all. He cried out to the Nine Righteous Gods. He offered prayer and sacrifice. Maena-Illakun was the first of all votaries, the world's first priest. He did exactly what he was told. And his skull tumbled through the afternoon sky.

Timsha, the Sacrifice, was the third of mankind to die. His lifeblood poured out over the lands, into the rivers, falling with the rain, but it mixed with the spittle of Death, who is Surat-Kemad, the Crocodile-Who-Waits. Therefore all flesh-creatures are mortal, because they have the spittle of Surat-Kemad in them, which dilutes the lifeblood of Timsha.

Here is what the priests will never tell you, what the gods command that they keep secret: there was a fourth brother, called Dalshepsut, which means Quiet One. He did not die with the rest. No, he sat alone in the darkness, contemplating the dooms of the others while the cold, foul breath of Surat-Kemad blew over him. He cursed the indifferent cruelty of the gods.

Dalshepsut whispered to the Shadow Titans, and a whisper sufficed. They rose up out of the abyss before him, scattering the foam of stars across the night sky, and he saw them clearly and trembled in their terrible gaze.

But he was brave enough to speak further, and the Titans replied, and a bargain was struck. Dalshepsut climbed the mountainous back of Arvadas and was cupped in the hands of Sedengul; and Vedatis breathed a wind which carried Dalshepsut to the place where the sky and the mountains meet. There, high above the Earth, the fourth brother found a silver cup.

'Go,' the Shadow Titans commanded him, 'and fill the cup with the world's pain. Drink from it and be made strong. Only when you have gathered every drop of blood shed by the sword and the spear and by stones, by the torturer's lash and by the torture of childbirth, every stain of bursting diseases; only when the world no longer suffers shall Dalshepsut weaken and die. Not until then.'

And Dalshepsut did not die, and Dalshepsut waxed strong, though he is often weary and puts off one body after another the way a traveller discards an old, worn-out cloak for a new one. He walks among us yet, and even when men know what he is and try to slay him, when his own blood fills the cup of pain, Dalshepsut continues; for he is within our minds, beneath the covering of our flesh.

Dalshepsut is the oldest of all sorcerers, whose sorcery shall not fail until the end of time, the first and truest servant of the Shadow Titans.

But, secretly, the Shadow Titans fear him and even worship him.

This is the faith and hope of the sorcerer.

I wrote this for you while you were asleep, Sekenre, my son.

Chapter 13: Time to Leave

I slept for what felt like weeks; brief periods of wakefulness followed long, delirious dreaming, recollections of memories and adventures that were often not my own. I dreamed of my mother once, but younger than I'd ever known her, scarcely older than my present age, and naked beside me, whispering, soft to the touch. I awoke with a shout, trembling, soaked in sweat. That had been Vashtem's dream.

Takpetor came several times with the physician in tow. I never knew his name; he was a completely bald, grave-faced man who never responded to my questions, who handled me like a prized *object* to be carefully repaired. I don't think he saw me as a human being at all, but as a weapon, the most deadly in the Queen's arsenal. So his was an important task, almost a sacred trust, but an impersonal one.

The two of them, with or without the help of other servants, sponge-bathed me, changed bandages, inspected my wounds, spooned broth when I couldn't find the strength to eat. I watched all this with a hazy detachment, unable to comprehend how seriously injured I had been, how near I had been to death from simple blood-loss.

When I tried to speak, the doctor would merely avert his gaze and pretend he hadn't heard. Takpetor said little either. He brushed off all my inquiries with phrases like, 'Her Divinity is pleased' or 'Her Eternity thinks of you often.'

I asked about Tica, and all he said was, 'The Princess Royal is likewise grateful to you.'

I tried to take hope from that, but I knew it was just a formula.

Sometimes my memory blacked out for what must have been hours at a time. I'd find myself among the books, in the middle of some volume I had never read before. I'd flip back to what I must have read just then, and Sekenre at least didn't recognize it.

Or I'd awake seated at a table, in my hands a bottle containing one of the soul-captives. If anything had been said between us, I didn't remember it.

Again, a gap of indeterminate time, and I was standing before the mirror, naked to the waist, examining the livid, half-healed scar like a huge sun-burst on my right shoulder and the deep traceries all over the upper part of my arm where the leather apron hadn't covered it. Such was the calligraphy of pain, the history of my career recorded in my own flesh. Perhaps one of my other selves saw the pattern, divined a secret there. Or the Sybil did. I did not.

I'd open my own notebooks and discover things there which I hadn't written. Yes, Father, I found your little story, and I studied it for a long time. But you know that.

This followed it:

> *Out of the darkness, light is rising,*
> *Out of the light, the sacred Earth.*
> *Out of the Earth, the holy River,*
> *From mud of the River, arise the gods.*
> *Out of the god-dreams, mankind wakens,*
> *Out of the man-dreams, returns the dark.*
> *Out of the darkness, Death arises,*
> *In dread of Death, the sorcerer dreams.*

I think the peculiar script was Tannivar's. I could barely make it out.

All these things were disturbing, yes, but worst of all was the time I awoke in the cellar, my hands dirty from having rubbed them, perhaps lovingly, over the side of the furnace. I wept and ran from the place, crashing into apparatus, entangling myself in chains and manacles. Upstairs, I piled more and more atop the trapdoor. I frantically searched for hammer and nails to fasten it shut, but there was nothing. I fainted, exhausted, and Takpetor found me that way. He seemed genuinely frightened. A slave ran for the doctor, who showed no emotion at all. My wrist throbbed hideously. I think I had broken it again.

But I did mend, slowly, and those within me receded. Sekenre wore the body. No one else.

I started writing in this book again. If I kept my wrist bandaged tightly, I could hold a pen, at least well enough to do plain text. But I didn't attempt any elaborate initial letters.

Lekkanut-Na spoke to me one day, in her old manner, the frog-voice coming out of my own throat.

'Sekenre, you're still a mess.' Her tone was of an amused but scolding parent.

I allowed her to continue. It felt right.

'Who cares?' I said.

'Well, if no one else, *I* do.'

I had been nowhere and seen no one. The doctor ceased his visits. Even Takpetor hadn't shown himself for a while. There were only the servants, silent, virtually invisible. They'd leave a basket of food at my door or take dirty laundry if there was any.

Winter had arrived. Sometimes I sat in the garden in the afternoons, but dressed more warmly. The skies were often overcast. The rains had just begun, often no more than a spray from the gray sky, or a mist that the sun didn't burn off. But if I sat there, no one interrupted me. I was completely alone.

Only by means of the mirror did I learn that the Zargati host was long since scattered, bands of the invaders slipping away in the night, more often than not caught in ambush and massacred by the Queen's counter-attacking soldiers.

The Zargati king Habu-Ita-Zhad, the Bloody Lion, hung impaled on a stake before the city to feast the flies and buzzards, but no one else. The other barbarians were merely butchered. They always fought to the death, and could not be taken as slaves.

Some practical-minded official ordered all the other stakes taken down, sawed into logs, and carted into the city for fuel. Wood is, after all, scarce in the Delta.

And far to the south, the black nations beyond the desert rose up and utterly destroyed the Zargati oppressors, until what few survived lived as robbers, as scavengers, competing with jackals for carrion.

How did the people of the south learn so quickly what had happened in the Delta? Someone else's mirror, I supposed. Someone else's sorcery. I didn't care. I put all such matters from my mind. I had so much to do, and, indeed, as Lekkanut-Na had told me, very little time left.

Still, she was almost a friend, a comfortable presence. I let her nag me.

'Get up, Sekenre. You're completely appalling. *Look* at yourself.'

The mirror hovered in the middle of the laboratory. With a thought, I turned it so I could see the reflection from my table and high stool.

'A mess,' said Lekkanut-Na. 'I mean, there are sorcerers who are elegant, who are even accounted dandies, who are bejewelled and refined like intricate gems slowly polished over the centuries. Every aspect of them shows it, speech, dress, grooming, manner, merely the way they stand or turn their head, but, no, not *Sekenre*—'

I slid from the stool. The mirror approached me. I looked at myself and saw that my hair was hopelessly tangled, that my cheeks and chin were stained with ink from my having idly touched myself with blackened fingers. Somehow I always managed to get ink all over myself, though my pages were immaculate, as were the other books.

The outsized neck of the shirt I wore exposed my whole chest. Streaks there, too. I vaguely remembered spilling a bottle of ink, desperately wiping it off the tabletop with my shirt-tail while setting the page I was working on out of harm's way.

Lekkanut-Na was right. I was a mess: trousers rolled up, dirty knees, grubby feet almost as black as my hands.

I shrugged. 'Well, I've been busy.'

'You forget to eat. You only sleep when you fall over from exhaustion. It's a wonder you remember to—'

'Well, if I don't eat, I won't have to.'

Had she been able to control my hands, she would have poked me.

'You don't smell particularly bad somehow. I think you've dried out. You're covered with dust. I lay in dust for hundreds of years, Sekenre. I'm tired of it.'

I let her use my hands. She pulled off my shirt. I stood there, hugging my shoulders against the chill. I had to admit I looked haggard, shadowed around the eyes, as gaunt as I had ever been, every rib showing.

'Ghastly,' she said.

'Well,' I said, forcing a smile. 'What do you recommend?'

'Start with a bath. Definitely that first.'

'But, the Ceremony of the Nine Angles—'

'—would kill you if you were interrupted by, for instance, fainting from hunger and lack of sleep in the middle of it. You haven't begun it. You've only studied the procedure. It's safe to pause here. Take my word for it.'

'You were the one who said I didn't have much time.'

'I also said that in sorcery the pace of time is different. When you go on for centuries, a few hours may sometimes be allowed to slip by. This afternoon, Sekenre, you have my permission to dawdle.'

'Doing what?'

'*Bathing.* That first.'

So I stepped outside. For once the sun had broken through the clouds. The light dazzled me. I all but groped my way across the garden to the bath house. The attendant there was asleep in a swinging chair hung from a tree. But he heard me coming, dropped down, muttered obsequiously, and scrambled down into the lower chamber to put logs on the fire. He probably thought my appearance appalling too, but being a slave voiced no opinion.

He shut the door from the outside. Sorcerers, I was beginning to appreciate, always bathe in secret, to conceal their peculiarities, transformations, strengths, and vulnerabilities.

I regarded my assorted wounds and scars, and for a moment the amusing tone of the whole sequence of events changed. I was afraid. I could only consider that I had gained so many marks of, ah, distinction in less than a year. What sort of malformed, mutilated wreck would I be in a hundred years, or even five?

Could I some day remove the magic, let the blood flow, and heal normally? That would be dangerous. I'd be helpless all the while. And what if the arrow-hole in my side were, in fact, fatal?

No more lying about naked in the sun, whether Lekkanut-Na enjoyed it or not.

I closed the shutters and even the skylight, and bathed alone in the dark, with only a single lamp flickering by the water's edge.

I lay back in the warm water and let myself float. Lekkanut-Na was content. I drifted off to sleep, slipped under the water, and sat up, sputtering.

Then, lamp in hand, I padded into the adjoining chamber and slid into another tiled pool, where the water was so frigid I gasped, interrupting Lekkanut-Na, who softly sang some old song I didn't know.

I sat in the darkness, teeth chattering. I thought I heard a footstep and looked up.

'It's just the wind,' she said.

'What wind? In here?'

'Try to relax. After we're done here, you will rest until this evening, *eat a decent meal for once,* and tonight we'll go into the city. Have you considered, Sekenre, that you've dwelt here for many months, but still the City of the Delta is completely unknown to you?'

'Ah, no.'

'Well, *do* consider. *I* feel like a prisoner here, Sekenre. I don't know about you. But if you can invade the enemy's camp with your mirror, you should be able to slip out of the palace every once in a while. Don't be afraid to use your powers frivolously when the occasion warrants it.'

'What?'

'You are *so* solemn, *so* serious, young man. It isn't natural—'

'Oh—?'

'Will it be monosyllables from now on, then? Well, while you're *oh*ing and *what*ing and *ah, no*ing, consider the history of the noted Vadlaeric, a sorcerer of Perthinos—'

'Where?'

'Far away, Sekenre. Never mind. What matters is that his particular path to sorcery was *laughter*. The Cackling One, they called Vadlaeric. It *is* possible for a sorcerer to laugh, to be merry, to be more than a somber, overwrought bore. I bet you don't even know what a *joke* is, Sekenre?'

'I don't have much occasion for joking,' I said.

'Your vocabulary's getting better, anyway. Huh? What? Ah, no . . .'

But I didn't manage to rest easily that afternoon. I lay down on my bed in the library, and dreamed that I was in the bottle with Haryn-Isha, the Soul-of-a-Fish who swam in blood—

I fled from him, trying to walk on the surface of the sea of blood inside the bottle, sinking down, splashing, sputtering. I wore Moon's over-sized sorcerer's robe, which had become soaked in blood, dragging me down. I couldn't get it off.

Haryn-Isha rose up, a skinless, eyeless horror with jaws stretched wide as a crocodile's, calling my name, even my secret, true-name: 'Heron. Come here, Heron-boy. This is the end of the story of the Heron-boy who pretended he was what he was not—'

He caught my feet in his jaws. All the while the huge figures of Vashtem and Tannivar and the mountain of flesh that was Lekkanut-Na towered over me, distorted by the glass of the bottle. I called out to them, but if they heard me, they merely heard the squeakings of an insect-like Sekenre inside the bottle on the tabletop before them, a curious specimen, nothing more. They spoke among themselves in voices like distant thunder.

I awoke, sweating and shaken. Lekkanut-Na assumed the body. She made me get up, strip everything off, and take a quick sponge bath, to get rid of the sweat.

'We can't have you smelling like a stable, not tonight.'

'Oh.'

'As articulate as ever, I see. Well, get dressed, not as a sorcerer, but as Sekenre, so you won't be noticed. That's your strength and your protection. I think you know that. Everyone underestimates you. They wouldn't if you were five years older and built like a hero. So don't feel bad about your appearance.'

'How could I? I've never had any other.' I laughed softly.

'Sekenre, if I didn't know you better, I'd think you were trying to make a joke.'

'Oh.'

'Never mind. Get dressed.'

I didn't have much to choose from, the coat and trousers Tica had bought for me in Thadistaphon, one of my predecessor's plain shirts which I could stuff down inside the trousers. My shoes. No jewelry at all. I tied my hair behind my head with a string.

'Now what?' I said.

'We're going into the city, Sekenre. It is a night of festival, of rejoicing that the rains have come, also, this year, that the city has been saved from the Zargati. You're going to *enjoy yourself,* whether you like it or not.'

I shrugged. She wouldn't be denied.

'Now look at yourself,' she said. 'What do you see?'

I stood before the mirror. Here was an ordinary young man who might have been either a Reedlander or Deltan, well enough dressed to be respectable, but probably not rich.

Then the image changed, and thousands of shining motes swam in utter darkness, as if the stars really were how the poets describe them, bubbles drifting in the foam of eternity.

They weren't stars. The lights resolved themselves into thousands of paper lanterns, some of them cut or painted into the shapes of birds, strange beasts, or ludicrous faces, strung from rooftop to rooftop, or held aloft on sticks by revellers in fantastic costumes. Here, a man dressed as a huge, silver-winged serpent, there, a clown walking above the crowd on stilts, his garb all streamers and glitter. A masked woman whirled in a frenzied dance, her gown seemingly ablaze with brilliant light. And among these were the plain-clad folk of the City of the Delta, many youths, and running, shouting children.

'*There,*' Lekkanut-Na said, pointing with my hand to an open space by a doorway, behind a row of barrels. I reached into the mirror, caught hold of the rim of a barrel, and pulled myself through.

The sudden noise of the festival was like an explosion, the music and laughter echoing like thunder in the narrow street. I walked from behind the barrels. No one had noticed my advent. I moved into the crowd, into the cool evening air.

I must have spent at least an hour merely wandering, gaping at the costumes, and the multitudes of masks, at the images of the many gods and demigods borne above the heads of the crowd on the shoulders of devotees. This endless mass of humanity was like a sea. I let the tide take me, and we spilled out into one of the great public squares of the capital. I stood still, clinging to a post, jostled by passers-by as I stared up in amazement at the huge temples with their polished black pillars gleaming by torchlight, at the countless larger-than-life statues of kings and heroes and nobles which so crowded the rooftops that they seemed another festival crowd in their own right, gazing down on us from the heavens. Indeed, many of them might have held the stars in their hands; but actually they only held more lanterns.

Someone caught me by the shoulder, whirling me around. I broke free, alarmed. I stepped back and found myself confronting a squat bearded man with a broad grin on his face. He held a cluster of multi-colored masks set on sticks.

'Take one,' he said. 'For you.'

Puzzled, I selected one. I twirled it. I saw that it was made of stiff paper and painted, with some kind of sparkling chips set in the paint.

'That'll be one fish.'

'What?' I had no idea what he meant. Was it some obscure custom in the Delta to trade masks for fish? I certainly hadn't thought to bring any *fish* along, living or dead.

(Within me, Lekkanut-Na chuckled, infinitely amused.)

The man made an exaggerated frown. 'You have *none?* Alas, poor boy.'

'I don't know what you mean—'

'Not from around here?'

'No, from Reedland.'

Again he frowned and shrugged in his comic way. 'Well then, poor boy from Reedland, let me explain to you that in the City of the Delta *this* is the only kind of fish anybody cares about –' He held up a small coin.

I'd never had occasion to spend money since my arrival in the city, but I had a little purse with me, on a thong around my neck. That had been Lekkanut-Na's idea. I drew it out of my shirt and went through such wealth as I found until I produced a copper piece which indeed had a fish on it. I had no idea what the fish signified. In the dark, I couldn't read the inscription. I had no idea what the coin was worth either, but I gave it to the man, whereupon he vanished into the crowd so quickly that it almost seemed – I told myself jokingly – magical.

Canopied booths filled the vast forum, like a shabby, brightly-decorated city-within-a-city. I wandered through the lanes and passages, coming to open spaces where acrobats tumbled or strong men lifted absurd weights. One performer in particular caught my attention: an unbelievably huge, fat, sweating fellow grunting as he heaved aloft on his shoulders a bronze statue of a similarly huge, fat, foolish-faced man with a basket in his arms. The crowd laughed and cheered when someone tossed a coin into the bronze basket. Sometimes someone tossed a stone instead. The athlete bared his teeth, hissing, but the crowd only laughed and cheered some more. The point seemed to be that if he dropped the statue, everyone would scramble for the money. If not, he could keep it. He seemed determined to keep it.

An older woman with a mask like mine leaned over and spoke to me through the mask.

'It's an allegory of human vanity.'

'Oh.'

I slipped away. For all that the weight-lifter gleamed with sweat, I was starting to shiver. The night air was colder than I'd expected. I laced up the front of my shirt and wished I'd worn something heavier.

I paid another fish-coin and was admitted into a tent, having no idea what I was to see. Musicians perched in high chairs played on reed pipes. Grotesquely deformed people did a kind of dance in a circle of dirt, some without arms or legs wriggling like worms. A sad-faced girl about my own age fluttered useless, translucent wings as she staggered stiffly around and around in a trance, her eyes closed. Vestigial arms no longer than my fingers twitched at her shoulders, the tiny hands clutching and unclutching.

(*Cast-offs from failed magical experiments,* said Lekkanut-Na within me, *here for the ignorant to gawk at. I suppose the only alternative is for them to starve, but unless you're really fascinated, let's go.*)

I left, ashamed at having been there, trying to hide behind my paper mask. I noticed for the first time that the face was that of a fish. A fish costing a fish. If it was a joke, I didn't get it.

Many more revellers carried such masks. Outside the tent, I encountered a dozen or so young men and women, aristocrats from the look of them. They all bowed before me, making elaborate gestures I tried to imitate. They spoke words I didn't know, not another language, it seemed, but some sort of special vocabulary I was supposed to recognize. The women held out costly gifts, jewelry, a silver dagger, a golden mirror, while the men asked the same incomprehensible questions, waiting for a response.

When it was clear I wasn't following, the women put the gifts away.

'He isn't of the wind,' someone said.

'Or of the cloud.'

'Or of the water.'

'Another fake.'

They went away, bursting into laughter a short distance off. I lowered my mask and stared after them. I still hadn't the slightest idea what any of it meant.

I slipped the mask under my belt. Overhead, the sky suddenly burst with thunderous light, and for a few seconds a winged dragon whirled and writhed, then faded into darkness a little at a time. His tail lingered longer than the rest. Cinders rained gently down.

The crowd gaped at the wonder of it, laughing and cheering. Nearby, a small child cried.

The dragon was a marvel, I decided, but the true wonder of this night was that I could mix with all these people and no one shrieked with dread to discover among them Sekenre, the terrible sorcerer, slayer of kings, the boy who spoke with corpses.

No, none of that. Just a boy who mangled the common city tongue with his Reedlandish accent.

I felt light-headed, *free*, as if heavy shackles had dropped off me.

Still I wandered, once spending two more fish for what was indeed a fish, sweetened and served on a skewer. Grease ran down my chin. I wiped it with my sleeve.

For a while I watched a religious drama performed by brightly-garbed and masked players on a wheeled stage which moved slowly through the crowd. It was impossible to follow the story without, literally, following the cart. I did so, but didn't understand much anyway, though the characters were familiar enough: the crocodile-headed man was unquestionably supposed to be Surat-Kemad, the lady in blue, Shedelvendra the Mother of Waters, the child bearing the leaf and the leafless branch symbolizing the passage of time.

I went into another tent. (*You'll like this better,* Lekkanut-Na said inside my mind.)

Inside, laughing, shouting children ran around and mock-fought and gradually settled into seats. I noticed, too, a few people my own age, or even older, but most of the audience were children. I glanced down once, to reassure myself that I was indeed wearing shoes and thus had passed into manhood. I blushed at how foolish I was being. Here in the Delta, it didn't matter what you wore on your feet. You were of a given age and considered an adult, or you were not. I was now by my count sixteen and a few months, though I knew I was small and could be taken for much younger. But no one cared.

A conjurer emerged onto a rickety stage, doing standard tricks which I suppose must be universal: pretending to find a coin or an egg or a wriggling, live fish in a customer's ear, birds fluttering from his sleeves, swallowing fire and breathing it out again. He told jokes. The audience laughed. I even understood a few of them.

Suddenly I realized that the conjurer's gaze was upon me.

Everyone turned to look. I stood with my hands in my pockets, trying to be inconspicuous.

'My boy, my boy,' he said, pointing. 'You there. Why so glum? Don't you know how to smile? Come here.'

Dozens of hands propelled me forward. The children clapped and cheered. The conjurer took my by the arm and hauled me up onto the platform with him.

'Well,' he said, 'I shall have to conjure happiness into you.' I could smell wine on his breath. He was more than a little drunk, I could tell, and possessed no trace of true magic, let alone sorcery. The joke was very much on him. This amusing fraud had found himself a genuine sorcerer. For once I remembered what Lekkanut-Na had said about using one's powers frivolously when the occasion warranted.

'Smile!' the conjurer said. He squeezed my face. The children found that uproarious. I pulled away, unsmiling.

He produced a pigeon out of my sleeve, but the bird was made of paper. Inside was a piece of candy, which he pressed into my hands. I slipped it into my jacket pocket for later.

The conjurer regarded me with that same ridiculously forlorn expression the mask-seller had used. The audience laughed.

'Let me try again.'

He eased a bright blue scarf out of his own ear with long, exaggerated motions, pretending to wince at the effort.

What followed was my doing: The blue scarf was tied to a red one, then a yellow, then a green, each of which came to life as if laid over the faces of laughing children. The cloth faces actually *laughed,* as did the children in the front row, who recognized their own images. Next came a white scarf in the likeness of a boy in the back who made funny faces and shouted. The white scarf shouted.

The conjurer grew ever more alarmed, but he kept on pulling out scarves. I played the role of his assistant, holding up the long strings of them so the onlookers could see the faces clearly. I spread the scarves over the platform stage, then made my way through the now compliant crowd and hung strings of scarves from the tent-posts. Now the laughter was redoubled, and still the poor conjurer frantically pulled scarves out of his ear, his eyes wide with fear now, the scarves flopping at his feet like beached fish, wriggling overhead, laughing and chattering back.

At the very last, out came two much larger scarves. I held up my own. It hung down past my knees, a huge image of my own face. The last scarf was in the likeness of the conjurer. I gave it to him. He took it with limp fingers.

'That's *incredible!*' my scarf said. 'How did you *do* that?'

'Foolish boy!' his scarf replied gravely. 'I am a mighty magician. I cannot reveal my secrets to mere rabble! Be gone!'

I stuffed my scarf into my jacket, bowed politely, and slipped down behind the stage and out the back of the tent.

And then? Did I smile at last? Did I double over in uncontrolled hilarity at my little joke? Certainly Lekkanut-Na thought it was funny. But what of Sekenre? Ah, mystery of mysteries, ever to remain one of sorcery's most esoteric secrets!

I wished Tica could have been with me, to see it all.

Outside, the crowd began to thin. It seemed later than it should have been, almost dawn. The mist in the air gave way to a light, steady drizzle. I hugged myself against the cold. The dampness made my throat raw.

I wondered if I had merely lost track of time. But I think it was more, as the masked lady had explained, an allegory, of my own life and folly. For behold, the sorcerer may emerge from the shadows for a little while, but he is like the elegantly clad, perfumed corpse come from the grave to attend a festival. Behind his wit, his pleasantries, the strangeness of sorcery lingers. The shadows soon close over him again.

It was time to leave. I wandered through the city, alone again in deserted streets. The statues on the rooftops, their lanterns now extinguished, became once more dark colossi, indifferent to all below.

The winter rains had truly arrived. Now the downpour fell ever harder. I ran to the shelter of the porch of a small, round temple, and stood there among the pillars while the wind drove the rain in waving sheets. Water lapped at my feet. I stepped back, into the darkness, now thoroughly wet, cold, beginning to cough from the dampness that had settled inside me. It was time to return to the palace, to get warm and dry, but then I realized that there was no easy, magical solution. I couldn't use a puddle as a mirror. There wasn't enough light.

Thunder rumbled far away, drawing slowly nearer as the storm's fury grew.

I closed my hands together and tried to make the magical fire flow through me. But I was too cold, too tired. My concentration faltered.

I slid down, crouching behind a pillar to hide from the worst of the rain, afraid that I'd have to spend the night here, or else go to the palace gate at this hour and try to convince the guards that I was who I claimed to be.

Then I folded my hands once more, opened them, and two tiny white flames flickered on either palm. By this I could see just a little of the temple porch, the base of the next pillar over, and some of the reliefs on the door: a winged maiden, a serpent with an eagle's head, a fish walking on human legs.

A footstep shuffled nearby. I cupped my hands to hide the flames. Gradually I realized that I was not alone, that many figures stood among the pillars all around me. The air took on a heavy, wet stench, like old leather or decaying straw.

Lightning lit up the whole sky, and I knew what temple this was: the great figure of Surat-Kemad extended all the way up the bronze door, writhing among the other reliefs. This was a shrine of Death and those on the porch with me were corpses, or ghosts, some sort of revenants of the unconsecrated dead who flocked to the temple at this hour to be reconciled with the god. But the door was barred. The priests had gone home. This porch was now part of *Leshé,* on the borderland of dreams and death, where visions came.

Around me, the dead spoke in the language of the dead:

'Brothers, we shall find Vashtem soon. I smell him. He is near.'

'The betrayer, the blasphemer, who sought to hide in the belly of Surat-Hemad.'

'Even Vashtem, who dared speak the Great Name.'

'Even Vashtem, who is many others.'

'We shall be avenged soon.'

'Let him become as one of us. That shall be the beginning of his punishment.'

In my fear I clasped my hands together, extinguishing the flames.

'. . . near . . .'

'. . . very soon . . .'

'. . . torments awaiting him . . .'

Now the storm was directly overhead. A thunderous flash illuminated the whole city as bright as day. I could see down a long street, into the great forum where the festival had been held, and out across the rooftops, far, far—

The corpses turned toward me, like bundles of rags and sticks shifting in the wind.

In that instant, I think they recognized me. But in that instant, too, I saw myself reflected in rainwater, and behind me, in the reflection, I made out the Queen's garden, that platform where I used to lie in the sun; now row upon row of hedges weaving in the wind; dead flowers, mud.

I leapt through.

It was time to leave.

But first, I must tell of one more thing, a foolish thing I did, less out of hope, I think, than to convince myself it was time to go.

Or at last that is how it seems now. It eases the pain to remember it that way.

The following afternoon, the sky was almost clear, the sun intermittently bright, though the air was cool from the onset of the winter rains. It would rain every day for months now.

But, when it wasn't raining, the Queen, the Princess Royal, and their attendants still walked in the garden, enjoying such respite as there was.

My sorcerer's mirror showed me as much. I spied on them. Then I went to meet them, stepping through the mirror, emerging behind a hedge.

When I came face-to-face with the royal party, the guards first lowered their spears to block me, then raised them again, nervously.

I nodded, to the Queen, then to Tica. The Princess Royal stood stiffly, hands folded before her, wearing an elaborate gown with a stiff lace collar, silver serpent-necklaces arranged down her front in careful sequence. I peered into her painted face for even a trace of the Tica with whom I had travelled along the River. I wasn't sure any of her remained. She regarded me without expression.

I was well aware of how incongruous I looked in such company, barefoot because my shoes were still soaked from last night's excursion, wearing my predecessor's plain, ill-fitting clothing, the long scarf around my neck because I'd caught cold. I didn't care.

'Sekenre,' the Queen said. 'We did not summon you.'

I shrugged. 'I know. But I wanted to talk to you.'

Some of the Queen's women gasped at this effrontery. A eunuch looked to her, as if for a signal. The guards stood at attention, impassive.

'Very well, then,' said the Queen.

'I mean alone, you and me and Tica.'

No one reacted to this further lapse of etiquette.

Queen Hapsenecuit nodded. 'Very well, then.' She waved her attendants off, took Tica by the hand, and walked a short way. I followed, the guards behind me. We came to an enclosure of hedges. The guards remained outside. I went in, hesitantly, and found the Queen and the Princess Royal side-by-side seated on a bench, making room for me to sit beside Tica.

There, alone, Queen Hapsenecuit became Lady Necu again. She sighed.

'Sekenre, I am afraid we'll never make a courtier out of you. You have no sense of propriety or style.'

Tica smiled, then covered her mouth with her hand.

'I wanted . . . It's hard to say.'

'You'll have to, Sekenre.' the Queen said. 'This was your idea, not mine.'

'I don't know how, really.'

283

'Try using words. You're rather good with them sometimes.'

Tica laughed this time, but broke off suddenly. She sat very upright, very still, staring down into her lap.

I fumbled in my pockets for a little leather box. I gave it to Tica.

'This is for you,' I said.

She accepted it, startled, and opened it. A blue-winged butterfly emerged, a thing of paper and wires but animate. It alighted on her hand and sat there, opening and closing its wings slowly.

'Oh! It's lovely!'

'I made that for you. Give it a name, and it'll always come when you call.'

The Queen shifted impatiently. 'Sekenre, if all you wanted to do was present my daughter with a gift, you could have passed it on through the chamberlains.'

'No, I—'

'Oh, Sekenre,' said Tica, 'it is a beautiful wedding-present. Thank you.'

That startled me as if I'd been hit. '*Wedding* present?'

'Sekenre?' said Tica. 'Didn't you know?'

I turned to the Queen helplessly. She cleared her throat and spoke like a herald, louder than she had to. 'The Princess Kanratica is to marry the Prince Royal Wenamon, Fifth of that revered name, three weeks from today, at the Feast of the River's Rising.' In a more natural voice she added, 'My diviners tell me it is a most propitious time.'

I didn't know what to say. Nothing made sense. The dead king's *grandson?* 'But ... but ... he's only *five years old.*'

'In a dynastic marriage, Sekenre, such inconveniences must be tolerated. Time will correct them.'

'But Tica and I—'

The Queen laughed gently, not maliciously, then turned to me, shaking her head slowly. Tica, between us, nudged the butterfly back into the box with her finger and snapped the lid shut. She sat still and red-faced, her hands folded tightly over the box in her lap.

'She and you *what*, Sekenre? What could you have possibly

imagined? You may be a sorcerer, but you are still very young, younger, I think, even than your years. In the first pangs of what you think is love, you suddenly imagine you're fit to marry a princess. Is that what you came here to ask me? Yes, it is. I won't even pose that as a question. I see it all. The obsession has been in the back of your mind, at least, for a long time. Admit it. In odd moments, whenever you're not distracted by sorcery, you think of my daughter. Isn't that so?'

'Yes, it is,' I said meekly.

'But can't you see, dear child, that all political considerations aside, your peculiar condition makes you entirely unsuitable to be her husband?'

I couldn't meet the Queen's gaze. I stared down at the ground.

'I don't know what you mean.'

'I am certain that you *do.*' With a sudden grunt at the effort, she reached across Tica and grabbed hold of my trouser leg, pulling me around sideways until my leg was in Tica's lap. I was so amazed that I made no resistance at all, even when Hapsenecuit pulled up the trouser leg and ran her hand over my bare shin and calf. Tica was fully as astonished as I, utterly motionless, staring.

'It's been a while since I was of such an age,' the Queen said, 'or since I had anything to do with boys of such an age, Sekenre, but you are now, by my count, past sixteen, and in the remote depths of my memory I seem to recall that boys past sixteen start to develop hair on their legs.'

Again this was so ludicrous, so incongruous, that I couldn't find any words. I thought the Queen had gone mad. Time was suspended, there, in that impossible instant.

But she spoke sanely enough, and, I think, with genuine sadness in her voice.

'Sekenre, do not deceive yourself. You know better than I do what effect sorcery has on the sorcerer. You will live for centuries if you are not slain. From the instant you became a sorcerer, time stopped for you. You ceased to age physically. You will always be as you are, as you were when you slew your father and became what you have become. It is common knowledge about sorcerers. Think what it means. If you married my daughter, what would you do? Remain young while she grew old, pretend to be her son, then her grandson, then preside over her funeral as if not a day had passed in your endless youth? That would be a cruel thing for both of you. And wouldn't it be worse for any children you might have, for your son to seem older than his father, to grow gray and bent and shuffle off into death while his father was still a boy—?'

She was right of course. I broke free and ran out of the hedges, past the startled guards, my face streaming with the tears which, as common knowledge has it, no sorcerer is able to weep.

Time to leave. There could be no more delay in my education as a sorcerer, my final initiation into the mysteries of darkness. No turning back. I would attend the College of Shadows, to learn, to master, to kill, or to die. It had to be done. There was no other way.

But where is this college?

Why, it is wherever there are shadows, wherever the mind turns toward the hidden darkness, all around us, invisible except to those eyes which are opened.

But the sorcerer needs to be prudent about where he enters the college. The beginning point of the journey must be chosen well.

So I packed what I wanted from Moon's laboratory: a satchel of spare clothes, a blanket, provisions of bread, cheese, smoked meat, a flask of sweet, Deltan wine, plus my pens, inks, and precious manuscripts, these in a waterproofed leather satchel all their own.

I took none of his books, nothing from the tons of apparatus he had left me. That was not my way. If I was ever to be more than a trickster and occasional assassin, I would have to find my individual path into sorcery.

That insight was, I think, the first step on my journey, right there, the product of my own thought rather than someone else's. Before, I had been a vessel filled up by others. No more.

I sat at my desk in Moon's laboratory. The sorcerer's mirror floated in the air before me, quivering slightly. I did not gaze into it even once, but concentrated on my work, writing the last page of the tale of my life, bringing my book up to date, shaping my whole self into words. This, this book, this became Sekenre, these characters before your eyes now, Reader. I found true magic in their *making*.

With infinite care, I illuminated the capital which begins this chapter, drawing a little picture inside the letter, recalling from memory every detail of a certain room, with its shelves and books and whispering bottles, with the long couch in the middle of the floor where once the priests of the City of Reeds dressed a fearsome corpse, replacing his eyes with coins.

The hours passed, and after a while I could smell the wind blowing in off the marshes and hear the calls of the river birds. The day faded. I looked up, searching for a candle, and discovered that, already, I was no longer in the royal palace in the City of the Delta, but in the workroom of my father's house where it stood like a wading heron, somewhere among the reeds along the bank of the Great River.

Chapter 14: The Gatekeeper

Whir-click-click. Wheeze.

I looked up suddenly, more startled than alarmed. I sat at my father's desk now, pen still in hand, parchment page spread before me with the ink of its illuminated capital still gleaming wet.

Whir. Click. Click.

My cloth satchel containing provisions hung from my left shoulder. I let it slide to the floor, then put the pen down, careful not to damage the page. The water-proofed leather manuscript satchel lay in my lap. I lowered it to the floor also.

Whir.

I slid my chair back and stood up. The noise came from the darkened far end of the room, from somewhere among the shelves of bottles, the bookshelves, the untidy heaps of wooden crates. As always, the room seemed to have changed subtly since the last time I had been there.

Whir. Click.

I fumbled for a candle in the desk drawers, found one, and clapped my right hand open and closed very quickly. A tiny blue flame rose from my palm. I lit the candle with it, then closed my hand again.

I too had changed subtly. That trick was new, trivial, but part of the deliberate use of body-light where before it merely burst forth like sweat.

Click.

'Who is there?' I said in a voice barely above a whisper, raising the candle.

A fragment of darkness separated itself from the surrounding gloom, and what might have been an old man stood before me.

'I am the gatekeeper,' he said, speaking Reedlandish in an accent I'd never heard before. 'If you seek admittance to the College of Shadows, you must find your way past me.'

'This is my father's house. I grew up here.'

'It also is the anteroom to the Invisible Lodge, the place of countless names.' He drew nearer. I began to doubt that he was a human being at all. His face moved like a parchment mask as he spoke, but it didn't move quite ... properly. It is hard to describe. His skin seemed to fold and wrinkle in the wrong places. His eyes were black, featureless voids.

'I am ...' I hesitated to give even my common name. This was some kind of test. I could yield no advantage, however slight.

I held out my right hand as if to take his in greeting.

'You are the young man with the pierced wrist. Further description is as yet unnecessary.'

I made a fist and withdrew my hand. The arrow-scar showed, but the gatekeeper's eyesight had to be far better than mine to make out such detail in the semi-darkness.

'I do indeed seek admittance,' I said. 'I am a sorcerer and the son of a sorcerer.'

'Ah.' *Whirr. Click.*

The gatekeeper now stood in front of me, the desk between us. As he held up his own right hand, I saw that it wasn't a living extremity at all, but a contrivance of metal rods, springs, and leather. It twisted strangely at the wrist, making the sounds I'd heard.

Click. He reached down as if to touch my manuscript, index finger hovering above the illuminated capital. I felt a flash of anger, then fear. I didn't know what I would do if he smeared the capital. But his hand just hovered there. I glared at it.

'A sorcerer needs to be careful about where he reaches with his hand,' he said, slowly raising the contrivance to point at my face.

But I didn't think him merely someone who had lost a hand. His whole body seemed as vaguely *wrong* as his face, proportioned and jointed and moving with indefinable strangeness, as if beneath his dark robe he were no more than a clockwork thing of rods and wires and gears, weights rising and falling on delicate chains, water or sand dribbling through glass veins.

Nor did I believe his remark was intended as a warning, well-intentioned or otherwise. Sorcery is never that simple. Some things recur in a sorcerer's life, disappearing and reappearing for no apparent reason, but with symbolic import, like auspices forming in clouds even as the priest studies them.

I stood as I do when I'm uneasy, hands clutching my sides, scrunching my toes inside my shoes; waiting for him to do something more. I expected a faint touch inside my mind, a vision of some sort, or a further apparition.

But the only sensation was of my other selves stirring within me, peering out eagerly, as if they were crowded around a tiny window.

Suddenly Dekac-Natae-Tsah, called Moon, manifested himself as I tried to speak. Dry wind rushed up out of my throat, like smoke from a chimney. I coughed and doubled over, eyes watering. Moon forced me upright, held me rigid, and a beam of light shot from my mouth, penetrating the gatekeeper, revealing him to be not even a thing of gears and rods, but spiderwebs and dust, a shadow given motion, but no more alive than a shadow.

The mechanical hand fell onto the desk with a thud. The gatekeeper's face fluttered to the floor. Nothing more remained of him.

Incredible as it sounds, the first thing I did was to rescue my manuscript. I tossed the hand aside, then held the page up to the window, where the fading light showed that my carefully-wrought capital had indeed been smeared.

I put it down, sighing. Only then did I consider the possibility of further enemies hiding in the darkness, of further traps. But nothing was apparent, here, now. I could safely stand at the desk for a few minutes, at least.

I raised my own hand to my mouth, in a half-conscious effort to prevent any more surprises. I felt Moon settling down within me, laughing.

'I too am part of the common enterprise now, Sekenre, son of Vashtem,' he said.

I exhaled slowly. No more smoke. No more burning light. Only breath.

I took a silent poll of Vashtem, Tannivar, Orkanre, Talno, Lekkanut-Na, and all the rest. Had I passed the test in their opinion, or failed? Was I within the Shadowed College now, or still on the doorstep?

Their thoughts remained hidden. I couldn't compel them to speak.

I wondered if Moon's action had been to protect us, or to prevent me from discovering something. He was part of me, true, but I had killed him, and he might still seek revenge.

I busied myself with the parchment page, fitting it into the carrying-box for unfinished sheets. I would repair the capital later. The damage wasn't too bad, and the rest of the text was all right. I put the box in my waterproof satchel, held the satchel under my arm, and slung the other satchel over my shoulder.

I stepped away from the desk and retrieved the mechanical hand, peeling back the leather skin to reveal its mechanism, a thing complex and undeniably clever, but merely an inanimate device and of no great interest. The paper mask was less impressive but more enigmatic, a mere sheet with crudely-drawn features and holes for the eyes. It had lost all semblance of a living face.

I was home again, here in my father's house. No, in *my* house, which I had inherited from my father. For a little while at least, I was not a sorcerer in the anteroom of the College of Shadows, but Sekenre, who had come home.

I explored cautiously, checking for uninvited and unexpected inhabitants to be sure, but I went over the place lovingly, touching familiar objects, standing in familiar rooms, remembering.

Back in the workroom, I picked up the bottle containing what had once been the Zargati sorcerer Haryn-Isha, whose secret name meant Soul-of-a-Fish.

'How are you swimming now, Fish?' I said.

The thing in the bottle screamed in its tiny, piping voice and flopped against the glass. Revolted, I replaced the bottle on the shelf.

For the most part, the house was as I had last left it. Time moved with infinitesimal slowness here, so that the frozen flames around the doorway had changed their shapes, but nothing more seemed consumed. Over the millennia they would eat away at the house like a cancer, but for now they hung motionless in the air, gleaming like almost translucently thin metal.

I opened a door I hadn't touched in years and gazed into my parents' bedroom. The unused bed was a vague shape in the darkness. The place smelled of dampness and dust. Neither my father nor my mother had slept here since I was a small child, since Father's true sorcery had begun to manifest itself so fearsomely and Mother moved in with me and Hamakina.

I went to my own bedroom next. It too remained as I'd left it, the light of the newly-risen moon shining through the open window I'd been unable to close as arrows streamed in. Hamakina had been dragged to her death through that window, by Vashtem, my father.

The huge, flaming shaft still impaled the bed, as if to destroy utterly everything that remained of my former life, to tell me that, no, I would never be able to live here again, to be what I had once been.

I tried yet again to pull it out, but I wasn't strong enough.

I gave up. I would abandon this room. But first, heart racing, I went to my desk and opened the school-bag which I'd left there so long ago. I trembled as I saw that the pages of my book were unharmed, and I wept softly when I came to the final page, where the arrow had found my wrist even as I wrote, the dried blood among the letters somehow completing the talismanic meaning of that particular passage.

I put the first four chapters of my tale in with the rest, in the waterproof satchel, then fumbled in the old bag for what remained: pens, stoppered bottles of ink, a small knife, some coins, a wooden cult-statue of Bel-He—

I almost wrote *Hemad,* in Deltan fashion. No, let it be Bel-*Kemad,* as we say in Reedland, the forgiving god, Lord of the Springtime.

I rummaged around, gathered some of my own clothes into my luggage, then retreated into my parents' dark bedroom and sat down on the unused bed amid the dust. I waited for what felt like hours for something to happen.

The old lure of inertia had returned. Why couldn't I just remain here, become merely Sekenre of Reedland again? In the morning I'd wake up, go into the kitchen for breakfast, and my mother and sister would be there, and we'd continue happily, as we always had. Perhaps Hamakina and I would walk into the city later, to study with Velachronos the scribe, or just to wander along the streets and look into the booths at things we couldn't afford to buy.

No. I knew better. I had reached the College of Shadows, here, in my father's and mother's old bedroom. What I felt was surely another test, or a trap set by some enemy. If I gave in, if I forgot myself, I'd soon find myself in a bottle, or else I'd become part of my own murderer. I didn't doubt that for an instant.

I, Sekenre, realized this on my own. No one else warned me. I came to this conclusion by myself, who am more than just a mask worn by my father, or a bottle containing other sorcerers.

I chose to enter the College of Shadows, and I had chosen, for better or worse, to find my entrance through my own house, where the very associations of the place, its familiarity, were both temptation and strength.

It had to be more than an elaborate excuse to come back here and recover my old manuscript, for all that now seemed infinitely precious to me. No, I, Sekenre, did not believe that Sekenre was that stupid. Having mastered my art, having returned from the College of Shadows, I could have come for the manuscript any time I chose.

'Therefore, Sekenre,' my father said within me, *'you should put the manuscript back in your room and return for it later.'*

I clutched the waterproof satchel in my lap defensively.

Hours passed without incident. I lit a candle, placed it on my mother's nightstand, laid the manuscript-satchel across my knees as a desk, and wrote a few paragraphs of this account. Under such conditions I couldn't attempt to fix the smeared capital, though.

Once something that might have been a bird fluttered outside the shuttered window. I didn't get up to go see.

Later, I studied the faint light seeping in through the shutter-slats. This was only the moon drifting through the night sky.

I yawned, at last confident that there would be no more challenges this night. I put the manuscript away, placed both the manuscript bag and the clothing bag by the bedside where I could grab them quickly, then shook the dust out of the top blanket and made ready to sleep.

But first, a precaution. I wove sorcerer's silk all around the bed.

I haven't mentioned this before. It is a secret of ancient magic, but not a particularly great one. I am not afraid to reveal that as you learn to control the body's fire, you can stretch the flames of your hands out into delicate, burning silk, invisible to the untrained eye. The sleeping sorcerer surrounds himself with it. Any intruder touching it gets scorched, or, if the sorcerer is feeling malicious, trapped and burned to death, for all that the flames are illusions. The sorcerer is like a spider resting in his web. The slightest vibration will awaken him.

Web completed, I lay down, exhausted, to sleep in my parents' bed and dream the dreams that come *within* that larger, never-ending dream which is sorcery itself.

These are the dreams of Sekenre the sorcerer, on his first night in the College of Shadows:

Cool, damp wind blew over my face. I sat up, opened my eyes, and saw that I was no longer in the house at all. The dusty bed rested among reeds. Overhead, more stars than I had ever seen before burned brilliantly, as if I had always been half-blind before, had never really seen the sky, and now all its splendor was revealed.

Did I truly wake, or dream? The distinction is meaningless.

For the longest time I sat listening to the wind rattle the

reeds and the night birds trilling. Then, suddenly, a *heron* thundered aloft in startled flight.

A barefoot figure in a white robe approached the bed, walking on the water's surface, ripples spreading where he stepped. He wore a lunar mask of beaten, tarnished silver.

Still, I thought I knew him.

'Father.'

The reply was in the Deltan tongue, the voice another's.

'I am Talno, who resides within Vashtem. Such is my prison, for Vashtem slew me.'

He spread his wrinkled hands. Blood poured from gaping wounds in his palms, then began to stream down from the eyeholes in the mask.

'Rise,' he said. 'You must make a brief journey.'

So I slid from the bed, onto what should have been the floor, but sank knee-deep in brackish water. I was forgetting myself. I still had shoes on. I crawled back onto the bed, dripping, removed my shoes, left them on the bed, and once more stepped down.

The surface held me. Talno regarded me impassively through his bleeding mask. Imitating his gesture, I spread my arms, my own scarred palms upraised. White fire rose from my hands.

We walked through the chilly night amid the reeds, speaking of magic, while the stars above us slowly wheeled toward the dawn and the River rippled with reflected light. I held my hands out in front of me to light our way.

'Your father killed me more than a century ago,' Talno said. 'I do not forgive him, nor do I any longer hate him. A sorcerer is purged of such emotions. He is a hollow reed, through which the wind of sorcery blows, on which the gods and titans play their own incomprehensible music.'

I did not dispute with him, though I doubted all sorcerers achieved such an ideal. 'What must I do,' I asked, 'to be certain of my survival in the College of Shadows?'

'Nothing is certain. I survived it, or did I? Are my memories false, my subsequent career before I encountered your father all imaginary? And *imagined by whom?* I can never know.'

'I must continue on the course I have begun,' I said. 'Can you help me— ?'

'Many others have gone the way before you, before Vashtem set foot on that same path—'.

'And I?'

'You must continue, as you have already realized. I may only recount how far I progressed, on my own, before I could go no further.'

'Then recount it,' I said.

He parted the reeds with his hands and light burst upon us, dazzling me. I reached out, caught hold of his sleeve, and let him lead me while I covered my eyes with my other hand. We walked through fire, across a sea of flaming, bubbling oil, the heat and smoke smothering me, the heat ever more painfully intense with each step. But the fire did not burn us.

We stopped before three screaming, writhing women bound to stakes. Their flesh melted and ran like wax. Their faces were so disfigured I couldn't tell if they were young or old, or even what color they had been.

I understood that these three had been here a long time, that they were unable to die.

'These were my gatekeepers,' said Talno. 'From them I learned a certain holy name and the feasibility of a certain enterprise, to which your father later devoted himself once he stole my life from me.'

'*And then what?*' I had to shout to make myself heard over the roaring flames and screaming women.

'You ask too many questions, Sekenre, son of my murderer,' Talno shouted back. 'My ability to answer them is limited. *And then what?* You find out for yourself. To what end did your father labor so relentlessly before circumstances interrupted him? Ask *him.* You might more profitably ask me who are these three before us. They are my mother and my two aunts, all three of them powerful sorceresses, who would have used me as I used them, as your father used you. Can I not relieve their pain? No, I cannot. Alive, they would destroy us. Dead, they would become part of us, Sekenre, and overwhelm us from within. So these fires must burn until your father's project is complete, at least; if not, throughout eternity. There is no morality in any of this, if that's what you would ask of me next, no right and wrong. These three are no more deserving of punishment than you or I, nor are they any less deserving. It merely must be so.'

Lungs burning, I coughed, then shouted, 'Tell me everything you know about this –' I raised my hand to make the Voorish sign.

Talno only laughed. 'You can't command me like a corpse, Sekenre. I'm not merely *dead*. The corpse you compel is *inside you*.'

He and the flames vanished. I stood alone in darkness among reeds, blind for a moment as my eyes adjusted. Then I saw the stars again and shivered in the frigid night air.

'Sekenre.'

I looked up. The masked, robed figure stood a distance off, clear of the reeds, on the open river. Even from where I stood, I could see the bloody streaks on the mask, but I knew this was no longer Talno.

I let the newcomer approach, the motion beneath the robe now a clumsy, broad waddle. The stranger was enormously fat, with feet swollen the size of melons.

'Lekkanut-Na.'

We did not walk, but sat down on the surface of the water as if on smooth, cold stone, playing a game with tiny blue and white flames on a board neither of us could see. Lekkanut-Na remembered her girlhood in some western, desert land, and sand and dust blew over us, out of the reeds.

She did not even speak. Her memories arose unbidden in my own mind, and it seemed that I was the one who had travelled by caravan for many weeks, each day searching the horizon for a first glimpse of the famous City of the Delta. But a sorceress murdered that girl-traveller in an oasis. The two became one, and journeyed on, into deeper sorcery. Which was the original Lekkanut-Na, I could not tell.

Then the sorceress walked through the city, even as Sekenre was to do centuries later, awe-stricken at the grandeur around her. I remembered this, and I remembered, too, how the composite I knew as Lekkanut-Na found the entrance to the College of Shadows in the vaults beneath the city, among the mummified sorcerers neither dead nor alive. She took a mummy for her mentor and learned many things, while the mummy looked on her hungrily as she waxed in power and understanding. But he waited too long to devour her. She devoured him instead. This done, she could never emerge from the shadows, never become again that girl who crossed the desert, or even the sorceress who walked the streets of the city. Therefore she caused herself to be buried in a secret tomb beneath a mountain far away, where she lay in absolute darkness as her spirit invaded the dreams of mankind, rummaging through souls as she searched for something she could not define.

Here the memories broke into disjointed fragments. I ceased to be Lekkanut-Na and became Sekenre again, sitting in the darkness on the river.

For the first time Lekkanut-Na actually spoke, not out of my mouth but through the mask, in her familiar bullfrog voice.

'What I sought, Vashtem found. My murder was but another stage in his journey. He was very close to his final goal before the end came for him. Therefore he was the dread and envy of all sorcerers everywhere.'

She touched a blue flame with her finger, moving it among my white flames, the blue flame flickering as if she'd blown on it, the white absolutely still.

'But what *is* it? I have to know.'

'Ask him what the sorcerer most desires. That is the key.'

I lifted a white flame onto my fingertip and set it at the edge of the invisible board.

'You're a sorcerer. Don't you know?'

'So are you, Sekenre. Don't *you?*'

I folded my arms and leaned over the game board, rocking slowly back and forth.

'I want to go back,' I said, 'to the way things were before—'

'I want to be that girl in the desert again, too, but I can't. I know it. You know it. We must look to the future. Our *minds* never grow younger, even if our bodies remain the same, or if we exchange them for other bodies like cloaks. No, that's not it. Tell me something else.'

'I want to be free from fear,' I said.

She laughed in her throaty, croaking way, and clapped the invisible game-board shut, extinguishing the flames. 'Yes. Exactly.'

Then she was gone. The masked, robed figure stood up and helped me to my feet. Blood dried on the silver cheeks. Someone else spoke. The robe hung loose, as if draped over a stick, then filled out again, changing, shifting. Thus I conferred with Orkanre and Tannivar the Parricide and with Vare, son of Jotu, a shaman from the wind-swept and barren lands of the far north, whom Talno had slain and never revealed until now.

Moon, whose true name is Dekac-Natae-Tsah, emerged once more, the mask unable to conceal the entirety of his malformed face; Moon disguised as the moon. I think he appreciated the irony. He spoke of the lands beyond death, which I had already visited. But they were different through his eyes. He suggested that no two travellers see or experience the same things in *Leshé*. In a vision within his own death, he had penetrated into the very heart of the Devouring God, but the light blinded him and the thunder deafened him.

Enough of this, I thought to myself. I dismissed Moon, and he departed.

'Father,' I said aloud. 'Vashtem whom *I* have slain, come to me. I summon you.'

Once more, we walked. He spoke through the mask, echoing the words of Talno. 'You cannot command that which is inside you, Sekenre, not until you learn to command yourself. First, purge yourself of anger, grief, love, longing, joy, sorrow, everything. They were but stones tied around your neck. Be rid of them.'

'Father?'

'Son.'

We paused at the edge of the reeds. All around us, black, misshapen birds waded, dipping into the Great River's muddy bottom with long, limp beaks and pink faces like fleshless human skulls.

He put his hands on my shoulders and gazed into my eyes.

Once more, the silver mask wept blood. His touch was dry and hard. I shivered in the frigid breeze.

'Do you still love me, Sekenre?' he said at last.

I was astonished. Only after a few seconds was I able to say, 'Why do you still care? I thought you had purged yourself.'

'Just answer my question.'

'I don't know anymore.'

'This indecision will be your death, boy. Make up your mind.'

'I can't. Not yet.'

'Ah.'

He took me by the right hand and we walked some more, ripples widening before us. Ahead, I could make out the house among the reeds, black against the glowing sky, like an enormous spider crouching at the River's edge.

'Father, you must tell me your secret. What were you working on? What were you after?'

'It was as you have said. I wanted to be free from fear.'

I stood still, pulling him to a stop.

'Is that all?'

His reaction was startling. He yanked me around, squeezing my hand until it hurt, then caught my left hand and crushed that too. He knelt, gazing up into my face, then pulled me down to kneel with him. He let go of my hands and ran his own over the surface of the water, searching for something.

'Is that *all?*' he shrilled, his voice so agitated it seemed to break. 'Is that *all?* Yes, that is all. That is quite enough. For, you see, I *found the way.*'

'What?'

Still he groped over the smooth surface of the water. I knelt motionless, bewildered.

'I achieved,' he said, 'what others had merely glimpsed from afar. I murdered selectively, taking into myself anyone whose progress had been greater than my own. Thus I was able to build on the efforts of many, befriending each of them first, working as a colleague, then killing. Yes. That was how I did it. I betrayed them all, those within me, more in the bottles. You've met ... Never trust a sorcerer, Sekenre.'

'Father, *you* are a sorcerer.'

'So are you, Sekenre. Ah, here we go—'

'What is— ?'

With a grunt and a mighty heave, he threw open a huge door set in the surface of the water, revealing a rectangle of faint light. Water dripped slowly over the edges, pattering somewhere far below.

'Come on,' he said. I crouched there as he climbed down, his moon-mask setting into the dark water. Then I lowered myself through the doorway gingerly, groping around with my feet for support, unwilling to just let go and drop I knew not how far.

Father caught me by the legs, and I slid down into his arms.

After a few seconds, my eyes adjusted. In diffuse twilight we two sat on the back of a large stone statue of Surat-Kemad which seemed affixed horizontally to the wall, snout downward.

Recognition was slow in coming as I took in the jumble of our surroundings: the battered staircase which coiled around and around and ended sideways in mid-air, the tumbled bookshelves, heaps of plaster, fallen beams, stray bones, and broken bottles. Colored-glass windows decorated with fishes and birds dangled open above from the apparent ceiling, on either side of the doorway through which I had emerged.

A lantern still dangled from the god's teeth, but it was rusted now. Otherwise, not much had changed since the last time I'd been here.

'Father, do you know this place?'

'Yes, I know it.'

'And what of the man who lived here, Aukin, son of Nevat?'

Father eased his way down from the statue, dropping a short space to the top of a cabinet, then climbing down to the debris-littered floor which had once been a wall before Aukin's house had somehow been rolled over on its side. I followed, wary of broken glass.

'I have no idea. I have been . . . variously distracted since I met him last.'

'When did you visit him?'

'Many times.'

'Why?'

He turned to me, angry beneath his mask. 'For my own reasons.'

Now it was my turn to be angry. I seized his arm. He merely paused, as if it had been his own choice to do so.

'I've come to the College of Shadows,' I said. 'I will have to live among many other sorcerers, all of them more than eager to devour me like dogfish when a minnow swims among them. I will be tested. Father, unless you tell me the truth, everything you know, unless there are no secrets at all between us anymore, unless I can see what you saw and understand what you were working toward and why the others were so afraid of you, then I might as well let them kill me right away, because I'll surely fail. You've told me to make up my mind regarding you. There. I have. If I end up in someone else's bottle, where does that get you?'

He broke away, then took my hand gently.

'Everything you say is true, Sekenre. Come, let me show you what I can.'

We made our way carefully through the wreckage of Aukin's tumbled-over house. I wondered briefly whether or not Father, who was in spirit-form, could cut his feet on the glass. He was likewise barefoot, having walked on water as I had. Then again, I was in spirit-form, too. Wasn't I? Certainly my body felt solid enough as I stepped from board to stone to clear floor, climbing over the headless bird-statue Aukin had used as a chair.

Father opened a sideways door, lowering it down against the wall. I bent over and peered through, into the sideways forest I had seen once before, where the trees seemed to float horizontally, the earth was a vast cliff-face to my right, and twilight suffused through the leaves from the left as brilliantly-plumed, almost luminous birds cawed and fluttered in the branches.

We watched for a while. The sun never grew any brighter, the dawn never giving birth to day. I understood, then, that it wasn't merely Aukin's house which lay tumbled on its side and broken, but his whole world.

'This way,' Father said, and we crawled through. I felt myself tumbling. My stomach lurched as all sense of up and down was yanked away. I found myself sitting at the base of a tree, staring up into the green canopy so impossibly far overheard. I got up slowly.

The air was chilly, though not as bad as it had been on the river. Only now did it occur to me to button up my jacket.

'Come on, Sekenre.'

I followed Father, hands in my pockets. The ground beneath my feet was moist and soft and cold, covered, not with leaves or fronds, but hair-like strands that fell from the trees, sprinkling down gently into my upturned face even as I walked.

Transformations began. First I was a boy in a long jacket who ran barefoot through a forest of needles, through the endless forest, along corridors of green and brown, startling the birds overhead, scattering strange beasts before me. Father ran at my side, robe fluttering, his mask bobbing up and down.

Then I had become a young deer, swift as the wind, straining to keep up with a great, silver stag.

And we were two birds, I a heron, incongruously out of its marshland home, he a silver eagle, feathers gleaming like polished metal. The heron is a slow, plodding flyer. It can never overtake the eagle. Father circled back again and again, urging me on. We flew low, weaving among the tree trunks, never attempting to reach through the green rooftop of the world.

Somehow I knew the way, I *remembered* it, where to turn among the great trees, the way down the rocky hillside where the trees hung horizontally once more and a brook flowed silently beneath them, eternally hidden from the light. I knew the way as, at last, the sun did seem to break through in a blinding burst, as the forest began to die, as we glided over dead stumps, down an all but endless slope into utter desolation, as we struggled against hot wind and swirling clouds of ash. Molten stone ran in rivulets, down into a valley of fire.

'*This is the heart of the forest, Sekenre, where dreams are born and die, where visions are forged. I found my way this far, as no other sorcerer ever has. Here. It's not a forest, of course, any more than it's a desert or the fire is really fire. But the human mind grasps the unknowable in this fashion, painting it with familiar symbols.*'

He spoke inside my mind now. His eagle-form could only shriek against the wind.

I replied, 'What is here? I don't see anything.'

Lightning flashed out of the sullen gray sky.

'*Don't you realize where we are?*'

'No.'

'*We have reached the borderland of* Akimshé, *ineffable holiness, where not even the gods see clearly, where gods and worlds are born. This is the region beyond* Tashé, *which men call Death. We are in the very heart of Surat-Kemad.*'

'I don't understand. We are *un*holy. How is it possible— ?'

'*That's the outrageous wonder of it, Sekenre. That's the secret. I came here the first time like a burglar, to steal the secret of the gods. Even Aukin, son of Nevat did not know how to do it, though I went through his door, into his forest.*'

'But what happened? You failed somehow. You didn't get it.'

The wind seized us, and we descended in an ever more rapid spiral into the valley of flame. I cried out in sudden fear, my heron-voice squalling, but I felt no fear in Father's thoughts. He expected this. It was merely part of the way.

Below, the fire darkened into a deep red, thinning out as if the whole valley had become the surface of an oily pool, and now the wind dispersed the flames. We splashed through the surface but were not burnt. For an instant I glimpsed the outstretched jaws of Surat-Kemad, whose mouth is the earth and sky, whose teeth are the stars, and I heard the deep, slow throbbing of his heart.

Then we were among the stars, hurtling across a frigid abyss of utter darkness, where the stars were mere pinpricks of light; and the darkness folded onto itself, becoming the forest again, or a ghost of the forest, where dark stone trees rose into limitless gloom. The wind bore us between the massive trunks, across valleys which gaped like mouths amid ragged hills. Enormous stone gods crouched on the ridges, their heads turning toward us as we passed, grinding with the rumble of an earthquake.

'Father,' I called out with my thoughts. 'You evaded my question. You have to tell me everything.'

'I am showing you everything as best I know how.'

'Then answer my question.'

'What question, Sekenre?'

'Why did you fail?'

He seemed to sigh, inside my mind. I envisioned him shrugging, turning away, refusing to meet my gaze.

'Everything will be revealed to you, Sekenre. Be patient.'

Ahead, brilliant light increased beyond the last of the stone gods, like a sunrise rushing upon us.

'I have another question, Father.'

'Ask it if you must.'

His silver wings gleamed in the light. He circled like a kite in the wind, twirling back as the heron-Sekenre strained to catch up with him.

'Will all of this truly make us free from fear?'

'That is the goal of all sorcery, isn't it, Sekenre? You kill your enemies because you have to, because you're afraid they'll kill you first. And they will, because they are similarly afraid. To transcend the endless cycle of murder, you must become immortal. Not of extended lifespan as any sorcerer is, but truly immortal, one who cannot be killed. That means a god, my son. You are as stone to your enemies' feeble knives. All knowledge opens up. You usurp holiness itself. You steal your way into Akimshé, as I did. Oh, how it terrified the others.'

'But you didn't succeed.'

'I had won the game. All the pieces were mine. But someone tipped the board over.'

'How could this happen? What was your weakness?'

'You, Sekenre. As you discerned, I did not fully purge myself. I couldn't. I loved you too much. It broke my concentration.'

I screamed defiance in my heron-voice, trying to deny what could not be denied. He wasn't listening.

* * *

And *next?*

The hand falters. The mind goes numb. The eye cannot see, nor can the tongue say, nor the ear hear, nor the memory recall—

Akimshé. Unutterable holiness, the light beyond dazzling blindness.

Father cried out in amazement and alarm, and the others within me screamed in terror—

I fell into the light, no longer a heron, but Sekenre, tumbling into an endless, burning blossom, a rose of fire with suns and worlds flickering in and out of existence like sparks from the petals, the petals peeling back layer upon layer, fire revealing fire, until *eyes* opened, huge and dark against the impossible light, and a mouth, gaping. The flower had become a face, inhuman, devouring, mad.

I fell into the light—

And in a timeless eternity, in time less than counting, I walked in every land, lived in every epoch, touched every world in all the heavens, and I spoke with the very gods in the speech which cannot be formed into human words nor transcribed into human letters. Surat-Kemad was within me as one of my many selves, as were Bel-Kemad with his birds and the terrible, forlorn Malevendra, the Hag of Vengeance.

But still, there was something I could not grasp. I was like a bird fluttering against a window-pane, trying to reach the light—

I plunged through the right eye of the demon face, into blackness more profound than may be imagined, but at last I came to rest lying on my back in shallow water while glowing foam rose and fell on gentle waves as they broke along a shore. I thought the foam the stars, the shore Eternity, the waves the brief moments of our lives; but as Father had explained, we tend to grasp for familiar symbols when regarding the incomprehensible.

The Sybil stood over me, her face glowing faintly in the darkness like the moon behind clouds. She watched me intently for a minute or two, but did not speak.

A footstep splashed by my ear. I sat up. The Sybil was

gone. Father leaned down, took me under the arms, and hauled me to my feet. I stood dripping wet, but for once the water was pleasantly warm.

We did not walk on the water this time, but waded, splashing along a darkened beach as stars appeared in the sky one by one.

'It is as I had dared to hope. No, better. You will be a great sorcerer, Sekenre. You took *me* farther than I ever got by myself.' He put his arm around me and held me close to his side. I tensed, but did not break away. His body felt misshapen, lumpy in the wrong places, jointed strangely, and his hands were claws, cruel and sharp. His gait was the sideways waddle of the *evatim*. For an instant I didn't believe he was my father at all. I looked down to see if he had a tail.

'Father, you failed at what you tried to do. Why do you think I'll succeed?'

'Because you will not be distracted as I was. You won't have to love anyone.'

'I think you're lying. I don't believe you.'

He hugged me to him, then let me go. I walked by his side, ankle-deep in warm water. Yet I shivered.

'I had intended your sister as my receptacle, Sekenre. When she came of age, I would arrange for her to kill me, have her serve me poison perhaps. I begat her for that purpose and for no other. Therefore, to me, she was but a thing. I did not love her. You, however, were my son. You, Sekenre, were the one who overturned the board after I had won the game.'

'I didn't know.'

He patted me on the back. His clawed hands tore my jacket. 'Never mind. Things seem to have worked themselves out anyway.'

'I don't know what you mean, Father.' But in flashes of confused memories which were not my own, I did know.

'Soon a new god will be born, formed out of the fires of *Akimshé,* as all gods are, but shaped by sorcery, not by prayer, not even by the prayers of the other gods. This one is a rogue. It will be filled with the soul of the sorcerer who calls it forth. Go back into your memories, Sekenre. Use the rite of *Tazen-Dha* and tell me what you see.'

He led me onto the beach. I knelt in the sand and performed the rite of *Tazen-Dha,* which may not be described fully, moving my hands through the angles, creating within my mind a kind of house, a little image of my father's house where every room, every chair, every desk or barrel or broom propped in a corner represented a thought or memory. Therefore to walk into one of those rooms or sit in a chair or pick up a broom is to unlock powerful forces, more than the conscious mind may apprehend. This is one of the sorcerer's innermost secrets. It is the vastness of his soul.

I cannot say more, but to report that my *Tazen-Dha* house was filled with babbling voices, with rushing spirits, with faces drifting in smoke. In my *Tazen-Dha* house books, chairs, cups, many familiar objects floated in the air of their own accord. Some of them spoke. The door to my own room suddenly swelled outward like a bubble in liquid wax. A pair of hands formed, reaching for me, and a face, the soft flesh *tearing* open to reveal blood-red eyes.

'Help me,' the thing said. 'Please. I have lost my way.'

'No,' I replied. 'I cannot help you. I don't see any hope for you.'

I reached for the door-latch, but the door swung inward before I could touch it.

My bedroom was suffused with brilliant light. I squinted to make out a small figure hunched at my desk, scribbling away on a long, curling strip of paper. I *remembered* this act of writing. I knew what words the pen would create, what *had been* created in some other time, some other past when what was now begun was already completed and I had held the pen myself.

I felt the words forming in my mind, in the divine script, the language of the gods, but they didn't say anything at all. The holy scribe was an idiot, an empty vessel to be filled.

Then all those within me awoke at once, rising up in a frenzy: Vashtem and Tannivar and Balredon, Orkanre, Lekkanut-Na, Talno, Vare, son of Jotu, and many more I had never suspected, sorcerers within sorcerers within sorcerers, receding to infinity like reflections in a house walled entirely with mirrors.

They were tearing me apart, fighting for control.

Vashtem wore the body, and spoke.

'I have come at last—'

Orkanre wore the body.

'I shall arrive soon.'

And Lekkanut-Na:

'I am risen into the light—'

Tannivar wore the body and screamed, falling to his knees, covering his face with his hands.

'Father, forgive me—'

Dekac-Natae-Tsah laughed. A vision came to him of the moon drifting from behind a bloody cloud, waxing from crescent into fullness in seconds.

Sekenre reached up from where he lay on the floor and touched the edge of the desk. The seated one looked down, face impossibly bright, like a rose of fire, burning petals peeling back like pages flipping in the wind, somehow not diminishing as each layer fell away.

The fiery face was my own, Sekenre staring down at Sekenre, eyes wide, face sculpted of living fire, but still Sekenre, with the Sybil's mark half hidden by hair hanging over his forehead, the crescent arrow-scar on his right cheek clearly visible.

The holy scribe, the illuminated Sekenre, looked into my eyes and babbled words without meaning, shrieking in the last extremity of pain.

I heard my father calling from far away, but could not answer him.

Touch awoke me, before sight or sound: something cold and hard pressing against my skin. I drifted up slowly out of my dream, each new sensation becoming part of that dream, then lingering behind like driftwood as the dream receded like a tide. Father called me from somewhere. But my more immediate concern was why my bare buttocks and shoulders were sliding down cold glass.

I sat still in utter darkness, fully awake now, naked, certain that this was no dream or vision. I reached out on either side to touch a curving wall of glass. I tried to stand, hit my head, slipped, and fell down clumsily.

I was imprisoned in a sphere. So, I wondered in a curiously analytical frame of mind, how was I able to breathe? I groped around for air-holes, but found none.

Still I saw absolutely nothing. The sudden dread came to me that I had been blinded. I pressed my fingers to my eyelids and saw flashes of drifting light.

But after a while I noticed that one of the lights didn't drift, instead drawing steadily nearer, flickering: a candle held in a pale fleshy hand. The candle lit more candles in a circle around me, until I could see that I was still in my parents' bedroom, suspended over the bed in a glass bubble. The candles rested atop the covers on plates taken from the kitchen. My clothing lay scattered across the floor. Both satchels had been dumped out, the pages of my book spilled in a heap, though everything else – coins, knives, brushes, ink-pots, the image of Bel-Kemad – was arranged in neat rows.

Something stood up, having lit the last candle. My first impression was of a dark, shaggy beast, but gradually, as my eyes adjusted, I made out a heavy, intensely ugly woman smeared with blood and filth, seemingly naked and fully as malformed as one of those foreign cult-statues with a hundred breasts. But as she leaned into the light I saw that she was elaborately garbed in human body parts, taken, no doubt, from her enemies: a necklace of teeth and ears, leathery, boneless arms draped over her shoulders like a tattered cloth, dozens of hands rising upright from her back, clutched into tight fists. Her skirt, which concealed nothing, consisted of dried penises strung together with hide thongs.

She smiled at me, her black, filed teeth a startling contrast to her fish-belly-pale face.

'I am the gatekeeper of the College of Shadows,' she said in unaccented Reedlandish. 'You are Sekenre. I know your name and you don't know mine.' She laughed, as if this were somehow enormously funny. She pointed to the sphere, the candles, to my things scattered across the floor. 'It makes me stronger. Doesn't it? Eh? I think so. Ha! Stupid Sekenre!'

She squatted before me, gazing up maliciously. The hands on her back unclenched, revealing tiny faces set in the palms. Smoke rose from each of the miniature mouths, swirling around her. The faces screamed, their voices like the faint whistlings of the denizens of my father's bottle collection. This, no doubt, was something similar.

I sat cross-legged, covering myself with my hand out of instinctive modesty.

She laughed at that too. 'I've already looked at every part of you, Sekenre, and touched whatever I pleased. That's why I keep you naked. Sorcerers hide too many things on themselves, one way or another. Tattoos are the common trick. I knew a sorcerer once who had branded his magic onto himself with iron. For all the good it did him. I killed him like the rest. The marks on you don't matter. Oh, should you be in there long enough to need to piss, just do it. Water passes out of the glass as easily as air comes in. Does it . . . *relieve* . . . you to know that?' Again she laughed, as if she'd said something wondrously funny.

I regarded her impassively, wondering to myself how she could say that the Sybil's mark on my forehead was of no significance.

'I name you – Death-Clad.'

'I spit on the name,' she said, and spat. 'So it has no power over me. Surprised?'

'Still, it is convenient. I have to call you something.'

'Call me what you like, Sekenre. I don't think we'll be talking together very long.'

'What do you want of me?'

Her humor vanished like a mask she'd ripped off and flung aside. She heaved herself up, then leaned over the candles and pressed her face against the glass, snarling. Her foul breath and the smoke from the tiny mouths filled the sphere. I drew back, gagging.

'I want everything that's inside you, Sekenre. You're too weak and stupid to defend yourself. Your stupid web was like a spider's to me. I just pushed it out of my way. Stupid Sekenre, you're like a jar filled with gold coins. I'll turn you upside down and dump you out. As for what's left of you then,

I'll keep you around' – she stood back, arms outstretched, so I could see her raiment fully – 'if I feel like it.'

'Why don't you just— ?'

She laughed once more. *'Kill* you? I could have killed you any time, stupid Sekenre. But I didn't choose to. Do you think I just *murder* people? I'm not like you, Sekenre. I am *one* person. I *wear* as many as I like, but I don't let them become *part* of me the way you do. They're all *alive*. I never *kill* anyone. So I'll have plenty of time to make you tell me all your secrets, beginning with your true name.'

'And if I refuse?'

'You could hurt quite a lot, Sekenre. You might feel more pain than you ever thought possible.'

'I don't doubt your skill.'

She scratched the glass idly with one finger. Her nails were thick and sharp, like claws. 'Then get on with it!'

I pointed to my book, its pages heaped on the floor.

'You have my magic right there.'

She looked down, seized a handful of manuscript pages, crumpled them, and turned to me sharply. 'This trash?'

'I am known as Sekenre the Illuminator,' I said, ironically naming myself thus for the first time. 'My magic is a matter of paper and colored pigments, raised gold leaf, swirling lines and finely-wrought letters with little pictures inside them. I can capture souls that way. It is a very great magic. It freezes time.'

'What?' She threw away all the pages but one, and held that one perilously close to a candle, squinting, turning the page sideways, upside down, sideways again.

I watched her intently, my contempt and excitement rising. For all her monstrous power, was it possible that Death-Clad was illiterate? She knew my name, but I knew of her incredible shortcoming. We were evenly matched.

She held up the page to the glass. 'Show me.'

I glanced at the page. It was from chapter two of my memoir.

'That tells the story of my early life,' I said. 'It wouldn't interest you.'

I winced as she crumpled it up and threw it away.

'Don't lie to me. You'd be surprised *how little* of your body needs to be undamaged for you to be able to tell me what I want to know.'

'I am not lying,' I said, swallowing hard. My throat was dry and sore. I hugged my sides. Every minute, the air seemed to grow colder. But my enemy showed no sign of discomfort. 'If I'm to demonstrate my secrets, I'll need a few things.'

She regarded me suspiciously.

'Like what?'

Once more, I indicated the materials on the floor. 'Ink, paper, a pen, a flat surface on which to write.'

She tapped a blackened hook of a fingernail on the glass. 'Why are you giving up so easily?'

'What choice have I?'

'None.'

'Then I might as well avoid the pain.'

She smiled and spoke very slowly. 'Only if I let you.'

'Again,' I said, 'what choice have I?'

'You are a weakling and a coward, not just stupid, Sekenre. You have no choice at all.' She ran her nail along the curve of the glass. 'Oh, very well.' She jerked the nail up suddenly.

The glass ceased to exist, and I fell to the bed, bouncing in a cloud of dust. Candles scattered to the floor. Those that still burned, she put out with her bare feet.

'Stay where you are,' she said. 'Tell me what you need.'

I pointed to the stoutest and sharpest of my pens, not a quill, but a wooden shaft with a metal point set in it. Ordinarily such an instrument is used only for the broadest strokes, not for illumination, but she handed it to me without question, along with a stoppered bottle of ink and a blank sheet of paper.

'I need something hard and flat to write on.'

Death-Clad had obvious difficulty understanding this. She paused for a long time, shuffling back and forth, her hideous adornment writhing with a life of its own, the many hands clasping and unclasping, the tiny mouths hissing, trailing smoke. Then she reached down, picked up the water-proofed manuscript satchel itself, and irritably threw it to me. I caught it, and laid it across my lap. Now I was shivering in the intense cold. It was hard to keep the writing surface still.

'Come closer,' I said. 'You have to see this.'

She circled around behind me, then leaned over and caught both my shoulders, squeezing so hard with her clawed hands that she drew blood. I did my best to ignore the pain and restrain my revulsion when she crawled onto the bed and began to lick the blood from the wounds. She hunched against me, her ghastly trophies wriggling against my back and sides. Her body gave off no warmth at all, her touch and stench that of a corpse.

'You've got to see—'

She grunted and caught me by the back of the neck. Her grip was enormously strong. She could have killed me in an instant.

Gasping, barely able to breathe, I drew a serpent on the paper in my lap. I curled its tail into its mouth. Death-Clad followed the pen with her gaze, fascinated. She let go of my neck and slid a greasy arm down over my shoulder to trace the serpent with her fingernail.

Now was the time to risk all. I wrote within the circle of the serpent, in large and plain Reedlandish script, YOU ARE AN IGNORANT SAVAGE.

Death-Clad hissed and raked my back with her nails. I felt blood trickling.

'It is . . . very powerful magic,' I said, afraid that somehow she *could* read after all and that my little ruse was finished. But she did not react further. 'But there is more. Here are the very words of life and death.' Indeed, for me, they were. I wrote in Reedlandish and again in Deltan: BUGGER YOURSELF, SCUMBAG.

She breathed hard, entranced, perhaps even in awe of this magic. My gamble was rewarded. I knew for certain now that Death-Clad was as I had dared to hope, completely illiterate. She continued to watch what my hands were doing with utter amazement. I concentrated on what I was doing, trying to ignore her foulness.

More words followed, trailing up and down the page, assuming amusing shapes, twisting upside down, their letters sometimes inside out or reversed. It was all the same to Death-Clad: nonsense syllables, rhymes from children's songs, insults, a list of every species of fish I knew, the names tightening into a spiral which became a hopeless, illegible mess. The calligraphy was terrible. The huge pen-point smeared the ink. I tried to work it sideways, to make the line thinner, but ink splattered. Still, Death-Clad couldn't tell the difference.

At last I drew a tiny spider with the word DEATH held in its clutches.

'Here is the ultimate secret,' I said, pointing to the spider. 'Look at it very, very closely. Then you will know everything I do, and you can do what you want with me.'

Snorting, she crawled around and leaned over into my lap like a dog about to lick something out of a bucket. She blocked my own view of the page. I saw that the smoking hands were no garment at all, but grafted into her back. I sat very still, jaw clenched, trying very hard to stay in control of myself as she caressed my legs and arms and chest. Very deliberately I turned the pen in my hand until I held the point upward.

'Look,' I said. 'Study it as carefully as you can.'

'Don't try to trick me—'

'If you are patient, all my magical secrets will come to you.'

'I am not patient. I don't have to be patient.' She sank a claw into my thigh and ripped.

I let out an involuntary yell and at the same instant caught hold of my enemy's hair with my left hand, yanking her head up. With my right hand, I rammed the pen as deeply as I could into her left eye.

Now she was screaming with dozens of voices, all the secondary faces squealing like tortured animals as we rolled and wrestled over the bed. I locked my legs around her sides and held on, shoving the pen in further, holding her away from me as she snapped and drooled and ground her teeth but could not connect. Her flailing claws tore my shoulders and sides. I screamed too, but I clung to her grimly as we tumbled to the floor.

I landed on top of her, all my weight on the pen. The impact drove it deep into her skull. Her grip relaxed. I held the pen with both hands and leaned on it, forcing the tip out through the top of her skull. Then I let go and quickly rolled aside and lay still, gasping, while she flapped and thrashed like a beached fish, spouting blood from her eye and mouth, struggling to speak, her final curses reduced to a wheezing gurgle.

Her many hands scratched the floor with their fingernails, then were still.

When I felt certain she was dead, I crawled over her and prodded her with one foot.

All her mouths drooled blood and filth, but she did not move. Her face had gone slack, distorted by the pen. Only one inch of the handle still protruded from her eye.

Suddenly I felt very weak and fell onto one side. I heaved up what little I had eaten in the past day or so. All I wanted to do was lie still, right there on the floor in the bitter cold. Somehow I thought the oozing blood from my several deep gashes would keep me warm. I was getting light-headed, as if I were drunk and afraid and trying to grope my way out of a nightmare. Every time I moved, some invisible torturer drove red-hot knives into my shoulders.

But the presence of this obscenity in my father's house, beside the very bed on which I and my sister had been conceived and born, I could not allow to continue even for an instant, despite any pain or cold. I staggered to my feet, grabbed my enemy by the ankles, and hauled her over to the window. I fumbled with the shutters and swung them wide, then clung to the window sill, blasted by a wind colder than any I had ever known, blinded by brilliant white light.

Yet I couldn't allow myself to stop with the task half done, with that awful *thing* still inside the house. Gasping, barely able to see, I heaved Death-Clad up until I had her head through the window, then her arms, then the middle of her body. She seemed heavier by the instant, soft, almost boneless, impossible to manipulate, but I shifted her weight, driven to frenzy by the pain of the effort, and at last she tumbled through.

I listened for the splash as she hit the river, but there was only a muted thud.

Puzzled, I clung once more to the window sill, leaning out, not quite able to kneel because I was too short to reach the floor with my knees. Gradually my eyes adjusted. There was no sign of the corpse. I gazed out over a strange landscape of white fields and sweeping valleys and ragged, black ridges and peaks. The house had moved again, and was now far from the Great River, perched high among the mountains.

Sunlight glared from the hillsides, brighter than the worst of any desert, but the air was filled with whirling, tiny flakes which melted into water when I caught them in my hand.

(*It's called* snow, *child,*' said Balredon within my mind.)

I was burning with the cold. Indeed, I noticed, in a detached, abstracted way, faint steam rose from my bare skin.

(*Get back inside and get dressed,*' Lekkanut-Na said. '*You'll be sick. You get sick easily enough as it is.*')

I tried to focus my thoughts. I was forgetting something.

I dropped down to the floor and started to crawl away from the window. Frigid air blew over me. I was so stiff I could hardly move.

What was I forgetting? My mind grasped at it, but the precise thought melted, like the *snow* in my hand. I had killed a sorcerer. Something about that. Something should have happened, but hadn't—

Death-Clad screamed inside my mind. I rolled over, thrashing on the floor, hands to my ears, helpless to shut out her voice.

It came to me. Kill a sorcerer and become a sorcerer. Yes. The most elementary fact of sorcery. I gritted my teeth and slashed at the air with claws I didn't have. I screamed in my own voice, in hers, and I understood that somehow she had still been alive when she had gone through the window, despite everything, and had only died just now, in the deep *snow* below.

She and I were one, and my name was Kareda-Raza, which means Fire-in-Darkness and my common name was Gredama. Familiar scenes came flooding back: the river, the marshes, a forest of posts beneath a wooden city.

That shocked me more than anything. Gredama, Fire-in-Darkness, was a Reedlander, who had once dwelt among those very pilings beneath the City of Reeds where my friends had played and explored and performed our own secret and terribly important childhood rites.

But her childhood games were somewhat different, as she flayed children alive, ever so precisely cutting away parts of the body, removing whole organs and limbs while life yet remained; mastering the arts of pain. That was her strength: the agony of others, torture and mutilation. That was her power and her lust. She knew nothing else, scorning those who practiced any other sort of magic.

As a small girl she experimented with animals first, then with children her own age, progressing to sailors she lured to their doom by offering herself to them in vaguely-defined ways. In time she was the terror who came in the night, from whom no rich man, no priest, no lord was ever safe; she who left behind bloody hides or faces or genitals nailed to doors.

What I had done to the Zargati wizard Dog-Face was trifling to her. She had performed worse before she was ten years old. When she was twenty, Surat-Kemad appeared to her, blessed her, and bestowed on her a secret name. Thereafter, she walked with the *evatim,* conversing with them in their own language, for she was a very special servant of the Lord of Death, an initiate into mysteries no human being had ever known. A hundred years and more she had gone on thus, becoming what she had been when I encountered her.

Now she was a part of me, raging in my mind, threatening to overwhelm all else by her sheer malevolence, pouring out gloating memories of all the pain she had inflicted, counting her thousands of victims who still suffered, alive in some other place, blinded, skinned, burning with inconceivable pain, *unable to die.* This was the joy of Gredama, of Kareda-Raza, whom Sekenre had inaccurately dubbed Death-Clad. No, she was Armored-In-the-Pain-Of-Others. Pain was her joy and her whole life.

Screaming, I called aloud to Father, to Balredon, to the Sybil, to anyone who could free me from the horror of *being* Kareda-Raza. But my words were mere babble. I glimpsed the Sybil in her house amid her webs of bones, stirring, her face like a moon in a dark sky. Babble. The words did not form. I couldn't focus my thoughts well enough to address her.

She vanished. Father rose up within me. He moved swiftly, and it was he who smote Kareda-Raza and drove her down deep within my mind. I grasped the thought, the image of a massive dungeon door. I willed it to close. I imagined its thunderous clang. Father barred the door with a heavy iron slab. He turned the key in the massive lock. Balredon and Orkanre and all the rest labored to heave stones to fill in the entire tunnel leading to that door.

Lekkanut-Na comforted me. 'Remember that you are Sekenre,' she said.

Kareda-Raza's thoughts and memories were like a fading echo in a cave, diminishing but never quite gone.

'That was crudely done,' said Father, aloud, speaking through my mouth. My throat was sore, hoarse. I lay face-down on the floor, arms crossed against my chest. I tried to get up, but couldn't. I rolled onto my back. I was almost completely numb with cold now. I couldn't tell if I'd stopped bleeding or not.

'It was the best I could manage,' I croaked. 'I thought I pulled it off . . . rather well.'

'At least you formed the plan yourself and executed it,' said Lekkanut-Na, likewise aloud. 'That must count for something.'

'Yes, that is the important thing,' said Vashtem. 'You still have much to learn, Sekenre, as I am sure you are aware. Perhaps the very crudity of your scheme saved you. She was expecting you to assault her with magic, not a pen. Your chief advantage remains that people underestimate you.'

'I guess so . . .' My speech broke off in a fit of coughing.

'Dress yourself,' said Lekkanut-Na within my mind.

But, cold as I was, my limbs and joints stiff, my sides sticky with half-dried blood, the first thing I did was gather up the pages of my precious book, straightening out the crumpled leaves as best I could, frantically counting and collating to make sure I had them all, even though my fingers could scarcely grasp the sheets.

The book was all there. I felt more relieved than I could

completely comprehend. I searched around for the wooden box with the one unfinished page in it, the one I'd been working on before I arrived. I had to wriggle under the bed to retrieve it. I stretched, and felt a sharp pain as a gash in my side tore open.

Only after I had replaced manuscript, pens, coins, and the image of Bel-Kemad in the waterproofed bag did I truly realize that I was still naked, that I was bleeding from a dozen places, and that it was so bitterly cold that I could hardly move.

I tore up one of my old shirts and tried to bandage myself. I decided none of my injuries were life-threatening, uncomfortable as they might be. I wouldn't have to heal myself with the body's fire this time and yield up that much more of my physical self to magic. There would be yet more scars, but no new vulnerabilities.

I dressed as warmly as I could, loincloth, two pairs of trousers, one shirt of my own first, then three of Moon's enormous tunics extending down to my knees. My stiff fingers labored to roll the sleeves up to the proper length. I struggled into the gaudy, now torn jacket Tica had selected for me in Thadistaphon, wincing at the effort. Drying blood had glued the undershirt to my back.

My throat seemed lined with hot sand, grinding painfully whenever I swallowed. I wrapped the scarf I'd taken from the festival conjurer around my neck several times, then stuffed the remainder into my shirt.

Now, where were my shoes? I couldn't find them. I crawled around. I came upon one, then the other. They still smelled of river mud, but had somehow become hard, almost like wood, and cold to the touch. I held them, unable to understand.

(*'Frozen,'* said Balredon within my mind. *'That's ice. You'll have to learn these things.'*)

Actually, I had seen frost before, on rare, cold winter days in Reedland. But there was no time to argue.

I didn't know what good frozen shoes would be or how to get them unfrozen. I'd work on it later. I gathered the rest of my things into the second bag and put the shoes in on top.

Still I was almost too cold to move. I pulled the top blanket off the dusty bed and wrapped myself in it.

I stood up for a moment, thinking to go somewhere, but the cold floor so burned my exposed feet that I could only think to sit down again, to huddle inside the blanket. The wind blew *snow* in through the open window, but I didn't feel strong enough to get up and close it. Gradually the sky clouded over. The sun disappeared, and the *snow* fell in a thick, silent shower. I sat watching, fascinated by its strangeness and beauty, clutching the blanket and both satchels to myself, slowly swaying back and forth.

Then there was someone else in the room with me, and a woman's voice said, 'Welcome, Sekenre the Illuminator.'

'Who are you?' I said dully, without looking up.

'I am the gatekeeper. I have found you worthy to enter into the College of Shadows.'

Chapter 15: The College of Shadows

I gazed at the newcomer, bleary-eyed. I was weary of strangeness, but so accustomed to it by now that I thought nothing could surprise me anymore.

Still, her aspect was hardly reassuring.

My first impression was of a great mass of multi-colored birds, all crushed together, then molded like dough into the shape of a woman. But as she moved, I saw that, no, this was merely a complicated gown composed entirely of the bodies of small birds, feathers cunningly woven, tiny bones like delicate embroidery, skulls and feet strung around her neck and wrists like jewelry made of thorns. The feathers stirred with a life of their own, like a huddled flock breathing in sleep.

I couldn't tell her apparent age – but what is age to a sorcerer? – though it might have been thirty or so: a long, intensely pale, unlined face, ink-black hair and eyes in utter, striking contrast. She seemed subtly ancient, possibly several centuries old. Were she a painted letter on the page, it would have been a matter of a distinct, but almost indefinable calligraphic style.

'Illuminator,' she said. 'Now that you have come among us, you are a full member of our fellowship. Come and meet the others.'

At first I thought she was breathing smoke. Then I saw that my breath was likewise clouded. The cold. In winter, sometimes—

I tried to get up steadily, to conceal any sign of weakness or confusion, but my legs almost folded under me. She caught me under both arms and held me upright. I let out an involuntary gasp. The motion had opened the wound in my thigh. Blood ran down my leg. I hung there in her arms, clutching the blanket and my two satchels, gazing down at the little red stream that trickled across my right foot. My body didn't seem real to me. The pain receded into the general numbness and cold.

The newcomer straightened me up. I seemed to be drifting in her arms, light as smoke, out of the bedroom, down the hall, past the open door of my father's study.

She paused once to regard the frozen flames around the doorway, then to gaze into my bedroom, but said nothing.

We continued. She merely led me by one arm now. I stood by her side on the porch outside. I pulled away from her. Just then, I didn't want to be touched.

I took both satchels in one hand and grabbed hold of the railing with the other. Now *snow* filled the air and a shadow fell across the land, until the mountainsides and sweeping valleys faded into muted silvery-blue, the great, distant peaks lost amid swirling clouds. Down below I made out a detail I had missed before, a gleaming curve of *ice* stretching as far as I could see. I wondered if in this inhospitable place the Great River itself had become *frozen.*

Black birds circled among the peaks, just below the clouds. They must have been enormous to remain visible at such a distance.

'Mountain eagles,' my companion said, 'the messengers of Regun-Temad, who is himself the courier of Death. He has much business here.'

I was puzzled both by what she said and how she said it. She spoke Reedlandish in an accent I didn't recognize, and she used what must have been the divine aftername, *Temad,* quite distinct from the familiar *Kemad* or the Deltan *Hemad.*

And what business could Death have here? I saw no dwelling but my own, perched on a snowy slope in absurd incongruity to the landscape. We were alone but for the eagles.

'Where are we?' I said.

'No longer in any *specific* place, in the geographical sense . . . no, this is not a country anyone reaches by an overland journey, no matter how long he travels. Ask neither *where* nor *when,* Sekenre. We are beyond both place and time. Think of it that way. Otherwise, all I can tell you is that it probably resembles my homeland more than it does yours.'

'And who are you? You know my name but I don't know yours.'

She smiled, but without mirth. 'You are testing me. You think I am a fool like that girl you bested on your way here.'

'No, I—'

'Then you know better than to ask names casually, here among so many other sorcerers. I overheard yours. That is perhaps your misfortune, perhaps not.'

I looked up at the clouds, the mountains, and the black specks that were eagles.

'I don't see any other sorcerers.'

She laughed again, genuinely this time. 'Why do you think it's called the Invisible Lodge?'

'But— ?'

'That's a joke, Sekenre. Even we sorcerers have our private sense of humor.'

'If you have no name, how may I address you?'

'Call me merely the Devourer of Birds.'

'As you wish,' I said, nodding as if this were what I expected. 'Shall we go on our way?'

But I didn't know where we were supposed to go, and in any case there was no sensation in my feet. It was like walking on stilts, as if my legs were made of wood from the knees down. I clung to the railing, trying just to remain upright, feeling light-headed from exhaustion and loss of blood. If I was still bleeding somewhere, I couldn't tell.

Devourer of Birds put her arms around me once more. I struggled feebly to get away, but she held on, burying my face in her strange raiment. I stood in that strange embrace, trying to puzzle out the secret of her name. The meaning was there, just out of my reach, like a coin gleaming up through muddy water. But I couldn't figure the riddle out.

Gently, she directed me to the edge of the porch, then eased me down onto the mountainside, into the snow. We walked for a time, knee-deep in it, my blanket dragging across the white surface as I clutched it and my two bags to my chest in a hopeless attempt to keep warm.

I dropped one of the bags. She picked it up and carried it. My *frozen* fingers told me nothing, but I looked and saw that she had the one filled with spare clothing. I still held the manuscript. I found that endlessly comforting.

'Your physical needs will be tended to,' she said. 'Then you will take instruction with the others.'

'But isn't it true that everyone here ... desires the death of everyone else? It has never been clear to me how sorcerers co-operate, even on everyday things.'

We descended a long slope. I stumbled and fell many times, clinging desperately to the manuscript satchel, more than once losing the blanket. Each time, Devourer-of-Birds would lift me up, wrap me in the blanket again, and we would continue. I was like a clumsy puppet in her hands.

'Think of us,' she said, 'as a band of thieves trapped in a cave filled with unimaginable treasure. As long as they're trapped, the thieves work together in the common interest of all, to find food and water, to tend one another's wounds, even to sing and joke and drive the fear of their predicament away. They are a brotherhood of necessity. But when they find a way out, oh, *then* things change, and every thief seeks to carry off as much as he can and prevent the others from getting the rest.'

'The gatekeeper ...' My teeth chattered so badly I couldn't finish speaking. It was hard to remember what I wanted to say.

'The gatekeeper was a foolish girl who thought she had learned enough and took you for an easy graduation exercise. She was wrong, of course, as you know already, as you will examine at your leisure for the rest of your life, Sekenre. But her attempt was, by the custom of the College, right and proper. She declared for you. Whenever a newcomer arrives, it is a challenge for one of us to take up. But only one. I, for instance, am not allowed to kill you just now, if that is what you are thinking. I am sure it is. I don't blame you. But there are rules here. We thieves co-operate within our cave.'

I wanted to believe her. I wanted to ask her who enforced

the rules. But my throat was raw and burning, my face so numb I couldn't feel my lips moving.

Darkness rose like a mist, indefinable, not truly a mist, or a cloud, or shadow, just a diminishing of light as the sky shifted from steely gray to almost black. I couldn't see the eagles anymore. Far away, wind shrieked among the peaks.

We walked into an ever-narrowing ravine, out of the wind. Gradually the way became a wooden trench, then a boardwalk by a peaked roof.

Once we encountered a girl about my own age who drifted inches above the boards, her legs ending irregularly in mid-air, the stump of one a little longer than the other. A fragment of hand and forearm floated in front of her. I couldn't tell if the hand was even attached at the wrist.

I shook my head, blinking, not sure I saw what I thought I did: the upper and lower halves of her body separated by a distinct gap. An almost animate darkness surrounded her, an attending shadow, or black smoke, or just a dark, filmy garment.

I saw her face clearly enough, an expressionless, two-dimensional cut-out hovering in the air.

And again, the Devourer and I struggled through deep snow. She bore me in her arms now, as if I were a small child, lifting my weight effortlessly. I clung to her, one arm around her back, the other holding both the satchels atop me beneath the blanket.

Amid the snow we came upon another denizen of this place, another member, I assumed, of the Invisible Lodge, this time a silver-haired, long-bearded man of obviously vast age, so gaunt he seemed little more than a skeleton as he stood naked to the wind and cold, stiff as a wooden ikon, his arms outstretched, his skin almost blue.

Devourer of Birds called out something to him. He made no reply.

'That one has removed himself far from us,' she said. 'I do not think he'll ever master his particular species of sorcery. He seeks to clothe himself in the whole world. The earth and sky are his flesh, so he can feel and touch everything, everywhere. That is the theory of it, anyway.'

I coughed hard and leaned over to spit out a gob of saliva. 'I wouldn't want to do it like that,' I gasped.

'No, I think the first thing you need as a sorcerer is a set of warm clothes.'

I breathed hard, trying very hard to focus my thoughts, to assemble my words. 'But, if anyone . . . if you . . . you could give me a cloak and weave my death into it. Maybe my shirt would turn into fire while I slept wearing it . . .'

'Sekenre,' she said sternly, as if I had given offense. 'Would you rather freeze?'

'I—' I coughed again. Something broke loose in my head. Now my nose was stopped up and my eyes ran with water. I spat, swallowed, then lay back, eyes closed, and concentrated on just breathing.

'You can't go walking barefoot in the snow, Sekenre. First you freeze. Then the frozen parts turn black, and black rot spreads. The choice becomes amputation or death.'

'Can that . . . really . . . happen?'

'You're from a hot country, aren't you?'

'Yes.'

'It can happen. It will happen if you don't get yourself a decent pair of shoes.'

That was too much. I think I was becoming delirious, or else I just needed some release after all I had been through. I trembled in her arms so violently she almost dropped me. I wept until I could feel the warm tears on my cheeks. I rocked back and forth as she held me, *laughing* hysterically like a complete lunatic. At last, gasping, I managed to say, 'Yes, yes . . . that's the story of my life . . . the epic quest for a good pair of shoes!'

I went into a kind of spasm, and tumbled from her arms. I found myself face-down in the snow, half-buried, sucking in searing lungfuls of frigid air.

She grabbed me by the collar and hauled me upright. I sat there, sputtering, wheezing, and laughing.

In all the time I knew her, in all my stay at the College of Shadows, I never again saw Devourer of Birds at a loss. Only then. She stood over me in complete befuddlement.

'Did I say something funny?'

I tried to explain, but could only cough. The pain in my throat was worse than ever. It felt like I'd swallowed splintering wood.

There is a gap in my memory after that. I think Orkanre rose up to wear the body, to guard against treachery, rules or no rules. I felt myself in the Devourer's arms once more, my face pressed against her feather-gown. I don't think she wore anything under it. Her body seemed neither warm or cold. There was no sensation at all touching her.

Soon great lanterns floated in the darkness, bobbing like glowing midnight blossoms on the river. Lanterns big as houses hung from the clouds on chains. I heard the eagles crying out, somewhere far away. I might have seen the sun once, far away, gleaming fitfully through the clouds like a tarnished penny, fading to blood-red, gone.

Now gleaming marble pillars rose on every side – white, black, some veined with many colors – *they* seemed to be holding up the sky. Stone columns, made by men or gods. Not the mountains.

Still the Devourer-of-Birds carried me through the snow, down a rough and rocky slope, between the marble columns while fur-muffled figures walked alongside us, a short distance off.

Then the floor was as smooth as the polished columns. I turned in the Devourer's arms and looked down to see my own face staring up at me, drifting along beneath a dark ceiling.

I saw her face too, pale as the Sybil's, like the moon in the night sky.

And in a kind of dream I sensed the Sybil stirring among her bones and debris. She held the thread of my life in her hands, but merely watched it trail away into the darkness like a fishing line.

I was truly amazed to awaken in my own body, free of apparent restraint, no one's prisoner. But it was the pain that woke me up, my hands and feet burning from within in a manner I didn't understand. I held my hands to my face. My fingers were stiff and cold. I tried to say something, but managed only a hoarse croak, then a wet, violent coughing. It took me several minutes to make sense of any of this.

Flames crackled off to my right, giving off the pleasant smell of wood smoke.

I hadn't been killed. Possibly the Devourer of Birds had actually told me the truth, about the thieves in the cave, or else my other selves had successfully warded off any attack. Or, I was like a book not yet opened, and no one cared to murder me until they had a better idea of what the result would be. Then again – and this seemed the most likely explanation – the sorcerers outside my body were surely as jealous of one another as those within. The many would not allow a single one to carry off the prize. No one had yet outwitted all the others. For a while, I would be allowed to live.

But, to more immediate matters. I lay on a soft couch, beneath blankets and furs, still terribly cold, my extremities aching terribly as sensation returned, the clothes I wore damp as – now I understood it – my body's heat turned the *snow* into water.

I sneezed, then coughed. I was sick from the cold. I knew that much. I felt it all the way into my chest.

I closed my eyes and lay back, trying to think, but someone put a hand under my head and raised me up, then pressed a cup to my lips. The drink was warm and sweet.

Poison? I thought not. None of those within me sensed any danger. No, not yet.

Once more I dozed off, and when next I awoke I was atop the furs, unable to offer any resistance as many hands peeled off layer after layer of wet clothing. At last someone undid my loincloth and pulled it gently away.

I looked up, too sick to be ashamed that I was naked in front of all these people. A dozen or so sorcerers crowded around me like vultures contemplating a meal. I grabbed a blanket and tried to roll myself up in it. Someone forced me to lie still, and they saw every mark upon me, every scar.

But I wasn't cold. This was a hot place. The couch had been moved so near a fireplace that I actually streamed with sweat. Devourer of Birds laid my wet clothing over a wooden rack. I noticed that she'd taken out my shoes and placed them on the hearth. They looked soggy now.

I reached down and touched the smooth marble floor, then gazed up at pillars higher than any even in the palace of the City of the Delta. The lanterns did indeed float among them. They were indeed as large as houses. Once I saw a winged man leap out of a window outlined in fire, then soar upward, trailing sparks, to vanish into the immeasurable distance beneath the ceiling.

A warty, hairy-faced dwarf rolled me onto one side and applied something acrid-smelling and greasy to some of my injuries. A bald woman in close-fitting crocodile hide leaned over and touched each mark on my body with a flickering serpent's tongue, her breath nearly scalding me.

When she was done, no one resisted my efforts to wrap myself in a blanket.

'The pattern is not complete,' the crocodile-woman said aloud, but seemingly to herself. She spoke the language of the dead.

Only the mark on my forehead, the Sybil's mark, she did not touch.

A man in a gleaming black robe held an hourglass. He turned it over, and the glass filled with pure white fire.

The others sat on the floor around me. Now it was my turn to examine them from where I lay. Some were visibly deformed by their magic. As I looked, I was less sure that the lizard-tongued woman *wore* the crocodile hide, rather than it being her own skin. A sorcerer behind her had the head of a bird, flicking constantly from side to side, brilliant blue feathers ruffled, eyes wide with perpetual astonishment. I couldn't tell if it had once been a man or a woman.

Several others appeared outwardly normal, complete human beings. But I knew enough of sorcery to disregard that. After all, could not Sekenre, the slayer of kings, pass on the street for an ordinary Reedlandish boy?

A red-bearded, pink-faced man drew near me and whispered. 'I be your friend,' he said in garbled, barely intelligible Deltan. His breath stank. His teeth were filed to points, like a Zargati. At first I thought he had been hideously burned, but then I realized that his skin color was merely that of some exotic barbarian race.

When I made no reply, he punched me lightly on the shoulder, grinned broadly, and said, 'Stand you beside me and all good. Help I you against them, who yours and mine enemies.'

The rest of the company laughed.

Devourer of Birds approached and the others stood or shuffled respectfully aside. I noted that with interest.

She knelt by my couch, her back to the fire, her feathers – which had now evolved into a kind of cloak – suffused with light.

'Hello,' I said. My voice had degenerated into a gurgle.

'Don't say anything, Sekenre.' She opened something flat and wooden, one hinged panel, then another, revealing mirrored inner surfaces, similar to the device I'd used telling fortunes to raise money for Lady Necu, back in Thadistaphon so long ago.

The Devourer held it up so that my face appeared in the center panel.

Vashtem, my father, seized the body suddenly. He cried out and reached up to swat the mirror away. But the sorceress easily jerked it out of my reach. She spoke a few sharp words. The others restrained me with no great effort, while she held her triple mirror once more before my face.

Father let go and I was Sekenre again. I stared at myself in the glass. On either side of my face, others appeared one by one, as if summoned and dismissed in turn, some familiar, some not, faces I had seen only in dreams or in someone else's memories: Orkanre and Talno and Balredon and Tannivar and Lekkanut-Na and many, many more, their victims, and my own. Moon regarded me impassively, and even the Zargati Haryn-Isha appeared, for all that he was still alive in a bottle back in Father's laboratory.

So the sorcerers searched the depths of me, to see what and whom I contained. Only Vashtem did not appear. I don't know how he concealed himself. But he had always been the master sorcerer, more powerful, cleverer, wiser than any single rival. Somehow he managed.

At last the side-mirrors went dark. Only Sekenre was reflected in the central glass.

'Ah,' said Devourer of Birds, closing the mirror-book.

They left me alone for days afterward. The next time I awoke, I was dressed in my own clothes, which had been dried by the fire and felt wonderfully warm against my skin. Blankets and furs covered me once more. A bowl of soup steamed on a table by the couch. But I was afraid of poison and did not eat. Still my throat tormented me hideously every time I tried to swallow. I shivered, alternately cold and slick with sweat. I knew I had a quite natural fever, that this was no magic. It was in the interest of the sorcerers for me to recover. If I died on my own, without being slain – what? All the 'treasure' I contained would be wasted, like wine spilled on desert sand.

Therefore it seemed only logical that someone would break the rules and poison me.

Time passed. I didn't eat. Food appeared, grew cold, and was removed. I awoke with my throat parched, my lips cracked, and this time I risked all and drank from a goblet left for me. The stuff inside tasted like honey and soothed my throat. A little later I sat up and picked at some cold meat.

Later still, I discovered my two satchels placed neatly on the floor by the end of the couch. I reached down and picked up the manuscript-bag, opened it, and checked to see that my book was all right. All the pages seemed to be there, though I didn't take them out and count them. As soon as possible I would have to examine the whole thing with painstaking care, since an enemy might have penned a single character somewhere in the middle which could change the meaning of the entire text, cripple me, or bring about my death. But for the moment, I did what I should have done long before. I wove strands of sorcerer's silk over the opening of the bag, so that I would know if anyone got into it.

My cloth shoes were placed neatly by the bags, but heavy, fur-lined boots had also been provided. I examined both first for subtle traps – magical patterns, tiny, poisoned barbs, or whatever – then tried the boots on and stood up, unsteadily, feeling very light, as if only such massive footwear anchored me to the floor. A similarly heavy fur coat lay draped over a chair. I searched it too, put it on, and stepped away from the couch.

The fire had been allowed to burn down. A few feet away from the fireplace, and the room grew intensely cold. A few more and the firelight receded into the darkness much more quickly than it should have, until the coals smoldered like distant stars, almost too faint to see. I leaned against a pillar, much too weak to go anywhere, sniffling, wiping my nose on my coat sleeve every once in a while. Overhead, something huge and dark passed, flapping like a tent in the wind. I had the impression of an enormous bird or bat, vanishing into the darkness among the columns.

I turned back toward the fire and took a step, and another, and another. The light continued to fade. Something was wrong with the space here. Distances weren't right. Darkness closed in around me. I ran as hard as I could, panting, gasping, increasingly afraid, until at last I caught hold of the back of the couch, then staggered around to the front and fell face down on the bedding, as exhausted as if I had been on a long journey.

Again I awoke. The fire burned vigorously this time, but I sat a distance from it in a high-backed wooden chair. I felt vaguely damp, and looked down to discover that my new boots were caked with mud. My hands, too, were muddy between the fingers and under the nails. I tasted salt in my mouth.

Vashtem stirred within me, cursing under his breath – my breath, in white puffs – at this puny, almost useless body which would have to serve his purpose for the time being.

'Father?' I whispered hoarsely.

'Shut up, son.'

I remembered then: Vashtem wearing the body, dragging himself through darkness for hours, sometimes walking, sometimes on all fours, often clinging to stone walls or iron fixtures to keep himself from fainting.

I sensed his purpose, as the memory became a kind of dream and I lived it again, but Vashtem concealed his secret even from Sekenre, and mere fragments of the adventure remained, fleeting glimpses: Candles lit at the touch of a hand, arranged carefully in twin rows on either side of a black sarcophagus; then Vashtem rifling through a vast library, cursing as his stiff, cold, boy's fingers made him clumsy. Sekenre was the one who was sick. He felt the pain. Vashtem didn't care.

He blew away dust and coughed, clutching the side of a bookshelf. Then he found the volume he wanted and opened it. Sekenre the Illuminator, in the memory itself, at the time this had really happened, started in amazement at the sight of page after page of intricate, impenetrable characters in hair-thin, raised silver.

Another gap. Darkness. Vashtem stood by the shore of a black, misty lake. Far away, ruined stone buildings barely protruded above the motionless water, like jagged, rotting teeth.

The moon rose, like a huge paper mask, but made no reflection.

The air was warm here. The body streamed sweat under the heavy fur coat. Vashtem didn't care about that either.

He listened for a long time to what might have been mere silence, to some sound that I, Sekenre-within-Vashtem, could not hear. Whether he was pleased or displeased, whether he had accomplished his mission or not, I couldn't tell.

I think he smiled at first, then, incredibly even to himself, wept those tears allegedly impossible for a full-fledged sorcerer. He touched fingers to his soft, unformed, boy's face, then touched his tongue, puzzling over the taste of his own tears.

Vashtem struggled to remember something. I couldn't make it out. He crouched down, searching for himself in the black water, but his face was no more mirrored there than the moon's.

More incredibly, he knelt down in the mud at the water's edge, hands upraised and apart, and began to pray, first to the Titans, then, as he grew bolder, as any regret or doubt receded, to the gods, whom he dared address as *brothers*.

And he listened to the long silence.

At the end of the dream, Vashtem rode through the reeds

at the water's edge astride a naked man as enormously fat as Lekkanut-Na, a great mountain of muddy, damp, cold flesh wallowing on all fours, half-covered with the dripping moss that streamed out of his mouth, his ears, his hair, his armpits and his rear.

The naked man rolled his head upward once, glaring with recognition and unending hatred.

'Ah, my old master,' Vashtem said. 'I have learned so much from you. Now I am returned at last. I want you to be proud of me.'

The fat man rolled over suddenly, making slurping, sucking sounds, mud spewing from his mouth. Vashtem leapt clear nimbly, splashing. Water filled the fur boots.

The fat man was scaled on the underside, like a fish. He thrashed helplessly, reaching for Vashtem, fingers as thick as my forearm clasping and unclasping.

Vashtem held a sharp, wooden stake. He brushed the fat man's hands aside easily. For all his apparent mass, the former master was barely substantial, like an inflated skin.

The fat man whimpered as Vashtem drove the stake into his throat. The sheer size of the rolling, thrashing body made it difficult to manage, but there was no strength in it. Vashtem dug his boots into the mud for purchase, then leaned his hundred-pound-if-that boy's body against the stake, cursing to himself that it might not be enough.

It was. The fat man tried once more to speak, but managed only a bloody gurgle. In the end, he sank down into the mud, his eyes still alive, hating, filled with terror as the water closed over his face.

Vashtem left him like that.

I jerked my head up, looking around, startled, taking a minute to re-orient myself. I sat on the couch by the fire, one of the furs crumpled up in my lap. My muddy boots had made a puddle among the bedclothes. I slipped them off and padded barefoot over to the fireplace and left them there to dry.

My hands were muddy too. But I didn't have any way to clean them other than to wipe as much as I could off on my coat, then spit, and wipe some more.

(*'Sekenre, I think you're always going to be a mess,'* said Lekkanut-Na within me. *'I think you're doomed to inelegance.'*)

'Maybe,' I said aloud.

I felt well enough to get on with my more serious task. Seated among the bedclothes, I opened the book-satchel and spread the first few pages out before me. I placed a globe of magical fire overhead so I could see better, then, with great care, I went through the text, running over the letters, not with my finger as many readers do, but with the handle of my longest calligraphic brush.

Touching the brush to page five brought a sudden pop and a whiff of smoke. Something like a tiny serpent with a human face arced up from the paper, caught hold of the brush handle in its teeth, and whirled around and around, hissing, shooting off sparks. I tossed it and the brush into the fireplace, then sat still, considering what I had found.

Somebody wanted to kill me. That was no surprise. But there is a time and a place for murder in the College of Shadows, as Devourer of Birds had told me, and a sorcerer must challenge another first, 'declare for him,' as she'd put it, and the winner graduates.

Possibly she hadn't told me everything. Possibly someone was cheating. It had been a feeble attempt, but an attempt nonetheless.

Father had broken a few rules in his time. He had *not* murdered his master, for all that he had overcome him. How, then, did Vashtem manage to leave? By murdering someone else unannounced?

I called him up within my mind, but he would not come.

'Father,' I said within myself, *'if I am to succeed, I must know everything you do. As I told you before, there must be no secrets between us.'*

But he would not answer.

I reached into my bag for another brush, then paused. What if the bag itself contained a trap? Where would this end? I got up, went over to the fire, pulled a smoldering stick out, and used that to probe the inside of the bag.

Nothing. I dumped the contents out onto the bedclothes,

wrapping my hands in cloth before stacking the entire manuscript to one side, then carefully examining everything else: pens, brushes, ink bottles, the box with the unfinished page in it, even the handful of coins one by one.

The statue of Bel-Kemad was missing. Futilely, I slid my hand around inside the bag, as if it might still be there, but invisible.

Of course, sorcerers do not worship the gods. Often, they fear them. Whoever had rummaged through my things might well have thrown the statue into the fire.

(What had Father been doing in my dream? Was that prayer, or a challenge? I asked. But he concealed himself even from me, as he had from the Devourer's mirror.)

I sat still for a long time, trying to figure all this out, all the while hurt, angry, and afraid that someone had tried to turn something as intimate as my manuscript against me. I felt violated.

What now? Obsessively, I went on through the rest of the book, until at last I was confident there were no more alterations. Then I put the manuscript away, resealed the bag, and sat back, shivering once more. The fever had returned. I was, as it seemed I always would be, completely exhausted.

But I didn't sleep. One by one I called my more familiar selves forward into my mind and interviewed Orkanre, Tannivar, Balredon, and Lekkanut-Na, all of whom freely spoke of their experiences in the College of Shadows.

No one agreed on anything. Tannivar's entire time had consisted of wandering through a dark forest. He heard many voices, uncovered many secrets, learned, slew, and departed, but never actually *saw* another sorcerer. Orkanre had drifted in a small boat on a fog-shrouded lake, while others congregated around him, walking on water, or in boats. He, too, was instructed. He drowned his master with his hands, while the others looked on. Lekkanut-Na was already entombed when she reached the College, and so attended only in her dreams.

Father came forward and volunteered some information: that he had begun as I had, in his own study, in his own house. Unlike me, he had never stepped outside. Nor had the house moved to any remote clime. Some of those sounds and smells from behind his door which had so disturbed me as a child were the result of his class exercises. One of the gatekeepers was in a bottle on his shelf.

(*'You see, my son, I enrolled toward the end of my career, not at the beginning as most sorcerers do. I had already achieved greatness before I even arrived. Does that startle you?'*)

'Then why am I here now?' I said aloud.

(*'For each sorcerer, the necessities are different. For each, the College of Shadows is a kind of consummation, after which the sorcerer is whole and complete. In my case, the path was long and tangled and took many years. In yours, the consummation must be accomplished quickly, urgently. You know perfectly well why.'*)

'Yes, I know perfectly well.'

The Palace of Sorcerers, for so I find it convenient to name it, cannot be readily described. In all my time there, as a student of the College of Shadows, I never grasped the entirety of it. Shape, layout, architectural plan all eluded me, as if they were one more mystery to be fathomed in the course of one's apprenticeship.

I questioned Devourer of Birds and she replied that this was indeed the case. A legendary sorcerer known only as the Builder had constructed it as part of his own attempt to master the magical arts. So great was his skill, so tireless his patience, so vast the product of his labor, that the rest of us could wander through his rooms and halls for centuries if we chose, gazing out the windows into many lands and worlds. Some speculated that the whole thing was intended as a clockwork mechanism of virtually infinite complexity – she paused here to explain about *mechanical* clocks that foreigners build, quite unlike the familiar Reedlandish sand or water clocks.

'The two of us talking here,' she said as we walked through a darkened room amid drifting bubbles of light, 'the others wandering about, the murders, the spells we cast, the books we read, everything that goes on here is all part of the Builder's device. We are but cogs and wheels and screws.

When he is finished building, when the pieces begin to perform their functions . . . who knows?'

I hefted my bags and my muddy boots from one shoulder to the other. I carried them tied together, and wore my cloth shoes, having wrapped my feet against the cold in strips torn from bedclothes. I didn't want to leave anything behind where someone could tamper with it.

I shrugged. 'How do we know the clock isn't working already?'

'How indeed? Possibly it is already doing what it's supposed to do. Have you ever encountered anything more about this, Sekenre, in your reading?'

'Ah . . . no.' Possibly I had, but every sorcerer has his secrets, especially at the College of Shadows.

'There are stories,' she said.

'Tell me some.'

'The first is that when the clock strikes midnight, the world's last hour has come, and even the gods and titans will die as Surat-Temad devours the universe, leaving only the Builder. He is a manifestation or agent of some force beyond all others, greater even than Surat-Temad. He shall raise his hand, speak the secret name which is the death-of-Death, and even the Crocodile-Headed One shall dissolve into primal mist, into nothingness.'

'But why?'

Devourer of Birds smiled. Her face seemed to wrinkle, almost crack. But somehow I felt that her smile was genuine, that now she was at her ease and amused with me, as a wise and learned queen might be with a peasant boy who asks naive questions.

'The prevailing school of thought holds that the God Who Is Greater Than Gods has tired of the universe as it now is. He wants his sleep. But the universe is like an endless racket outside his window. He needs silence. Then he can dream creation anew, wholly different, wholly strange.'

'Won't that make more noise outside his window?'

The Devourer actually *laughed* and sounded very, very human just then, as if her sorcery were no more than a charade, now ended.

'Yes, Sekenre, I suppose it will.'

'And the other stories?'

She paused, her mind on something else. We had come to a pool set in the middle of the floor where luminous golden fish drifted in the black water, whispering softly. I could almost make out their words.

The Devourer turned away from the fish and continued on her way. I looked back once and saw that the fish had begun to change into glowing, naked people, none of them taller than the length of my hand.

'Come, Sekenre.'

I hurried after her.

'Ah yes,' she said, 'more stories. Some say that the Builder was an intensely moral and upright artisan, not at all wicked like you or me –' she smiled at me with just a trace of malice, then went on – 'who accidentally ran down a sorcerer one day while driving his cart. Oh, he tried to give every aid and comfort. He cradled the dying sorcerer's head in his hands as the man – or maybe it was a woman – lay beneath the wheel of the cart, but, wouldn't you know it? The sorcerer died anyway and passed into his slayer. Our hero found himself here, at the College of Shadows. Completely horrified at the prospect of endless killing, he employed his artisan's skills – possibly he was a carpenter, or a carver of some sort – to find another way out. Therefore he builds and builds, hoping that one day he can open a door and step through into his home town, and return to being a simple and virtuous man without enemies. They say he's still working at it. Therefore the palace grows and grows. Often you discover a room no one has ever seen before.'

'Or at least no one has reported it to anyone else.'

'Yes, that could be.'

Such are the secrets of the sorcerer.

(*Father, did you find another way out?*)

(*How do you know I ever left? Suppose the entire world was cobbled together by this builder, even into the heart of Surat-Kemad. The College of Shadows might well go on forever.*)

* * *

I don't know which, if either, of the stories is true. The former explains the vastness and mystery of the place. The latter offers hope. Surely each sorcerer, deep within himself, longs to return to his former state, to be an ordinary human being again. He toys with the idea. He torments himself with false optimism, then tries to dismiss the story, give it a cynical ending, with the deluded Builder working futilely until the end of time, adding more and more rooms to the Palace of Sorcerers.

('*He's looking for the latrine, Sekenre,*' said Lekkanut-Na, '*and doomed by a particularly insidious curse never to find it.*')

('Shut up. Stop laughing. That's not funny.')

I never found my way back to the fireplace and the couch. I wandered through more rooms than I could count. Sometimes I slept on the floor, wrapped in my fur coat, sometimes on a bench, once beside a fountain of ghostly fire, pale white, silent flames giving off only a trace of heat.

That morning I awoke and found a naked man sitting in the fountain. The flames burned him. I saw his flesh bubble, blacken, and fall away. His hair exploded in a single burst and his bald scalp began to peel.

I forgot myself. I thought to rescue him. I reached into the fire, then drew my hand out again in dreadful fascination, now all but forgetting the burning man as I watched the flames spread slowly up my sleeve, sizzling, only slightly warm.

'I'd smother that if I were you,' the man in the fountain said. 'It *will* hurt you after a while. You'll end up where I am.'

Quickly I extinguished the flames in the folds of my coat. My bare hand tingled, as if it had been washed in alcohol. I regarded the burning man as his face dropped away like melting wax. One of his eyeballs popped.

'Don't you feel any pain?' I asked.

'Yes, but I have learned to ignore it. The sorcerer must be oblivious to physical discomfort. Pain is merely irrelevant.'

I stood there watching, unable to turn away, as the flames

consumed him completely, and the shrivelled husk of his body sank down out of sight.

Nauseous, I hurried from the room.

I never learned to ignore discomfort – the fever, aches, throbbing pain from the wound in my thigh which didn't seem to be healing properly, and the omnipresent cold. It was always wretchedly cold in the Palace of Sorcerers unless one stood right up against a fire. I could never truly get warm, or clean. The best I could do to wash was to grab a handful of snow from an open window and wipe myself down with it. I was also slowly starving. Any sudden exertion became a risk that I would faint and be killed or enslaved while helpless.

I read a story once about a sorcerer lost in the desert, who lay down and shrivelled up like a dried seed, returning to life five hundred years later when travellers found him and touched water to his lips. I could see that happening to me. More than once I dreamt of it. I'd be no more than a heap of rubbish in a corner of one of the enormous rooms, rags, skin stretched over a few bones, a tangle of hair, unnoticed for five hundred years or more.

But I continued on my way, and the fever left me in its own time, neither magicked away nor ignored. I felt empty, as if the wind blew right through me.

I began to explore, making notes about each room I visited:

A bedroom with lace canopies and intricately-carven chairs, a lady's stand with bottles and a mirror, lamps drifting in the air like bubbles. But when I stepped into that room, the lamps crashed to the floor. The bed and the chairs melted with startling swiftness, for they were made of ice so delicate that the heat of my body was enough to destroy them.

Then, a series of colored rooms, red, blue, green, white, gold: and finally black, suffused with subtle light, empty but for a single mask set on the wall in the black room. I touched the mask, then lifted it from its peg. The thing was strangely wrought of some light metal I couldn't identify. If it concealed any secret, I didn't find it. I even put the mask on and peered out through its wide, startled eyes. But I only saw the black room. So I replaced the mask on its peg and left.

Once I turned suddenly in a dim corridor and stared in amazement as my way seemed blocked by thousands of pale giants congregated together: kings and queens in heavy robes, fierce warriors in battle stance, solemn sages, a naked, impossibly muscular man holding up some invisible weight; and among these, grotesque cripples, eyeless people, hunchbacks; a human worm without arms or legs but with vestigial fins runing up his back; even a young girl holding her detached, screaming head aloft in her hands.

All of them stood before me, utterly motionless, utterly silent, but somehow so real that I believed them to be living beings until I reached out, touched the nearest, and felt stone.

Even then I wasn't sure. Nothing is impossible in the College of Shadows. I ran my hand over the perfectly polished, pure marble, and it trembled slightly, as if stirring to life.

I drew my hand back and waited. Nothing happened.

Shadows shifted, light streaming into some distant room at the far end of the corridor, through a skylight I couldn't see.

I had to crawl and wriggle between those marble legs, like a marsh rat in a clump of grass, and as I did I slowly came to realize the most amazing thing of all, that these carvings, the corridor and the wider room the corridor opened up into were *of one piece,* chipped from a single, mountainous block of stone.

That was too crazy. I thought I must be delirious. I rested between a giant's feet, waiting for my mind to clear.

From far away came the *plink-plink-plink* of a hammer striking a chisel. I struggled toward it, many times forced to turn aside and take a circuitous course, or even doubling back as the sound seemed to come from one direction, then another. The room was *huge.* The carving must have taken centuries. Still the hammering echoed all around me. Shadows lengthened, deepened. Night fell. I lay still in darkness as the hammering continued without pause. I couldn't sleep at all, but gazed at the stars for hours through the glass roof.

In the darkness, I am certain, the statues *did* move, their stone limbs and necks grinding, as the monsters towering over me conversed among themselves in low whispers, in some secret language of stone.

I clung to the spiny back of some half-human beast, fearful of being crushed as the statues shifted.

The hammering continued without pause.

Perhaps I did sleep for a while and dream that Vashtem my father stood beside me, in his white robe and silver mask.

'This is not the way for you, Sekenre,' he said.

'Why not?' I said, as faintly as I could, lest the giants overhear.

'You haven't the patience. Nor have I.'

Slowly the darkness faded into gray. Father was no longer with me. I strained to make out the great, inert shapes of the stone giants once more, slowly defining themselves in the gloom.

I rose, still very cold, feeling faint, my injured leg so sore I could barely stand, but I forced my way along, crawling up the back of an enormous stone crocodile. When I reached its head, the hammer sound was suddenly sharper, and to my immediate right.

There, through a mazeway of stone bodies and limbs, framed between two stooping marble eagles, stood an old man with hair and beard as white as the marble, clad in a soiled white smock and torn leather apron, with hammer in one hand and chisel in the other, carving a *door* out of the rough, solid stone of the far wall.

I watched for a while, puzzled that he would spend such time and effort on embellishments, swirling designs of roses and leaves, before he finished the basic outline of the door itself.

Had I been carving, I would have settled for a plain rectangle of a door, a knob, hinges, anything I could open as quickly as possible.

I looked on in awe, then felt an intense urge to flee. (*'Get control of yourself!'* said Lekkanut-Na. She seemed more curious about this place than any of the others. But Father and Orkanre stirred awake within me.)

I crept nearer, close enough to see the chips fly, to hear them rattle as they hit the floor.

But the carver was briefly hidden from view as I passed behind the seated figure of a horse-headed god, and when I emerged again, he was gone.

I ran my fingers over the door, marvelling at the delicacy of the design. But I could not open it, or even detect the crack between the door and the wall, if there was one.

I could only wonder: Had I seen the Builder himself and frightened him away before he could complete this door? Or had it merely been a fellow sorcerer, who worked magic through arduous carving, even as I did through letters, and who didn't care to reveal his art to me?

A sorcerer must have his secrets, after all.

So, in darkness and in light, but always intensely cold, the Palace of Sorcerers extended forever, its corridors and rooms multiplied like reflections in an endless maze of mirrors. I lost all sense of time. Hours or even days might pass without my encountering another sorcerer, then suddenly I'd turn a corner or open a door and find a whole crowd of them working together, or a single one at study or ease.

I seldom spoke to them. I would pass on by them slowly, as if with great dignity, but really to conceal how physically weak I was.

Possibly among sorcerers, even starvation is an art. The naked man in the snow probably hadn't eaten or truly slept in years. Like the burning man, he had transcended all such considerations.

I couldn't do that, any more than I could ask some other sorcerer for a spare loaf of bread. Why should he give it to me? Why should he not poison it and announce, as I began to eat, that he'd declared for me?

I stood in a doorway looking out onto a roof and surprised the Devourer of Birds as she summoned thousands of tiny birds out of the air, finches, sparrows, and little humming things no larger than bees. Their song was like high-pitched thunder, the air trembling with their wingbeats. They swarmed around her as thick as smoke, chirping, whistling, screeching as she replied to them in the same speech; as her face seemed to float in a raging sea of feathers; as she took birds into her hands one by one, twisting their necks, then biting them until blood and feathers matted her chin.

I was so famished then that I thought I would eat a bird, raw, one among the many thousands. No one would notice. I stepped out onto the roof and grabbed for a bird.

But they rose like a whirlwind, exploding into my face so that I had to shield my eyes with my hands. I fell back through the doorway. When I could see again, when they were gone, there was the Devourer of Birds on all fours before me, rooting among dead birds, grunting and snorting like some scavenging beast as she tore them apart with her hands and teeth, sometimes chewing them to a pulp and spitting them out again, sometimes swallowing, sometimes pausing to examine the interior of a tiny body as if it held some vast and inscrutable significance, which I had no doubt it did.

After several minutes she looked up, her face filthy, feathers matted around her mouth like a beard.

Once more she smiled.

'Do I disgust you, Sekenre? Each sorcerer finds a unique path to sorcery. This is merely mine.'

Eventually I discovered the kitchen. I couldn't concentrate on sorcery. I only thought of food. I knew I was dying, that I had been ten days, possibly more without anything more than occasional handfuls of snow. My body seemed but a bundle of twigs, held together by my heavy coat, somehow still animated by some energy other than my own.

Then I opened a plain wooden door, and stood there clinging to the doorway, amazed at the sight of ovens, pots simmering on fires, baskets of bread on the floor, bowls of fruit set on tables, long benches ready to accommodate a hundred diners.

The kitchen was empty. Possibly my coming had frightened off the cooks. I couldn't see why they should be afraid of me.

Possibly it was all an illusion, conjured by my drifting mind.

Or else I had created it, out of genuine sorcery.

Or someone else had, and everything was poisoned.

I sat down at one of the tables, exhausted, trying to sort out the meaning of all this. At last I took a chance, picked a piece of some unfamiliar fruit, and bit into it. The taste was sweet and moist and good, but almost at once my stomach cramped painfully. I threw the fruit away and fell back over the bench onto the floor.

'Who is challenging me . . .?' I gasped aloud.

(*'I don't think anyone is,'* said Lekkanut-Na within me. *'I think you're so far gone that you'll have to learn to eat all over again. Wait a few minutes, then try some broth. Then rest. Don't take solids for a while.'*)

I obeyed her, sipped wonderful soup from one of the simmering pots, then lay down on a bench and slept. If any other sorcerers came to eat while I was there, they did not interfere with me.

When I was ready to leave, I said aloud, 'How will I find this again?'

'You merely will,' said Lekkanut-Na aloud, using my voice.

Perhaps by this same principle, I found the library. My own path to sorcery, after all, is one of words, of illuminated letters and painted images. I had to have books. So I dreamed of books and awoke to find myself in a vast, frigid cavern, sitting up on a stone bench in the uncertain light as brass lamps shaped like fat-bellied serpents smoked and flickered overhead. As far as I could see, cubbyholes and shelves stretched upward into the gloom, cut out of the living rock.

I took down a book from the nearest shelf, but it was written in a language I didn't know, so I replaced it and took out another, and another. I ranged along the shelves, sometimes climbing up the front of them, sometimes reaching in as far as I could reach for some scroll or codex, only to find it hopelessly worn or worm-eaten or frozen into a solid mass of paper and ice.

I almost stumbled over a frozen corpse which sat hunched on the floor, its blue-black face gouged and mutilated, both eyes gone, nose like a second gaping mouth, lipless mouth stretched into an eternal grin. I shuddered in disgust, stepped back, and reached at random into a shelf and pulled out an oversized scroll.

'No,' someone said. I looked up with a start. A tall, thin, pale-faced man in a black robe and skull-cap stood beside me. 'You'll never find anything that way.' The stranger spoke heavily accented Deltan, his breath puffing white.

'How do you know what I'm looking for?'

'Any book you might want . . .' He swept his hand through the air. 'Anything at all, is here. Ah, but finding it is another matter. The Library of Shadows is infinite. It contains every book ever written, and books not yet written, even some which, in fact, will never be written. Every time you put one back on the shelf, it disappears, or maybe turns into something else. Perhaps it will reappear three shelves away, or nowhere at all for a thousand years. Perhaps it will never reappear at all.' Now his tone was almost cheerfully matter-of-fact, like a helpful stranger on a city street giving directions. 'Therefore you must ask help of our friend the librarian here. Like this.' He produced a metal rod from inside his robe, heated it in the flame of the nearest lamp, then plunged it into the face of the seated corpse. Frozen flesh hissed. The corpse whimpered, then staggered to its feet, limbs creaking.

'Pain is the key,' the black-robed man said. 'It unlocks many doors.'

The corpse swayed, seemingly about to fall apart.

'Now ask for a book,' the man said.

I hesitated only for a second, then requested a legendary item I wasn't sure even existed, though I had seen reference to it, even extracts from its text in other works. I remember Tannivar puzzling over it in his own writings.

'Give me *The Book of Blood*,' I said.

Perhaps such a book didn't exist, but the corpse fetched it for me anyway. In less than a minute I held the actual, original *Book of Blood* in my hands: the work of a young sorcerer from a far, western isle, a talented, excessive, almost whimsical youth who had carved occult secrets and wild tales into his own flesh. His suffering approached infinity, but his magic sustained him. His power grew as he mutilated himself, as every inch of his body was covered with intricate characters, the text always shifting, until no page was ever the same twice. This book, created from the author's eternal agony, was the model of this very library, its archetype, perhaps the only book actually here, manifested in a million shelves in a million different forms.

In the end, the author had caused himself to be cut to pieces, his still living skin bound into the massive codex now in my hands.

The book was warm to the touch, and faintly throbbing as I held it. I turned to a random page. Two living eyes opened in the middle of swirling, red calligraphy. Blood poured over my hands, soaking my sleeves. The book screamed.

Thus I came to know the terrible secrets of *The Book of Blood.*

'Ah,' said the black-clad stranger. 'An intriguing choice.'

Before I could reply, the air rippled as if he had passed through a curtain, and I was alone once more. He had left his iron rod behind on the floor. I stooped over and picked it up in a fold of my coat.

So my researches continued in the Library of Shadows. I did what I had to, prodding the dead librarian again and again. In the books he brought, I read the deepest secrets of sorcery. I sat still for what must have been days, bundled against the cold, once more forgetting – and Lekkanut-Na still chided me – to eat or sleep until I was ready to fall over. Then I would wander among the shelves and find a passage into the kitchen, eat, rest a while, and return to the library.

Pain was more than the key. It was, for so many, for the author of *The Book of Blood* most especially, but also for the man I'd seen in the fountain and for the one who stood naked in the snow, the *way* to mastery. I understood that for all a naked Sekenre looked like something a cat had played with, my own wounds and scars were less than a beginning, a few random specks of ink on an otherwise blank page.

Pain can yield up powerful sorcery. It is a true and valid key to the mysteries, yes, but the the mutilations are infinite; the sorcerer is reshaped until no trace of the original person remains. This much the youth from the western isle learned as he screamed in his agony, as he simultaneously *welcomed* each new injury which rendered *The Book of Blood* closer to completion.

At times I was afraid that no other course lay open to any of us here at the College of Shadows. The rest was self-delusion. Only by suffering could we gain mastery of our powers. I asked my father about this, and he would not deny it.

I read much about the land of the dead and the secret ways of the dead, how corpses have their own rites no living person has ever seen – this, of course, in a book written by a corpse – I coughed from flakes of mummy-gauze swirling in the air as I turned the pages. I spent weeks unravelling a cipher which enabled me to learn the secret name of the God of Sorcerers, the usurping deity who is to come.

Father directed my efforts now, duplicating the path of his own explorations, until I understood fully what he had revealed to me already, and what he intended.

Now I knew the object of all his life, all his desperate researches, all his experiments: I knew how Vashtem had intended to raise up the God of Sorcerers and slay that god, becoming divine himself, an avatar, achieving the sorcerer's ultimate goal.

I knew how he would be free from fear.

But, despite everything, the scheme was impossible for me to accept. I wasn't even angry, let alone filled with awe and dread. It was a wild fantasy, a madman's raving, nothing Sekenre could ever actually *do*. Sekenre hoped and planned to go on with his life, somehow, despite the muddle sorcery had made of things. He would return to Reedland one day. He would live in the house by the River's edge, alone, resigned to a life without any possibility of friendship or love, and write beautifully-lettered books. He had no aspirations to godhood.

Within, Vashtem waited and manipulated his instrument. He didn't care what Sekenre thought.

Now all my other selves were awake, watching.

I even felt the Sybil holding the thread of my life, weighing it carefully.

I was finished in the library. But before I left for the last time, I did something my father could not understand. He said as much. ('Stop wasting time, Sekenre! Get on with your business.') Despite him, I crouched down before the corpse-librarian and spoke to him gently in the language of the dead.

'I know the way to the dark land,' I said. 'Let me guide you.'

'Can you? Can you relieve my pain at last?'

'Yes, I can, but if worse awaits you in the belly of Surat-Kemad, I cannot help you there.'

The corpse rose to its feet without being prodded. 'I am not afraid.'

I took the cold, rotting hand in my own and led the dead man out of the library, into a long, low hall filled with squat pillars. As we walked, he told me his name, which was Hevados, and of his native country – some barbarian region beyond the crescent sea, called the Land of Pines – and how like any man he had once dwelt in the sunlight beneath the blue sky, beneath the warm sun. More than anything else, he missed the sun. He wept for it. He remembered how he had toiled in the sun's heat, plowing the earth. But his wife and children died in a famine, and in his despair, Hevados turned to sorcery, calling a demoness to himself as he lay by night in the middle of his barren field.

He wasn't very talented. Before long an enemy beguiled him, but did not slay him, for all his body soon died of cold and starvation here in the Palace of Sorcerers.

'I think it is cold here,' he said, 'because the sorcerers are dead, all of them, and without the cold their souls would rot.'

'Am I dead then?' I asked him.

'You speak the language of corpses.'

He shook his head with sorrow and anger and went on long and bitterly. Still I walked with him, holding his hand, listening, trying not to cry out as his grip became like a vise. In his rage, he was crushing my hand. Somehow I knew that more was at stake than was readily apparent. If I screamed, I would yield to him and become like him. Someone had placed him here as a trap for me. I knew what that meant. I had been weighted and tested and the largely invisible members of the Invisible Lodge had decided what to do with me. Or at least one of them had, not necessarily the black-robed man either, who might have been their dupe, or only an illusion.

Hevados was breaking my right hand, the hand I held a pen with. Blood oozed from beneath my fingernails.

Pain unlocks doors. It also closes them forever.

With my hand destroyed, if I were unable to write, what would be left of Sekenre the Illuminator?

It was all I could do to recite the service for the dead, to speak the words of the passage out of life, to bid Hevados in a steady voice to journey on a little ways more, into the place Surat-Kemad had prepared for him.

As we walked amid the pillars in the deepening gloom, then in total darkness, I could smell mud and marsh-water, the damp air inexpressibly cold, like the swamps of Reedland on the harshest winter days. But there was more, something only one such as I could know from experience, the distinct smell of death and decay which characterizes the borderland of *Leshé*.

Then Hevados ceased his angry tirade, let go of my hand, touched me gently on the shoulder, and whispered 'Thank you,' not in the tongue of the dead, but in surprisingly pure Reedlandish. He left me in the dark, among the pillars, on the frontier of the kingdom of Surat-Kemad.

As I stood nursing my throbbing hand, I heard his footsteps splash along the water's edge. Then he stopped and spoke one last time from a far distance.

'Beware the gatekeeper,' he said.

What more can be said of the College of Shadows? Everything and nothing. It goes on and on, and so did my stay there. Not all can be committed to writing, even by the slowly healing hand of the Illuminator.

Let me try:

All sense of time faded away. I spent weeks or months or maybe even years wandering by myself through corridors and rooms, circling back to the kitchen when I needed to, leaning out of a window for snow when I wanted to drink or wash. If one place interested me, if it contained some particular marvel, I would linger there until I had learned all I could from it.

I conversed with human-faced stone beasts that paced back and forth in a stone garden, with drifting motes of light in the dark, with an enormous leviathan that swam beneath the palace, beneath the world itself, and whispered up through a shaft so deep that the monster's words took half an hour to reach me, and my replies half an hour to return.

My fellow sorcerers mostly avoided me, or else the rooms and halls were simply so vast that I did not encounter them.

I remained cold, stiff, and sore, always at the verge of exhaustion. My wounds healed slowly. I wondered if Kareda-Raza's talons had been venom-tipped. Deep within my mind she remained silent, sullen, revealing nothing. But I had almost learned to ignore such things after all. The Palace of Sorcerers was a marvel of uninhabitability, a monument to discomfort: endless drafty halls, little rooms with huge fireplaces that heated up like furnaces, benches hard and rough, stairways steep and slippery, without railings.

Yet I adapted. I claimed a sunlit room in a tower for myself, set up a board between two urns, and made a desk. For a long while I sat there, writing in the book of my life in the tiniest lettering I could manage, to hoard my precious supply of unused sheets; defining and strengthening myself by the sorcery of letters. There were no further attempts to pollute my text. No one attacked me on my own ground, through the medium of my own words. At times that puzzled me. At times it made sense.

But someone did stab me in the back during a lecture. On rare occasions we student sorcerers would gather in a common room. Somehow we all knew the time and place as wordlessly as a bird knows when and where to migrate. In some vast hall or cramped chamber, or even on a mountaintop, the sorcerous host would assemble, a dozen, a hundred, a thousand, or just two or three, as the population of the Invisible Lodge fluctuated.

So we came together like the rich young men of the Delta gathering to hear some fashionable philosopher, and listened as some visiting master sorcerer or even a demon might expound on the true meaning of the Nine Angles or the dreams of the dead or the unbinding of names.

This time, though, the teacher was our own Devourer of Birds. She demonstrated the sorcerer's cabinet, opening drawers which never contained the same thing twice and which release certain death on the uninvited or unwary.

And someone stabbed me in the back with a long, reinforced dagger, the kind foot-soldiers use to penetrate armor or gut a cavalryman's horse from underneath.

But I was already adept at bi-location, and the knife went through my false image as if through smoke and pierced the sorcerer standing in front of it, while I watched from across the room. Instead of Sekenre, an enormously tall, black-skinned man in a gleaming silver robe crumpled to the floor, the knife's point protruding out of his chest, smoke hissing from the wound.

The murderer stood over the body and grinned. I recognized him: the pale-faced, red-haired barbarian with filed teeth who had claimed to be my friend on the day of my arrival.

Then someone garroted the red-haired savage with a wire, while a third person struck off his head and arms with a cleaver and ran out of the room with these trophies wrapped in a bloody apron.

The other sorcerers drew away in disgust at the crudity of such proceedings.

'*If* we may continue . . .' Devourer of Birds said testily.

And again we gathered, at a certain turning of the year, to partake in the secret worship of the Shadow Titans, which even I, Sekenre the Illuminator, may not set down in any detail.

In the shadow of the gods, we worshipped them, for sorcery is a thing of shadow, not of light, and the gods are of the light.

In the night, when the moon hid her face and only the stars beheld us, many hundreds of sorcerers gathered along the ridges of the mountains. Flying creatures, night-gaunts, terrors filled the air, but in utter silence, their cries unheard, their wings muted.

Very slowly, below us, the earth dissolved away, and the valley filled with the black ocean of the night sky, foam of drifting stars lapping at our feet.

And the Titans appeared, like great, swimming monsters breaching from unimaginable depths, one by one: Tanilgetro, whose steed is the earthquake; Ishamander, who is Wrath; Sedengul, sower of chaos, the Father of Storms; Arvadas, the Lord of Lust; Lady Jaedelmar, who knows all things forbidden by the gods; Thia-Medak, who binds the stolen dead; Gegliel, who cut out the eyes of Surat-Kemad and wears them around his neck; Kimos the Maker, who creates what the gods would leave uncreated; and, at the very last, the wildest and fiercest of them all, Vedatis, Titan of Dreams, who invades the minds of the Nine Gods of Righteousness and troubles their repose.

Vedatis rose up. His face filled the sky.

To me at least – I think only for my ears – he spoke a single word:

'Vashtem.'

The mountains shook. The sky split with the thunder of his speech. Wind whirled me about, and I fell down faint. When I awoke, I lay on the floor of my tower room, cold air blowing over my face, brilliant sunlight dazzling my eyes. Father relinquished the body then; I was myself. I sat up and saw that my hands were caked in blood and ash. He never told me what he had done.

I came to know with absolute certainty that it was my writing which defined Sekenre the Illuminator, the endless care I put into forming each letter flawlessly, the painted capitals, the tiny pictures of birds and fishes and serpents in the margins, the very precise formulae which formed a subtext of color and shape and emphasis.

Such was my place in the scheme of things. I *seized* those persons and things around me, gaining power over them even as I introduced them into this narrative. *Naming* a secret name will hold someone fast, but *shaping* the name, stroke upon stroke, swirling curves turning back into themselves – that, *that* can bind forever.

Therefore I write:

Tannivar the Parricide.

Orkanre.

Lekkanut-Na.

Talno.

Balredon.

Dekac-Natae-Tsah, who is called Moon.

Kareda-Raza, who is Gredama, the sorceress of pain and mutilation.

And, most especially I write the name of *Vashtem,* who is my father, *Vashtem,* who murdered my mother, *Vashtem* who begat my sister solely to be the vehicle for his subsequent adventures, *Vashtem,* who hides within me, concealed from his brother sorcerers, scheming yet.

I write them, and mine is the hand which shapes their names, and I am the master of them.

Thus, in the College of Shadows, we master sorcery as we master ourselves.

With even greater care than I have taken with all the others, I write the name of *Sekenre.*

The Devourer of Birds began visiting me often. I continued my work as she looked on, sometimes writing for hours without saying anything. She would merely stand there, her feathers quivering slightly in the breeze from the open window, watching as I shaped the letters and filled the pages.

'What is in your book?' she asked me one day.

I looked up at her, startled. It hadn't occurred to me that she might be unable to read my native script, for all that she spoke Reedlandish and was clearly no illiterate, vicious imbecile like Kareda-Raza. How curious that two sorceresses in a row should be vulnerable in the same way. How truly *obscene* that those two should have anything at all in common.

I weighed my response very carefully. 'A story,' I said. 'I can't tell it to you until it is done. That's part of the magic.'

She nodded. 'Yes, a sorcerer must keep secrets, mustn't he?'

On another occasion, after equally careful consideration, I invited her to write something of her own on the page. She took the pen from me, paused, biting her lip, then drew a tiny bird where I indicated she should, amid a swirl of letters and flourishes. She smiled and returned the pen to me. I smiled back.

And later still, she asked me, 'Sekenre, what do you miss most?'

'Most what?'

'From the time before. When you were not yet a sorcerer.'

I couldn't force my throat to form the words. I swallowed hard, just trying to breathe. Oh, she had wounded me more deeply than if she had stabbed me with a knife, and I simply sat there, clutching the edge of my makeshift desk, my knees trembling, tears streaming down my face.

For a long time I made no reply at all, but drew dozens of tiny birds on the page, trailing behind the larger, much cruder bird she had drawn. It took all the power of my will to keep my hand steady.

I don't think she understood what she had done, what I felt. When I didn't answer she merely shrugged and walked over to the window, rustling her feather cape like enormous, dark wings.

'You and I have much in common, Sekenre,' she said, gazing out at the sky. 'I am ... I was ... no, I still am a human being. I miss my friends, the women who were girls when I was a girl, who grew up and raised children and loved their husbands. I remember ... lots of things ... songs, games, walking along the streets on the festival days with the other girls, while men drove herds of goats into town to be slaughtered and the older women labored to bake bread and boys were put to work stringing up the bright banners. But we girls were free ... for a little while. It was the custom. I wonder, Sekenre, is it likewise possible for a sorcerer to be free for a little while?'

'I don't know.'

'Maybe we can find out.'

She went on for a long time, recalling her life in a town called Kadisphon high among the mountains to the south where the Great River is born among spray-filled gorges; a strange place of stone houses perched on cliffs, of winding trails that seem to go on forever or else drop off, suddenly and treacherously, into space; where grimly masked priests leave sacrifices, even human beings, buried on the mountaintops for the gods and avatars who descend in the night.

She named the gods in the manner of her country and spoke of Regun-*Temad,* the black-winged, eagle-headed messenger of Death.

Above the clouds, in the stone villages among the mountain passes, there are sorcerers aplenty. When she was still an ordinary woman of middle years, before assuming the aspect and name of the Devourer, she had killed a sorcerer in revenge for the death of her lover.

She offered herself to the sorcerer in his bed, but her mouth was filled with poison. When they kissed, she spat the poison down his throat. She had taken the antidote and survived, while the sorcerer rolled to the floor, gasping. She stood over him, nauseated but triumphant for just an instant before she felt the dead man's soul pouring into her, and the hater and the hated became one. That, of course, was the beginning.

'It is hard for me, Sekenre,' she said, 'even as it is for you.'

I noted that she had not revealed any magic, any names. I continued outlining the little birds with gold ink.

'What do you plan to do?' she asked me after a while.

'Do when?'

'When you leave the College of Shadows.'

(*'Be careful, you idiot!'* Father hissed within me. His warning was apt. Inadvertently or not, the Devourer had found my true weakness, not that I got sick too easily or was so small and skinny, but that I had been so famished for any human companionship that I wanted so terribly, so recklessly, to confide in her, to release myself, to tell her everything.)

'When I leave,' I said slowly, 'what I really want to do is *get all this business over with—*'

The Devourer leaned forward intently.

I said nothing more.

'What business is that, Sekenre?' she asked calmly, sweetly, in a tone my mother might have used when I was small and needed to be comforted.

I put my pen down and shrugged. 'Well, I feel as if my life has not been going on at all for a long time now. Everything has been one long interruption, not part of my life at all. When I get it over with, finished, I can go back to what I want to do.'

'And what is that, Sekenre?'

I looked into her eyes. I saw the predator there, but felt no fear at all, only sorrow that I could not have her as a friend, that I was still alone.

'I guess I'll find out when the time comes.'

The faintest flicker of anger showed in her expression. Then she stood absolutely still, gazing out the window into the distance, her pale face gleaming like marble in the bright sunlight.

I resumed my illumination, filling the entire page with the name *Devourer of Birds,* the characters and their signs and their aspects formed out of tiny birds. At times they almost seemed alive, swirling around on the page before me in a spiral of brilliant colors. I could almost hear their song.

(*'What are you doing?'* Father demanded.)

('Don't you know? Isn't my every thought open to you, Father?')

(Angrily: *'I asked you . . .'*)

('You'll just have to trust me. You made me a sorcerer. Now let me be one.')

(*'Never trust a sorcerer, Sekenre.'*)

('Then don't trust me. Leave me alone.')

When I paused in my work, the Devourer of Birds took me aside to play *madrokae,* a board-game in which one moves animal-headed pieces up and down a wooden slope, in and out of cubbyholes and caves. It was a game from her country, not Reedland, so she won every time, but it *was* a game, and she gained no power over me. It was a merely *human* diversion, not a thing of sorcery.

We regarded one another warily, pretending every sort of pleasantry. As much as it pained me, this was a kind of duel, how serious I wasn't sure yet, but a duel nonetheless, a contest in studied hypocrisy. Perhaps the loser would be the one who forgot that.

We walked through corridors, then a gallery of huge, stooping human and bestial figures formed out of colored wall-tiles, and out through a door onto the bare mountain beneath the brilliant, blue sky. Both of us paused then, leaning against an outcropping, admiring the barren white world that stretched before us, gleaming in the sun. The air, surprisingly, wasn't particularly cold.

'What you said before moved me, Sekenre,' she said. 'My life has been similarly interrupted, so that I, too, would like to complete this business of sorcery and get on with living.'

It was entirely possible she was telling the truth. Even in sorcery, truth can be a weapon. You can use it like any other.

'Oh? How long have you been trying?'

'A very long time. But I haven't given up hope. And you?'

'I haven't either.'

She gathered snow in her hands, compacting it between her palms. 'Don't you sometimes just want to *throw*' – she heaved the streaming snowball into space – 'it all away?'

'Yes.'

'Then why don't you?'

'Why don't *you?*' I said.

'I'm afraid to, Sekenre. We are all afraid. Surely you know that. Why do you even ask?'

I took her hand in mine. Responding, she drew me to her. We stood side-by-side like lovers.

She whispered, 'Who are you, Sekenre, really?'

'What do you mean? I am Sekenre, son of –' She stiffened. Within me, Father cried out in alarm. She had almost tricked me. 'Son of many,' I said. 'I contain multitudes. Who are you, really?'

She let go of my hand and hugged herself as if suddenly cold. For once I found the direct sunlight almost too warm.

'I have *devoured* multitudes. I am the daughter of mystery.'

'And I am the son.'

She laughed. 'Ah. Does that make us brother and sister?'

I shrugged. 'I don't know.'

She hurled another snowball, watching its path as it streaked down into a drift below.

'Let's throw it all away, Sekenre.'

'Yes. Let's.'

I hurled a snowball, and she threw another, and I another, and another, until we both fell down, gasping for breath, laughing like two children at the end of an exhilarating, immensely satisfying game. She held one last snowball and took a bite out of it, then offered it to me.

I shook my head and she tossed it after the rest.

'What now?' she asked.

The sun was low in the western sky. 'I suppose we'd better get back.'

She put her arm around me and pulled me to her once more. 'In some ways you are genuinely a child, Sekenre. It is time for you to become a man—'

She opened her plumage, revealing a normal woman's body without any flaw, malformation, or even scars. She tugged my clothing off me, and we lay together as man and woman, naked on her bed of feathers, streaming with sweat and melted snow even as the shadows lengthened and the evening air grew cold.

One part of me asked what this new game was. Another part knew. Afterward, she lay with her face inches from mine, smiling gently, running her finger through my hair and down the side of my cheek.

'I missed that most of all,' she said.

(*'Sekenre,'* Father said sternly, inside my mind.)

('Did that fascinate you, Father? Did it remind you of Mother?')

(*'Sekenre!'*)

('Trust me, Father. I know what I am doing.' But he did not trust me, and tried to seize the body. I *resisted,* hurling him back, and he lay within me, astonished and furious.)

(*'You wretched fool! Have you considered the consequences of your actions?'*)

('Have you considered the consequences of yours, Father?')

The Devourer of Birds kissed me on the forehead. 'What are you thinking, Sekenre? You seemed far away for a moment there.' She ran her hand down my chest, onto my stomach, then further down. I shivered.

Everything was clear to me now. All the pieces came together.

I sat up suddenly, and got out my manuscript-satchel, which lay among my clothes. I never risked leaving it out of my sight.

'What are you *doing?*' she said with genuine surprise and irritation.

'Here. Look at this.' I got out the page of illuminated birds and held them up to the fading sun. The colors gleamed red, gold, silver. 'Isn't that lovely? It's for you. A gift.'

'Never mind that,' she said. She put her arms around me and drew me down to her, encircling me with her legs.

Truly I had become a sorcerer. I did not weep for what I was about to do, nor did I betray myself by a sigh or a change of expression, or even a pause in the rhythm of my body.

I willed the tiny birds to come alive, to drift across the page, which now lay atop the snow. I commanded them to swallow the sunlight. Once I turned and caught a glimpse of the illuminated figures glowing like coals fanned by a bellows. The Devourer turned my head away and held me in a long, deep kiss.

At last I pulled free. I squatted atop her now, raised up on my arms, gazing into her inscrutable eyes.

I remembered what the corpse-librarian had said just before he had departed the world. I asked the Devourer of Birds a certain question. To this day I do not understand why she answered me truthfully. She trembled, holding on to my arms tightly. Perhaps she was even weeping as she spoke.

'Yes, I am the gatekeeper,' she said.

I felt a sudden chill, far more than the wind on my bare back.

'It's time for me to leave here,' I said. 'I have to go out through the gate.'

'Sekenre, you know what that means.'

'Yes. I am sorry it has to be you.'

'And I am sorry for you, Sekenre. You made me remember things I thought I had forgotten. I am grateful to you for that. I truly am.'

'We might have been friends under other circumstances,' I said.

'Can't we still, for a while? Must our friendship end right now?'

'I think it must.'

'Nonsense, Sekenre.' She pulled me down to her, one arm over my back. With the other hand she reached down between my legs, to hold me there. She whispered in my ear, 'I have declared for you, Sekenre.'

'And I for you. Right now. I am sure the others can hear us.'

She squeezed my groin hard and sank her teeth into my ear. I struggled to break free. I struck her across the face with an elbow. She rolled over on top of me, forcing me down into her feather-cloak, which suddenly closed over me like water, and I was falling in darkness amid millions of shrieking black birds, a thundering, swirling mass, a tempest of feathers and claws and almost human screaming.

I rolled into a ball, tumbling over and over, trying to protect my face and groin, and I felt them yanking at my hair, ripping and pecking away at my back, sides, buttocks, and legs.

I opened my eyes once and saw the Devourer, standing over me with her arms upraised, her whole body glowing with light as she mouthed words I could not make out.

Then she spoke to me clearly, by some inner voice.

'Goodbye, Sekenre. Or perhaps it should be hello. Soon, you and I will be more intimate than ever before.'

'Yes, we will!' I shouted back.

Our minds met. She opened to me, ravenous for my dying soul to pour into her. I felt her triumph, then hesitation, followed by sudden alarm as an image formed in my mind and hers, of another light, of painted birds on a page gorged with the heat of the sun, of smoke rising from the parchment—

She understood. It was too late. She screamed as the parchment began to burn.

I had not learned her true name, but still I'd captured her essence, building on the name *Devourer* with so much delicate penmanship and brushwork, imitating the single bird-image she herself had carelessly drawn. That was enough.

Now her pale flesh burst afire, boiling, popping, streaming, peeling away while she grabbed hold of me once more, locked her arms around me, and we two rolled in the snow, burning and screaming amid the swarming birds as she cursed and called out my name many, many times, and at the very last, pleaded, whether for mercy or forgiveness, I couldn't tell.

At last I lay by myself, cold and wet and hurting all over.

I sat up in silence and opened my eyes. Ashes and feathers rained down. I sat naked in snow blackened by the bodies of dead, smoldering birds.

The left ear pained me the worst of all. I reached up, and my fingers came away bloody. She'd bitten part of it off.

Again my first thought was for my manuscript. I fumbled around amid the shredded ruin of my clothes, tossing bird corpses aside, and took the satchel in both hands.

I sat still, shivering, coughing from the ash and feathers. Only after a long while did I turn to where the Devourer of Birds lay beside me, her body black and incredibly shrunken. I reached out to touch her shoulder and the skin came away, revealing greasy redness underneath.

'Sekenre . . .' she said, hissing between her teeth, her voice sibilant and distorted. Her face was a cracked, charred skull. 'I am glad . . . to be going with you . . . it is what we all want, isn't it?'

'I hope you will be free from fear,' I said.

Smoke rose from her gaping mouth. She made a wet, gurgling sound.

Then she died and was part of me, one more in the company of Vashtem and Talno and Balredon and Lekkanut-Na; and now I understood and *remembered* how she saw through the eyes of a million birds all over the world as her spirit soared; and how, for forty-three years before the infection of sorcery claimed her, her name had been Julna Tarmina and she had lived in Kadisphon, high in the mountains near the source of the Great River. Her husband died, and when her children were grown and gone, she began to take handsome young men as lovers. I reminded her, in particular, of the last of them, after whom a sorcerer lusted. But it was the custom of this sorcerer to devour his lovers, both male and female, after ravishing them; and so he had.

What followed, I already knew, but now I shared the memories themselves, reliving everything.

The sorcerer's name was Regnato Barat, and his hideous memories, too, were mine, for he was contained within Julna. Regnato Barat had raised rape and cannibalism to the level of true sorcery, by which he had grown very powerful. Now he assaulted me with loving, endlessly detailed recollections of his deeds.

I called on the others to lock him in the same mental dungeon with Kareda-Raza, the sorceress of pain. What a perfect pair those two made. Shut away, they lingered within me, and I felt soiled by their presence.

Father spoke aloud, with my mouth.

'That was quite expertly done, I must admit.'

Once more I was wretched and hurt and too weak to stand, covered with my own blood. My face and hands were burnt, much of my hair seared away. I was missing part of an ear.

'Was it really?'

'I have said that it was.'

I forced myself onto hands and knees, crawling through the snow to recover what I could of my clothes, then sitting again as I struggled into what remained of my trousers, one shoe, and my heavy coat. I never found the shirt I'd been wearing. Thus clad, my satchel clutched firmly under one arm, I caught hold of a rock and pulled myself into a standing position, then began to stagger back to the Palace of Sorcerers.

I let Father direct me. He wore the body for a time as we

made our way through many corridors and halls. I thought to return to my tower room, to recover the rest of my luggage, the other bag with the spare clothes in it, but he did not pause until he reached a vast hall lined with sorcerer's mirrors.

I had won the right to depart from the College of Shadows, but had been too dazed to remember where the exit was. Now Father relinquished the body and I walked past mirror after mirror, reflected again and again. For the first time in a long while I thought of *Tica,* who always chided me about my appearance, and I wondered what she would make of me in my present state. I observed with almost amused detachment that I didn't have any eyebrows, but I assumed they'd grow back eventually – or perhaps not. That is the way of sorcery, to scar, to mark, to disfigure the flesh and the spirit both.

Then Father walked beside me, in the mirrors, and with him were Talno and Balredon and the rest. Lekkanut-Na filled an entire mirror by herself, trailing behind us like a drifting cloud.

And there were many more, faces I did not know, even the loathsome Regnato Barat, a squat, pale man with dark, curly hair and a matted beard. He glared at me out of the darkness, as if from the other end of a long tunnel. After a minute, Kareda-Raza appeared beside him.

I reached a place where the mirrors formed a semi-circle. Before me, reflected in all of them, my various selves waited, and for an instant, behind them, deeper within the reflections, stood many more figures, sorcerers and sorceresses by the countless hundreds, their hands upraised to salute and bid farewell to one who has passed the final test of the College of Shadows.

'Come here, Sekenre,' my father said from out of the glass.

I approached the mirror in which he alone stood. He stepped aside, vanishing. I beheld the familiar study in my own house, Father's old workroom with its shelves and books and bottles and the couch on which he had died, all illuminated by the motionless flames which rimmed the doorway like tinsel.

He reached through the mirror as if around a corner and caught hold of my coat.

'No more dallying,' he said. 'We must complete what we have begun.'

He yanked me off my feet, through the mirror.

Chapter 16: The God of Sorcerers

That couch was almost irresistibly inviting. My body yearned
to fall into its soft embrace and just lie there, perhaps forever.
I was cold and exhausted, a mass of cuts, bruises, and burns,
barely able to stand.

But there could be no delay now. Father didn't have to
remind me. I *knew* that every sorcerer in the world would
soon be aware of what I had done, what I had set out to
do. The College of Shadows would send out the alarm, in
dreams, in apparitions, into the minds of sorcerers as an
unbidden thought. As soon as I approached my goal the
others would be certain of what they surely suspected, that
Vashtem had returned to the Invisible Lodge, that he had
walked its halls for a second time and graduated through a
second murder. To tarry now was to lose all.

I gently placed my satchel on the couch and turned
away.

The attacks began at once. The house creaked and shifted.
its many voices cried out. Shrill, whistling wind circled,
probing, rattling shutters, then found an opening and wriggled
inside like a serpent of air. Papers and dust rose whirling
inside the workroom. Bottles trembled on shelves. Two or
three books and a candlestick fell.

I made a sign, and the wind was still.

Outside in the corridor, a heavy beam fell with a crash. I
smelled smoke and felt the heat of the renewed fires.

Another sign slowed the flames, but they remained brilliantly
alive, pulsating, as if I were inside the heart of a fiery beast.

I rummaged frantically through my father's desk, dumping
out drawers. Something shattered, and a malformed, squealing
thing scurried between my feet and off into the gloom.

'Sekenre! Stop what you're doing!'

The voice resonated within me more intimately than my own thoughts.

I turned, startled. A decayed corpse stood in the doorway, dripping river mud from long, tangled strands of hair and from ragged clothing, the whole figure illuminated – yes, that is precisely the correct word – by the muted fires, like a cryptic letter on a page rimmed in gold.

One of those within me, perhaps I myself, knew who this person was, knew this was more than a friend—

But someone else – Father, did you do it? – waved my hand and spoke with my voice, unbinding time once more, for an instant only as the flames leapt up, roaring, hissing as they devoured the damp corpse, and soon the visitant lay on the threshold of the workroom, a smoking heap of bones. Gagging from the thick black smoke, I put the flames to sleep once more. But I felt time slipping away from me, like grains of sand through my fingertips. I didn't know if I could make that particular magic hold much longer.

The memory of the corpse's voice, the inner recognition, pierced me like a sudden pain. I had to sit down. I slid into my father's chair and just for a second or two, rested my head on his desk.

Part of me was somehow insanely sure that this had been my *mother* whom I had so casually destroyed. Another argued, no, that's crazy; it's impossible. She and I had parted far away, in the land of the dead, from which no one but a sorcerer ever returns.

This was one more trap laid for me by some enemy. I had overcome it, as a sorcerer properly should.

Father, within me, remained enigmatically silent.

I fumbled around among the papers atop his desk and found what I had been looking for, a multi-faceted green stone the size of a duck's egg.

I sat up, staggered to my feet, and lurched away from the desk, clomping about the room in my single shoe. Irritably, I kicked the shoe off. My heavy coat tore at my flesh. I tossed it aside and stood more than half naked in the bitter cold, shaking a couple more dead birds out of the ruin of my trousers.

Clasping the stone between folded hands, I stepped over the smoldering corpse and out into the corridor, where I confronted one of the crocodilian *evatim,* but the creature merely hissed and backed away from me, its tail weaving from side to side, its eyes glowing like dying coals.

My chest felt clogged with ice. I struggled to breathe, my throat again raw with the cold, while my underarms had become slick with sweat. I shivered uncontrollably, almost dropping the stone several times, stumbling against the walls and the somnolent flames.

'Sekenre, come and play with me!' It was my sister's voice. I ignored her.

'Sekenre, I have come to take you back. Let us continue our lessons.' Velachronos, my old teacher, stood in my way. I walked *through* him and he burst like a soap bubble. In the last instant I saw the wound by which he had died, gaping from his throat like a second mouth.

Something massive dropped to the floor behind me, at the far end of the corridor. I turned to see what might have been a dark sack, or an almost shapeless body drag itself (or be dragged) around a corner and out of sight. Flames flickered as it passed.

I reached my own bedroom, elbowing the door open. All was as before, the huge wooden arrow thrust through the collapsed bed, the floor strewn with debris, my writing desk upright, as I had set it the last time I was here.

I placed the stone firmly in the inkwell, then dragged the desk over to the window.

I threw open the shutters and leaned out across the desk, barechested into a blast of snow and frigid air. Something about the size of my outstretched hand fluttered in front of my face, squeaking my name. It exploded in flame when I brushed it away.

In the black midnight outside, the wind howled among the ridges, speaking in voices I could almost make out. Above, the sky streamed with broken clouds, intermittently revealing stars and the waning moon. Auroras flickered madly from horizon to horizon.

Something rustled just below. I gazed down and saw the

snow flowing like a stream around the foundations of the house; and I somehow understood that this was no stream at all, but a living serpent made of ice, circling again and again, growing stronger with each revolution, its great head drifting by like a boat as I watched, floating on the surface of the snow, its dark eyes gleaming and impenetrable.

Along the ridges, gathered as they had been in worship of the Shadow Titans, the sorcerers stood, torches and lanterns in hand, waiting.

I reached down and touched two specific facets of the stone in the inkwell.

(*'When you have truly mastered its use,'* my father said within me, *'You won't need to touch it. Thought alone will suffice.'*)

I knew that. I wondered why he had chosen this instant for such pedantry.

I let my fingers fall away, and looked down at the stone. Two facets gleamed so brilliantly I had to turn aside.

The mountaintop vanished. The wounded house, filled with fire, bristling with arrows, weighted down with its burden of ghosts, lumbered through space and time at my command, every beam, every board grinding and creaking in protest. I heard deep resounding crashes as if whole rooms had caved in. Perhaps they had. I couldn't stop to find out as I stood like the captain at the helm of his ship, gazing out into a sea of darkness, into the flickering auroras.

I shivered more as the sweat dried on my sides, but the cold had noticeably diminished. At last, as the auroras faded, the sun rose slowly ahead of me, pale blue and orange spreading across the horizon like spilled paint; and I beheld the Great River from some unknown vantage point along its curving shore.

Now the air was pleasantly warm. I leaned over the desk, onto the windowsill, enjoying the sensation of the morning breeze on my face.

But I knew I could not stay here. Yet, before I touched the stone again, I lowered a bucket out the window on a rope, drew up water, and washed myself, standing naked in the middle of the floor. Then I dried myself gingerly on a torn blanket and put on a loose, ankle-length robe, all I could wear without discomfort. My arms and shoulders especially were badly burned and had begun to blister. It was painful to move.

I could only pause a few minutes. Within me, Father scolded me for wasting time on such matters. I ignored him as I quickly cut the remains of my hair short, to keep it out of my eyes, and wrapped a strip of cloth around my scorched forehead.

Still, I desperately wanted to rest, but dared not.

I forced myself back to the window and leaned over the desk once more.

(*'You know, Sekenre, your suspicions may have been right all along. The true calligraphy of your magic isn't on the page, but carved and burnt into your own flesh.'*)

'Maybe,' was all I could think to say, aloud.

(*'Truly,'* Father continued within me, *'Like so many sorcerers, you are marked, transformed by your adventures. Perhaps the book of Sekenre is written, not in ink, but in scars.'*)

'So someone can flay me and file me away in the sorcerers' library? No, Father, I think not.'

(*'In the end, such details do not matter.'*)

'They do to me.'

Black eagles circled in the sky, cawing like crows.

I touched the stone once more, and the view from the window receded into darkness and flickering lights.

So the house moved on, dragging itself like a monster spider with half its legs broken. Once more the sky lightened. The boards beneath my feet heaved and jolted to one side. The desk fell over, but I held onto the stone as I tumbled to the floor. For a moment I lay still, listening to the house settle unevenly into mud and rock. Above me, heavy beams and furniture crashed against the upper floors. Dust and splinters rained down into my face. I coughed and wiped my face with my free hand.

I didn't bother with the desk this time, but merely stood at the window, clutching the stone. I gazed out on the City of the Delta as an imperial bireme swelled toward me, its straining sail marked with the double device of the eagle and the crocodile: double death, of the air and the river.

Again and again I fingered the green stone, and the house manifested itself in many lands. I even beheld Reedland, and what must have been my home, the City of Reeds, though it was little more than a cluster of wood-and-thatch huts on stilts and a couple of ramshackle wharfs. The one large ship anchored there flew banners displaying an owl-motif of some forgotten local king.

I was gazing into the remote past, centuries before my own lifetime, before Sestobast the First had united all Riverland into the Hegemony of the Delta.

(*'Keep going,'* Father said inside my mind. *'You know where we must arrive.'*)

'Yes, I know,' I said aloud.

Beyond the window, the scene changed as rapidly as the flipping pages of a codex book: rolling riverscapes, snow-capped mountains where black eagles soared, an endless forest scarlet and golden with the colors of some unimaginable northern autumn; and for a long time, only wind-swept desert, a featureless sea of sand.

I grew weary leaning on the window sill, brought up a chair, and sat there, the stone in my lap, running my fingers over its many polished sides. The floor swayed gently like the deck of a ship on the river.

I began to nod off to sleep. I jerked my head back up, once, twice; then I understood what I truly must do.

It was time to dream. I hurled the house far into the darkness, falling for hours in utter silence. I slept, leaning over the armrest of my chair, but my mind was active as my body rested, yes, for this was a sorcerer's dream, a deliberate thing.

I dreamt that I sat at my writing desk, laboring for an immeasurable time, dipping pens in many colors of ink, blotting, scraping away mistakes, writing again, until I had condensed the entirety of my narrative into a single, plainly-rendered letter.

As Father had said, the apprentice sorcerer uses complicated apparatus. Had I been skilled with that stone, I would have only needed to think of it. In the infancy of my magic, I had written the whole book of my life to define myself, to preserve that which is Sekenre against all dangers, some subtle and ineffable resonance rendering the whole of all the letters and flourishes and pictures greater than the sum of the parts.

My book's meaning lay not in what it said, but in what it *was*. In what I was, what I had become in the making of it.

A single letter.

In my dream I traced it out clearly in black ink with an ordinary pen, the letter *tchod,* which occurs in both the Deltan and Reedlandish scripts, but is unknown to the barbarians: an *X* shape with a dot in the upper triangle, like the head of a tiny figure with arms and legs outstretched. It is called the Dancing One, also the Suppliant, and has many other names. *Tchod* denotes many things: patience, long waiting, sudden fulfillment, sorrow, subtle and quiet joy, the triumph that is only seen in retrospect. So many words contain the *tchod* that a list of them would fill a book.

Only *tchod.* Here was the essence of Sekenre.

I awoke from my dream and found myself, not in the chair but standing over the righted desk. But I had not written anything yet. Pen and paper waited.

I made the *tchod,* blew on it until the ink was dry, and folded the paper carefully, never creasing the letter. Then I sat down in the chair before the darkened window, the flames glowing softly at my back, the paper between my folded hands, and I dreamed of brilliant, featureless fire.

When next I awoke, Father stood over me, having formed himself out of smoke. Through him, I saw the window, and beyond, only a gray sky.

'Get up,' he said. 'We have arrived.'

But I did not rise immediately. I sat still, comfortable for once and free of any pain, dully surprised to discover that I now wore the silver mask of the Moon, and that my father's sword lay across my knees.

I stood, holding the sword up to examine it in the uncertain light. The weapon was alive with energy of its own, every delicate silver inlay, every inscription and carved flourish glowing as if molten. Yet the metal was cold to the touch. I held the sword in my right hand, the paper containing the *tchod* in my left. There was no scabbard. I looked around for the green stone, but realized I wouldn't be needing it any longer.

'Come,' Father said, his voice almost breaking with excitement. 'Come with me. Yes. Now. I want to tell you the very last of the tales of the Heron Boy. I'll tell it as we walk. Hurry. Hurry.' He reached to take me by the arm, but his hand was of smoke and could not grasp me.

I followed him through the house, stepping over debris where the ceilings had fallen or floors had heaved up and split. Everything was silent now, but for occasional creaks and pops of wood settling.

In the kitchen, all the cupboards had flown open and the floor was ankle-deep in shards. I walked gingerly among them in my bare feet, not even wishing for shoes, because I knew that ours was to be a magic walk, on water or fire or air, and flesh must touch.

The porch outside was simply gone, perhaps fallen away in the course of the journey here, into some prior landscape. Now Father and I climbed down onto a plain of featureless dust. I stood for a moment, looking around, but perceived only desolation in every direction. Even the air was dead, without any scent of mud or pollen or smoke. The ground I stood on gave no sensation at all, as if my feet were numb.

'What is this place?' I asked. 'It's as if it never was alive, and never will be.'

'Oh no, my son, it *will* be. It definitely will be. This is merely the familiar world, the Earth, but at the beginning of time, before creation, before the gods walked over it. Imagine that.'

'Why are we here?'

He began walking in long, vigorous strides, his smoke-clothing streaming as he leaned into a non-existent wind. I hurried after him. Once he looked back at me, and I saw his face. A second time, he wore a silver mask, like my own.

'I think you know perfectly well why we're here,' he called

out. 'Yes. Yes. You've reached this place before, though by a different route. As we continue our journey, the landscape will become familiar enough.'

Breathing hard, I struggled to keep up with him. I whirled around once, and saw that the house had diminished – much too quickly, it seemed – into a black dot on the horizon. More than ever it looked like a black, maimed spider crouching there, something you might find shrivelled and dead in the dust of a window-sill.

We walked on for what might have been hours or even days. I had no way of knowing, and felt neither weariness nor cold nor hunger nor thirst; nor even the ground beneath my feet. Only the sword in my right hand, the paper in my left, and the silver mask chafing my face were real to me in an empty world.

Light spread across the horizon, like a slow sunrise.

'There. Look,' Father said, pointing.

I didn't see anything but the light, and said as much, but he neither argued nor explained. And as we walked, he grew ever more loquacious.

'That sword, *my* sword . . . oh, the joke of it all is that to the sorcerer, that sword should be *invisible*. It is antithetical to sorcery, the weapon of a Knight Inquisitor. You know that, son. An instrument consecrated to the Nine Gods of Righteousness, to mankind's endless struggle against nightmare madness, against the darkness, chaos, the Shadow Titans, and, incidentally, against you and me, Sekenre. It is tempered in the blood of dying sorcerers, for it has slain many, and by this blade they have truly *died,* coming to an end rather than passing into the slayer. A Knight Inquisitor devotes himself to cleansing the world of such as ourselves, Sekenre, to the extermination of the wild things. Oh, that's a jest. Oh, that's so terribly, terribly funny.'

I hefted the sword. 'I don't understand. I can see it. So can you.'

Like an eager child he raced in front of me and turned, running backward, facing me as he went, his mask jiggling up and down. Behind him, the glow on the horizon increased, the rising sun outlining him in brilliant light, turning him into fire.

'Exquisite,' he said. 'Ah. When I thought I could put aside sorcery, I became a Knight Inquisitor. When I thought I could put aside righteousness, I lapsed into sorcery once again. Both were but means to my greater end. Thus I retain some characteristics of each. So do you. You understand that now, don't you, Sekenre? Well, never mind. Here is the rest of the story of the Heron Boy. This is what all his previous adventures lead up to: He wandered for many years among the birds, impersonating a bird, but each morning, when the others took flight, he was left behind knee-deep in mud, flapping his arms ridiculously. So he ventured among mankind, yet never settled in any place, nor was he able to love a human woman, nor did he serve any king. He was utterly alone. But, in a dream perhaps, or because it was his fate or the whim of some god, he came to a place of secret fires. There he was reborn, like a broken blade melted down and forged anew. He became something which was neither boy nor heron, but more than either, his dual nature perfectly united for the first time. Thus he was unique, alone as before, but now immune to all longings, all sorrows, for he possessed an entire universe within his own mind and required nothing more.'

Now brilliant lights rose from below the horizon, sparks, explosions, sunbursts. I trudged on. Father trotted backward, in front of me.

Now the sun itself rose, its face that of a man, too brilliant to look upon. I wept and averted my gaze, shielding my eyes with the hand that held the sword.

And the sun spoke, in the language of the gods, which may not be written down or even approximated, which may not, by human beings at least, even be remembered. But the import was that now, with this rising, Time had begun, duration, hours, minutes, seconds poured out onto the sandy world like wine from a jar. Amid the desolation and the light, the gods themselves were coming to birth, for we were in the holy realm, Father and I. We had stolen like burglars into *Akimshé*.

Father's smoky form could no longer sustain itself, and he was within my mind once more.

'What you never told me,' I said, staggering forward, 'was whether or not the Heron Boy was any happier in his new form, after the change.'

Father spoke with my own voice, my throat now hoarse and dry from the dust and increasing heat. 'He is part of our dreams now. Sorcerers know him. He whispers to them in the night. I have held long and intricate conversation with him myself, but he does not speak of happiness.'

'Really? Never?'

'Never. Nor unhappiness either.'

It is impossible to truly relate what happened next. I fumble, approximate—

For the eye has not seen, nor the ear heard, nor can the mind conceive—

Father and I witnessed the birth of the gods, there, at the beginning of Time, on the first day of the world. I descended into a valley of fire, as brilliant, white lava streamed around me and molten rock bubbled over my bare feet. Yet I was not burnt as walked down that endless slope, as I crossed a river of fire. For once the passage was easy, without struggle or pain as I focussed my mind on the *tchod* and contemplated its mysteries.

We reached that place Father had barely glimpsed on his own, that utmost culmination of his labors and his journeys which he called, metaphorically, the Heart of the Forest. In truth it has no name, for no one has ever seen its entirety to give it a name—

The very core of the universe, where the flames themselves are made up of billions of suns and worlds—

Here the silver eyes of my battered mask wept molten tears—

Here I gazed with more than human sight from atop a ridge, overlooking a lake of white fire, slowly apprehending that the ridgeline formed the backbone of a god, that the surrounding mountains were the god's ribs, that rising smoke and splattering lava coalesced into the divine flesh. Then the earth convulsed and I was hurled into the air like a stray cinder from a furnace as the skeleton came together, bone unto glowing bone, flesh slowly gathering together like the petals of an indescribably huge, fiery blossom closing back to bud again, layer folding upon layer to form a single body, and a face I dared not look upon.

And I saw Surat-Kemad rising out of the fire and smoke of heaven, a vast crocodile, his mouth disgorging stars.

('Sekenre, listen to me,' Father said inside my head – then someone cut him off. All my captive selves were awake now, fighting inside me. I ignored them, pressing on to my goal. I felt Father vanquish Orkanre and Regnato Barat the cannibal. The others circled him, like fighters in a pit, seeking an opening.)

Still I walked through fire and blinding light, leaning against roaring winds, the letter *tchod* upraised in my left hand, the sword of the Knight Inquisitor in my right.

Light gave way to darkness as suddenly as the closing of a book. Without slowing my stride, I made my way through the utter blackness which is also *Akimshé,* indescribable holiness. At last a single, flickering point of light appeared, resolving into my father's house now all aglow as fire poured from every window but did not consume the structure.

Without scabbard or pockets, I could only shift both paper and sword to my left hand, and climb as best I could with my right, hooking my left arm or elbow over to haul myself up over the fallen timbers where the porch had once been. I entered the house. All the rooms blazed with light now, everything submerged in stationary fire. Father's workshop echoed with faint screams, as little dark things thumped against the insides of the trembling bottles.

Vashtem seized the body, shoving Sekenre aside, returning to his laboratory in triumph, to his sanctuary, his holy of holies, trembling in anticipation at the climax of all his labors, all his sufferings, his treacheries, his many murders.

It was all for this. For so many centuries he had lived and worked and suffered and even died in anticipation of a future, which now had arrived. This instant.

He opened the door to Sekenre's room, surveying the toppled desk, the ruined bed, the debris and flames. In the chair by the window sat a sleeping form clad in white robe and silver mask, but without sword or paper in its softly glowing hands.

Vashtem, my father, held the sword on high, ready to strike. But his arm trembled. He hesitated.

('Father, what are you doing?' I shouted within him.)

'What I always intended to do,' he replied in a boy's voice, trembling, the voice almost breaking. 'Sekenre, I wanted to leave you out of all this. I had intended your sister to be my instrument, not you. But it hasn't worked out that way, has it?'

The form in the chair sat up in a sudden fright. Its mask fell off, revealing a face sculpted out of delicate flames, the fiery flesh peeling away, layer by layer, like a flower *opening*, losing all definition as it did so, burning ever more brightly. Its features were Vashtem's, for just an instant, then my mother's, then Hamakina's, and countless others I had known or never known, strangers, even beasts and demons, the various forms flickering, vanishing, reshaping themselves almost too quickly for the eye to follow.

It turned stupidly toward me, a mindless thing, empty. It spoke in meaningless words of thunder. The house shook and swayed like a ship in a stormy sea.

The burning face was my own.

Father raised the sword one last time.

And I, Sekenre, sorcerer and murderer of sorcerers, deftly reached into his mind and snatched control of the body from him, like seizing the reins of a horse.

He screamed through my mouth and staggered back, dropping both sword and folded paper, but I was Sekenre again, rolling on the floor, limbs flailing as Vashtem and Talno and Balredon and Lekkanut-Na and all the rest struggled against me and against one another, even those Father had seemingly vanquished returning into the fray. I gasped. I heaved up, then fell limp, then twisted in uncontrollable spasms. The room blurred, swam, went dark, and my eyesight returned as they shouted and struck and hurled magic at one another, all inside my head. White flames snapped and hissed from my palms. Smoke poured out of my mouth.

I thought of an image: *Splat!* We would explode like

overripe fruit, a smear of flesh and gore on the walls and ceiling, while the newborn god rose into strength and full divinity, oblivious of this absurd, incoherent creature at its feet.

(*'Sekenre! Don't fight me! Let me kill it now! Kill a god and become a god! You'll be part of it. I promise!'*)

Patiently, I fought for control. I was a sorcerer now, not the mere glove worn by a sorcerer. I clung to my inner *self,* reciting the dholish formulae I had learned in the College of Shadows, not because I particularly needed them just now, but to focus my mind, to distract the others—

And I felt the indescribable *lust* of sorcery more powerfully than ever before. I was just like my father. I knew it, with terrible certainty. It was so awfully *funny,* so humorously horrible that I couldn't restrain my hoarse laughter or my wracking sobs.

I managed to sit up. I recovered the fallen paper and held it up for the god-thing to see.

'Here I am,' I said. 'Look.' There was powerful magic in the *tchod,* sufficient to bind a brainless god, I thought.

But it took the paper from me, burning my hand with its touch, setting my sleeve afire, the paper itself disintegrating in a burst of flame, ashes drifting, while the letter *tchod* remained floating in the air, written in brilliant light.

(*'Sekenre! Do what you have to do!'*)

('What do I have to do, father? I don't remember anymore.')

(*'Yes, you do, Sekenre,'* said Lekkanut-Na suddenly, within me. *'We all do. But I should be the one to help you. We're friends, aren't we?'* And in that instant I knew she was no more a friend than any of the others.)

Kareda-Raza, the sorceress of pain, nearly got the better of all of us. She merely *discarded* a detail of magic, dropping it like a cloak.

No more was the body shielded from the fires of *Akimshé.*

Now I was the one screaming on the floor, my clothing burnt away in an instant, my flesh hissing, bubbling, blazing like a torch in the endless, merciless agony which did not consume.

I thought of the three burning women, Talno's mentors
and victims—

And I couldn't think of anything at all—

Kareda-Raza gorged herself relentlessly on pain, any pain,
all pain, even her own, relishing my suffering as it became
her own, as she seized the body and stood up, naked and
outlined in flame, sword in hand, confronting the newborn
god who backed away from her in instinctive fright.

Somehow it knew that hers would be a godhead of relentless
cruelty, from which not even the other gods would be free.

Within Kareda-Raza, I yielded, not to her, but to my father,
deliberately joining myself to him.

We two were one, twice as powerful as any of the others.
This changed configuration caught Kareda-Raza off guard,
just for an instant.

And in that instant, Father snatched up the sword and
plunged it into my own heart.

I shouted in alarm and amazement and fell to my knees.
Kareda-Raza shrieked in wordless rage.

There was no blood. The fires of my flesh went out. I knelt
in the middle of the floor, naked, smoking, in wordless pain,
gaping at the sword sunk to the hilt into my chest. I couldn't
tell if it protruded from my back. Probably.

Father made the Voorish sign to bind the dead, and
managed to gasp from my parched throat, 'Kareda-Raza,
now die. Die for the last time.'

Then he drew the sword out, and the next thing I knew I
was lying on my back on the floor, not sure who I was or
whether I was dead or alive, numb beyond all amazement at
this final revelation of how a sorcerer who has once been a
Knight Inquisitor – unique; there has never been another –
may use a holy instrument to kill another sorcerer within
himself.

Kareda-Raza was truly gone, the contents of her mind no
more than a memory among many. *She* no longer dwelt
within me.

(*'Now let us complete our task, Sekenre,'* Father said.)

I tried to get up. I wasn't sure if I had been hideously
burned or not. My clothes were gone. My hair might have

been completely burnt off. I was numb all over, my skin vaguely tingling. The only pain was in my hand, where the godling had touched me.

And what of that? What of the newborn god, the god of sorcerers, whose birth my father had foreseen and, in some way even I didn't understand, *shaped?* Somehow Father had bound and stunted this divine infant, until it was within our power.

The glowing figure was now twice the size it had been, naked as I was, burning within, but softly, like a paper lantern come alive in human shape. It knelt over me, drooling liquid fire, which hissed on my chest, my stomach, my thigh as I screamed in the sudden renewed pain and rolled out of its way.

Father and I closed our hand over the grip of the sword. We rolled again and sat, back to the wall, gazing up at the luminous giant which now hunched low beneath the ceiling, expanding like an inflated skin even as I watched, filling the whole room.

I seized the reins, control, the body, back from Father.

(*'Kill it, you fool! Strike!'*)

('I'm not sure I can, Father. I have too long considered what it would mean.')

(*'You stupid brat! No time for argument! It means the triumph of sorcery over the Nine Gods. It means the victor fills the world with magic. It means you'll never be afraid again, Sekenre. Have you considered that? Have you really considered it?'*)

The new god followed the letter *tchod* with its hands, like a child trying to catch a butterfly.

('Father, why did you fail to win on your own?')

(*'Because I—'*)

('I never believed your last answer, that you broke your concentration. Because you loved me too much?')

(*'Sekenre, for the very last time, ever, I ask you this.* Do you love your father? *I have always told you that you must, in the end, make up your mind.'*)

I was choking on smoke. I held up a hand to shield my face from raining cinders. Now there was more pain, as the cinders burned me all over. This was not the holy, unconsuming fire of *Akimshé,* but mere wood burning, splinters of the house.

I managed to speak aloud, not in my mind, but in my own voice, tears streaming down my cheeks. The god-thing above me paused, turning its head sideways to listen, as if spoken words were a novelty to it.

'Father,' I said. 'I am unable to hate you. I truly am. Possibly that means I love you. I don't know anymore. I loved Mother and I loved Hamakina, and even Tica. The Lady Hapsenecuit ... I can't say. She was kind, even when she used me for her own ends ... Were you ever kind to those you made your instruments, Father? But love, hate, do not matter, not one, not the other ... You know as well as I do that the sorcerer must be purged clean of love and hatred, even of fear. You know that to achieve this idea one must become perfect—'

'Like the Heron Boy at the end of the story,' Vashtem said, aloud, with my voice.

The god-thing listened, squatting beneath the ceiling, filling the room with pure white fire as I huddled between its feet. Perhaps it could understand what Vashtem and I said. Who can know if it had thoughts at all? A god, in the beginning, is like a storm, gathering, swirling, waxing ever stronger, but only defining itself gradually.

Think of it as a whirlwind of divine fire, come alive.

'Kill it, Sekenre,' Father said, speaking through my mouth. 'Kill it now. I cannot compel you. You have grown too strong for that. I can only ... advise. Sekenre, you must do it. You cannot be fulfilled any other way.'

I trembled with the sorcerer's lust, even as he did, but still something stayed my hand.

'I can't. I truly cannot.'

'You don't mean that.'

'I do, Father. Goodbye.'

'Sekenre! I forbid—!'

Sobbing those tears no sorcerer is supposed to have, there in the room of fire, huddled at the feet of a god, seizing the Knight Inquisitor's sword which no sorcerer is supposed to be able to see, let alone wield, I did what I had to do, what Vashtem had shown me how to do when he destroyed Kareda-Raza.

I drove the sword into myself, up through the roof of my mouth, into the skull – impossible, yes, but the blade pierced the spirit, going *between* the flesh without touching it, as if through a barred window – Vashtem understood this, in his final terror, and supplied the metaphor as his very last thought.

He screamed within me, silently, as the silver holiness touched him, and then was utterly, truly gone, whether into the Land of the Dead or out of existence altogether like a burst bubble, I did not know.

I could only remember him.

I drew the sword out and lay back against the wall, the weapon dropping from my limb fingers. Abstractly, as if it were something conveyed to me by remote means, I watched the newborn god leaning down over me with nearly cupped hands, about to trap the drifting *tchod*.

Searing spittle dripped onto my chest. I put both hands to my forehead, covering the Sybil's mark, and called out, both with my voice and in my mind, *'Sybil! Come to me! This is the last time! Now!'*

And she came, from the darkness of her secret abode, scurrying like a pale spider up the black threads she had been weaving for so long. She was with me in my mind.

I looked up once more and saw the god-creature frozen above me, motionless between one instant and the next.

Time had stopped.

I closed my eyes and seemed to be sitting beside the Sybil in the shadows, amid bones and debris and swaying ropes, in air thick with the odors of decay and of river mud.

Her face shone like the moon through thick clouds.

'Sekenre, this is the final time you may call on me, before you are utterly and irrevocably mine. Why have you summoned me?'

'Because I am afraid.'

'You have been afraid many times. Now your salvation is at hand. You still have the sword. Snatch it up. Do what your father told you. Slay a god and become a god. That is

386

what you want. I do not phrase it as a question, Sekenre. It *is* what you desire above all else.'

'Yes, Sybil,' I said, weeping, glorying in the fact that I *could* weep. 'That is what I want. I lied to my father. He always told me never to trust a sorcerer ... but he believed me when he shouldn't have. I *am* able to do it. And that is what I am afraid of. I want the very same thing my father did, so desperately that ... I'll become pure, without hate or love or anything ... not Sekenre anymore ... just a *force* ... and by winning, I will lose everything. I think Father knew that, but he couldn't turn away from the path he had been on for so long.'

She put her hand on mine. She closed my fingers over the sword.

'Nor can you turn away,' she said. 'There is no other recourse left, but to complete what Vashtem began. But I shall take care of you at the very end. Trust me. Work with me. Obey, and this shall be the last of the miracles I promised you when you came to my house.'

'Why are you doing this, Sybil?'

'Sekenre, why do you illuminate a page with swirls and colors and little pictures, when you could get the meaning of the text across just as well in plain letters? For that same reason I embellish the lives I weave. It makes my work more interesting.'

Time resumed.

The god-thing reached down. I knew with absolute certainty that if it crushed and extinguished the *tchod,* I would die as completely as my father had, leaving behind no more than a burnt-out husk. I *knew,* because I'd read it somewhere or the other sorcerers within me said so or the Sybil told me. Perhaps I could hear the babbling thoughts of the newborn god.

Therefore I called upon the *tchod,* addressing it by the alternate, secret name of the letter, drawing it to myself until it sank into my chest, hissing like the mark of a branding iron.

I'd failed to understand, before. The letter on the paper was useless. The floating letter was worse, a terrible vulnerability. I had to be united with it, and now I was. I was the *tchod* and the *tchod* was Sekenre. So I defined myself in sudden pain.

I grabbed the sword and struck off the gigantic, glowing hand. Liquid fire poured out on me. I screamed and staggered back, as the divine monster howled and stood up, crashing through the ceiling, showering me with debris. Something heavy hit me and I was hurled to one side. My right shoulder felt broken. I shifted the sword from right hand to left, and I did not falter now, but leapt up, oblivious to blinding light and searing fire, and drove the sword into the creature's groin. It fell to its knees, roaring, thundering down in an avalanche of sparks and splintered wood.

I stood to meet it, driving myself and the sword into its startled embrace like a single instrument.

And the god-thing died. Its inner light went out. Its body became dark and hard and brittle, like poorly-fired clay, and broke into a thousand pieces.

For an instant I stood alone and naked and hurting in the darkening room, as cinders and sparks settled around me.

'Sybil?' I said. 'What happens now?'

Chapter 17: A Long Time Watching

Here are the dreams of Sekenre the god, written down by Sekenre, who is not a god. Not anymore. At least I don't think so. I struggle to recall what memory cannot hold; to express something for which no words are adequate.

Did I wake or dream?

The fires diminished, the flames of the burning house now a dull red, almost motionless once more.

Did I dream as I stood there in the semi-darkness, as the dead thing which had once been divine lay at my feet like a husk of charred paper?

I touched it with my sword and it broke up into a formless heap.

Did I dream as pure light suddenly streamed from my many wounds, as the arrow-hole in my side roared like a furnace mouth?

I stood transfigured in light, like a statue of brilliantly gleaming metal. And I heard the startled, even frightened whispers of the gods as they leaned forward in the couches in Heaven, incredulous at what they saw. How extraordinary, how terrifying to them that one created *by* the gods had travelled back in time prior to that very creation – before any human being walked upon the Earth – and had now *become* one of the divine company, one of the creators. An irresolvable paradox.

I heard Surat-Kemad stirring from his endless sleep in the River's mud. I heard the rising thunder of his heart.

There was no pain now. My body felt like a piece of ash rising in a hot wind, effortless and directionless. I saw the inevitability of what had been, what was, and what was to come, all of it flowing like the eternal course of the Great River.

Therefore I walked to the doorway of my father's house, and I stood on the threshold, beholding the River beneath me and the stars above. New stars rose slowly out of the dark water, smoldering to life; and the breath of Heaven stirred the River's surface, and new gods and spirits yet unborn began to dream.

I witnessed the sunrise on the first day of the world. The gods walked across the featureless Earth, stirring the dust with their feet, sowing living things as a farmer sows seed.

But the Earth itself did not live, and the seed fell on barren ground. Birds and beasts withered into frail husks, into dust.

I felt the seed falling on my own bare skin like a rain of sand, as if the earth and my flesh were one and the same, dry and hard and cracked.

And in the evening of the first day, the gods beheld their shadows rising up to mock them. These were the Titans, the living darkness, whom generations of sorcerers would come to worship, in defiance of the affrighted gods.

I too feared them, for the thoughts of the gods were my own thoughts.

I stood at the lip of the abyss where the porch had once been, high above the river, far beneath the sky and the faces of the gods, and I held my father's holy sword aloft and cried out, *'Here I am, gods, I am one of you! I am Sekenre, the sorcerer-god! Fear not, I who shall be the greatest among you shall protect you! I am the god who casts no shadow. There is no Titan in the shape of Sekenre, therefore I do not fear the Titans.'*

Such effrontery. Did I really mean what I said? What would Vashtem have done? I reached within my mind to ask him, but he was silent, of course. He wasn't there anymore.

I stood there throughout the night, my pierced flesh pouring light into the darkness, dispelling the shadows, filling the world like a second sunrise.

In the day I stood there, smoke rising from me in a long, black column.

The god within me spoke out of his own furious pride. The boy Sekenre and the other sorcerers were all shouted into silence. The god spoke. Newborn, the god proclaimed what Sekenre had once called the sorcerer's lust. This god would tear down the skies. He would remake the world. He would devour all the gods and make them part of himself.

Then, and only then, could he be free from fear.

The gods in Heaven heard me. How could they not, for their voice was mine and my voice was theirs? I looked up into the evening twilight, and I saw them conferring behind the sunset. I saw them stand up from their thrones, the newly-formed constellations spreading and rippling in their cloaks.

And I heard them judge Sekenre upstart and pretender and thief, whose godhood had been won through murder.

(*'Father?'* I called out within my mind. *'Is this what you wanted? Is this what you foresaw?'* But he did not answer. He was not there.)

The other gods cast me down, with thunder, with hail, with raging winds, shaking the whole Earth. Pain returned. The light of my body was extinguished and blood poured from my side, from my pierced wrist, from so many other places, splashing down over my feet.

The sword slipped from limp fingers and fell twirling into the darkness below.

I dropped to my knees, then tumbled forward out of the house, but was caught among the broken timbers where the porch had once been, and dangled there like a doll some child has cast away because the stuffing which gave it shape is leaking out.

Regun-Kemad, the eagle-headed one, came to me, his black wings spread wide, and he spoke the god-tongue: *'Behold, thou art flesh, and flesh must die, for my master Surat-Kemad hungers.'*

The Dark Messenger's terrible beak gaped, and he reached for me with taloned hands.

But a light streaked toward me out of the darkness, across the rippling water, bobbing up and down like a paper lantern carried by someone running. Death's servant turned, startled. I raised my head, drawing on my last reserves of strength, and saw the Sybil standing there on the surface of the water. She placed herself between Regun-Kemad and myself. She parried his talon-thrusts with my father's silver sword, battling Death on my behalf, her face shining like the newly-risen winter moon, pale, white, her features perfectly defined.

This too seemed a dream to me, but such distinctions had lost all meaning. I drifted, like flotsam tangled among old pilings, while the Sybil and the Eagle-God whirled around me in a kind of dance, darkness encircling light, light encircling darkness, each grasping the other by the wrist, perfectly matched, in balance, locked together.

I recognized them of course. I had seen them back in Arnatisphon, the City of Reeds: two masked performers, dark and light, who honor the Child of Thorns in rites of immemorial antiquity.

Let me tell you all about that rite. I was present at its inception. I alone understand its full meaning.

'*Sekenre.*' The Sybil's voice spoke inside my mind, amidst my dream of pain and darkness. 'Release yourself. Let go. Let the holy blood spill out of you. Do not struggle, but instead relinquish all that you have stolen. Cling only to that which is Sekenre. Remember your childhood. Remember the first letters you formed on the page. Remember games, old stories, anything. Be brave and patient and strong. You have endured much, Sekenre. Now endure this last ordeal and all shall be resolved, as I have promised.'

I tried to reach out to her, possessed by some mad urge to touch her, as if that would comfort me and give me strength, but instead I lost my precarious balance among the timbers and tumbled into the river without even a splash, sinking for a thousand years, it seemed, in cold and utter darkness, as the blood of godhood streamed out of me and the Great River flowed in my veins. I saw the unborn stars drifting beside me like impossible, underwater lanterns. I saw the dreaming gods there, and their dreams were like lines spoken in a drama performed somewhere far away in the night, where I could not see the stage or even hear very much of what was said.

Still the Sybil and the Messenger of Death danced their dance around me, while I tried to ignore them and focus my thoughts on some obscure person called Sekenre. It was like finding a single droplet in a raging sea.

But I found him, and he guided me to himself. I wanted to rage at the gods. I wanted to call the Titans to my aid. I wanted to work great feats of sorcery, but Sekenre, within me, said, 'No. Don't. Just wait.'

Sekenre was strong enough. He waited.

Memories flickered and gleamed and vanished, like shards of glass, falling:

A little boy named Sekenre standing on the porch of a house, gazing out over the Great River, looking at the many ships for a time, then turning to follow the sinking sun amid the cat-tails and reeds of an endless marsh. Someone tall and strong held me by the hand and stood with me, watching the red sky fade into purple, then black.

Gone.

Older now, a boy among other boys, paddling boats between the massive pilings on which the City of Reeds is built, coming at last to that secret place where the Wooden King lies almost buried in the mud. We moored our boats, at lunch while seated between the spikes of the rotting wooden crown, then carved our names on the top of the king's head. Later, as we paddled away, I looked back at the huge, blind face as it faded into the perpetual gloom of the undercity. My boy-self and my dreaming-self both pondered the mystery of this king for a long time, but neither of us knew him. He lingered from another epoch, forever strange and alone.

Still Sekenre drifted deep within the Great River, neither dead nor alive, neither breathing nor drowned; for I was a god, and gods do not die by drowning. My blood stained the waters and touched the banks, and for the first time the Earth lived. Reeds and grasses grew from the mud in the shallows. Fishes darted, startled into existence. Herons waded there, like automatons newly released into motion.

I rolled over onto my back in the frigid darkness and for a time I seemed to leave my body altogether. I saw it, pale and small, turning with the current as the river bore it onward, and I watched the moon-faced Sybil and the Eagle-God circling. For a time they vanished into the night and the distance, and I did not see them.

I was in the house of Velachronos the scribe, seated at

a high desk, working intently on an illumination. Sunlight streamed through broad, open windows, but there was no breeze. The air was hot, still. My hair clung to my sweaty forehead. My shirt stuck to my back. Repeatedly I wiped my hands on my trousers so the ink wouldn't be smeared. I felt light-headed, weary, but I didn't want to stop working. I clung to the legs of my stool with my toes, lest I lose my perch. This project I was working on was important, some delicate, intricate piece I had to finish before my master looked in on me again.

In the next room, he was teaching my sister to sing.

With infinite patience, I constructed the enormously complex figure on the page, linking countless tiny lines, then illuminating the pattern with specks of gold and silver and long, broad sweeps of brilliant blue.

It was a portrait of a round-faced, wide-eyed boy with tangled, dark hair, his expression pained and startled, as if he had no idea how he had gotten there; and at the same time the drawing depicted a kind of landscape, of cities and hills and forests, of rivers filled with fish, with ships upon the waters; and the setting sun was there, and the rising sun, and the reeds of an endless marsh; and, rigid and stylized as holy ikons, the faces of the gods were there too; all these contained within the flesh of the boy, drifting in his blood which poured out from countless wounds and streamed into the illuminated border of the page; the blood, the boy, this great composite forming something more abstract—

A single letter, which the dreaming Sekenre recognized at once.

It was the *tchod.*

Come, let me expound, expostulate, explicate.

Let Child Thorn tell you what it means.

Surat-Kemad, the great crocodile, who is Death, vomited me up. The river turned suddenly, pouring over a cataract, splashing among boulders, and the furious current heaved me onto the land.

There I lay in burning sunlight, in the freezing night, naked and motionless while my blood stained the rocks and seeped into the earth, as birds and beasts rose out of the mud and came to drink from the wound in my side. There the Sybil and Regun-Kemad wrestled over my fate; those two dancing yet, a swirl of dark clouds, the silver sword gleaming just beyond the horizon, like the lightning flash of a distant storm.

Waking, dreaming, all as one. This is *tchod:*

The Child of Thorns, who dies continuously without ever ending his life, who endures forever and is always a child.

The Suffering One, whose holy blood brings all gifts.

These are his mysteries.

Mankind walked upon the Earth in those days and came to the river's edge to drink. There the first men and women found me, lying in the mud amid boulders, while rain poured onto my face. A hundred wild faces gathered about me, looking down in wonder, but they could not speak, for words were not yet known to them.

Two hundred hands bore me up. A hundred shoulders carried me like driftwood on a heaving ocean. I was placed in a tree, cast there, heaved up, impaled on thorns, every part of my body pierced through, my arms and legs outstretched to form the figure *tchod,* which is like an *X* with a dot between the two upper bars to represent the victim's head.

I screamed in the unendurable agony of it, but I could not writhe; I could not move; the thorns held me fast.

At the sound of my cries, the host of mankind turned toward me, amazed. Thus our ancestors learned speech. Thus the gods spoke to them through my mouth and every word in every language is but a refinement of the screams of Sekenre, who is the Thorn Child.

The gods bade the first men take my blood in their cupped hands and carry it to every part of the world; and where my blood fell, there was I, the Child of Thorns, on the river, crossing the sea, amid distant islands, high among mountains, in the depths of the forests, amid the thundering herds of the grasslands.

Again the sun set, and in the darkness wind raged around me and the Eagle of Death drew very close. But when daylight returned and the sky was fair, then the Sybil was just beneath my feet as I hung in the thorn tree, continuing her dance, her combat for my sake, speaking words of hope.

Black birds rested on my shoulders, gazing hungrily into my face. Beasts and men came to me, to be washed in my blood, to drink of it to gaze up in amazement at the thorns protruding from my flesh like so many spearheads.

Wise men asked prophecies of me, and somehow I answered them, in mysterious signs written in droplets of blood on the ground, or in dreams. But when I tried to speak, I had no breath. Blood dripped down over my chin. I could only open and close my eyes slowly to show that I was alive. All the while my hair grew longer and was transformed into vines and trees, filling the holy grove.

So I became a treasure, guarded by priests, attended by hundreds of acolytes. Centuries passed, and still Regun-Kemad, Death's Messenger, and the Sybil contended over me, while the nations of mankind grew fruitful and spread over the whole Earth.

And I saw the time when the skies were black with the passage of dragons. Regun-Kemad had summoned them to his aid, against the Sybil, and the world trembled with the thunder of their wings. But the Sybil summoned heroes, who tempered their new-forged swords in my blood and slew the dragons. The skies brightened once more.

Still cities rose, and fell, as warring nations dashed themselves against nations like waves in a furious tide. The spirits of the fallen gathered before me, to know of Child Thorn the meaning of their own pain. In dreams I addressed them in the language of the dead, directing them into the mouth and belly of the All-Devouring, Surat-Kemad, whose beating heart seemed to throb forever inside my own head.

And more:

The Sybil called out to me, *'Sekenre, think of Sekenre,'* and I was able to recall walking along the River with two women. Sekenre-in-the-dream knew them, but Sekenre-the-dreamer could only grasp helplessly at their puzzling, frustrating familiarity.

The Sybil called out, *'Heron, think of Heron,'* and I remembered wading among the reeds at the water's edge, my bare feet sinking into the cool mud.

Then she called out a third time, bestowing on me a new,

secret name; the true name of the reborn Sekenre, of the Thorn Child, even as *Heron* was the true and secret name Vashtem gave to his son.

Heron ceased to be a secret at all. The reader of my book may know it. The other, I may not repeat or write down.

At long last my blood ceased to flow. The divinity within me had run out. What remained, I did not know, but the dreams and prophecies ceased and the holy grove withered. Then bronze-clad legions marched from beyond the horizon, slew the priests and acolytes, cut down the thorn tree, and bore me off in a golden litter as prized booty. In a city of green stone I was shut up in a tomb carven into the shape of my gaunt, distorted, sprawling self; and as more years passed, or I dreamed of more years, many kings came to rest beside me in tombs more magnificent than my own, until I was surrounded by a labyrinth filled with brick and stone lions, enthroned colossi, and countless pillars.

When the desert sand blew among what shards remained of that green-stone city, when the names of the kings were forgotten by all but the eternal, murmuring waters of the Great River, still I lay there in the cool darkness, listening to the prayers of the faithful few who kept watch over the holy tombs even after we who lay within had become an ineffable mystery to all mankind.

Wind and sand wiped the faces off our effigies, and featureless, we regarded eternity.

Once I saw a ragged, almost naked, badly sunburnt boy climbing across my stone face like an ant, gazing down into my stone eyes as if into a pair of bottomless wells. I wanted to call out to him, to demand his name, which was somehow terribly important; why, I didn't know.

So I stirred within my sarcophagus, and the Sybil stood on my right hand, the Messenger of Death on the other.

'*Sekenre,*' the Sybil said. I reached out with my wounded right arm, and took her hand in mine.

'*Sekenre. Get up now.*'

The pain was, after so long, completely gone, replaced by utterly novel sensations I struggled to define: the closeness of the air as my lungs struggled for breath. The odors of dust and ancient, dry stone. The touch of the cool, smooth slab on which I lay. The Sybil's fingers gently caressing my arrow-pierced wrist.

To my left, Regun-Kemad screeched angrily and was gone, stirring a frigid, acrid draught with his passage.

'Sekenre, climb into the light,' the Sybil said, speaking both aloud and inside my mind simultaneously.

The light was before me, above me, like a pinprick in the roof of a dark tent; no, a candle, flickering; then a torch; the rising sun between two mountains, bursting into the world, dazzling me. I climbed. For a time, the Sybil was with me, urging me on, helping me with a gentle shove, steadying me when I stumbled. I couldn't see her. I saw only the light, slowly widening before me.

I crawled through sumptuous dust, over dry stone, my every scraping movement echoing in the darkness far below. I might have ascended a staircase. One more I slipped, nearly fell, and the Sybil caught me under the arms.

Then I was alone. I groped around for the Sybil, but instead discovered a round, smooth orifice like the opening of a large earthen jar.

'Go on, Sekenre. You must.'

She spoke inside my mind only, fading. Those were her final words to me.

I crawled out of the mouth of some reclining stone effigy, into warmth and sunlight. I stood up for a moment, regarding the half-buried, skeletal limbs, the round, featureless face; and then I lost my footing and slid down bumpily into sand. I sat where I had fallen for a long time, my back against warm stone, my eyes closed against the burning daylight. I listened to the wind, to the birds cawing, to the sound of water lapping far away. I enjoyed the touch of the gentle breeze on my bare skin.

Sekenre came to me in a kind of waking dream, standing before me on the bright sand. How wasted away he looked, naked, dirty, covered with scars, his hair a tangled mass almost down to his waist. His legs trembled, knees knocking together. He tried to say something but I couldn't make it out. He sounded lost and afraid.

Tannivar the Parricide stood before me, clad all in black. He asked me if I knew where his father was.

'No,' I said aloud. 'I don't even know where *my* father is.'

'Don't you?' said Lekkanut-Na. I couldn't see her. Perhaps she was behind the tomb from which I had emerged, or still within it. 'Don't you, Sekenre?'

In addressing me thus, she gave me back a name, my first name, and once more I was Sekenre, who remembered. Slowly I understood that it was *I* who was famished and scarred and lost.

The Great River called me. When at last the sun went down into the western desert, I was able to see. I groped among fallen slabs, among pillars and seated effigies of stone. Birds shrieked at me from atop palm trees.

Someone caught me by the shoulder, whirling me around. It was an old man, naked as I, burnt almost black by the sun, his body gnarled like ancient wood.

'You!' sputtered through rotting teeth. 'You *have* returned. My Master, why did you torment me before, when I alone of all the others have remained faithful? Am I not worthy? In the end, there was no one to take my place. No one else remembered the rites, the prayers. Therefore I could not leave. Weary as I was, *I could not die.* Now my vigil is at an end, after many centuries. Holy One, will you release me at last?'

I could only gape at him. I had no idea what he was talking about. Then Balredon reminded me, whispering inside my mind.

I held up my right hand. Blood still trickled from the wound on my wrist.

'Will you remake the heavens and the earth?' the old man asked. 'Will you overthrow the very gods, now that you have awakened?'

'I don't know.'

'That is what we believe, Holy Lord. No, excuse me, that is what *I alone* believe, because there are no others of the brotherhood left. That is my faith, that the Sleeping God would cast down the proud, that he would renew the sacred grove. For hope of these things, I have endured for so long.'

'I don't think your effort has been in vain,' I said.

He fell to his knees, covering his face with his hands, weeping softly. Then he reached up to touch my side, drawing his fingers away tipped in red. He gazed in wonder, then closed his eyes and touched his fingers to his forehead, very, very gently.

His body collapsed into itself like a thing of charred paper disturbed by a wind.

'Be now released,' I said to him in the language of the dead.

Later, exhausted, light-headed, and terribly thirsty, I fell down at the river's edge and lay on my belly to drink. I saw my face reflected in the water, in the fading twilight, but the image rippled and became a huge fish, larger than I. I reached down to touch the fish, and the very last drop of divine blood fell from my wounded wrist, into the water, and the fish spoke to me, saying, 'Sekenre, son of Vashtem who is no more, go into the City of the Delta where your friend Kanratica and her mother Hapsenecuit have need of you.'

I drew the figure of the *tchod* with my finger in the mud, but the lapping water erased it.

Then I slept, my face half buried in mud, and I dreamed of the Sybil back in her dark, swaying domain beneath the City of Reeds, ropes creaking and bones rattling all around her as she worked busily to straighten and rearrange the threads of her weaving, from which she had just untangled an enormous knot.

Chapter 18: The Return of the Thorn Child

I must have been lying there for most of a day before travellers found me. I felt myself lifted up out of the mud and laid out on my back on warm, hard sand. Someone started washing me with a wet cloth.

I opened my eyes and saw a dozen faces gazing down at me, black men with flared noses and blue-dyed, pointed beards. I let out a cry and started to struggle, certain that these were Zargati, that they had a sharpened stake waiting for me.

(*Is it possible to kill a god?* I asked myself. I didn't feel like a god. I had never felt less like one. But no matter, a god can suffer for a long time, dead or not.)

Strong, firm hands held me in place. Someone spoke in reassuring tones, in words I couldn't make out. A round-faced, balding man smiled at me. His teeth were not filed in Zargati fashion but, it seemed at first, to be made of gold. Then he smiled again and I saw that they were only partially golden, capped or plated somehow.

He spoke the Deltan tongue, in an accent I didn't recognize.

'Do not be afraid. I am a physician.'

Most of the others seemed to be his colleagues. He addressed them in a completely foreign language, instructing them to turn me this way or that, as all of them examined me, touching my many scars, shaking their heads in wonder at what they saw, making little sighs or clucking noises. Then they laid me down again. One of them rummaged in a bag, got out a strip of linen, and wrapped it around me to cover my loins.

I raised myself on my elbows, to see what they saw: that I wasn't bleeding anymore, that huge, ugly wounds sufficient to have killed me a dozen times had closed, even the one in my side. It was as much a source of amazement to me as it was to them.

The golden-toothed man gingerly reached down to touch the scar over my heart, where the sword had gone in, and examined several more on my chest and stomach, where thorns had passed all the way through my body. With an extended finger he traced the letter *tchod* which was burned into my chest. He kneaded my flesh between his fingers, as if trying to convince himself it was real. Several of his companions winced.

He spoke to them once more in their own language, then said to me in Deltan, 'This is very strange. You should be dead. I cannot explain it.'

All I could think to say was, 'Maybe ...' Exhausted, I sprawled back on the sand.

He forced a laugh, followed by a wide, golden grin, and then he put a strong arm around my shoulders, lifting me up into a sitting position. 'No, boy. Whatever you are, you are definitely not dead. It is an inexplicable marvel, but it is true.' His eyes were wide. From his face and from a subtle quavering in his voice, I could tell that he was on the verge of awe, as if he suspected, somehow, some small part of my true history.

But he put aside whatever dread he might have felt and spoke a curt order to his fellows, and two of them lifted me to my feet, and we walked a short way to their encampment. A fire smoldered under palm trees. Tethered camels stood a way off.

All the black men wore sleeveless, knee-length tunics of blue cloth, beautifully embroidered in many colors; round, wide-brimmed hats; bronze or silver armlets, necklaces, and many rings. I was given one of the tunics, so large on me it came to my ankles and fit like a loose robe, but no hat or jewelry. I sat with them around their fire and shared their dinner with them: bread, cheese, smoked meat, some intensely sweet, dried fruit I'd never tasted before, and a little wine. The wine made me sleepy, but someone shook me and held me upright.

'Your must tell us something of yourself,' the leader said. He introduced himself as Arnegazad, which, in the language of his people, he explained, meant gazelle.

I forgot myself. I must have been half delirious. I laughed.

'What is so funny?' he asked, but he was not angry.

'I've never seen anyone who looked less like his name.' Indeed this squat, heavily-built man was an unlikely gazelle.

He leaned forward and gazed into my eyes intently. 'And you? Do *you* look like your name?'

'My name is –' I almost told him my secret name, *Heron,* caught myself, then realized that it wasn't a secret anymore and it would be perfectly safe to argue that someone as skinny as me did somewhat resemble a wading heron. I didn't know what to say. I only shook my head and sat rocking back and forth, hugging my knees. 'My name is Sekenre. I don't really know what it means.'

Arnegazad grinned, flashing gold. 'At least I understand my own name. I have the advantage, don't you think?'

I could only drop my head down and gaze at the sand.

There were no more questions for a while as someone plied my hair with a brush, working out the worst of the tangles. One after another, they ran their fingers through it, as if examining a rare silk. To these men, waist-length, straight hair must have seemed nearly as remarkable as my impossible scars. They surely thought me a Heaven-sent freak, a prodigy to be studied and interpreted in the days to come.

I didn't care. I was too tired. Even the light meal made my stomach heavy. I would have fallen face-down into the fire if someone hadn't caught me.

That night I dreamed that I was still the Thorn Child, suspended on my tree, thorns protruding from beneath my collarbone, neatly hooking me like a fish on a line. I streamed blood, and shifted very slightly in my pain, sighing. Blood oozed from my mouth. The Thorn Child dreamed that he was a boy called Sekenre, who camped by the bank of the Great River in the care of kindly, exotically foreign physicians. Sekenre dreamed he was the Thorn Child.

In the morning twilight, I sat very still while the others still slept, watching the sun rise across the river, trying to

403

figure out whether I was Sekenre awakening from a dream or the Thorn Child descending into one. Since then I have never been sure. I can find no proof. Perhaps I hang on the tree even now, and only dream that I write these words.

I rode a camel, seated almost in Arnegazad's lap.

'Will you travel with us, Sekenre?'

I thought of the random casting, the 'wizard's never-ending game,' as one source called it, *tanal madt.* I thought of the Sybil, weaving.

'I already am . . . I—'

'But you are not a captive, Sekenre. You may leave us if you wish. We are going to the City of the Delta, where, so we have been told, the king has taken ill, and there is a great reward offered for any doctor who can cure him.'

The fish in the pool had told me to go to the City of the Delta, if I hadn't hallucinated the whole episode.

'I'm going there, too.'

Arnegazad clasped my shoulder and shook me gently. 'We are agreed, then. You shall be our companion on the way, Sekenre.'

(King? I thought to myself. What king? Had Queen Hapsenecuit married? But then, I realized, I had no idea what year this was, for I had travelled both backward and forward in time, to my considerable confusion. But I didn't want to reveal too much. I did not ask.)

When we camped the next evening, I decided to tell something of myself; not all, but just enough to convince Arnegazad that I was mad. Then he would try to cure me. Perhaps he would succeed. What a profound thing, I reflected, to be cured of the truth.

But he foresaw and defeated my stratagem.

'These are my brothers, Delregazad and Kedrigazad.' The two of them bowed and seated themselves on either side of me as we gathered around our fire. The others were introduced, cousins, colleagues, even the apprentice Karimazad, who was off watering the camels. They told me about their native country, Tsongatoko, which comes out as Land of Black

Trees in our tongue. Why it is called that, I learned much later. Tsongatoko lies a great distance beyond the Southern, or White Fire Desert, where few Riverlanders have ever ventured.

There were actually fourteen in the present company, counting the apprentice. They were indeed, as had been my first impression, kindly, learned men. They had come to heal the king of the Delta.

'But how did you know he was sick, so far away?'

Delregazad broke in. He was thinner, younger, more long-faced than his brother Arnegazad. He seemed very intense, relentlessly serious. 'A magician saw – in his mirror – the king had been wasting away slowly for a long time.'

'Don't you have such mirrors in your country?' said Arnegazad, casually, as if the question had only just occurred to him. If course it hadn't. He smiled, expectant but also subtly amused, as if he already knew what I was going to say.

'Yes,' I answered softly. 'I am such a magician myself.'

'Are you *indeed?*' said Delregazad.

That was my cue. I related to them much of my adventures, but not all. I omitted everything that had happened in the College of Shadows, and the fact that there were still other sorcerers somnolent within me, and, more importantly – though I think Arnegazad was probing in precisely this direction – that I had been touched by the divine, had actually been, sort of, a god. The memories stirred together in my mind like different colors of paint in a pot. My narrative doubtless made very little sense. I concluded with the admission that I had slept for a long time in a tomb.

Everyone was silent for a long while after that. I listened to the night birds calling one another as they floated on the river.

Arnegazad regarded me inscrutably, and finally asked, 'What was your father's specialty? You were not clear about that.'

'Specialty?'

'Each sorcerer, so you have said, discovers the unique and individual form of his own sorcery. What was his?'

It was a startling question. In one sense, I'd never actually thoght of it. In another, I'd seldom thought of anything else.

'I suppose,' I said after considerable hesitation, 'his specialty was treason. Taking others into his confidence. Learning from them. Using them as his instruments, then murdering them when it suited his purpose.'

'But,' said the younger brother, Delregazad, 'don't all sorcerers do that?'

The others eyed me a little fearfully. I looked like a child to them, but I had admitted to being a murderer. I was not merely a magician, who might be harmless or even holy, but a sorcerer, who is unquestionably neither.

'Yes,' I said, 'but for my father, murder was his main course of action, not just an expedient. He refined it into an art.'

'Ah,' said Delregazad, sitting back.

Again there was awkward silence. Once more Arnegazad broke it.

'And what form did *your* sorcery take, Sekenre?'

'Calligraphy. Letters on the page.'

'Really?' This too he absorbed inscrutably. I didn't think he believed me. I sat there glumly, waiting for him to say, *No, Sekenre, your true talent is suffering. Your calligraphy is written all over your body. See how full the page is already.*

But he said nothing.

A while later, someone brought me a bowl of water.

'Look into it,' said Arnegazad. 'Tell us what you see.'

It was an obvious test, but I did what I was told, making fire with my hands to the muted gasps of the onlookers, lowering my hands into the bowl until the water was suffused with a white glow.

I beheld many things, from many points of view. Then I let out a cry and deliberately spilled the water in my lap.

'I can't tell you –' I was weeping. Arnegazad reached out and touched my cheek, then drew his finger away, examining the specimen of my tears minutely.

'I did not know that sorcerers could do this,' he said.

The following morning we came to the burnt ruin of a town.

Uprooted stakes lay in heaps by the riverbank, but the place no longer smelled of death or of burning, only of dust.

That afternoon we reached another town, which had been burnt also, but was slowly being rebuilt by the few surviving inhabitants. Arnegazad bade the rest of us wait while he had a long conference with what remained of the town council, three old men who argued and gesticulated wildly. Finally we were ushered onto a small boat crewed by a single riverman and his son, while the rest of the people kept a distance from us, as if afraid. We sat amid the luggage and ate a frugal meal on the water. I thought to ask what had become of the camels. They were worth far more than mere passage. But I kept silent.

Arnegazad spoke to his companions in their own language, then turned to me.

'I am afraid our mission is fruitless. The king is dead already.'

'Wha – what king was that?'

Arnegazad looked at me strangely. 'Why, Wenamon the Fourth, naturally.'

Did you know you're looking at his murderer?

I swallowed hard and said, 'Then why do you continue? Why don't you return home?'

Arnegazad merely shrugged. 'We've come so far. We've always wanted to see the famous City of the Delta.'

Delregazad touched him on the shoulder and whispered something.

'Besides which, Sekenre,' Arnegazad continued, 'we might yet have something to do there. I think you have something you must do.'

'Yes,' I said softly.

'That's what you saw in the bowl last night.'

'Yes.'

Suffice it to say that we journeyed on in our small boat past several more towns, some of them ruined, some not, encountering very little traffic on the river. When the City of the Delta was in sight, I asked to be put ashore. There I parted from the Tsongatokoi physicians with declarations of friendship and the hope that we might meet again.

Suffice it to say I had something I had to do.

I entered the palace itself by means of the sorcerer's mirror, using a rain puddle in the shadow of the royal stables. There I found two buckets and a yoke, all I needed. I took my bright tunic off, folding it neatly behind some barrels in case I should be able to retrieve it. I smeared myself with mud.

Then, naked but for a loincloth, covered with dirt, the yoke and buckets over my shoulders, I walked right into the dungeons as if I were invisible. No guard challenged me. I passed a crowd of them seated at a table, drinking and playing knucklebones. They didn't look up. In the damp, foul-smelling depths, as I began to pass occupied cells, no prisoner called out to me.

That is the one advantage of being as I am. Were I a giant, or an elegantly dressed sorcerer, I would have attracted attention, but no one takes a scrawny, grubby boy seriously. Probably a servant's brat, or more likely a slave. If he has a lot of scars, well, slaves are often beaten. I could go anywhere I wanted, as long as I stayed out of the fine halls.

Unseen, I scooped up a certain ring of keys, continued onward, and opened a certain cell.

I put the buckets down gently and peered into the darkness. The only light came from a hole in the ceiling, which led, not outside, but to the room above. The place smelled like a latrine.

I made a flame in the palm of my hand and beheld the prisoner dangling from chains against the far wall: gaunt, naked, covered with filth and welts and open wounds, her hair even longer than mine, down past her waist in a matted tangle. She stirred as I approached her, moaning softly, shaking her head to get the hair out of the way so she could see.

I held the flame up close. Her face was swollen, puffy, and blackened where she had been beaten recently. She gazed at me, barely able to open her pain-glazed eyes.

'It can't be Sekenre,' she said. 'I am dead. You are dead, too.'

'Tica, it is I. Truly, it is.'

'You are not lying?'

'No, Tica, I'm not.'

I extinguished my light, fumbling in the darkness with keys and shackles. I tried to hold her up as she fell, but the two of us tumbled to the muddy floor in a heap. We lay there a minute in several inches of cold muck. She clung to my chest like a drowning woman holding on to a log.

She did not weep. I think she was beyond all weeping.

I wriggled out from under her and got to my knees.

'Think you can stand up?'

'Yes . . .'

I helped her to her feet, slinging one of her arms over my shoulder as we staggered toward the door.

I left her clinging to the doorway while I went back for the buckets and yoke.

'What are those for?'

'Do you think you can carry one?'

She lurched toward me, catching hold of my shoulders with both hands, embracing me, knocking both yoke and buckets to the floor. We stood there for a moment. I let her rest on my shoulder, holding her up without too much difficulty. She was no heavier than me now, though a full head taller.

Clearly she wasn't strong enough to carry a couple of slop buckets and walk past the guards as if she'd done it every day. This wasn't going to work. I'd have to use the sorcerer's mirror, despite the risk – no, the nearcertainty – that some sorcerer would be watching the dungeons, even if none had been watching the stables.

'Water,' I whispered. 'I'll just need a little water. Then we can get out of here.'

She dropped to her hands and knees, and crawled a little way back into the darkness of her cell, then returned, gasping at the effort. She handed me a cup containing two or three inches of what must have been water.

'My week's ration,' she said. 'If they didn't piss in it.'

As a precaution, I ushered her back into the cell and closed the door behind us.

'It'll only be a minute more,' I said. I sat in the mud with one of the buckets in my lap, shivering from the damp and the cold. I poured the water into the bottom to make a broader surface than the cup allowed, swirling it around to break up the scum. This time I leaned down and breathed until the water glowed.

'I never saw you do it like that before,' Tica said.

'I've learned a few things. But, wait—'

As I feared, a balding, gray-haired man glared at me from out of the bucket. I spoke to him harshly, in the language of the dead.

'Do not molest us. We only wish to depart. Interference will cost thee dearly.' Then I repeated certain secret words I had learned at the College of Shadows and made up a few additional ones, implying that I knew vastly more. I recited a few lines of horrific verse from the litanies of the Blood Kings of Ta-Yed Hzan in their own tongue, all this courtesy of Tannivar the Parricide who had once visited that realm of eternal ice and darkness.

The other sorcerer made a sign with his hand and vanished.

'Come on, now,' I said. I set the bucket on the floor, then clasped Tica from behind, my arms under hers. I held her tightly, leaned forward, and the two of us tumbled into the glowing water.

We landed with a splash among reeds at the river's edge. I sat up, sputtering. Tica lay face down beside me. I rolled her over, then took her under the arms again and dragged her to the bank. She coughed and spat up mud, then lay still, eyes closed, but breathing softly as I cupped clear water in my hands and washed her many hurts. As I worked, evening fell. Night birds circled overhead. Near at hand, a wading heron paused to watch me. I took it as a good sign.

When I had done what I could, I washed myself, and we two lay side by side, wet and shivering in the evening breeze.

'You never asked me,' Tica said at last, 'what happened to Mother.'

'I was afraid to.'

'What do you think? The Green faction reasserted itself shortly after you ... disappeared. Mother screamed for you as the soldiers came for her. But you weren't there to help—'

I didn't know what to say. I took her hand in mine. She moved closer to me, for warmth.

'I don't think you could have helped very much . . .' she said, staring up at the emerging stars. 'People said that the Queen . . . Mother – and I, too – were usurpers, unholy, wicked, that we had stolen the throne by sorcery and murder. What could I say in reply? We *had.*'

After a long pause I said, 'What will you do now, Tica? Will you try to become queen yourself?'

Now she began to weep, a little at first, then great hoarse, heaving sighs. 'No . . . no . . . I don't want to . . .'

'What, then?'

'I don't know, Sekenre. What will *you* do?'

I put my arm around her shoulders. She flinched, but let me stay. She rested her head against my chest. 'Where is the Queen, your mother?'

'Over the city gate. On a spike. Her head, anyway.'

I felt white-hot rage. I had never known such anger before, ever, despite all I had been through.

I let go of Tica and sat up. 'They should *not* have done that,' I said. 'Truly, they should *not.*'

'What will you do, Sekenre?'

I rose to my feet. 'Rest here,' I said. 'Just rest and wait as long as it takes. I'll be back soon.'

We were not far from the city. I walked through the night, as the stars wheeled overhead, counting one hour, then two, then three by the clock of the sky. When the city came into view, I crouched down among some trees and waited, my teeth chattering in the chilly air. Caravaneers camped around the main gate, waiting to be admitted in the morning. In the night's last hour, when all were asleep, I passed silently through the camp and stood before twin towers that flanked the city's gate.

Queen Hapsenecuit's head rested on a spike directly over the gate. Her face had been eaten away by crows, but she still wore her crown.

411

And her spirit was there. I saw it with my sorcerer's vision. It dangled by the neck like a rag doll, impaled under the chin, twisting in the breeze.

I summoned her in the language of the dead, releasing her from her defiled body. She came down. But it was I who shook and wept.

I mourned for the Queen even as her ghost stood beside me.

'I hate them *all* for this. I *hate* them. I hate them for what they did to Tica!'

Hapsenecuit reached out to touch me. Her hand passed through my arm as if through smoke.

'Sekenre, you did not love me, nor I you. I used you as an instrument, like so many others. Surely you knew—'

'I don't know what I feel right now,' I said. 'But it hurts worse than anything.'

'Sekenre, please—'

Furious, I gave the Sorcerer's Shout, and the gateway of the city collapsed in a heap of stones, the twin towers tottering toward one another. At once came cries from within, screams, lanterns lit. Behind us, the caravaneers woke up in confusion, struggling to control their terrified animals.

I drew breath to shout again, to wipe the whole city off the face of the Earth. I could do it, I who had murdered sorcerers and kings, who had challenged the very gods—

But, still very much a queen, Hapsenecuit commanded me. 'Sekenre, give it up. This is not your quarrel. Everything, the outcome, the consequences of my actions – it was all inevitable. Do not punish people for what is inevitable.'

'Everything is inevitable,' I said sullenly.

'Everything. At least it seems that way to me.'

In my mind, for an instant, I saw the Sybil, weaving in her darkened house. Bitterly, I hoped she was finding her work interesting.

I backed away from the gate. In the confusion of alarm and rescue, no one noticed me any more than they had in the dungeons. No one else could see the Queen's ghost.

The eastern sky brightened into dawn, and Hapsenecuit

started to fade away. But before she was gone, I took her by the hand. If I concentrated very hard, I could feel her, as if I held on to the morning breeze. I spoke to her in the language of the dead, leading her to the Great River's edge and out onto the water, reciting as I did the service for the dead. The city faded away behind me. At the very last, we were in darkness once more, beneath the never-fading stars of *Leshé,* where dreams and death come together like black currents conjoining. I sent her into the belly of Surat-Kemad, into the world beyond the world, and she left me there in the darkness, alone.

Translucent white birds waded nearby. A ship passed me, also translucent. I could see the rowers within its sides, their living souls flickering like candle flames. If any aboard saw me, I must have seemed a ghost, or just a patch of morning mist. No one called out.

Later, I returned to the City of the Delta, making my way through the crowd at the collapsed gate. Soldiers tried to restrain the crowd, saying it had been an earthquake, but no one believed them. Fortune-tellers and magicians gathered, making nonsensical proclamations, but fortunately there were no sorcerers, who might have seen the truth.

Inside, the crowds were tolerant enough of a mad, magical boy who careened all but naked around the great forum, running in circles around the pillars of the temples of the gods, his wild hair streaming as he shouted portentous absurdities and did tricks with fire and smoke that rose from his hands. He earned a few coins that way. In the heat of the afternoon, when everyone else was resting, the mad child became suddenly sane and went among the merchants' booths, purchasing simple clothing for two and provisions for a journey. No one questioned him there either. Business hadn't been good of late. A customer was, after all, a customer.

I knew Tica was feeling better when she started to fuss over me. 'You're such a *mess,* Sekenre,' she would say, 'still a little boy in so many ways. I don't care where you've been or what you've done.' She cut my hair short, in the Deltan fashion. She was always brushing dust off me and straightening my clothing. If my hands or even feet got dirty, she made me wash at once. 'You have to be *presentable,'* she kept repeating.

We wandered along the river, heading south, away from the Delta, back the way we had come along the western bank. Here the land itself seemed scarred by the passage of the Zargati. We could walk for days without seeing another living person, passing only the ruins and ash-heaps of towns. But, further south, below the bend in the river, the scourge had been lighter. There were survivors. Larger towns had endured sieges, while villagers took shelter behind the town walls.

So I prophesied, while Tica danced or played upon the tambang or the zootibar. Sometimes people asked me to lay my hands on them and drive out their evils, and sometimes, indeed, I was successful.

We made enough to live. We claimed to be brother and sister.

In Thanisphon, near the border of Reedland, we met fourteen blue-bearded, black men clad in bright tunics.

'Arnegazad!' I shouted as I ran to embrace him. He laughed and hugged me tightly, lifting me off my feet and whirling me around. It was a joyous meeting.

'Have you completed your task in the City of the Delta?' he asked as his colleagues gathered around.

Tica stood off at a distance and regarded them shyly.

'Yes. As best I could.'

'Tell us about it later. Or not at all, as you please.' Once more Arnegazad smiled, gleaming gold.

I introduced Tica, then asked of my friend's fortunes.

Arnegazad rolled his eyes. 'Alas, no fortunes for us. Doors shut in our faces. Even stones thrown at us. No one in the Delta would hire the greatest physician in the world if his skin happens to be black.'

'They remember the Zargati,' said Tica, 'and they're still afraid.'

'Can they really be so ignorant?' Delregazad broke in with characteristic fury. 'Do they mistake us for *savages* merely because of our color?'

I shrugged, looking at the ground. 'Maybe . . .'

Arnegazad shook me by the shoulder. 'But never mind

that now!' He led us to a tavern, where we all sat down to dinner, in the course of which he said, 'Having seen the famous City of the Delta and not being overly impressed, my brothers and I long for our own country. Would you care to accompany us?'

So Tica and I travelled with them, by a route that must have been more leisurely than their original journey, for it took nearly a year. We retrieved the camels from the town where we had left them, the black men giving up much of their jewelry in exchange for the beasts' upkeep, and for supplies. We spent over a month crossing the White Fire Desert, though there was some respite in the third week by a lake among some hills. The short, brown men who lived by the lake welcomed us and traded fish and grain for bright Tsongatokoi cloth; but we had to go on, across yet another desert unknown to familiar geographies, called, in the Tsongatokoi language, *Weka-Hu-Tanna,* which means Anvil of the Sun. There is no name for it in Deltan or Reedlandish.

After much hardship, after Tica and I had been burnt nearly as dark as our companions by the heat of the Sun's Anvil, we came at last to Tsongatoko, the Land of Black Trees, where cities lie deep within steaming jungles and people live *inside* huge ebony trunks and build houses among the upper branches. By means of song and special instruments, Tsongatokoi priests can shape the growth of the trees. No one drives a nail or saws a board. That would be blasphemy in a country where the forest is the direct and conscious manifestation of the gods.

If you learn to listen, the forest speaks, in its own special language. Tsongatokoi sages spend lifetimes mastering the vocabulary.

The forest contains, too, a great library, where all the texts are marked in colored inks on the inside of a single, undying tree, not carven, but painted there, like calligraphy on a vast page. As the tree grows, so does the accumulated knowledge of Tsongatoko. Sometimes words, sentences, or even whole books appear spontaneously. Sometimes unseen hands correct or change what human scribes have written.

Again, the sages of Tsongatoko spend lifetimes learning to read what is written.

High among the branches, I found a dangling wicker cage containing a naked, incredibly shrivelled and aged man. At first I was shocked to see him treated thus, but the wind stirred the treetops, and in the uncertain light of evening twilight I saw that the door to the cage was not fastened in any way.

I sensed something very powerful here, not sorcery, but truest, holy magic.

The ancient one stirred. As I drew closer I saw that he was of a race unknown to me, possibly not even human at all. His skin was gray-blue, his face strangely ridged above the eyes, his cheekbones and chin protruding severely.

As he stirred, I saw to my amazement that he was winged.

He opened his cat-like, yellow eyes and regarded me.

And he spoke to me in the language of the dead, uttering my true, secret name, the one the Sybil had given me, addressing me thus as he said, 'Find the third path, the middle way between sanctity and sorcery. On the right hand, there is thaumaturgy, miracle-working which comes from the gods. On the left, sorcery, evil; murder, endless fear and pain, as you well know. Find the middle way. Thus I charge thee.'

I was so terrified of him that I nearly lost my footing and fell to my death. Instead I clung to a broad branch and lay still, streaming sweat, trembling. Only when night hid the winged man from me was I able to creep to safety.

That night, the last before Tica and I were to depart from Tsongatoko, I dreamed of the Sybil for the first time in a long while. I saw her as always, weaving, the threads pouring out of her hands into the darkness below. She hummed softly to herself, intent on what she was doing. I felt no urge to interrupt.

What more?

Tica grew older, of course, while I did not. For a brief while, we presented ourselves as man and wife, but then I posed as her son and eventually her grandson. In time the strangeness and discomfort became too great for her, and she left me to dwell with another man called Nahrin in a house by the Great River. I didn't try to hold her. I think she was happy with Nahrin, who aged as she did, by whom she had several sons.

So I lived alone in the desert for some years, puzzling out the meaning of what I had seen and done, conversing with Lekkanut-Na and Orkanre and the others who still remained within me. Deprived of a goal, they didn't fight me any more. They were like a library of books within my head. I could open them and read as I chose.

I wrote much, but only on wind-blown sand. I had not yet found the middle way.

And I remembered Tica. She remembered me. How could she forget, when before we parted I begot a son on her whom she raised as her own? His name was Miriban, and late in her life, when Miriban was already old enough to be my apparent father, she sent him to fetch me.

'Mother is gravely ill,' was all he said to me. 'She wants to see you.'

I returned to her house, which was not my own, a place I had visited but rarely.

Nahrin, I discovered, had died. The children of Nahrin and Tica were grown, but they had gathered here now. As I entered the house, they all fell silent, regarding me with awe. I was shown out onto the porch, where the aged Tica lay in a hammock. I sat by her in a wicker chair.

It was evening. As the sun set, I swung the hammock gently. She reached down and ran her fingers through my hair, which had grown long again.

'How are you, Sekenre?'

'I haven't changed.'

She smiled. This was an old joke between us.

She found a tangle and gave a sharp tug.

'Sekenre, you're still a mess.'

I held her hand between mine. 'It doesn't matter,' I said.

'No, I don't suppose it really does.'

'Are you dying?' I asked.

'I don't know. Perhaps. What is old age but dying, day by

day? If I am dying, I want to be with you, Sekenre, on the river, as we once were. Go tell Miriban to fetch a boat.'

'Now?'

'Yes, now, Sekenre. Quite possibly, there will be no other time.'

The sons were alarmed and dismayed, but they heeded their mother's wishes. I stole away with her in the night, drifting in a boat, seated with her head in my lap. Above us, the stars turned slowly in their courses, to mark the hours.

'When I dream of you,' she said, 'it's always like this. I want to remember when we were first friends, on the water.'

'I do, too,' I said.

She turned with more vigor than I expected from her, and faced me. 'Oh, Sekenre, does any of it mean anything? Anything at all?'

'Only the Sybil knows.'

'And you, Sekenre?'

'As you say, I'm a mess. I've made a mess of things. All I've managed to do is stay alive. I am still Sekenre. I haven't been changed into something else. That must count for something.'

'I think it counts for everything,' she said.

In the darkness, as we drifted around a bend in the river, we came upon a ruined building on stilts among the reeds, looming like a huge spider, glowing from within from countless fires like luminous eyes.

Tica had never actually *seen* it before, but she recognized it as surely as I did, from my telling, perhaps even from dreams I had shared with her.

'Holy gods!' she cried out. 'It can't be!'

I stood up in astonishment.

It was my father's house.

She wept and pleaded with me as I poled the boat closer. She clung to me as I moored it to one of the pilings.

'Don't go inside, Sekenre! I'm afraid you won't come back. It'll swallow you up.'

'I have to,' I said. I knew this was no random thing. It was the Sybil's weaving. It had to be dealt with. 'Please wait for me. I won't be long.' I climbed up onto the remains of the porch.

The Sorcerer to His Long-Lost Love

Come to me by moonlight,
when the wind is in the trees,
and follow me in silence yet
and linger among these
fallen idols of lost gods
and fanes where wild thorns grow,
where once we walked and once we paused
a thousand years ago.

Now I conjure you amid
this city of the dead:
Rise from your grave by moonlight,
before the night has fled,
and for an instant resurrect
the love we used to know,
when we two dwelt among these stones
a thousand years ago.

– from the notebooks of Sekenre the Illuminator

I spoke a word, unbinding time, and the long-delayed fires leapt up, roaring with delight, and the beacon of the burning house lit up the night sky like a sudden and impossible sunrise.

Tica and I floated on the water, watching.

That was how I cast off the heritage of my father.

I don't know how long I was inside that house. Time passed differently for me, I think. It felt like many days, a long time, though it may have been only an hour. The thought of Tica lying below, the terrible dread that she might die before I could return to her, that special pain saved me in the end.

The house did indeed try to swallow me up, tempting me with sights, with sounds, with memories, as I went from room to room, exploring, rummaging through cupboards and trunks, trying to discover, at last, the meaning of this symbol on the page of my life, this inscrutable hieroglyph, this *tchod*—

I listened to its many voices. Phantoms appeared. The damned spirits within my father's bottles called out to me, cursing or begging for mercy or just babbling insanely.

Here, the house seemed to be saying. *Here, Sekenre, you may be as you once were. Here, dwell in your own room, sleep in your own bed, write at your desk by the window; forget everything else that ever happened as a bad dream—*

I nearly yielded as I contemplated the treasures there in my father's workroom, the magical books, the apparatus, the talismans and charms. If I remained, the damage would repair itself. The house would heal and become, once more, the vessel of a mighty sorcerer, capable of leaping through eons and between the worlds.

I thought to bring Tica inside with me, but I knew she wouldn't like that.

In the end I took with me only a few things, my precious, long-lost but never forgotten satchel containing the manuscript of the tale of my life, which I resolved to bring up to date and one day transcribe onto the library wall in Tsongatoko; also my pens and inks, some clothing, a handful of coins from a jar my mother kept under her bed, and one of her *hevats* that I found in the attic, a delicate, articulated figure of a bird; not a heron, but a swan, with painted wings.

Tica cried out, wept, and embraced me as I descended into the waiting boat.

As we drifted away, I asked her to forgive me, but she only said, 'Sekenre, I haven't heard the Crocodile's heartbeat ⸢ yet. Dying can wait till later.'